The LAST
Best Quest
EVER

F.T. LUKENS

SIMON & SCHUSTER

London   New York   Amsterdam/Antwerp   Sydney/Melbourne   Toronto   New Delhi

First published in Great Britain in 2026 by Simon & Schuster UK Ltd

First published in the USA in 2026 by Margaret K. McElderry Books,
an imprint of Simon & Schuster Children's Publishing Division,
1230 Avenue of the Americas, New York, New York 10020

1 3 5 7 9 10 8 6 4 2

Simon & Schuster UK Ltd
1st Floor, 222 Gray's Inn Road
London WC1X 8HB

www.simonandschuster.co.uk
www.simonandschuster.com.au
www.simonandschuster.co.in

Simon & Schuster Australia, Sydney
Simon & Schuster India, New Delhi

The authorised representative in the EEA is Simon & Schuster Netherlands BV,
Herculesplein 96, 3584 AA Utrecht, Netherlands.
info@simonandschuster.nl

A CIP catalogue record for this book
is available from the British Library.

PB ISBN 978-1-3985-4732-2
eBook ISBN 978-1-3985-4733-9
eAudio ISBN 978-1-3985-4734-6

Printed and Bound in the UK using 100% Renewable Electricity
at CPI Group (UK) Ltd

MIX
Paper | Supporting
responsible forestry
FSC
www.fsc.org   FSC® C013604

The LAST
Best Quest
EVER

Also by F.T. Lukens

So This Is Ever After
In Deeper Waters
Spell Bound
Otherworldly
Love at Second Sight

For anyone who has ever felt like an impostor

1

IF I HAD LEARNED ANYTHING IN MY YEARS OF QUESTING, IT WAS THAT members of the royal court always appreciated a grand entrance.

They were gluttons for pageantry and suspense. They salivated over any spectacle and devoured drama and pomp. And since the upper class didn't have to work for a living, unlike lowly peasants such as myself, they had endless hours to fill with various forms of entertainment. Gossip, secret liaisons, and treason were the normal fare, but even elaborate plans for a coup d'état became boring after a while. Thus, they invented different avenues of distraction, diversion, and amusement.

The kingdom's monarchs organized all manner of competitions and celebrations, much to the delight of the lords, ladies, and lieges of the court. They gorged themselves on lavish feasts, sophisticated fashion, and complicated dancing. And, of course, there were the tournaments. The monarchs loved to watch knights pummel one another with dull swords or spear one another with pointy sticks while hurtling at full speed on horseback. Unfortunately for the spectators, the court couldn't indulge in sword fights and jousting matches daily, or there would be no knights to defend against the threat of warlords, bandits, and the sporadic vengeful gnome. So they had to turn to other sources of daring entertainment.

That's where I came in.

I was an expert at questing, the broad term for a variety of daring and courageous tasks, including monster hunting, magic or divine object retrieval or destruction (depending on the day), and the occasional VIR (very important royal) recovery mission. (Princess Avriel was very excited when I showed up to rescue her from the swamp sprites instead of Lord Ethan, as he harbored a very large and very unrequited crush on her and had vowed to be her champion despite his utter lack of prowess when it came to feats of rescue or romance.)

Anyway, I was great at winning quest competitions. The best at it, in fact, in the entire kingdom. Exalted throughout all the land. And though I wasn't someone who enjoyed prolonged attention, it was an act I was willing to play for the gold.

For a time.

With my vast experience in these matters, I knew that absolutely nothing topped a theatrical last-second entrance.

Which was how I came to be there, impatiently waiting outside the closed double doors of the castle's great hall for my final performance. I pressed my ear to the glossy polished wood while I listened for the best moment to announce my arrival. If this was to be the last time I would enter the presence of royalty as the most decorated quest competitor in all of Avoury, I would do so in style. Magnificent, boorish, boasting style. Even if it meant upstaging my opposition, and especially if it irritated my fiercest competitor.

Princet Aven was fun to tease.

"Well, as no one else has returned from the Dark Wood," the king's voice rang out, "then I believe I must declare Princet Aven the—"

Ah, my cue. I rammed my shoulder against the heavy door so it swung wide open, startling the guards and the banner bearers, and cutting the king off mid-sentence. The ornately carved handle slammed into the stone wall, the impact reverberating amid the gasps of the court as I took a brash step over the threshold. I swept my brown hair to the side, revealing my blood-splattered face, and tossed the tattered hem of my cloak over my shoulder to full effect. Between the sword at my side and my dirtied leather armor, I appeared gruesome and battle worn as I stood proudly at the back of the hall, every inch the mighty adventurer the bards proclaimed me to be.

"Sorry I'm late," I called as I strode in, lugging the heavy corpse of a monstrous spider behind me by its own web, which was kind of poetic in a macabre and gross way. "I was a little caught up." The crowd stared at me in stunned silence. "Caught up. Get it?" I sighed. The castle court had no sense of humor. "The spiderweb?" I jiggled the thick strands entwined around my hands for emphasis. A twitter of disgusted laughter echoed throughout the chamber but abruptly changed to horrified gasps when one of the long, hairy legs of the spider twitched. The thud of a liege fainting followed shortly after.

I gripped the sticky fibers I'd looped over my shoulder and dragged the creature across the stone with a foul scrape and squelch. The ribbon of carpet that led to the royal dais bunched beneath the eight-legged carcass, while a wide swath of black blood and green, viscous venom seeped from beneath it, spreading out toward the jeweled toes of the courtiers, who pressed handkerchiefs over their mouths to ward off the stench.

Yeah. It was dead. *Very* dead, despite the occasional postmortem spasm. And heavy.

I grinned as my gaze slid to Princet Aven. My stomach leaped gleefully at their attractive pout, their fair skin reddening with annoyance as they crossed their arms over their pristine royal outfit. Aven had a wheelbarrow of smaller spiders, adolescents compared with the one I was dragging toward the raised thrones of the king and queen. Not a bad showing for the second best, and if I had been one minute later, they'd have won the challenge and the court's favor this time.

There were other participants lined up behind Aven, some with a smattering of dead spiders and one with a large bat. Lord Ethan, with his ridiculous curled mustache, had obviously missed the entire point of the adventure, which was to cull the Dark Wood's man-eating spider population down to a manageable level.

The Dark Wood was thick and wild, and during peak foliage season it was so dense that light scarcely broke through the canopy of leaves. The populace thought it cursed, but the path cutting through it was the shortest way between the farms and ports on the northern edge of the continent and the rest of the kingdom. Taking the route through the wood took a third of the time it would take to venture around the perimeter—which for a trader or a farmer was no menial deviation.

Unfortunately, the spider population had exploded as an unhappy herald of spring. I and my fellow questers had been tasked with bringing back as many dead creatures as possible to create a safer way through the wood for the prime trading months of the spring and summer. The reward was a sack of gold and the esteem of the kingdom.

It was the perfect last quest. A way to earn a bit of gold and one last chorus of enthusiastic huzzahs.

I paused next to Princet Aven and bowed to the king and queen, seated on their thrones atop the raised platform. The bulbous body of my bounty smelled like death, the stink wafting anew each time I moved it. It was positively vile. But the king stared, delighted, and the queen giggled as I dropped the web to the floor with a loud splat.

"I apologize for my tardiness, Your Majesties." I bowed again at the waist. "This," I said with a gesture toward the body, "was difficult to lug all the way from the depths of the Dark Wood."

Aven rolled their blue eyes and dropped their arms with a soft huff. I ignored them, though I inwardly preened.

"You're forgiven, of course, Ellinore," the queen said. "Especially as you have brought a fine specimen."

The king gestured to the stone wall behind them, where a gigantic bear rug hung above a recessed stone shelf. The ledge held a quill from a manticore, a magnificent pearl from the Eastern Sea, a silver thimble from the swamp sprites, and a scale from the famed Golden Dragon, about the size of a small shield, which gleamed in the sunlight. "Yes. The fangs will make an excellent addition to the other trophies you have brought to us."

I internally flinched but hid my distaste behind a wide smile. "I agree, Your Majesty." One of the spider's brittle legs cracked and fell off, eliciting another waft of death so overpowering that I clamped my mouth shut to keep from vomiting.

The king wrinkled his nose. "A quite pungent creature."

I laughed through my clenched teeth. "Yes. Well, it's dead. That's what happens."

"Of course." The king's gaze cut to Aven, standing by my side. "I was just about to declare my dear brother's only child, Princet Aven, the winner of this little competition, as they have killed the most spiders. But we cannot deny that once again you have prevailed."

"Wait. How did she win?" Aven asked, gesturing to the corpse behind me. "That's one spider. The quest was to kill many spiders. To decrease the population." They pointed at their wheelbarrow. "Twelve is much greater than one."

"Princet Aven does have a point," the king said, stroking his gray beard. He was a stately man, a warrior in his day, and the sharpness of his blue eyes was rivaled only by Aven's. "The quest did specify quantity."

"Yes, Princet Aven does have a magnificent point," I said with a wink in their direction. "And while this is but one spider compared with Princet Aven's bounty, this is a mother spider. And all her eggs are also now . . . gone." Gone, but not dead. Merely relocated by a friend. But that bit of information would remain between myself, my friend, and the ancients. "And she cannot procreate again."

"Well done, Ellinore." The king cleared his throat and addressed the crowd. "Once again I hereby declare Ellinore the Brave—the Spider Slayer—the winner. She has triumphed in this quest!"

I beamed in spite of the name. I'd always despised epithets, but "the Spider Slayer" wasn't too awful. It was better than some of the other ones the king had bestowed on me previously. The crowd clapped politely as the rest of the competitors dispersed with grumbles and envious looks. Lord Ethan sniffed as he passed and checked his shoulder hard against mine, his steel armor knocking my already-loose leather pauldron askew. The prick. He had a chip on his shoulder larger than the dragon scale displayed on the shelf.

Aven didn't move from their position by the thrones and frowned as I accepted the sack of gold from a nearby page and a bouquet of colorful flowers from another, a mix of bright cosmos, delphiniums, and small pink roses. With my back straight, I endured the praise and adulation from those courageous enough to skirt around the stretch of the giant spider's legs to speak with me. They were mostly young lieges of the court, dressed fashionably, and blushing as they asked me about my adventure. There were a few older nobles as well, vying for me to move to their fiefs, though I had no intention of doing so. Interest finally began to dwindle, most likely because of my curt answers and forced, frozen smile. Or maybe it was the thick stench. Either way, I was left to make my escape.

That was when Aven chose their moment. "Like you need another purse of gold," they said as they bent their head close to mine, tone low but sharp. Their eyes glinted with a perceptiveness I didn't appreciate, and they exuded an aura that, thanks to the breadth of their shoulders and royal bearing, would eclipse mine in any other circumstance. "You've won the last five competitions. Isn't that enough?"

"Six competitions. And that's rich coming from you," I said, wedging the gold into the bag at my hip. "Literally."

"I would have donated it to charity, of course. Some worthy cause."

I tapped my chin in thought. "Do you consider your own coffers a worthy cause?" One fun fact about acting as Ellinore the Brave—she was kind of a jerk.

Aven scoffed. They brushed a piece of imaginary lint from their tunic sleeve, showing off the golden thread and intricate embroidery around the cuffs. Aven was the pinnacle of royalty, from the shine of their glossy black hair and the gold glint of the earrings that lined the curves of both their ears, to the makeup expertly applied around their eyes. Their sturdy leather boots were polished to a glow, and their trademark bow and quiver were made with the straightest wood and the finest feathers—peacock, pheasant, and raven alike.

Aven was currently last in line for the throne, the king's dead brother's only child, sometimes referred to as the Pointless Princet. With five cousins who were the children of the king and queen, they barely held a claim, and they'd fall even further down the rungs once the oldest cousin, Princet Avia, ascended the throne and named their own heirs. Maybe that was why Aven was perpetually in a bad mood.

"At least don't spend it all in the first tavern you find. Save some for a leatherworker and have that buckle fixed." Aven nodded toward my shoulder. "One firm hit and that pauldron will give."

Embarrassed, I clapped my free hand over the distressed strap of my armor. I knew the buckle and leather were on their last legs, but I didn't see the use in getting it repaired when this would be my last quest. And I hadn't thought anyone would notice. I lifted my chin and swished my long, loose hair, tangled as it was. "Well, maybe that will allow you the chance to actually best me."

"I'm serious."

"So am I. Here." I smacked the flowers against their chest. "These suit you more than they do me."

Aven's jaw clenched, and the tips of their ears turned red, a dead giveaway that I'd successfully annoyed them. They took the bouquet anyway. "You're infuriating."

"I aim to please," I said, a genuine smile stealing over my features. "Now if you'll excuse me, I'm going home. With my bag of shiny new coins."

I turned my back to them, all set to march right out of the throne room, until the king's voice stopped me in my tracks.

"Not staying for the feast, Ellinore?" the king called.

I went rigid as all the attention in the room swung back in my direction. I took a fortifying breath, plastered a pleasant smile on my face, then turned and faced the king. I bowed as elegantly as I could, which was not elegantly at all.

"No, Your Majesty. I've been in the Dark Wood for several days, and I would like to return home."

"You can stay here," the queen said, resting her hand on the arm of her throne, the flash of the jewels in her rings highlighting the cool undertones of her deep-brown skin. "You could quickly bathe and change into a spare gown and—"

"You're too kind, Your Majesty." A gown. As if. Who did she think I was? "But I've left my brother unsupervised for too long."

"I thought he was your twin," Aven said, their mouth pulling into a slow smirk. "Surely, he'd be fine for another day. He's almost an adult, after all."

"He is my twin. But there is no telling what kind of trouble he can find without me there." That was an understatement. I only hoped that the house was still standing.

"Ah, siblings," the king said. "I understand how troublesome they can be."

Aven's teasing expression turned cold and sour for the span of a blink, before smoothing into something bland and neutral. I hated watching their personality recede behind a blank mask, as it often did under the scrutiny of the court. It was one of the reasons I always teased them, to bring out the person I knew existed beneath it.

"Anyway," the king continued, "at least regale us with the tale of how you were able to slay this magnificent creature and her brood, so the bards may spin another rousing song of Ellinore the Brave."

My smile grew tight. My tongue was thick in my mouth as my mind whirred for a good answer. I'd hoped to make it out of the castle before anyone asked for details. "Right. A stirring tale for the bard." In the corner of the hall, a bard sat with his quill perched over a parchment, ready to take down my words, his lute propped nearby. Ugh. Bards were the worst. Almost as horrible as mages.

I coughed into my fist. "It was a short fight," I said finally, patting the sword at my side. "No match for the best steel in the kingdom. Again, thank you for the gift. I couldn't have defeated the creature without it."

I may have hated playing the social game, but I knew how to appeal to vanity. The sword had been a gift from the monarchs after the quest of the Golden Dragon and had been made by the finest swordsmith in all the kingdom. Maybe a bit of flattery and gratitude would distract them long enough to let me make my getaway.

"Oh, very good to hear our gift was of help," the queen said, drinking from a goblet worth more than the pouch I'd just received. "But I bet it was harrowing all the same."

"Yes! Very harrowing. Incredibly harrowing. The most harrowing. It was dark in the Dark Wood, obviously. I was very deep in the interior, and it was difficult to see. The spider did have the upper hand with the web and venomous fangs and all, but I landed several blows. I managed to defeat it and win. As I always do."

The bard scribbled furiously in the corner. Another round of polite applause swept through the room as the king and queen nodded their heads. Aven frowned while circling the spider, stepping over the river of ooze. They poked at a leg with a gloved finger, and the brittle limb creaked.

"Well, if the bard has any questions," I added hastily, taking a step backward, "he may contact me in my home village. Thank you."

"Wait," the king said with a chuckle. "Not so fast, Ellinore. Please, indulge us by answering one last question before you take your leave. What do you intend to do with the winnings?"

My throat went as dry as a desert. I gripped the hilt of my sword, my fingers curling around the leather. I licked my lips as the crowd leaned in, hanging by a thread for my answer.

"Retire."

The great hall fell morbidly silent. So quiet, the only sound was the audible gasp of a nearby servant. Aven snapped their head around, abandoning the spider's corpse.

"What?" they breathed.

Their question sparked a ripple of conversation that ran through the onlookers, courtiers and servants alike, while the king glowered down at me from his throne.

"Retire?" the king demanded. "From questing?"

"Yes," I said firmly.

Aven narrowed their eyes. "You're only seventeen."

A tingle of irritation worked down my spine at their tone, and the mention of my age. I was aware I was quite young to retire. And we were of a similar age. They'd had their eighteenth birthday a few months ago, and because they were royalty, there had been a big feast and competition. I had won, of course. Beating them on their birthday had been particularly satisfying. They'd gotten over it. Probably.

"Yes. But I've been questing for years, and to be honest, I'm exhausted."

"A rest, then," the queen said, smiling gently. "A well-earned respite until you return for the summer season." She touched her spouse's hand, which had curled into a fist. "And she'll return fitter and fiercer for it!"

I wanted to argue, to tell them I had no intention of returning for the summer tournaments, but that would just keep me here longer. I nodded.

"Yes. A rest."

The king clapped his hands. "Wonderful. Well, then, let us feast."

Before anyone else could stop me, I hurried down the carpet, dodging the ooze I'd dragged in, and made it out of the double doors into the castle's main hallway. I leaned against the cool stone and inhaled a steadying breath. I rubbed my hands over my face, my thin bracelet slipping down my wrist. Thank the ancients that would be the last time I'd have to pretend to be an extrovert. The last time I would have to pretend to be a hero.

"Ellinore the Brave?"

I startled, pushing myself from the wall, immediately transforming from haggard and exhausted Ellinore into the extraordinary champion everyone expected.

"Yes?" My voice squeaked in pitch. Yes. I was an *impressive* hero.

A girl approached me dressed in an elegant muted-green dress, which was stunning against the warm sepia tone of her skin. Her hair was twisted and styled in the popular way of the women of the court, a stark contrast to my tangled hair hanging in my face. Jewels adorned her fingers and her neck, and any composure I'd gathered fled in the face of her soft smile.

She offered me a cloth sack. "Food for your journey. From the feast."

"Oh, thank you." I took the bag gratefully, with an awkward, deferential nod. I may have been a decorated quester, but I was still a peasant.

"You're welcome. Thank you for . . . helping our traders and farmers. That spider was quite gruesome."

"Ah. Yes. That." Oh no, she wanted to talk about the quest. Must flee.

"I've greatly enjoyed hearing about your quests. You're so brave and admirable." She batted her long eyelashes. Oh no, this might be more than just quest talk. Must flee squared. "The tale about the Golden Dragon is my favorite."

"Oh, yes. That was a . . . great quest."

"I was wondering—"

"Well. Um . . . look at the time. I really must be going. Thanks for the food. Bye."

I brushed past her and all but ran toward the stables. I exited the castle, gracefully tripping down the stone steps of the entrance into the square courtyard, focused on escape.

Footsteps followed me as I crossed the cobblestones, and I desperately hoped it wasn't the courtier trying to engage in more conversation.

"You're lying," a voice said from behind me. Oh, it was worse than the courtier. It was Aven. I stopped in my tracks, stiffening in fear until they continued. "You have no intention of returning for the summer quests."

I sighed before I turned to face them. "I thought you'd be happy. You'll win for once."

Their ears glowed red, but it may have been the heat from the late-afternoon sun instead of their obvious irritation. The weather was warm for an early-spring day, and sweat gathered under my tunic. I couldn't wait to divest myself of my cuirass, tassets, and bracers. Not to mention the pauldron that was barely hanging on. I didn't know how Aven stood it in their brocaded layers and the high lace collar tight around their throat.

The courtyard was empty for the time of day; most of the servants who would normally be bustling by were occupied with the feast. Other than the whinnies from the nearby stable, and the occasional caw from a bird overhead, Aven and I were alone.

"You can't retire," they said.

Why did they always have to be so contrary *all the time*? "You may be royalty, but you're not the king. You can't order me not to, you know. I *am* retiring."

Their brow furrowed, dark eyebrows pulling together. "But you're the best."

"It's nice to hear you admit it."

"I've always admitted it," they rebutted quickly. "It's why I strive to be better. So I can beat you. One day."

My cheeks heated in the face of their sincerity. I hated how a well-placed compliment from them could unravel the solid façade I'd projected for the last several years. "Well. Now *you're* the best. Congratulations!" I gestured awkwardly with my hands to convey my false cheer.

"No." They shook their head. "I don't want to be the best because you've left. I want to be the best by beating you. In the summer competition."

I pressed my fingers into my eyes, which were stinging from both the sunlight and fatigue. "Princet Aven, I smell like dead spider, and I want to go home. Please have your existential crisis on your own time."

They blinked. "I'm not having an existential crisis."

"You literally are. In front of me. It's not cute." Actually, it was kind of cute, especially when the red of their ears deepened and a blush seeped into their pale cheeks.

"Retirement doesn't suit you. You'll be bored to tears in a week."

"I disagree." I crossed my arms. "I think it suits me fine. Great, even. It'll be fun and amazing."

"What do you even plan to do?"

"Garden," I said, lifting my chin. "Knit. Bake. Write. And grow old with a bunch of cats." I didn't mention the piece about figuring out who I was beneath the Ellinore the Brave mantle. Aven wouldn't understand. They were born royalty. They knew who they were and who they could be without ever having to question. I had made a life of pretending, of assuming a persona so my family had a chance at a better life. I was an actor, and I was at my breaking point.

"Garden? Cats? That's not you."

"You don't know me," I shot back. They had no right to say that. They only knew the part I played, not the real me. I barely knew who that was. "Don't pretend we're anything other than competitors."

They matched my defensive posture, their armguard catching on their ornate sleeve. "Fine. Leave. But mark my words, you'll be back. And I'll be ready."

"I won't, but whatever. Have fun, Princet Aven. Try not to die."

They squawked in offense as I hastily sped toward the stables.

My steed, a beautiful bay mare with a black mane, was as happy to see me as I was to see her. Declining the help of the stable hands, I pulled her out of the stall by her halter and adjusted my saddle, then tucked the new bag of gold and bundle of food into the saddlebag.

"Come on, Bluebell," I said, patting her neck. She nickered and pressed the smooth velvet of her nose against my hand. "Let's go visit our good friend. Then we'll ride home and make sure Zig isn't locked in a dungeon or back in the stocks."

I mounted and rode out of the castle grounds, under the portcullis, and over the drawbridge, until I was on the road headed to my home village on the outskirts of the castle's looming influence. Though Aven may have been watching, and though the competitions and contests had been good to me over the years and had allowed me to provide for my family, and though the bards had sung charitably of my feats, I didn't look back.

Not once.

2

"Hail the conquering hero!" I yelled as I squeezed my way
through the cavern tunnel. "Or, you know, a close approximation."

The cool stone wall scraped my grubby skin and rasped against my
leather armor. I still smelled, but I had found a sliver of soap in my saddlebag,
and I hoped to use it once I wiggled my way into my sometime accomplice's
home.

At no response, I called again. "Fine, not quite a *conquering* hero, but at
least I won!"

I turned a tight corner, then stumbled into a huge natural grotto. Over
the centuries an underground stream had worn away the rock, creating a large,
enclosed space with a towering ceiling. Rivulets of cool whitewater spilled
down one wall and dumped into a large pool off to the side. Stalactites of various sizes protruded from above, and slow drips ran down their lengths and fell
with splats to the hard ground. The floor was slick with spray and condensation, and I had to watch my step as I ventured farther.

The cool, damp air raised goose bumps along my arms. One beam of
setting sunlight spilled from a small hole in the rock near the highest point,
illuminating veins of glittering quartz and pyrite in the walls, but offered little
in the way of heat. Otherwise, there was no natural light, which made the shadows toward the back of the cave deep and dark.

"Dave?" I called, stepping farther into my friend's residence. "Are you here?" I squinted into the dark. "Dave?"

Feeling around the edge, I navigated to the spot where I usually slept when staying overnight, a carved-out bench in the wall with stolen blankets and a feather pillow.

"Dave?" I called again as I bumped around noisily until I found the torch I'd used the last time. Using the flint from my bag at my hip, I managed to light the tip of the burned cloth and wood. Holding it aloft, I turned and—

"Boo!"

I gasped, dropping the torch and yanking my sword from my scabbard, a shrill scream erupting from my throat.

Dave chuckled, falling over onto his side, while smoke billowed from the large nostrils in his snout. The golden scales of his belly gleamed in the sputtering firelight cast by the torch, much like the golden coins of his hoard in the recesses of his cave.

I pushed my hand against my chest, feeling the rabbit-beat of my heart under my palm. "What the fu—"

"Did I get you?" Dave asked as he sat up on his haunches and smiled, showing off the rows of razor-sharp teeth in his mouth.

"Yes!"

He chuckled under his breath. "Excellent. I'd been wanting to do that for ages."

"That was not funny!"

Dave shrugged, his wings shifting behind him. "It was hilarious. Did you hear the sound you made? The notoriously cool and composed Ellinore the Brave squealing in fright. The scandal! What would the populace think?"

"I almost skewered you!" I sheathed my sword as I scowled, choosing to ignore the dig about public opinion. "I could've hurt you."

Dave snorted, his tail swishing on the ground behind him. "I would've dodged."

"I can't believe I'm friends with you . . . you unhinged overgrown lizard." I scooped up the torch and held it aloft as Dave continued giggling under his hot breath.

"I'm a delight! A charming dragon who adores a good joke. Besides, I have to get my entertainment somehow, since I'm not allowed to play pranks on the human folk anymore."

"And rightfully so."

Dave was my second quest ever. Several years ago the king declared that the person who rid a neighboring village of a pesky dragon would receive an obscene amount of gold. I found Dave right on the outskirts of said town, eating sheep and terrorizing the populace with his awful pranks and jokes. I convinced him to make a deal. He'd stop his activities, and in exchange I'd split the royal reward with him. The bargain was in his best interest because there were about a dozen other questers bearing down on his location who would not hesitate to stab him with pointy weapons. In the end he made the wise choice and hid in a cave, daring to hunt and fly only at night, and only on the mountainsides, which afforded him a limited, but allegedly tasty, selection of wild game.

After we'd shaken hands—well, claws—I journeyed to the castle and told the king that the dragon had been vanquished. I used that term specifically because in the beginning of my career I tried to stick to little white lies, and not the intricate yarns I've had to spin since. Anyway, a single golden scale from beneath Dave's front leg proved what I'd said, and the king and queen bought my story. It was one of the better bard tales, since Dave had helped me embellish the details of what really happened.

"Did you do it?" I asked as I followed Dave deeper into the cavern.

He slithered ahead of me, his long, spiked tail dragging behind him. "Of course I did," he said, spine twisting as he looked over his shoulder, green eyes glittering. "But I can't believe you had me moving spider egg sacs. The task was vile and not one I'm willing to repeat."

"Yeah, well, it was that or dragging the dead momma spider for miles by her web. Which was equally disgusting."

Dave spat fire as he settled down in his usual spot and lit the other torches in the sconces on the walls. They flared to life and the entire cave was bathed in a gentle glow. He perched on the small hoard he kept in the main chamber, a pile of golden coins and jewels, modest compared with what I knew he kept in another section of the cave.

Dave's body was larger than that of a horse and much longer from snout to tail, but small for a dragon, or so I'd learned from scrolls. His scales were mostly gold, with a smattering of red and orange between his horns. A large, spiked barb adorned the tip of his tail, and he had two leathery wings folded at his back. He moved as if he didn't have bones, able to navigate the smallest nooks and crannies of the cavern system and sneak out the small back entrance when he needed. Lithe as he was, he was still impressive. He towered over me when he stood on his hind legs, even while I was atop Bluebell. He could be terrifying if he wanted, but as I'd come to learn, he preferred bad jokes and gold to breathing fire and eating people.

I settled in a wooden chair Dave kept for me, and tossed the torch off to the side. "At least tell me the egg sacs are safe and we didn't actually make the giant spiders of the world extinct."

"They're safe. There will be a mountain pass that will become inordinately dangerous for travelers in a few years, but for now all is fine." He looked at me expectantly, his clawed feet digging into the mound of gold as a cat would knead a blanket.

"Good. I don't need any more guilt." I dropped my saddlebag at my feet and stretched my arms above my head and yawned. "Remind me—are man-eating giant spiders ancients or folklores?"

"Folklores, I believe," Dave said. "Though I'm not sure if they possess any magic other than their ability to grow to large sizes."

"You don't know?"

He narrowed his eyes into slits. "I may be old, but I don't know everything."

"Whoa. I was just asking. I am merely glad that another folklore has a chance to live on. It feels like there are fewer and fewer out there."

"Maybe if the humans would cease killing the ancients and folklores for sport and coin, then there would be more."

"Yeah, I know," I said quietly. I always hated the way other questers often defaulted to *killing* rather than utilizing basic problem-solving or communication skills. It was a relief to be done with it. "Speaking of coin." Rummaging in my bag, I dug out the reward pouch. Dave's eyes glowed with interest as he watched me remove his share of the gold. When I tossed it onto his pile, a low, pleased rumble vibrated up from his gut into his throat. He grasped the coins with his front claws and tucked the gold under his belly. "Enjoy those, because they will be the last ones I bring for a long time."

Dave pulled his attention away from his newest acquisition and narrowed his eyes. "What do you mean?"

"I did it." I spread my arms. "Ellinore the Brave has officially retired. No more questing. No more lies. No more of any of it. I'm done."

A curl of judgmental smoke wafted from Dave's nose and from between the gaps in his sharp teeth. "What brought this on? I thought you liked questing."

"Well, yeah. It's fun in a disgusting way," I said, gesturing to the grit and grime clinging to my body. "But I finally had enough gold to purchase a house on the southeastern coast for my parents. Which was always the goal. I've sent them on their way. This," I said, hefting the pouch, "was one last fun hurrah."

"I thought we worked well together," Dave said with an exaggerated pout.

I touched the thin silver bracelet at my wrist, my way of calling Dave if needed. He'd gifted it to me after a disastrous quest that involved an enraged strix where I almost died. Come to find out, strixes were one of the few magical beings that didn't like to negotiate. Since then, all I needed was to rub the bracelet between my fingers with intent and Dave would come.

"We do work well together. And we'll always be friends, but I've reached my goal of helping my parents and my brother."

Dave scratched his cheek with the claw of his foreleg. "What about you?" he rumbled.

"What about me?" I asked. "I get to rest. I can shed this imposter's mantle of a supposed hero and go live in my family's cabin and . . . knit, and then I'll join my parents on the coast and just be Ellinore. Besides, it was only a matter of time before I was discovered bending the rules anyway. Aven almost caught on this time. They were so close to realizing that the giant spider had already been dead for days before I found it."

Dave sighed. "A sad end to a centuries-old creature."

"But hey, we've given a few of her children a chance. Aven and the others may have harvested a few of the smaller spiders, but one of those eggs might grow to her size and be terrorizing that canyon in a few decades."

Dave smiled at that, as close as a dragon could smile. "And what did dear Aven say about you quitting?" He waggled the curve of scales that acted as eyebrows.

I flinched, then bristled. My back stiffened as I straightened from my tired slump. "What does it matter what Aven said? Their opinion is of no interest to me."

Dave chuckled. "Sure."

"What?" I stood. "It's not. I don't care what spoiled royalty thinks."

"If that was the case, you wouldn't be worried about being deemed a fraud."

My mouth dropped open; then I snapped it shut. Shame made my face grow hot and my shoulders sag. "That's different. I don't want the entire kingdom to demand all their gold back once they've found out I'm a sham. That I'm not a real champion. That Ellinore the Brave is a construct composed of embellished bards' songs and the whimsy of a populace primed to believe in heroes and fairy tales."

"That's cynical even for you." Dave lazily eyed me from his pile. "Didn't the king and queen deem you the best quester in all the land?"

I raised a finger. "They're wrong. I was the best at *winning*. There's a subtle difference."

Dave stretched his long body. A golden goblet rolled from the small hoard, clinking over the other gold and jewels until it came to rest at my feet. My reflection in the glossy surface warped with the curve of the metal, creating a distorted caricature that felt like a mirror of my court persona.

He hummed a jaunty tune under his breath, one I recognized as a song about me. "Do you want the opinion of a very old and wise being?" he asked, blinking slowly.

"Why? Is there one around?" He growled in offense, and I held up my hands. "I mean . . . I guess."

"You're not an imposter, Ellinore," Dave said.

It was a nice sentiment, but Dave was my friend and thus obligated to say nice things about me. "I literally dragged an already-dead spider from the forest to win and had you move the egg sacs I supposedly destroyed. I not only lied but used an accomplice."

Dave smiled. "All the same. You are not a fraud. Yes, you've completed quests in your own special way, but you've completed them. You have done what was asked of you, just differently than what the royals expected. Take me, for example. You were sent to rid the kingdom of the dragon terrorizing a village. And you did. I'm not terrorizing anyone anymore." He grinned wide. "Other than you, of course."

I crossed my arms and sank down slowly into the chair. "Thanks, but I don't think wordplay is going to save me if they ever find out. Especially with the bigger tales the bards have concocted. I need to quit while I'm ahead. Before the clever untruths catch up to me. I finally have some time to figure out who I am without a sword and an epithet."

"It's your choice," Dave said. "But who will come tell me fun stories? You won't have any." He flashed a comically large pout. "And I won't get to travel as often as I do now."

"You can always come live by the sea."

Dave scoffed. "And leave my hoard? Now you're speaking nonsense."

"Well, until it's time for me to move, I promise to come visit when I can, and I'll tell you all about what Zig is up to."

"Oh, he is unruly. What has he done lately?"

"I don't know. He's been home alone ever since I was able to send my parents to their new life. I just hope he's not done something reckless and impulsive while I've been away."

"If he has," Dave said, "you can always leave and live here. I enjoy your company. But not when you smell so bad." He wrinkled his nose.

I sniffed and gagged. "Look. I'm aware. I was hoping you would heat the spring for me." I clasped my hands together and gave him my best pleading expression, complete with pouty lips and puppy eyes. Dave huffed, then sighed.

"Fine."

He trundled over to the spring, took a deep breath, and released a torrent of fire into the basin. Steam ballooned upward and the water bubbled with heat.

A bath would do wonders for my joints and for my mind. It would make the remaining short ride back to my village more pleasant. And once I returned home, I could really start to enjoy my retirement. With no more quests in my future, I could finally, finally relax and just be myself.

3

THE KINGDOM OF AVOURY COVERED THE ENTIRE CONTINENT—FROM the mostly uninhabitable western coastline to the mountains that spat fire in the northeast to the plains and forests of the midland to the almost always warm southern coast. It hadn't always been so expansive, but centuries had passed since Avoury was formed and the current succession of monarchs had come into power. It was a diverse kingdom that encompassed a wide range of communities—small farm villages, bustling trade towns, fishing settlements along the coasts, castles and keeps, thick forests (at least one of which was haunted), and rivers that connected them all. And while the entire land was solidified under one banner, life wasn't as harmonious as it could be. Most often because humans were jerks.

My home village sat exactly in the middle of the kingdom. Though it wasn't as large as the city that abutted the castle walls, it was a popular spot for travelers and traders due to its location along a river and a main road. As such, Traveler's Rest boasted three inns, four taverns, and a shrine to the white hart, our local deity dedicated to the safety of explorers and adventurers. A colorful market teemed with residents and visitors on most days, hosting wares from the local craftspeople and food from the outlying farms. Festivals with music, storytelling, dancing, and other forms of entertainment were held nearly every week. The town was a tourist haven.

In the late days of spring, it was positively hectic. And unfortunately, the quickest route from Dave's cavern to my family's small cabin on the outskirts was through the main square.

I lingered in the grotto overnight, choosing to eat and sleep in relative safety rather than risking it on the road. I even spent hours detangling my hair with a fine golden comb from Dave's hoard. The next day I hoped to time my ride so that I passed through town in the late afternoon, when everyone was either napping after their midday meal or preparing for the evening.

I tied my armor to the back of my saddle and pulled on a sturdy pair of trousers, a large, frayed tunic, and my boots. I wrapped myself in my tattered cloak with the hood pulled over my head in an attempt at anonymity. With my legendary quest record, I was the closest thing to a celebrity many of the towns-folk would ever see. And the last thing I wanted was a repeat of the badgering I'd received from Aven, once everyone learned of my retirement.

I curled my shoulders and slouched as I rode. It was one thing to have spent my teenage years fooling royalty and taking their gold—they had enough to hand out, and other than their riches, I held no love for them. But to have fooled the folks of my hometown into believing I was some manner of local hero—that guilt was a far heavier burden.

I deftly guided Bluebell over the trail leading in from the stretch of family farms on the periphery, down the main thoroughfare of hard-packed dirt, and into the center of town. She danced around muddy wheel ruts filled with this morning's spring rain as we traveled the thatched-roof-lined streets. My plan seemed to be working, as the canopied tables of wares were shuttered for the day, but I wasn't out of the woods yet. When I passed the local magistrate's office and found the pillory empty, I breathed out a sigh of relief.

"If I have told you once," came a voice from down the road, "I've told you thousands of times."

I snapped my head around and nudged Bluebell forward. The doors to the Winter Hart banged open, and a figure stumbled out. A short, balding man followed, shaking his fist and yelling. "No swindling in my place of business!"

"I wasn't swindling!"

The person gained his feet, and my stomach plummeted. I'd recognize that lanky frame anywhere.

Zig was my twin, younger than me by only a few minutes, though he acted as if the gap were much bigger. We looked alike, sharing the same brown hair and brown eyes. His was cut short, though, with bangs that fell across his forehead, and he was slightly taller than me, with the slim build of someone who hadn't ever held a sword—or worked a day in his life, for that matter. My shoulders were broader, my muscles thicker from all the questing, while he was lithe from running away from his problems.

Zig huffed as he straightened his vest and tucked his shirttails into his trousers. "I was merely engaging in a game of cards with fellow patrons. It's not my fault that they were so severely unlucky as to lose most of their coin and three of their prized sheep. Which I will promptly and kindly sell back to them once they have the means to purchase Bleep, Bloop, and Rainbow."

The tavern keeper scowled. "Unlucky, huh?"

"Yes," Zig said adamantly. "Pure, unadulterated bad luck. They must have broken a mirror." He snapped his fingers and pointed toward the door, beyond which the poor suckers were probably drowning their sorrow in ale. "Or a black cat crossed their path! I heard there was one prowling about the other night. Or maybe"—he leaned in and dramatically dropped his voice to a near whisper—"they were cursed by one of our many regional deities."

The tavern keeper's eyes narrowed. He stomped forward and grabbed Zig's wrist. Zig squeaked.

My brother might be a nuisance, but I wouldn't see him hurt. I urged Bluebell forward, hand on my sword, while Zig struggled in the other man's hold.

The tavern keeper shoved his free hand into Zig's sleeve and, after a moment, yanked something out, before releasing Zig with a push. He held up a bent card—the eye of newt.

Zig blanched, then let out a nervous chuckle. "How did that get there?"

"You are banned, Zig! Don't come into my tavern again for another month!"

"A month?" Zig whined. "But you have the best ale in town."

"A month!" the man said again, wagging his finger. "Why can't you be more like your sister? The pride of Traveler's Rest shouldn't have to endure a brother like you. You are lucky I don't take you to the magistrate. She'd likely throw you in Lord Henley's dungeon instead of just the pillory this time."

Zig lifted his chin, his lips pressed into a thin line, his brow drawn. He spread his arms and bowed. "Don't you know, I'm a twin. I'm inherently lucky. Born under fortunate stars and all. Luck will follow me all my days."

The tavern owner snorted. "You're a cheat."

"Well, even twins have to make their own luck sometimes." Quick as a hummingbird, Zig straightened and snatched the card from the owner's grasp. With a flourish of his fingers, it disappeared. "Fine," he said sharply. "A month."

He turned and stopped short. He narrowed his eyes, focusing on the spot where I'd paused to watch. "Sister," he said.

I sighed and tugged back my hood. "Brother," I replied.

"You're home."

"I am."

The tavern owner gasped. "Ellinore the Brave," he said with round eyes.

I winced.

"It would be an honor to have you drink in my tavern this afternoon."

I glanced at Zig, who crossed his arms over his chest. Try as he might to exude an unbothered appearance, the tavern keeper's words had poked at the only sore spot Zig possessed.

I tossed my braided hair over my shoulder. "I'm sorry. I would love to, but I'd like to have a celebratory drink with my brother, and well, sadly, he's banned."

Zig cocked his head to the side, his eyebrows raised in question.

"I will lift the ban!" the tavern owner said quickly, while waving his hands. "For the rest of the afternoon. Then he's banned again for a month."

"Zig?" I asked.

He sighed dramatically and turned slowly to face the owner. "I can't deny my sister the best ale in town, now can I?"

I dismounted from Bluebell, grabbed my sword from where I'd kept it near the pommel, then tied her off on a hitching post outside. I followed Zig into the tavern.

Despite the afternoon sun, the interior was dark, with scant natural light filtering in through gaps in the worn planks that made up the walls. The few windows were covered with cloth to keep out the flies, and candlelight flickered from waxy tapers that had melted to the tables. A banked fire glowed in the fireplace at the other end, keeping a kettle warm in the coals. The heels of my boots thunked against the wooden floor, the scattering of sawdust slightly muffling the sound. The air was thick with the smell of ale and pipe smoke and the unique pub scent of regret. A low hum of chatter arose as we entered.

We settled at a round table in the corner, and I propped my sword next to me as I tucked my back to the wall, giving myself a clear view of the room. Zig sat beside me, and I raised an eyebrow.

"I may not be a great adventurer or have an impressive sword gifted to me by royalty, but I know better than to turn my back to a crowd who have just lost a significant sum to me." He nodded toward a trio on the other side of the room who shot baleful glares in our direction. "Bleep, Bloop, and Rainbow's previous owners."

"You've somehow managed to add a whole new level to the term 'fleecing,'" I said with a roll of my eyes.

"I know. Impressive, right?"

"What are you going to do with three sheep, anyway?" I drummed my fingers on the table while I cast glances around the crowd. They stared at us, some sly, others bold.

The scrutiny did not bother Zig at all, but it made my skin crawl.

Zig shrugged at my question. "Sell them, I guess. Or keep them. I don't know. Winning sheep wasn't on my list of things to do today."

"What was on your list?"

"Occupy myself," he said with a grin. "In ways that I know Mom and Pop would not approve of, and neither would you, apparently."

I had sent my parents to their new house on the coast before I set out on the spider quest, with the promise I'd join them soon. Zig had chosen to stay behind. I'd thought his intention was to wait for me, but his statement proved otherwise.

"You could've gone with them."

He laughed, tossing his head back. "To do what? Watch the waves roll in, drop a line in the sea, or frolic on the beach? Oh wait, be grateful to my sister for providing a boring life for me? No thanks."

"But our family," I said, heart sinking. "We were all going. That was the plan."

Zig made a face. "That was *your* plan. Not mine. I'll stay here, where there is plenty to entertain me and I can earn my own living."

"You could earn a living there."

Zig's eyebrow twitched. "Yes, until all the sailors and fishermen become wise. Here there are tourists aplenty. A populace that is constantly changing is ripe for the picking."

I scoffed. "So, you have been swindling."

His eyes narrowed. "I don't swindle. I'm just good at playing games. It's not my fault that the folks I play against can't keep track of their own cards."

It wasn't worth arguing with Zig. I had never been able to talk him out of things when he had his mind set on them. He was stubborn. But I could be too. I'd get him to the coast even if I had to tie him in a sack and drag him there.

A pretty girl with blond hair served us two pints of ale, the froth spilling over the lips of the full tankards as she set them down. The girl straightened, then twisted her hands in her apron and stared at me with unblinking eyes. After a moment of silence, she retreated toward the bar.

Zig tented his fingers, a smirk playing around the edge of his mouth. "Looks like you have an adoring fan."

I glanced at the bar area and saw her openly staring at me. She smiled, wide and bright, showing off a row of pretty teeth, and twirled her hair around her finger.

Ugh. He was right. My annoyance with Zig was already simmering under my skin, and despite the night's rest in the grotto, exhaustion tugged behind my eyes. An encounter with a fan was the last thing I needed. I took a sip of the ale and began to plan my escape before she became emboldened and wanted to talk with me. The horror.

"Drink quickly so we can get out of here."

He raised a questioning eyebrow and grabbed his cup, taking a large gulp. "What? Did the Lady in the Sea ask for her pearl back?"

I didn't even know if the Lady in the Sea knew her pearl was missing. I'd found it when it had washed up on the shore after a terrible storm years ago.

"Or did the manticore want to defend its honor and challenge you to a fight?"

There was no fight with the manticore the first time, just the easiest riddle I'd ever solved. Well, Dave and I solved. The manticore probably gave us an easy one because Dave and he were fellow ancients.

"Or did the Harpy want revenge? Wait, did you kill that one? Or . . . what was that other one . . . the lion with the wings . . ." He tapped his fingers on the table. "Oh! The griffin."

I frowned. "Those creatures are all ancients, and if you had ever listened to our parents' tales, you would know it is nearly impossible to kill an ancient." I had once . . . inadvertently, at the very beginning of my career. A happy accident, some would say, that resulted in the large bearskin hung on the wall behind the thrones. It was my introduction to questing and the beginning of Lord Ethan's deep-seated hatred. "They are the closest things to deities that walk in our realm."

Zig took a swig of his drink. "Whatever." A coin appeared on the backs of his fingers, and he made it dance along his knuckles, before making it disappear into his palm with a twitch. "Why are you in such a pissy mood?"

I sagged against the back of the chair. "I'm tired."

"So you've said. Multiple times. Go home and take a nap."

"No, it's not that kind of tired." I shook my head. "I'm tired of it all, Zig. This was my last quest. I'm done."

"What? Now?" He gestured toward the pints of ale. "You're at the height of your fame. The court loves you. Bards spin tales. Fangirls swoon in your presence." He nodded to where the barmaid watched us intently.

She caught my gaze and flushed. Oh no, she looked like she was going to come over. I was horrible at dealing with fans and with people in general. I suddenly found myself wishing Aven were here. They were always better at socializing than I was. As much as I hated to admit it, they'd saved me at court more than once or twice.

"Why quit now?" Zig asked.

"Huh?" I asked.

Zig raised an eyebrow. "I said, why quit now that you are at peak celebrity?"

"It was never about glory or recognition."

"No, of course not," he said, and drank down the dregs of his cup.

"Look, I think we should go." I gathered my belongings just as a faint twang of plucked strings wafted across the room, and the low babble of conversation softened.

"Forgot you were perfect," he muttered.

"That's not true. I'm far from—"

"And now it's time to listen to the story," a bard began, his singsong voice and the strumming from his lute cutting me off, "of the Brave Ellinore at the start of her glory."

Zig and I both groaned.

"Oh, ancients save me," he said, covering his face with his hands.

"Ugh," I agreed. "I hate this one."

"It's literally about you."

"I know and it's ridiculous." *And it's all wrong,* I wanted to say, but the words stuck in my throat. That wasn't a public conversation. I didn't know how Zig would react when I finally told him the truth about my questing exploits. *If* I ever told him.

We were close once. Closer than regular siblings, being twins born only minutes apart. And Zig was right—we were lucky, according to our parents. For the first twelve years of our lives, we did everything together. We ran the fields behind our home, weaved flower crowns, and dodged bees as we stole honey from their hives. We played with baby goats and rolled in the mud with piglets. We giggled all through the day, and all through the night when we were supposed to be sleeping. But we grew up and grew apart after the events of the bard's song, the first time I'd been dragged in front of the royal court and been given a purse of gold. I had no idea how he would handle the truth of what I'd done since, or more specifically, hadn't done. If it would bring us closer or drive the final wedge between us.

I shuddered when the bard reached a high note on a false rhyme while regaling the crowd with the tale of the Ursa. Zig winced. He downed the remainder of my drink and then staggered to his feet.

"The one about the Golden Dragon is better," he muttered as he dropped a few coins onto the table.

I stood and grabbed his arm. He immediately wrenched out of my grasp.

"I'm leaving," he said. "Getting a head start on my month's ban. You stay, though. Have fun. Bask in the adoration of your fans."

I frowned, my middle twisting at Zig's thinly veiled resentment. The bard's voice took on a desperate edge as he saw Zig and me heading toward the exit, but I ignored him and followed Zig into the sunlit street.

"Let's go home." I grabbed Bluebell's reins. "We can talk. It'll be like old times."

Zig burst into obnoxious laughter. "You go home. I'm going to another tavern."

"Zig . . . ," I said with a sigh. "I've been away and—"

"Yes," he said, walking down the street toward the Green Serpent with long-legged strides, "you've been away. You left me to my own devices. And vices, I might add." He wagged a finger at me. He turned and walked backward, his brown eyes dagger-sharp despite the ale. "You go do your . . . noble thing and let me do my . . . not-so-noble things, and I'll see you when I see you. Okay? Okay."

Then he dashed through the door of the Green Serpent without so much as a goodbye.

4

I, Ellinore, *just* Ellinore, had spent the last two weeks of my life trying a variety of new things only to discover that I was completely horrible at all of them.

Not that I would admit it *ever*. Especially not to Zig or to Aven (if I saw them again) or to anyone who asked, really, because I had chosen this. I had *chosen* to garden and to knit and to cook and to write. It was just more difficult than I had anticipated. I'd hit a few snags, but I was certain I could figure it all out. Maybe.

I sprinkled water on my decidedly dead herb garden on the windowsill and looked out at the backyard, where the mud pit that was supposed to be rows of carrots and string beans mocked me. Okay, so I didn't have a green thumb.

I also didn't have the fine motor skills required for knitting. What I did have was a knotted tangle of yarn and two bent needles sitting uselessly on the table. The large jumble of string would have been a perfect plaything for the two stray kittens I'd adopted from the nearby farmer's barn, if they hadn't run off together on the second day they lived with me.

One of the sheep bleated contentedly in the yard, reminding me that my brother had been more successful with his newly acquired livestock than I had in all my domestic efforts.

Fine. Whatever. I had failed at the other things, but cooking . . . cooking I could maybe do. I'd roasted plenty of game over a campfire in my lifetime. And it hadn't been horrible. I'd survived.

I left the window and crossed to the hearth, where I peered into the pot. Well, that didn't look right.

I skimmed over the recipe that I'd purchased from a merchant a few days ago. It was supposed to be rabbit stew, but it looked more like . . . noxious sludge. I grabbed a long wooden spoon and tried to stir it. I wiggled the handle, attempting to lever the not-quite-soup into moving. With a grunt and my ample sword-arm strength, I tugged. The handle snapped in half, and the thick, viscous liquid didn't budge. The broken end of the spoon sank into the brew, like a stone slowly disappearing into a bubbling swamp. I cursed and threw the remnants of the shattered handle into the fire, before sighing and slumping onto the bench at the table. I covered my face with my hands and let out a frustrated scream.

I took a breath and composed myself. "Okay, no," I said out loud. "It's okay. This is not a pity party. I tried something new, and it didn't work." I stood and placed my hands on my hips. "It's okay."

I comforted myself with the knowledge that my parents had made it to their new home. A trader from the coastline had brought the message and delivered my mom's letter. It was a bright spot in an otherwise bleak spell, knowing that my parents could now enjoy the benefits of my winnings. Even if it had come at the cost of . . . my sense of self and any and all normal life skills.

"I think you're a lost cause," I said to the gelatinous stew currently destroying my mother's good pot. "Maybe I am too."

Rainbow bleated from the yard in agreement.

With a heavy sigh, I dumped whatever it was that I'd mistakenly conjured into the row of carrots (it couldn't hurt), then scrubbed the pot clean. Then I sat inside and drummed my fingers against the kitchen table, unsure of what to do next.

A journal of pristine parchment sat tauntingly blank in front of me, and a new quill and inkwell were within reach, waiting for me to take them and do some self-exploration. Small splats of ink stained my fingers as I dipped the quill into the well. I stalled. I set the quill down, then picked it up, then twirled it in my fingers, then set it down again. It was only a journal, meant for my own eyes, or maybe Zig's if I ever told him the truth. It shouldn't be so difficult, but I didn't know how to begin or what to write. I knew the truth about how all my supposed accolades had gone down, but there were so many lies tangled into who I was to everyone else, I didn't know what the real Ellinore looked like.

I stared into the distance for a few minutes, contemplating a nap, when the door creaked open and Zig slipped inside, wearing the same clothes from the day before, a sack in his hand. He raised an eyebrow at me. "Ah, you're home. Just where I left you."

I mustered my best annoyed look. "And you didn't come home last night."

He shrugged, then smiled, all teeth. "Would you like to know why?"

"No. Ancients, no."

My mom once said the cosmos had given her me to test her humility and had given her Zig to test her patience. I'd never quite understood what she meant until these last two weeks of living alone with Zig. And now I got it. I *so* got it. But I couldn't leave him, not until I convinced him to move to the new house.

He laughed as he kicked off his boots. "Did I hear shrieking earlier?" He ran a hand through his tousled hair before wandering over to where I sat. "I swore I heard a scream while I was walking home."

I crossed my arms over my chest. "No. There was no shrieking."

"Oh, must have been someone else." He lifted his nose and took a tentative sniff, then shuddered. "What's that smell?"

"Stew."

"No, it's not." He breathed deeply, then pinched his nose. "That smells like death."

"You're a jerk."

"As expected," he said. "I could say it's nice to know that you're not perfect at everything, but that would tip me from jerk into prick territory."

I bristled but didn't deign to respond.

He smiled, knowing he'd touched a nerve, then dropped the sack on the table with a thump and settled on the bench. He extended his hands above his head and yawned, grimacing as he stretched. "Ugh. My back. I shouldn't have slept on that floor."

"You could've come home."

"That still would entail sleeping on the floor."

"No, it would be sleeping on a mattress and blankets . . . on the floor."

The home where we'd grown up was a two-room cabin with a fireplace in one wall and a window in the other that looked out over the backyard and the well; a rough-hewn table in the living area, with a long bench on one side and two chairs; and one room with a hay-stuffed mattress. I'd taken my parents' old room since they left, and Zig still slept where we used to as children, on a mattress and a pile of blankets in a curtained-off area on the other side of the structure. Not that he slept at home often.

"It's a good thing I brought home lunch, or else you'd starve from obstinacy . . . and ineptitude." He reached into the bag and handed me an apple with a perfect red peel. He flapped open a cloth napkin and placed the rest of the contents on it—a hunk of cheese, slices of salted meat, a loaf of bread, another apple, and a large pile of thick-shelled nuts.

"Those better not be magic beans," I said.

Zig narrowed his eyes. "That was one time, and we were nine. Let it go. Besides, be grateful I brought you anything at all. Beggars can't be choosers, you know."

"I can pay you back—"

He shot me a glare. "I can treat my sister to lunch. I have my own money."

I bit back the comments about *how* he made that money because I was very much aware of how hypocritical that would be.

I sighed. "I tried, okay? Cooking is difficult."

His expression turned grim, as if he'd already noticed my struggles. Or maybe he was just hungover. "It smells about as difficult as the knitting looks," he said, holding the raggedy ball of yarn between two fingers, then tossing it aside. "You know . . . you can sit around and be miserable at the coast with our parents. You don't have to be here to do that."

I straightened from my slump. "What? I'm not miserable."

"Sure. Tell that to your dying plants." He jerked his thumb over his shoulder. A faint breeze blew in through the open shutters, rattling the stunted twigs of my herbs. Another cheerful bleat of the sheep echoed from the pasture.

"Anyway," he said, and took a bite of his own apple. "I don't get it. You were happy. You had a competitive situuation with that royal person."

I scoffed at that, but Zig continued undeterred.

"You had acclaim. You earned enough gold for five lifetimes. And you just quit? Like that?" He snapped his fingers. "Why?"

"It's complicated."

"Right." He cast a glance at my leather armor and sword propped in the corner. I'd not fixed the pauldron, but I'd cleaned and shined the armor. And of course polished and sharpened my sword. And hadn't touched it since. He frowned. "You can tell me, you know. I'd listen. I can't promise I won't judge, but I'd at least keep my mouth shut." He fiddled with his sleeve. "Did something happen?"

My eyes stung at Zig's sincere concern. It would be so easy to tell him. That I wasn't what everyone made me out to be. But it was all too fresh, too immediate, sparkling right under my skin. And I couldn't shake how he'd looked at me on the street two weeks before, like he despised me. I swallowed down the lump in my throat. "You wouldn't understand."

His expression shuttered, like a cloud passing over the sun. "Right. Of course. I'm not an adventurer. I'm not Ellinore the Brave." He said the title with such disdain, it made my heart ache. "I wouldn't get it."

"That's not what I meant," I said. "I don't really even understand myself." And that was the first full truth I'd said to him since I returned. I gestured to the blank parchment. "I'm trying to figure it out."

Zig touched the journal. "Wow," he said, staring down at the blank page, "you've been so prolific. I'm impressed."

I snatched the book from him, almost knocking over the inkwell in the process. "I'm organizing my thoughts before I start writing. I'm . . . preplanning."

"Sure," he said. "Other people call that procrastinating, but whatever.

Instead of writing about an adventure, why don't you get back out there and slay something?"

I took a vicious bite of bread and washed it down with a gulp of water from the tankard on the table.

"I'll slay *you*."

"Nice, Sister. Look, I may have the perfect next quest for you."

I paused. "What?"

Zig's hands danced over the worn wood, picking at the grain, his fingers tapping in anxious energy, a card flashing between his knuckles every now and then. His knee juddered beneath the table. His eye twitched, and between his fingers he twirled a pendant on a chain he wore.

"Out with it," I said, setting down a bit of the cheese. "What mischief have you done now?"

"Me?" he asked, feigning innocence. "Are you addressing me? Your brother, who has not done a single wrong thing in his entire life? Your blameless, innocent little brother?"

"You were in the stocks three days ago for selling fake treasure maps."

"Slander."

"Really?"

"Absolutely. That bard promised me those directions were real. I merely transcribed the information readily available in her song. If anyone was upset, they should've taken it up with her. Spreading misinformation like she was."

My stomach clenched when his scenario hit a little too close to home. "Right. On the day I returned, you were thrown out and banned from a tavern."

He threw up his hands. "It's not cheating. It's not my fault the other players sucked." He tore off a hunk of bread and took a bite. "By the way, that tavern owner has a poster of you tacked outside about how you love his ale. You should make him pay you for your endorsement. At the very least, for your image. It's called branding, and now that you are retired, you should really look into cultivating diverse revenue streams."

I narrowed my eyes. "You're avoiding the topic. A topic, I might add, that you brought up. So let me ask again—what have you done?"

"First, I just have a question for you, mighty Ellinore who has recently slain the giant spider of the Dark Wood and has completed other miraculous deeds, like tricking the Lady in the Sea for her pearl and saving a town from a volcano and blah, blah, blah."

"Nice."

He shrugged. "The accolades get long after a bit. Anyway, what do you know of the Elder Beast?"

I arched an eyebrow as alarm bells went off in my head. I took a swallow of water, then set down my tankard. Where would he have learned of the Elder Beast? I'd heard only a handful of stories that referenced the myth, and none of the books I'd read as a child even mentioned it. The Elder Beast wasn't a being that would come up in casual conversation. "Um . . . why?"

He plunked his elbow onto the table and held his chin in his hand. "Because I want to know." He prodded me with the toe of his boot, the pointy edge jabbing into my calf muscle. "So tell me."

"It's a beast."

"I gathered."

I shrugged. "I've only heard about it a few times. It's not a popular story subject. I don't know much about it."

"Oh, don't be difficult. I may not have been as enamored with mythical stories as a child as you were"—that was a lie, evident by all the "magical" items Zig had purchased with his chore money—"but I occasionally listened to the bards and storytellers. They sang of all kinds of beastly things in their songs. You must remember *something*."

"I'm not being difficult. I honestly know very little."

"Then tell me what you do know."

"Um . . . I think it's an ancient? Possibly a chimera, like a griffin or a manticore, in that it has attributes of a few different creatures. Like the legs of a bull and the face of a deer and the wings of an eagle. I'm not quite certain, but it sounds vaguely terrifying."

"Huh," Zig said. "You've never seen it, then? Never encountered it on an adventure?"

I laughed and bit into the cheese. "No. Never."

"Never?"

"Never. It's said to live in an invisible realm. No one has even claimed to have seen it for decades, probably longer. And if it's anything like the other beasts, it's dangerous. I doubt anyone who has beheld it survived long enough to tell anyone." I took another bite of cheese. "Why are you so interested, anyway?"

Zig's bright smile dropped away, replaced by a nervous tremble of his lips. He rubbed his hand over his stubbled chin, then through his hair, tugging on the ends with a fist.

"How . . . ," he said, voice a worried creak, "how would someone find it?"

"Did I mention it lives in an invisible realm? I've traveled the majority of this kingdom, and I've never seen it. I've barely heard of it, and as you pointed out, I was the one who sat rapt at the campfire during celebrations to listen to the storytellers when we were children. I was the one who read the scrolls that travelers would bring from other parts of the kingdom. I imagine someone would have to stumble upon it and live to tell the tale for anyone else to find it."

"Oh," he said, voice small. "That's . . . unfortunate."

I straightened from my slouch. The alarm bells rose in pitch and frequency, and my stomach clenched, chasing away my appetite. "Why, Zig? Why do you suddenly care about the Elder Beast?"

He licked his lips. Then raised his hands in a preemptive placating gesture. "Promise you won't get mad."

"No."

He frowned. "Aw, come on."

"No. What did you do?" I gripped the edge of the table, the beveled wood biting into my palms. "Does this have something to do with lunch? Tell me I didn't just eat Elder Beast."

"What?" He crinkled his nose. "No." He waved his hands and laughed. "You literally just said it's impossible to find. How would that meat be Elder Beast?"

"I don't know! Stranger things have happened!"

"Well, that's not one of them!" His voice went shrill.

"Then what? And don't lie," I said, pointing my finger at him.

He wilted, thin lips pressed into a line.

"Well, I happened to be in the Green Serpent, and I'd had a few tankards. And I overheard this council of mages gabbing on and on about needing a horn of some kind—"

"A horn?" I asked, cutting him off.

"Yeah." He shrugged.

"And you . . . walked out and left?" I crossed my fingers under the table, hoping that my brother had taken the prudent road for once.

He winced, then scratched the side of his head, his brown hair sticking on end. "I maybe made a bet with them."

And so much for hope. "You did *what*?" My voice went low and threatening.

"They said no one could defeat the Elder Beast. How no one would even dare try. Not even Ellinore the Brave, Strong, and Mighty, and this was *after* we all had to endure a bard singing about your greatest feats. They said if they had the creature's horn, they could make a thing that could help a lot of people. They promised a reward. A massive reward. And really? Besmirching your name and legacy right in front of me like that. What was I supposed to do?"

"Ignore them!" I slammed my hands on the table. Ink from the well sloshed over the lip, staining the edge of my journal. "You're supposed to ignore them and walk away."

He crossed his arms and pouted. "Well, I didn't. I told them my sister was Ellinore the Brave, the Righteous, and so on and so forth, and she could beat any man or beast set in front of her."

"You didn't," I whispered.

He nodded curtly. "And things happened to spiral from there."

"How so?"

"Well, there was a bit more mead involved and another horrific song. And I ended up wagering that you could find the beast, kill it, and bring back the horn, because you are the best at questing in the entire kingdom."

I closed my eyes and drew on every calming technique I knew—picturing cute, fluffy kittens, counting breaths, focusing on the sensation of my feet on the floor—before I reopened them. "Zig, it's, like, the second rule of questing to never trust a mage. They're dicks."

"What's the first rule?"

"Anything can become a weapon in a pinch."

Zig blinked. "Huh," he said, contemplative, then he shook his head. "Anyway, how am I supposed to know that? I don't go on quests. I don't talk with mages. I'm not you."

I frowned. "I know that. But it's a moot point anyway. I'm retired."

"I know. But they promised gold. You *know* that's my one weakness."

I bit my tongue to stop myself from listing his many weaknesses. I wouldn't be drawn into a petty fight over Zig's reckless behavior. That was the last thing I wanted, especially since I was still trying to convince him to move to the coast to be with me and our parents.

"Okay. So you made a bet. What were the stakes?"

At this, he sat up straight and his eyes sparkled. "Like I said, if you do it, they give us gold. Like, a lot of gold. So much gold."

"I have gold."

He shook his head. "Not the measly purses you won at court. More. So much more."

"And if I fail?"

"You won't."

"Zig," I said, exasperated, "I'm not going on a grand adventure to find the Elder Beast. I don't care for how much gold," I added when he opened his mouth to protest. "So let's pay the loser's share and move on with our lives. Then we can leave and join Mom and Pop."

Zig pressed his palm to his chest, his fingers curling in the fabric of his tunic. "I can't."

I dropped my head into my hand. "Zig, I know you don't want to move, but I think it would be good for our whole family and—"

"No. I *can't* pay the loser's share."

I snapped my head up. "What? Why? What did you promise them if I fail?"

He didn't answer right away, his mouth parted in worry, his eyes wide.

"Zig?" I prompted. "What did you wager?"

His throat bobbed. "Um . . . my heart?"

I jumped to my feet. The chair clattered behind me. "Your what?" My stomach dropped to the floor. "You didn't."

Zig stood. "I didn't mean to! They tricked me with their magical ways and their promises of a lot of money. And they kept sliding full mugs of mead in my direction, and the bard was droning on and on about how great you are, and I figured, *Why not? She's not busy right now anyway.* How was I supposed to know that killing the Elder Beast was, like, a difficult thing to do?"

"Because of the amount of money! That should've been the first clue!"

"Well! You're the best adventurer in the land! You've defeated a hundred malicious creatures. You've retrieved divine implements and saved princesses. You have songs written all about your feats that I'm forced to hear daily! I thought it was something within your area of expertise!"

I gritted my teeth. Placing my hands on the table, I hung my head, my tangled hair dangling in front of me, my shoulders bunched. I couldn't fault him for that. I hadn't confessed that the tales weren't true. I hadn't told him. This was my fault.

"Okay. It's okay." I pushed up and placed my hands on my hips. "We'll go talk to this council of mages and get this fixed. Easy peasy."

A stuttered sigh of relief blew past Zig's parted lips, and his body sagged. "You think that will work?"

"Yeah," I said with false confidence, rolling my shoulders and twisting my torso as I would do before facing down an opponent. "No big deal. Happens all the time."

"And if they don't listen?"

"I'm Ellinore the Strong. The Brave. The Mighty. Trust me."

He nodded. "Okay. Okay. Great."

I gripped his shoulder and squeezed. "No worries, Zig. We'll take care of it. It's fine."

He smiled tightly. "Okay. But, uh . . . just in case . . . can you take your sword?"

That was not a bad idea. I nodded. "Yeah."

"And brush your hair? Maybe wash up a bit and put on your boots?"

"Fine," I said, stalking toward the other room. "Then we'll go. And it will all work out."

It would be no problem. These mages would understand. Mistakes like this happened all the time. It was okay, wonderful even. An easy fix that would work itself out, and Zig and I would come back home and laugh like we did when we were children.

It'd all be fine.

5

OKAY, WELL, IT DIDN'T START OFF FINE.

After an unfruitful trip to the Green Serpent, Zig and I strode down the packed-dirt street of the town toward one of the inns. My sword hung heavy at my hip in its scabbard, and I grasped it with my sweaty palm, hand clenching the leather-wrapped hilt. I'd pulled my brown hair up in a high ponytail, breaking a few bristles of the brush while untangling the knots. And I'd changed into a fresh tunic and a pair of wide traveling trousers, but I'd forgone the armor. Because, hopefully, this could be a friendly meeting and end in a beneficial way for us all. Maybe this would even become something we'd laugh about later.

But I was not going to lie, I was a bit stressed.

"You let me do the talking," I instructed Zig, who was breathing heavily from keeping up with my frantic steps. "Keep your mouth shut."

"Why shouldn't I do the talking? I'm the personable twin. You just glare and growl at people."

"Because your talking got us in this mess to begin with," I said with a sharp glare. "And I do more than scowl at people at court when I'm there. I socialize." I imparted as much disdain as I could into the last word. I may have socialized mostly with Aven, if antagonistic bickering could count as socializing, but there were other times when I had to talk to the lieges and the king and queen. I had skills. Kind of.

"That's not what the bards say," Zig muttered.

I whirled on him, grabbing his sleeve. "I think you learned a lesson about trusting bards."

Zig raised his hands. "Fine. You do the talking."

We entered the Griff-Inn through the open front door. The building itself was a nondescript two-story structure with a small lobby area on the first floor and a handful of rooms on the second. In the back courtyard was a detached kitchen, where meals were cooked for the guests. A few teens about our age leaned against one of the walls, waiting to serve food or clean rooms.

Zig tapped my shoulder and pointed a finger at two men hunched over a round table, eating lunch. "That's them, by the way."

Even without Zig pointing them out, I could tell they were mages by their fanciful and impractical robes and their obnoxious hats. One wore a battered pointy thing over his long brown hair, while the other wore a hat adorned with a single feather that looked like it had been smashed into a pancake. They both had hideous goatees, and many jeweled rings sparkled on their fingers. Twin staves of ash, though differently carved, were propped up in the corner behind them, glittering jewels ornately attached to the ends.

They weren't really a *council*, though. "Council" was the collective noun for a group of mages. Like "bunch" for grapes or "murder" for crows. But there were only two of these gentlemen. A pair. A twosome. Even if "a duo of mages" didn't have the same authoritative ring to it.

"And then I pulled the chicken out of my robes!" the pointy-hat jerk with the dark mustache said, slamming his mug of mead down on the table.

"Did you actually magic a chicken?" the other asked. His flattened hat with the feather sat atop a nest of dark-blond curls.

Pointy-Hat shook his head, chuckling all the while. "No! It was the same chicken. I just found it wandering outside!"

They both erupted into theatrical laughter, throwing their heads back, clutching their stomachs as their leftover stew sloshed in their bowls. All the things I'd seen courtiers do when pretending to laugh at one of the king's awful dad jokes. Well, at least I knew the level of pomposity I'd have to deal with when talking to these two.

I approached their table, Zig crowding my back as he followed, and cleared my throat. I kept my spine straight, my shoulders back, and one hand on the hilt of my sword.

They glanced in my direction. "Oh," the pointy-hat one said. "We're fine, thank you, except maybe I would like a cup of mead to take up to my room."

"Same for me as well. And you can clear my plate. I'm not going to finish the stew. It was too bland."

"To put it mildly," the other said.

They brayed loudly at the bad pun, thus solidifying my theory that all mages were dicks.

"I'm not a waitress. I'm Ellinore the Brave. I believe you've made a wager with my brother." I grabbed Zig's arm and yanked him forward, his heels sliding across the wooden floor. We stood shoulder to shoulder as we stared down at the duo.

"You're Ellinore?" the squashed-hat mage asked. "The Mighty? The Strong?" He looked me up and down. "Are you certain?"

I bristled. I should've worn the armor. "Yes. And you are?"

The mage with the pointy hat smirked. "I'm Forto. And this is my younger brother, Quip."

"Okay. Great. Anyway, my own reckless brother here," I said, clapping my palm against the back of Zig's neck and shaking him like a naughty puppy, "apparently entered a bargain with the two of you regarding the Elder Beast. It was a mistake, and we are here to let you know that we're out."

"Out?" Forto asked. "What are you saying?"

"I'm saying that the bet was made in error. My brother spoke for me, which he had no authority to do. So . . ."—I gestured with my free hand—"undo it."

"Oh," he said with a nod and a huffed laugh. "He made a mistake. I understand. Younger brothers, am I right?" he said, pointing to Quip while wearing a sympathetic expression.

"Hey!" Quip said in protest, but I ignored his outburst.

Instead I let out an airy faux laugh as well. This was going better than I'd thought it would. Maybe we'd get out of this with no penalty at all. And the bag of gold I'd brought would be used for celebratory ale instead of buying my way out of Zig's mess. "Yes. Exactly. You understand. So just cancel the bargain and we'll be on our way."

Forto hummed. "Well, we can't."

"What do you mean?" My jovial tone petered out more with each subsequent syllable.

He shrugged. "We can't release your brother."

"Again, what do you mean you can't?" I slammed my palm against the table, my other hand firmly on the hilt of my sword. I leaned over them and gave them my best menacing look.

Quip flinched, but Forto met my glare with a steely gaze of his own. "It can't be undone."

"What's there to undo?"

He scoffed. "Your brother shook on the bargain. It's sealed in magic. We require the Elder Beast's horn in two weeks' time, then—"

"Two weeks' time?" I cut my gaze to Zig. He shrugged.

"Sixteen days, to be exact. But yes. We will either receive the Elder Beast's horn or your brother's heart."

I narrowed my eyes. "You wouldn't happen to mean 'hart,' as in 'deer,' would you?"

Quip scrunched his nose. "No."

"Oh, so you mean it like 'love,' right? His first true love? Or the heart of his personality. Could it be the heart of his humor? Because I wouldn't miss that at all." Zig shoved his elbow into my ribs. I grunted, then continued as if my annoying brother hadn't brought all this trouble on himself in the first place. "Not his actual physical heart."

Quip steepled his fingers and cleared his throat. "No. We do need a human heart freely given if we aren't able to procure the Elder Beast's horn. It wouldn't be the exact ingredient for the curse—" He let out a yelp, and the table wobbled from the force of his knee hitting the underside. "Cure! I meant cure. Potion. Elixir."

"Well, I refuse. This is obviously a case of coercion. You plied my brother with mead and took advantage. That's a clear violation of questing rules." Not really. I made that up, but the mages wouldn't know that. Probably.

Quip frowned. "We are not compelled to follow whatever rules your king and queen set for quests. We exist beyond their influence."

That was slightly worrying. Okay. New tactic. "My brother bargained that I would remove the Elder Beast's horn, and I won't. I won't do it. I'm retired. The deal is moot."

Forto chuckled. "That's not the way things work, Ellinore the Cowardly."

I didn't like his oily smirk. I didn't like his laugh. I didn't like how he obviously had the upper hand. And I hated his ridiculous hat.

I drew my sword, the sound of the steel sliding from the scabbard ceasing all other conversation in the inn. I pressed the tip to Quip's throat, but I addressed Forto.

"I refuse because I choose to do so," I said, the tip of my blade bobbing as Quip swallowed. A small bead of blood welled along the shiny edge and slid down his skin, until it pooled in the hollow. "You will find that ultimatums do not work with me. Release my brother from this sucker's bet, and I won't skewer your brother right here and right now."

Forto grinned. He quickly reached for his staff and thumped the end twice on the floor, and in a puff of smoke, his brother disappeared. My sword point dropped and banged on the edge of the table, blood splattering from the tip onto the chair. The acrid tang of magic, which smelled much like burning hair, wafted from the seat. Then, with another thud and a flash-bang of bright light and sound, Quip reappeared, standing behind Forto's shoulder. A trickle of blood wound down Quip's neck, and Forto glared at me with shimmering, unnaturally blue eyes that slowly bled back to brown.

"And you'll find that brute force doesn't work on us," he said.

I glared. I hated mages. It was often debated if they held any true magic or if they were smoke and mirrors wrapped up in gaudy packaging. In my experience, mages were the epitome of parlor tricks and tacky explosions, but unfortunately, these two might be the real thing.

I swung my sword around and leveled it at them again, both hands gripping the hilt.

"I have killed greater men and beasts than you," I said, voice a growl. That was a stretch. I'd killed exactly one. And I didn't know if I could kill these two, but that wouldn't stop me from trying. "Just ask any bard in the kingdom."

Forto clucked his tongue and shook his head. "Oh, Ellinore. Don't worry. With either the Elder Beast's horn or your brother's heart, you will still receive payment. The whole kingdom knows how you just love winning gold."

I clenched my teeth.

"Now, you have one day to decide. Elder Beast's horn or brother's heart." He examined his fingernails in a forced nonchalant way. "We look forward to your answer tomorrow."

And with a crackle of energy, a flash like lightning, and a cloud of smoke they were gone.

I lowered my sword and gaped. Zig bounced on his toes next to me.

"What happened to easy peasy?" he whispered.

My thought exactly. But what did I expect, dealing with mages? "Mages are dicks," I answered.

He nodded.

A person cleared his throat behind us. I slowly turned, sword still in hand, and faced a young man with an apron tied around his waist and a timid expression. He raised a single finger.

"Pardon me, but will you be paying for their meal?"

My mouth dropped open a second time. "What? No! Charge it to their room."

Then I grabbed Zig by the front of his shirt and pulled him out of the inn.

6

♧

"WHAT ARE YOU GOING TO DO?" ZIG ASKED AS HE ALL BUT RAN TO KEEP up with my strides. "Did you see that? They just popped out of existence!" He waved his hands, and a playing card appeared between his fingers. "I can make objects appear and disappear from sight but not evaporate altogether."

I ground my teeth. "I know." My mind spun with possibilities, but I came up empty. I couldn't fight the mages. They were powerful if they were able to vanish or teleport or whatever it was that they did. I'd not encountered mages before that were more than flamboyant acts of sleight of hand, and it worried me. I'd heard they existed, but they didn't frequent the court, preferring instead to stick to the outskirts of the realm and society, similar to how the ancients and folklores were pushed to the edges. That said, I had no idea if I could even vanquish a mage with a sword. Would I need a magic sword to do so? Would they just disappear again if I took a swing? Would I need an inordinate amount of luck even to get in a hit?

And as the last hour proved, I couldn't talk my way out of it either. There were no deals to be made other than the one they'd offered.

I was out of my depth. I needed help. Magical help.

"I need to go."

"Go?" Zig shouted. "Go where?"

"To talk to a friend."

"You can't leave me," Zig argued as I wrenched open the door to our cabin and began packing my saddlebag. "What if they come back? What if they try to take my heart now?"

"They won't," I said, shoving a money pouch into my bag. "They gave us a day."

"Yeah. A day. Where are you going that you'll be back in a day? You won't make it to the castle and back."

I grabbed the leftovers from lunch and wrapped them up, adding the bundle to the mishmash of objects I'd gathered in my panicked haste. "I'm not going to the castle."

"Then where are you going?"

"It's not far. Don't worry."

"Can I come with you?"

"No."

"Why not?"

"Because you can't."

"Ellinore," Zig pleaded as he followed me about the small room. "What am I going to do while you're gone?"

I turned and grabbed Zig by the front of his shirt, twisting the fabric in my fist. His face was ashen from fear, and his eyes were wide. The composure I tried to gather slipped as sweat trickled down my spine and my pulse thudded in my temples.

"You will sit in this cabin and wait for me! You will not talk to the mages before I return. And you will not cause any more trouble. Understand?"

He nodded quickly.

"Good." I released him, swung open the door, and marched out into the bright, sunny day.

I saddled Bluebell quickly, ignoring the bleating sheep as they butted against my legs. After I led her from the pasture, I swung up into my seat and took off at a gallop.

The landscape sped past me in the blurred colors of spring as I thundered out of town and down the road. Bluebell's reins creaked, the oiled leather biting into my palms as I clutched them. Her long stride ate up the distance, but it paled in comparison with the race of adrenaline in my veins. The sun beat hot on my face, my skin burning and tight, as the fabric of my tunic whipped and billowed around my body. A soft breeze slightly tempered the heat, bearing the sweet perfume of wild honeysuckle and azaleas as the wind swept across the flowering fields.

It felt like centuries passed before I spied the entrance to Dave's cavern, my body tense, my mind spinning with worst-case scenarios, but it had been only a few hours. When I dismounted, my thighs quivered from the strain. I led Bluebell into the shade of the rocky outcropping, next to a shallow stream, and tied her to a small tree. She drank greedily while I staggered into the gapped opening of the grotto.

"Dave!" I yelled, before I'd even rounded the corner into the cavern. "Dave!"

With the high afternoon sun, I didn't need a torch; the hole in the ceiling allowed enough light to reflect off the water and the veins of pyrite to illuminate the space with a soft glow.

Dave was asleep, the gold scales of his slack body blending in with the coins of the horde he was draped across, like gilded camouflage. The sound of his snore cut off abruptly, tipping into a strangled snort as I approached. He yawned, his jaw cracking, and a sliver of meaty flesh dangled between two of his lower teeth from his morning meal. He mumbled something about impertinent questers, then flopped to his other side, turning his back toward me.

"Dave!" I shouted, panic bleeding into my tone. "Zig made a bet with a duo of mages in a tavern. But not charlatan mages. Real mages. With magic. Real magic. And I have to get him out of it somehow. Because he wagered his heart! His stupid, reckless, good heart, and I don't know how to help him. I don't know how to save him." The words poured out of me in a torrent, tumbling over one another in my rush, barely intelligible. "And yes, he's annoying and impulsive and my exact opposite despite being my twin, but he is my brother. And I love him. I tried to negotiate with the mages, but they were awful and unyielding. They said the bet was sealed with magic, but magic can be broken, right? Maybe? Hopefully? Anyway, when I drew my sword, one of them disappeared. In a puff of smoke. Then reappeared! Like, popped back into existence. Then they gave me one day to agree to a foolish quest or they're going to hurt Zig. And I can't let that happen. I need your help!" My shout echoed down farther into the cavern, bouncing off the rock walls. My hands curled into fists, and my body vibrated with pent-up energy, like lightning, zinging from the tips of my fingers to the soles of my feet.

Dave snorted. "Is that a new tale by the castle bard?" he asked lazily. "If so, it needs work. Very cliché. Dramatic. And your delivery was awful. Where's the comedy? Where are the pauses for theatrical effect?"

I picked up the nearest object—a hefty, jeweled goblet—and flung it at him. It bounced harmlessly off his scale-armored back, right between his wings. "I'm serious!"

"And I'm napping," he grumbled. He rolled over onto his belly, eyes still firmly shut. A puff of smoke curled from his nostrils as he tucked his head under his wing. "Come back later."

"I don't have time for your antics. I need your advice. I need to know how to defeat these mages."

He groaned and stretched, tail swishing behind him. Coins clinked as they toppled and fell while he squirmed in his bed of gold. "And what do I know of mages?" he asked, words slightly slurred, as he was on the verge of falling back asleep.

"You are a very old and wise being; you must know something."

He let out a low chuckle. "Good try, Ellinore, but dragon magic is vastly different from hand waving while uttering spells." A tongue of fire flared from between his lips when he let out a deep sigh. "If you want my advice, give the mages what they want. Go on the quest. Complete the task they've asked of you."

"I'm retired."

He scoffed. "Fine. Then your brother loses his heart. I imagine that means he dies."

"Dave!"

"What?" Dave's eyes cracked open, revealing annoyed slits of glittering green. "That's my advice. Take it or leave it."

"Why are you being so grumpy?"

"Haven't you heard the adage about waking a sleeping dragon?"

I blinked. "No?"

"The prevailing advice is don't."

"But—"

"From what you've said," Dave interrupted me, fully conscious now and highly irritated, "these mages have a substantial amount of power, and Zig's bet was sealed in their magic. You should not trifle with them."

"So, what? I'm just supposed to complete their quest?"

"Yes."

I closed my eyes and groaned. Dave had all but confirmed my worst fear. That I would have to find the Elder Beast and take its horn. My shoulders dropped and I rubbed my hands over my face.

"What if I can't? What if this is beyond me?"

"If that is what you believe, then Zig's life is surely lost."

I stiffened and opened my eyes, staring at Dave's placid expression. "No. No, that's not an option. But I can't . . ." I swallowed down the anxiety that had built in my throat. "What if there is not a way out of this? This isn't . . . I won't be able to win this one by conveniently finding what I'm looking for washed up on a beach or hauling an already-dead carcass out of the woods or negotiating with swamp sprites. I'm not going to be able to barter or trade or"—I waved my hands, gesturing to the grotto and Dave's pile of gold—"make a beneficial deal."

Dave hummed. "I don't see how this is any different from your previous quests. You know the objective. You must find a way to complete it."

"Dave, this isn't a quest that a couple of pompous royals are sending me on for fun to make them look good, with a purse of coin for a prize. This is real life. Zig's life."

Smoke bloomed from between Dave's teeth, a sign of exasperation. "You're making this more complicated than it is. You don't want your brother to die, so you do what the mages have set forth for you to do. I don't understand—"

"Because I'm a fraud!" I yelled, my clenched fists shaking at my side. I took a breath and continued with an even tone. "I'm a liar and I'm a con. I am *not* the Ellinore the Brave from those stupid stories. She doesn't exist! There's not a real person who slays dragons and kills manticores and giant spiders. I'm a fake. And *this* . . . this is *actual* magic with *actual* consequences."

Dave eyed me as he unconsciously gathered wayward trinkets back into his heap with his front claws. "Do you think all heroes who have had songs written about them accomplished their great deeds? I know for a fact that Bartholomew Dragonslayer was a charlatan," Dave said, gesturing to himself.

"Did Bartholomew Dragonslayer admonish his brother for swindling others out of their gold, while also lying to that same brother for almost all of their teenage years, which led to his brother thinking Bartholomew was capable of things far greater than he actually was?" Dave flapped his wings, which in dragon body language was the equivalent of a nonchalant shrug. "Right. I thought so. Thanks for the fun history lesson, but it's not the same situation." I dropped into the chair at Dave's golden bedside. "I'm a hypocrite and a fake. There is no way I'm going to be able to trick the Elder Beast into giving me its horn."

Dave perked up immediately, lifting onto his haunches. "What did you say?"

"I said I can't luck my way into saving Zig. I can't do this. I'm an imposter, and everyone will know it when I ultimately fail." I dropped my head into my hands, tears brimming in my eyes. "And Zig will die."

"Not that part. That part is foolish, as you know you would never allow your brother to perish without doing everything possible to save him." Dave's tail swished in agitation. "The other part about the beast."

"The Elder Beast?" I raised my head. "Do you know anything about it?"

"The Elder Beast," Dave repeated in a soft, contemplative rumble. "Is that what the mages asked you to find?"

"Yeah. One of the most shrouded figures in the history of our world."

Dave hummed, the vibration of it echoing down the cavern. "And what do the mages want?"

"They want its horn. But there's almost no information available about it, just a few mentions in a handful of songs. Is it an ancient?"

Dave regarded me with a serious expression, one that set a chill in my blood. Dave was hardly ever serious. "No, it's not an ancient."

"Is it even real, then? Does it exist?" Trust the mages to send me on a snipe hunt. If that was the case, then maybe there could be a way out of the bargain if I provided proof that it wasn't an actual beast. I wondered if they would trust the word of a dragon? I could always lure the mages to Dave's cave, and he could tell them the Elder Beast wasn't real, break the magical bet, and then eat them. My brother would be saved. Dave would get a snack. Perfect. Problem solved.

"Oh, yes. It's real," Dave said. My heart sank. Well, there went that idea. "I've never encountered it, but it's real."

"Okay. I'm confused. It's not an ancient, but it has to be more powerful than a folklore for the mages to want it and for them to farm out the job to me. From the stories, it sounds like a chimera, so it's not an ordinary. What the hell is it, then?"

"A primordial."

All color drained from my face. My breath stuttered. "It's a god?"

"It's not a god," Dave said, regarding me with an intense gaze. "It's *the* god. The god-king of all creatures. The maker of all the animals in our world. All the ancients. All the folklores. All the ordinaries. Every single one, including me." His gaze traveled up and down my body. "Including you."

I stood from my chair in shock. "What? How? Huh?" My trembling legs barely held me as they shook like I was on the precipice of a rumbling volcano.

"Very articulate," Dave said with a haughty scoff. "The story of creation is an ancient belief. Far older than either of us. Parts of the myth have obviously not been passed down through human stories if you're unaware of the raw power of the Elder Beast." He gave me a significant look. "And the power of any portion of its body."

I hadn't thought of that at all. I'd been focused solely on saving Zig, not the implications of retrieving the horn. "What are you saying?"

Dave sighed, and tongues of flame licked the edges of his teeth. "I'm saying that handing over its horn to a duo of mages is handing that duo a monumental amount of power. *If* you could find the invisible realm, and *if* you could defeat the beast itself, allowing the mages to possess its horn is dangerous. For all of us."

My knees gave out. I fell to the rocky floor, landing on my backside. If what Dave said was true, there was an infinitesimal chance of success. And if I was successful, I could save my brother but doom the rest of the kingdom. Or the world. I closed my eyes and took a steadying breath. "It doesn't matter," I said, voice barely a whisper. "I have to save Zig. I can't . . . I can't let them have his heart."

I opened my eyes and came face-to-face with Dave's snout. He'd lowered his belly to the rocky floor, so his impressive maw was at my eye level. If Dave were any other dragon, this would be the last sight I'd ever see in my short life. But he wasn't just any dragon. He was my friend. "Are you sure you want to take that risk?" he asked, his voice a concerned rumble.

I didn't have an answer for that, other than one laced with obscenities. I gulped down my fears. All of them, and somehow made it to my feet. "Yes. How . . . how do I find the invisible realm?"

"I don't know."

"Okay. Great. Good start."

"But I'm positive we'll figure it out."

"We?"

"Yes. *We.* If you're taking on this ridiculously dangerous quest, I'm coming with you."

I winced. "Sir, you are a *dragon.* You're very conspicuous. I only called on you when I knew you wouldn't be seen, and if anyone found out you were traveling with me, it would put both of us in danger."

Dave lifted his nose high in the air. "We could only travel at night. And you could fly on my back and—"

"Dave. Be realistic."

"I could wear a *hat.* No one would know."

Laughter born of the absurd vision of Dave in a hat, and of the utter stress of finding and somehow defeating a primordial being, bubbled into my throat.

Dave was less than amused. "Laugh all you want. I would look dashing in a hat."

Suppressing my giggles, I bobbed my head in agreement. "I'm certain you would. But to keep us both safe—you from anyone looking for the glory of killing a dragon, and me from being dragged in front of the royal court for my deception several years ago—I think you must stay here."

"You'll call me if you need me, yes?"

I lifted my wrist, the slim silver bracelet glittering in the light. "I'll give it a tug and request your assistance, like I have before."

"Fine. I guess." He huffed in annoyed acceptance. "But if I'm not coming, you'll need more than a bracelet." Dave suddenly twisted away from me and slithered deeper into the cave, his form serpentine as he disappeared into the recesses.

I fell heavily into my chair and propped my elbow on my knee while waiting. I had no starting point, other than to tell the mages I had accepted their quest and then hunt down any clues from there. After a few moments Dave returned. He approached and dropped a sturdy vial of a glittering liquid at my feet.

"What's this?" I asked, picking it up and twirling it in the light. The vial was ornate, with a golden dragon encompassing the glass, but inside, a green elixir sloshed. A golden chain hooked to the stopper, long enough to wear under my armor.

"I can't join you, as you don't want your reputation to be jeopardized by the appearance of a large, unhinged golden lizard."

I smiled in spite of myself. "Thanks for your understanding."

He snorted. "But this quest is beyond what you've encountered before. It's dangerous out there. I don't want you to be alone. You can summon me with the bracelet, but just in case I can't arrive in time, take this."

"And what does it do?"

"It's a healing potion. It won't save you from death, and it certainly won't bring anyone back from the dead, but it will cure moderate ailments."

I slipped the chain over my head, the vial banging against my breastbone.

A tingle of magic, much like the one that emanated from the bracelet, brushed my skin with a gentle warmth. "Thank you for giving me another piece from your precious hoard."

"Don't be too flattered." He dropped back onto his golden pile, rolling around in the coins and jewels like a pig would roll in mud. "The bracelet is only silver, and the amount that tiny vial holds couldn't help me if it came down to it."

"Don't worry. I'm not."

He smiled, his tongue lolling out of his mouth. That piece of burned animal flesh was still caught in his teeth. Our relationship had been born from necessity—my need to complete a quest and his need to remain alive—but it had evolved over the years into a friendship marked by gentle teasing and comradery. We didn't do feelings often. If ever. But he was my longest friend . . . maybe even my only friend.

"Thank you," I said, mustering every ounce of sincerity I had. I tucked the vial under my shirt, the silver bracelet around my wrist slipping slightly down my arm, shining in the scant light like a beacon. "Really. I appreciate it."

"Don't get mushy."

I sighed and rolled my head back. "Fine. I'm leaving."

"Good. I hope not to hear from you until it's all over." He snuggled down into his nest of gold. "But," he said, voice low and soft, "if you need me . . ."

I waved over my shoulder as I exited the cave. "I won't," I called back, taking his cue. "No need to get sappy."

"Bye! Have fun finding the invisible realm and defeating the Elder Beast!"

I laughed, but the levity was short lived once I wiggled out of the cave into the light of day. I found Bluebell as I'd left her, saddled and munching on the long grass. Dragging her away from her lunch, I mounted the saddle and rode home, the sound of her hooves hitting the ground in beat with the worries pounding in my brain.

7

THE FOLLOWING MORNING I DONNED THE MANTLE OF ELLINORE THE Brave and strode into the Griff-Inn, Zig on my heels. I slammed the flat of my blade down on the table between the two mages. Quip flinched, knocking over his cup of water, but Forto didn't even look up from his meal despite the rattle of their breakfast dishes. A plate tipped to the side under the edge of my sword, and a runny egg slid over the lip and onto the table in a yolky puddle.

Forto looked up at me, unperturbed, even in the face of my resplendent leather armor and magnificently brushed and styled hair. He arched a thin eyebrow. "Yes?"

"I accept your ridiculous quest," I said with all the grace and aplomb I'd polished at the castle over the last few years. "I will find the Elder Beast and bring you its horn in exchange for the gold you promised my brother. And you will release him from the magical bargain."

"Very well," he said. Forto dabbed a napkin to each side of his mouth. "We accept."

Quip cleared his throat. "We look forward to your return in fifteen days."

"Sixteen days," I corrected. "That's what you said. I remember because it seemed like a weird number."

He grinned like a weasel. "It was sixteen days when your brother made the bargain. A day has already passed."

I narrowed my eyes. "Fine. Fifteen days."

"Excellent!" He removed a sheet of parchment from the sleeve of his robe and rubbed the heel of his hand over the rectangular area, shimmers of light glowing from between his fingers. A splash of ink appeared at each swipe of his palm, until a picture of a long candle with a flickering inky flame formed on the page. He daintily rolled the paper into a scroll and tied it with a blue ribbon. "This will keep you on task," he said, offering it to me. "Each day the candle will burn down a mark. You will need to be at this very inn before the flame burns out, or the magic will take your brother's heart."

Zig emitted a high-pitched distressed noise behind me.

I took the countdown scroll, examining it with a wary eye before stuffing it into the bag at my hip. I wasn't enthused to carry a magical item given to me by this guy, but it could come in handy.

"As long as you return with the horn in the allotted time, your brother will be saved."

"Great." I rolled my shoulders and cracked my neck. "Now that it's all settled, I have a quest to complete."

Forto raised his hand. "Just one more thing." He tucked his jeweled fingers into the interior of his robe under his collarbone and removed a battered scrap of fabric. He held it up. It was small, about the span of my hand, and it was vaguely oval in shape. It appeared to have been torn from a larger bolt of cloth, but the ragged edges had been worn down with time and touch.

"You will need this to find the Elder Beast."

I raised my eyebrows. "What is it?"

"A clue. Of a sort."

I gently took it from his fingers and flipped it over. The fabric was strangely smooth but blatantly bare. Not a hint of dye or threads or even a bead. Just a plain scrap of cloth. Annoyance welled up within me, as hot as Dave's breath. "It's blank," I said, handing it back. "It's of no use to me."

He scoffed. "Of course it's blank. It needs to be activated with magic."

"Well then, activate it and hand it over."

The mages exchanged a glance. Forto cleared his throat. "It must be activated with a power that we do not possess."

My frustration level rose, sloshing around my insides like the river after a hard rain. I wanted to throttle them both, erase their smug expressions and destroy their silly hats, maybe push their faces into their breakfast plates. But I couldn't risk aggravating them, so I took a deep breath.

"What kind of power, then?" I said, smiling through gritted teeth.

"We don't know," Quip said, earning a glare from Forto. "Just that it must be saturated with it, or it won't reveal its secrets."

"Again, that doesn't seem like much use to me. I don't have any magical ability, despite what some people think."

"Certainly, in all your travels, you've come across various forms of power." Forto stroked his mustache with his fingertips. I expected him to twirl the ends and laugh maniacally, as I'd heard villains often did in stories. He refrained, but I swore his fingers twitched, and a smile teased at the corners of his mouth. "That is, if the bards are to be believed."

My heart clenched. That jerk. Okay, just play it cool. "Yeah. I have. A lot. So fine. I'll take it."

I reached for it, but he snatched it back. "Wait, one last caveat."

"Oh, what now?" I blurted. "Let me guess, it was stolen from a faery's grove, so if I use it, a nasty horde of them will come after me. Was it ripped from the hand of some knight by a Harpy, and you took it from her, so she's always looking for it? Oh, will it only work if I mend it back into whatever larger piece it was torn from?"

Zig poked me in my back, right under the fraying strap of my pauldron.

"What?" I said, looking over my shoulder. Zig had parked himself on top of the neighboring table and was swinging his legs like a little kid, but his hands gripped the edge of the wood so tightly, his knuckles stood out as white bumps. "Magic always comes with a price," I told him. "Always. It's, like, rule three of questing."

Forto pouted. "She's right. Spell magic demands balance. Energy requires energy, be it from living things, the pull of the tides, or even from another spell. And that means if perchance you figure out how to activate this scrap, then that will decrease the time of your quest by three days."

"What?" I demanded. "You mean you'll skim three days off the allotted time?"

"We won't," Quip said to clarify, raising one finger. "The magic will."

"That's absurd," I shot back.

Forto shrugged. "Sorry."

He wasn't sorry. He was smirking, because this placed me in a difficult position. I had no idea where the Elder Beast was, and I didn't have any idea how or where to begin. Chances were I could spend more than a few days wandering around the countryside looking for directions. But I also didn't want to spend time trying to figure out how to activate the scrap, only to find out it was a false lead and lose three days of Zig's remaining time. No. I didn't want to be sidetracked. And these mages had already proven they were tricky. And jerks. They were definitely jerks. They would get a payoff either way—my brother's heart or the Elder Beast's horn.

"No thanks," I said, sheathing my sword and wincing at the dried yolk left on the edge. I'd have to wipe that down later. "We're good."

Forto didn't expect that. He tucked the scrap away with a huff and a frown. "Fine. Best of luck."

"Fuck off." I gestured for Zig to follow me out of the inn.

Zig jumped from his perch, promptly tripped on a wonky floorboard, fell into the table with the mages' breakfast plates, and sent a carafe of coffee flying. Coffee spilled all over the place, soaking Forto's robe.

Forto's face turned an interesting shade of red. "How dare you—"

"I'm so sorry!" Zig interrupted, grabbing a napkin and lurching forward, awkwardly patting down the front of the mage's robe.

"Get off of me, you utter imbecile."

Zig ignored him and continued to try to mop up the mess with the wet cloth napkin, while the mage attempted to bat Zig's hands away.

"I will take care of it myself! Off!"

"I'm sorry," Zig said again, taking a step back and waving the drenched napkin around. "I'm so sorry. My mistake. Your breakfast is on me." He took a few coins from the pouch at his side and set them on the table. "Here. This should cover it and the mess. Sorry again. Anyway, see you in fifteen days!"

Zig beat a hasty retreat and made a beeline for the door. I rolled my eyes and followed him out.

8

ᴢɪɢ ᴀɴᴅ I ᴡᴀʟᴋᴇᴅ ɪɴ ꜱɪʟᴇɴᴄᴇ ʙᴀᴄᴋ ᴛᴏ ᴏᴜʀ ʜᴏᴍᴇ, ᴏᴜʀ ʙᴏᴏᴛꜱ ᴋɪᴄᴋɪɴɢ up dust along the well-worn path. Guilt weighed on my shoulders at the situation, almost as heavy as the fear that I would fail.

Once the town was solidly in the distance behind us, Zig glanced over his shoulder and chuckled.

"What?" I asked.

"Those suckers," he said. "I can't believe they fell for the old trying-to-clean-up-a-spill routine. The second rule of questing may be to never trust a mage, but the first rule of preventing pickpockets is to never allow anyone to get too close."

I tipped my head back in exasperation and groaned. "What did you steal?" With my current luck, Zig had probably absconded with some priceless family heirloom from the innkeeper that was cursed, or a sausage that would upset his stomach later.

"Oh, only this." Zig whipped out the scrap of cloth that the mage had tucked away in his pocket after I refused it. Ah, that was somehow worse. The fabric now sported a blobby coffee stain, but upon close inspection, I saw it was the very same. Zig flapped it around like it was merely a wet washcloth instead of the only hint we had to the whereabouts of the Elder Beast. "I figured, why not? They don't need it, and I wagered that you were bluffing when you said you didn't know any magic that could activate it. And the reason you didn't take it was because you didn't want to be tempted to use it and scrub three days from the quest timeline. Am I right?"

I opened my mouth, then shut it. "You're right. I didn't want to be tempted. But I wasn't bluffing. I really don't have experience in their type of magic. I don't like mages. I tend to avoid them. For good reason," I added sharply.

Zig kicked a pebble from the path. "Well, who knows? Maybe we'll get desperate enough to try to use it."

That brought me up short. *"We?"* Oh no, that sentence sounded vaguely like Dave when he wanted to go on the quest.

Zig paused beside me. He pointed at me and then at his own chest. "We. As in us. As in Ellinore and Zig, brother and sister, on our first adventure together. It'll be fun! Like best-quest-ever kind of vibe."

I put my hands on my hips and took a centering breath. I'd taken several of those since this whole debacle started. "Well, first things first, Ellinore the Brave works alone. Sorry to burst whatever delusional bubble you were entertaining in that little brain of yours," I said, making a gesture toward his head. "But you're not coming with me. You're going to stay here and stay out of trouble. But most importantly, stay alive. Second, this fun adventure has last-quest-ever vibes. Get it?"

Zig straightened and puffed out his chest. "What? You can't make me stay home. It's my life."

"Exactly," I shouted. "It's your life. You'll only slow me down. And if you want to live, I need to move as fast as possible. You'll be a hindrance."

Zig scoffed. "I wouldn't be. I will enhance the experience."

I laughed, loud and obnoxious. "Enhance? What do you even bring to the table?"

Zig waved the cloth in my face. "I literally just stole this off a mage without him or anyone else noticing!"

Okay. Maybe he had a point. His particular set of skills might be useful in a pinch. And he wasn't a dragon, like Dave, who would cause a commotion; though with Zig, I could never predict if his shenanigans were to gain attention or avoid it.

"That's what I can bring," he continued. "You may not like it, but I'm excellent at what I do. Also, my social skills are leagues better than yours."

It was my turn to scoff. "Better? May I remind you that I navigated the royal court for years by myself." While lying the whole time, but he didn't need to know that just yet, if ever. "And I didn't make a single social faux pas." That I knew of.

Zig laughed. He nailed me with his elbow, but it merely glanced off my armor. "You beat Princet Aven on their birthday at their own tournament in front of their entire family."

"So?" I asked with a shrug.

"So you humiliated them. That was, like, the biggest misstep ever. Total asshole maneuver. It was talked about for weeks among the townspeople, even this far away from the castle, and let's just say it wasn't all good."

Huh. I didn't know that. No one had said anything to my face or had even hinted. But now that I thought about it, the bards hadn't written a word about that particular adventure. Had I really messed that up?

"I give you the social skills," I said, "but I don't know. I have always worked alone."

"Which is why I should come along. It will be new and different. And with both of us, I bet we cut the time of the quest in half. Like I said: Best. Quest. Ever."

Ugh. He was right, I guess. He did have a way with people. If he didn't, he'd be in the pillory more than he was out of it. I had to admit he had a certain kind of infuriating charm that I hadn't inherited. And it might be nice to have my brother along with me. Maybe I could convince him to travel to the coast when all was said and done.

If he was still alive.

"Fine," I said as we turned the corner around the hill, our cabin coming into sight. "But you listen to me. I'm the leader. You do what I say, when I say. No questions asked."

Zig flashed a wide grin but didn't answer. Instead he stopped short. "Hey, who is that?"

I whipped my gaze around and my breath caught in my throat. Princet

Aven stood at the fence beside our door, wrestling with one of the sheep. Their hands were wrapped around the bottom of their tunic, part of which was firmly in Rainbow's mouth.

"Let go. You're as stubborn as your owner, you woolly menace," they said as they tugged to free themself. They lifted their foot and placed it on the bottom slat of the fence and yanked. The black fabric tore out of Rainbow's mouth. Aven reeled backward, their arms windmilling, before losing their balance and landing on their backside. Rainbow bleated at them from the other side of the fence, which I completely accepted as her way of laughing at them. In return Aven stuck out their tongue. I stifled a chuckle behind my hand, amazed that Aven would dare do something so childish, even if they thought they didn't have an audience.

"Hey! Leave my sheep alone!" Zig yelled, breaking from my side in a run. "I won them fair and square. If Farmer John wants them back, then he is going to have to send more than a trumped-up squire from Lord Henley's keep to steal them. These sheep are mine, unless you happen to have a purse full of gold tucked somewhere in all that embroidery."

Aven jumped to their feet and brushed off their trousers, their cheeks flushed pink. They squared their shoulders and pulled themself to their full height. Even with their trousers covered in hay and dirt, and their tunic disheveled and missing a chunk at the bottom hem, they were as noble and beautiful as they'd been the day I left them in the courtyard of the castle.

"Squire?" they said, voice cracking in affront. "I'm not a squire."

"Then what are you?"

Aven puffed out their chest. "I'm a royal."

Zig frowned and eyed Aven up and down. "Are you certain?"

I pinched the bridge of my nose. "Zig," I said, amused at Aven's offended expression and Zig's absolute confusion, "meet Princet Aven."

Zig's mouth dropped. "Oh shit."

Oh shit, indeed.

Zig dropped into a hasty bow. "Um . . . you're welcome to the sheep, Your . . . Highness? Majesty? Grace?"

"Aven is fine," they said with a shake of their head, their glossy black hair falling perfectly across their brow, highlighting the vibrant blue of their eyes.

My stomach swooped. "What are you doing here?"

"Apparently, being accosted by a sheep," they said, appraising the state of their tunic mournfully.

Rainbow bleated in response.

Aven narrowed their eyes. "The king isn't overly fond of mutton chops, but I'm certain a feast could be *arranged*." They yanked a dagger from the folds of their clothes. "Your owner did give permission."

"Hey!" I squeezed between Aven and the fence, holding up my hands. "You don't need to get all aggro toward a sheep. She's just an ordinary being."

"Are you certain? She could be a fauness in disguise." Aven peered around my shoulder. "She's quite intelligent for a sheep."

"Takes after her owner!" Zig chirped as he leaned by the door of the house.

I rolled my eyes. "You do know how ridiculous it is to try to intimidate a sheep with verbal threats and a dagger, right?" Rainbow butted her head against the back of my leg, then proceeded to nibble on my trousers in an act of blatant betrayal. "She's only mildly irritating," I said, yanking my leg away before she could bite off a chunk of the fabric. "Which is another trait she inherited from her owner."

Zig frowned. "Hey!"

"*Anyway*, sheep aside, why are you here, Aven?"

Aven tucked the dagger away. A light blush had seeped into their cheeks, and they slid their abashed glare from the paddock and locked it on me. "You lied," they said, crossing their arms over their chest. "Lying to royalty is a criminal offense. I'm here to investigate the charges."

Zig's eyes widened, but he took the opportunity to bow quickly out of the conversation regarding criminality and ducked into our cabin, closing the door with a loud thud behind him. Coward.

As for myself, I wouldn't have minded following, and throwing a bar across the door, because I had no idea which lie Aven was referring to. There were many to choose from. My heart did a flip in my chest, and my palms grew sweaty. I crossed my arms in a mirror of their pose to hide the way I trembled, hoping to exude powerful warrior woman who knew how to use a sword. I think all I managed was girl who might possibly be constipated and maybe knew to use the pointy end of the weapon strapped to her hip.

I forced a laugh. "Lie to royalty. Me? Preposterous. I am astounded and insulted that you would even dare accuse me of such a thing." Ancients! I'd over-sold it. I was going to be marched back to the king and queen and made to repay all the gold that I didn't have any longer or spend my lifetime in a dungeon. "I mean, what lie?" I said with a scoff. "Lying is morally wrong and reprehensible and—"

"What is wrong with you?" Aven said, scrunching their nose.

"I'm on edge!"

"I can tell!" Aven dropped their arms. "I didn't mean to do that," they said, softer. "I was joking. That was a joke, as was the mutton remark. Ha ha. A playful, funny type of statement."

Now who was overselling?

"You are really bad at jokes." My voice came out entirely too breathy, but my body still thrummed with anxiety and the urgent need to overexplain.

"Noted," they said with a sigh. "I was referring to our last interaction at the castle. You declared, quite loudly, that you were planning to retire. But I . . . uh, *the king* heard through the very fast rumor network that you might have taken on another quest."

Huh. Word traveled surprisingly fast. "How does he even know about that?"

"Royals have their ways."

"Are you lot spying on me?"

Aven sputtered, "What? No." They laced their fingers together in front of them. "But is it true? Are you questing again?"

"What business is it of yours if I am or not?" And that was a little harsh. Maybe I did need Zig's social skills. "I mean . . . how did the Crown find out?"

"The news of your argument with the council of mages—"

"Duo of mages," I corrected quickly. "There's only two of them. And they wear ugly hats."

Aven scrunched their nose again, as if processing information. "Okay. The king and queen heard about the argument you had with a duo of badly dressed mages. They know as well as you do that you would never allow anything awful to befall your brother, so even without your declaration this morning, you were going to take on the quest."

"Okay. And that involves you how?"

"I'm coming with you." They cleared their throat. "By order of the king."

My heart stopped beating as my brain processed the shock. Aven? Coming with? How? Why? *What?* Luckily, my brain kicked back in, as did my now-thrumming heart.

"Absolutely not!" It was one thing to drag my foolish brother along on a quest, but it was entirely another to bring a quest rival, a royal person. Especially since there would be no way to hide that I had actually lied about the whole being-the-best-at-questing thing. "No way."

"It's a royal order. You don't have much of a choice, Ellinore."

Oh no. "Why would the king and queen be concerned that I've taken on a quest, anyway? Don't they have more-pressing worries? Aren't they ruling an entire kingdom?"

Aven huffed. "Do you not remember announcing your retirement in the middle of the great hall?"

"Um . . . yes?"

"And do you not remember my uncle's displeasure at hearing that, and how my aunt stepped in and said you'd be *resting* before the summer tournaments?"

"Yes?" I said, voice a squeak.

Aven crossed their arms, looking unfairly smug. "Taking on another quest is the opposite of resting and is in direct defiance of a royal's decree." They nonchalantly rubbed their knuckles on their fine sleeve. "Thus they sent me to accompany you. To supervise."

I sputtered in disbelief. I scrambled for a reason to keep Aven from joining.

"You would just get in the way."

Aven snorted, for real snorted, like a piglet with an attitude. "Get in the way? I'm the best chance you have at finding the Elder Beast."

"How?"

Aven's mouth pulled into a smug grin. "Because I know the last person who saw it. And I know where they live."

Well, shit.

"So if I allow you to tag along—"

"You're not *allowing* me. I'm coming if you like it or not," Aven said. "I will be observing, of course, by royal order."

My throat went as dry as the sand on the southern shore at noon. "Observing?" I managed.

"Yes. You're the best. I know that. I want to see for myself how you accomplish what you do. The king said that I could learn from you." They paused, back stiff, their face entirely red in what I supposed was embarrassment. "And the king has come to the conclusion that accompanying you is the best way for me to do so."

Okay. I would have to unpack the tremor in their voice later. I had a brother to save. And ancients forbid, Aven might be my only lead. But . . . I couldn't let them see how I accomplished things, because the king and queen would be absolutely livid. I'd end up in a dungeon or worse.

"You could just give me the information, and I'll complete the quest and come back and tell you everything."

Their brow furrowed. "Absolutely not," they parroted.

I crossed my arms. "So if I don't give in to you, you would let my brother die? You would be that cruel?"

They wavered. They rubbed the toe of their boot in the dirt, leaning too close to the fence, where Rainbow eagerly waited for another nibble at the fancy hem of their tunic. A flicker of indecision swept across their features, but then their royal blank mask slid into place. "It's go with me or don't go at all."

"What?" I yelled. "You can't keep me from—"

"I can. The Crown can. And they will," Aven said in the detached, imperious tone I'd heard them use on lords and ladies of the court. "You certainly wouldn't allow your stubbornness to impede finding the solution for your brother. Would you?"

My blood boiled. I'd never really disliked Aven. They were fun to tease, and they were a great competitor, having kept me on my toes a few times over the years. But in this moment I was kind of disgusted. "Okay," I ground out through clenched teeth. And despite my better judgment screaming at me to hit Aven over the head and search through their pockets and saddlebags for the information, then run, I acquiesced. "You can join us. But Zig comes first," I said, pointing my finger. "He's priority. If I feel that you are hindering me in any way, I'll cut you loose."

Aven raised their hands. "Understood."

"Okay." I swallowed the lump of anger that had formed in my throat. It wouldn't do me any good and would only distract me. "You're part of the team. Let me get packed and we'll be off."

Aven shook their head. "I just rode from the castle. My horse needs a good night's rest. And you probably have more to do than just pack. Like feed your suspect sheep." They cast a glance at the paddock, eyebrow raised as Bleep bleated in response and Rainbow stomped her feet.

I hated that they were right. I needed a good rest myself. I needed to pack. And I needed to figure out how to fake being an honest quester before both Aven and Zig figured out that I was the biggest fraud in the history of the kingdom.

"We'll meet at first light," I said.

Aven nodded. "I'll be at the Griff-Inn," they said with thinly veiled disbelief at the name. "Come find me in the morning."

"Okay. See you then."

Aven mounted their horse and tugged on the reins to point it in the direction of town.

"For the record," I said, "I *had* retired. I didn't lie about that."

Aven regarded me with an unreadable expression. "Good to know." Then they rode off down the path. I reluctantly headed inside, to find my brother with his ear pressed to the window, obviously eavesdropping.

"What are you doing?"

Zig jumped. He grinned. "So that was the infamous Princet Aven. How do you not have a crush on them? They're literally the image of royalty from the bards' tales. If they didn't already have massive heart eyes for you, I'd totally shoot my shot. They're hot, and I bet they have a ton of gold."

"Gross," I said, but with no bite. "And you're wrong. They do not have heart eyes for me. That's just how they are."

"Sure, believe that. I see why you two get along. You're like peas in an odd pod." Zig hummed as he stepped away from the window and began gathering items for the journey. "And did I hear they are joining us on our journey?"

"We *don't* get along. Or did you not hear them just threaten me . . . us?"

"Yeah, with a good time."

I didn't respond to that. Instead I sank heavily into the seat at the kitchen table and dropped my head into my hands. "Yes, they are accompanying us."

"That's great. Three is a lucky number." He stuffed a balled-up tunic into his bag. "I have a good feeling."

Ugh. I was glad he did. I would need all the luck I could get to save Zig and somehow keep Aven from finding out about my less-than-truthful ways of winning. Even without luck, I couldn't fail. Failing meant Zig's life. Succeeding meant handing over a powerful artifact to a duo of pricks. I knew which one was worse for me, but it was a roll of dice which was worse for the world at large.

But it was a risk I had to take.

9

~⁊~

I STARED DOWN AT THE PARCHMENT THE MAGE HAD GIVEN ME, WITH the magically drawn candle. It had burned down a mark, the flickering ink-flame blurring with movement as small drips of wax flowed slowly down the sides. It was like I was watching Zig's life melt away.

"Ready?" Zig asked, coming up behind me and yawning.

I hastily rolled the parchment candle and shoved it and the blank scrap of cloth into the bag at my hip.

"Yes," I said as we walked out our door.

After Aven had left for the inn the night before, Zig had gone out to find someone to either buy the sheep or take care of them while we were gone, and I had descended into a packing frenzy. This wasn't an ordinary quest, by any means. First, the stakes were much higher than a purse of gold. And second, I wouldn't be working alone. Which meant days of grungy, smelly Ellinore on the trail wouldn't do.

I then proceeded to shove enough items into my saddlebag for our days of questing. Thankfully, I'd just finished my cycle, but I squeezed as many small cloths as possible into the bottom, just in case. And on top, three extra changes of clothes, including additional breast bindings, which were essential under my armor. Plus, I added a full bar of soap wrapped in washcloths. I shoved a small sack of gold into the bag among the clothes.

As Zig and I walked outside, I inwardly cringed at the sight of my saddle-bags bulging at Bluebell's flank, stuffed full with more than I'd ever take traveling alone. My sword was strapped to the other side of my saddle. I hoped I wouldn't need to use it, but I was aware of the high chance I would.

"Do you have a weapon?" I asked abruptly in the silence of the rising dawn.

Zig arched an eyebrow. "A weapon?"

"Like a sword or a knife. I don't know, a pointy stick. Something more than a deck of cards or a pair of dice. A way to protect yourself in case we get into trouble."

"Are you expecting trouble?" he asked.

"Um . . . yes! First, I'm traveling with *you*, and your very existence courts trouble. And second, we're looking for a mythical creature! We're going to run into at least one dangerous situation."

"You'll save me," he said with a sassy grin and a punch to my arm.

"But what if we get separated?" I asked. "What if something happens to me and you need to protect yourself? What if you can't run away like you normally do? What if—"

"You're really worried about it, aren't you?" he asked.

"Yes!" I threw up my hands. "Of course I am. This whole quest is to save you. If I weren't worried about you, then I wouldn't even be doing this. You could at least have the courtesy to take this seriously."

Zig's eyes widened, and he held up his palms in a placating gesture. "Okay. I am. And yes, I have a small dagger." He did something complicated with his fingers, and a playing card popped from his sleeve. I arched an eyebrow until he tilted it up to reveal a blade no longer than my pointer finger, the handle tucked in close to his wrist. "I'm not as foolish as you think I am. I'm always armed just in case I piss off the wrong people."

I blew out my breath. "You could've just said yes."

"What's the fun in that?"

I returned the punch in the arm, but I did it with far more force. He winced and rubbed the spot while pouting.

"Okay. If you're ready, let's go."

I mounted Bluebell with ease, while Zig unsteadily hopped onto the back of a mule named Carrot that he'd somehow acquired. I didn't ask questions. At least the mule could help carry our gear, though I wasn't sure how fast she would be if we needed to push the pace. Zig's discomfort in the saddle suggested we wouldn't be able to move very quickly even if he had a horse.

I clicked my tongue and nudged Bluebell forward. Zig followed behind. It wasn't a long ride to the center of town, and soon we found ourselves outside the inn. Aven was waiting for us on the covered porch, steed already saddled and ready, despite the sky only just lightening with the dawn.

"Good morning," Aven said lazily, feet propped on the hitching post while they crunched on an apple. They were unfairly put together for it being so early. I'd barely managed to brush my hair, and Zig looked like he'd just rolled out of bed.

"Ready?" they asked. I noticed they had ditched the finer clothes they'd been wearing when they arrived, instead settling on a simple black belted tunic and black breeches. There was not a stitch of embroidery in sight, though their clothes were still far nicer than anything I owned.

I hunched down in my tattered hooded cloak, which covered my tunic and pair of sturdy traveling trousers. My armor was tied to the back of Bluebell because I wasn't expecting a fight on the first day.

"Yes. Once you tell us where we are going," I said.

Aven stood, their blue eyes bright in the rising sun. As they swung their own traveling cloak over their shoulders, I spied the leather guard strapped to their left arm, used to protect against the snap of a bowstring.

"I found a scroll tucked away in the palace archives," Aven explained as they mounted their impressive white stallion. They tucked their shiny black boots into the stirrups and placed their bow across the pommel of their saddle for quick retrieval. "And it said the last person to see the Elder Beast was a teenager who lived in the town of Ashin."

"Why does that sound familiar?" Zig asked.

Aven shrugged. "It's at the base of the Melting Peaks."

Zig snapped his fingers. "Oh, right!" He poked my arm—in reach, as he'd maneuvered Carrot close to my side. "Isn't that the place where you saved the village from the wrath of the mountain ancients by wrestling them into submission? The earth quaked and you stopped the eruption or whatever."

I bit back a groan. "Something like that," I said. It was actually a nest of fire salamanders causing a ruckus around the caldera that gave the mountains their name. Dave assisted me with herding the salamanders toward a less volatile environment. And while I was doing so, it just so happened that there was an earthquake. The townsfolk made up their own story, and I . . . didn't correct them.

The town of Ashin was rather isolated. Towering mountains blocked it on the northern border. To the east was the sea, and to the west and south was a long river. The headwaters of said river were boiling hot but cooled as the water flowed south. The quickest way to the town would be dangerous, but the safe route would take too long.

I knocked my heels against Bluebell's sides and pushed past my traveling companions to stand in the middle of the road. "It's not my favorite place. The ground tends to . . . rumble." Bluebell danced beneath me. She could feel the tension in my thighs, alerting her to my own anxiety, so she responded in kind. Zig fidgeted in his seat atop his mule, while Aven was unfairly calm. "Ashin is a two-day ride due northeast as the crow flies," I said, pulling the hood of my cloak up to shade my eyes in the face of the rising sun. "How certain are you about your information?"

Aven eyed me and I felt pinned. "Fairly certain."

I squinted at the horizon. "I'm not sure I can bet my brother's life on 'fairly certain.' We have fourteen days now. We're on a tight timeline."

"Do you have a better idea of a starting point?"

The image of the burning candle on the parchment wavered in my mind's eye. "No. I don't. I just want to make sure we're utilizing our time wisely."

"Do you think arguing is a good use, then?" Zig piped up behind me.

Aven smirked. "Your brother has a point."

I narrowed my eyes, shooting Aven a scathing look. "Fine."

"Good," Aven answered quickly.

"Okay."

Zig maneuvered Carrot between me and Aven, head swiveling between us. "Are we going?"

"Yes!" Ancients! I couldn't allow Aven to crawl under my skin so easily, or this would be a long trip. I schooled my expression. "Let's go find the Elder Beast."

And then we were off.

We rode for the morning, allowing our mounts to rest as needed. Carrot surprisingly kept up with us, despite Zig's complaints about the pace of our travel. I reminded him of his insistence on accompanying me on the quest, and he quieted to muttering disparaging remarks beneath his breath. We took lunch in a small clearing.

After, we found the main road and followed it east until we came to a crossroads.

I slowed Bluebell to a halt.

The fork to the right was the safer way toward the town, hooking to the south, then crossing the river into the outskirts of Ashin. But it was longer, by at least a day. The road to the left was much less traveled as of a few years ago and had become overgrown. But it was faster. Much faster.

"Why are we stopping? Are we camping here?" Zig asked, his hands clasped in a hopeful plea.

I didn't answer him.

"Ah, the crossroads," Aven said, pulling up beside me on their horse. "A difficult debate, to be sure, though"—they jerked their chin toward the rugged path—"crossing the Simmer *would* make for a rousing story for my uncle and the court bards." Their smug grin was annoyingly bright and . . . pretty.

My eye twitched, but Aven wasn't wrong. The exciting route was to the left. The right had calmer, cooler waters, several different crossings, and even a ferry we could use to travel into the town. If I were on my own, I'd take the safer path. But . . . Aven would be reporting to the king, and Zig was expecting the famous Ellinore the Brave. I had to think of what the bards would write, what the court would want to hear, and take the action they believed I would as the person they thought I was. Even if it was riskier.

And based on the stories, Ellinore the Brave wouldn't allow the chance of boiling alive to deter her from taking the faster route. Ellinore the Brave would go left. I swallowed. "We . . . need to conserve every minute." I tugged Bluebell's reins. "We'll take the left fork."

The line of Aven's shoulders went taut and their jaw clenched, almost as if they weren't expecting that decision. Though they nodded in acquiescence.

"Come on," I said. I didn't have time to decipher Aven. "Let's go."

We rode for several more hours, until the day turned to dusk. The Melting Peaks rose in the distance in front of us, the tops covered by a thick smog, a mixture of ash and smoke spitting from the cratered summit of the tallest peak.

"We'll have to cross the Simmer to enter Ashin," Aven said as we walked our horses down the overgrown dirt road, giving them a break.

"I know. We should stop for the night," I said. The sun was well below the horizon, only a few minutes of light left in the day. "We don't want to try to traverse it in the dark."

Aven nodded. "Agreed."

"Oh, thank the ancients," Zig said. He hugged Carrot's neck, hunched over the pommel of the saddle. "I think my legs fell off a few leagues back."

Aven huffed a laugh as we guided the horses and Carrot toward the forest, away from the main thoroughfare. It was dangerous to camp too close to the road at night, even as untraveled as it was. We found a nice clearing right on the edge of the wooded area, with a barrier of trees between us and the path. The cluster of trees to our back wasn't as deep as the Dark Wood, but it was dense all the same. I was glad we didn't venture farther in, as I felt a tingle at the base of my skull warning me that something lurked within.

Zig slid from Carrot in a heap, his legs giving out beneath him. He plopped over into the soft carpet of the forest floor, lying on his back and stretching out his limbs. "What is the Simmer, by the way? And why do we have to cross it?"

I dismounted, hopping to the soft layer of pine needles. "It's a river fed by hot springs on the way to Ashin."

"That sounds wonderful," Zig said with a groan.

"That would boil your flesh right off," Aven added as they tied their stallion to a nearby tree.

"Less wonderful, then."

"There are a few remaining bridges we can use to cross." I was sure there was at least one left. There had to be. I hadn't traveled to Ashin in years, and the last time, the Simmer didn't exist. But the road I'd chosen wasn't *completely* overgrown. Someone still had to travel this way. Maybe.

"Come on, Zig," Aven said, dropping their saddlebags to the ground. "Let's find kindling before it gets too dark."

"Don't go far," I cautioned as they set out. "Stay within eyesight. I don't want any of us lost."

"Yes, lead adventurer. Noted," Zig said, flashing a grin.

By the time we made camp and had a cheerful fire flickering, the deep dark of the night had spread over the world, the sky dotted with stars and the three sister moons. The mounts were tied off a few feet away, nibbling on a smattering of saplings they'd found. After a quick dinner of provisions, Zig promptly fell asleep in his bedroll. He wasn't accustomed to the rigors of travel like Aven and I were.

Aven sat next to me on a log, tossing twigs into the fire, while I leaned back on my elbows and stared at the sky. One of the moons hung waxing, dappling the world in a glowing silver and blue, while the other two shone as slivers.

"If we leave at dawn," I said, "we'll make Ashin before nightfall."

Aven hummed lowly. "Then we can find the eyewitness."

An owl hooted in the distance.

"Should we set up a watch?" they asked.

I tipped my head to respond, but my breath caught at the way the flames cast light and shadow across Aven's profile, splashing reds and oranges across their fair skin, playing along the sharp edge of their jaw.

I must have stared for too long without answering, because they turned toward me, their eyebrows raised.

"Ellinore?" Aven asked.

"Huh?"

"A watch?"

"Oh!" I started, then looked away and cleared my throat. "Sure. A watch would be good," I said, voice only slightly strangled. "I'll go first, and I'll wake you when I start to feel tired. But it might be a while, since I'm used to questing alone and don't sleep much." That was mostly true. Sometimes Dave would stick around after he helped and allow me to sleep, pressed against his warm side, but that was only when we were certain he wouldn't be seen. Otherwise, I fended for myself.

Aven sighed heavily.

"What?" I snapped at them. Probably unfairly, but I was annoyed and tired and had been caught . . . staring. "Does that plan not suit you?"

"It was nothing."

"That sigh was not nothing. What's wrong?"

Aven squirmed on the log. "Well, uh . . ." They cleared their throat. "I haven't stayed awake the entire night before."

I laughed. "Yeah, right. We completed the same quests. We were alone and out in the wilds for days, you must have . . ."

Their ears reddened.

"You didn't?" I squeaked with indignation. Were Aven's deeds as suspect as my own? Were they not the pinnacle of rule-following royalty?

Aven winced, nose wrinkling. "I'm royal. I never go anywhere alone. I always had a bodyguard. But I completed the tasks myself!"

I held up my hands. "I wasn't going to say otherwise."

"Yes. You were."

I grinned, because I had thought about it but bitten my tongue. I may have been a jerk and a liar, but I drew the line at hypocrite. Well, that wasn't quite true, but semantics.

"Wait. You were by yourself at my house."

Aven broke a stick. "The king sent me and knew I would be with you." They shrugged. "That seemed to be enough for my uncle."

"Wow. The king of Avoury thinks I'm good enough to protect the precious princet," I crowed. "I'm bodyguard material. The Crown trusts me with one of their own!"

Aven scowled. "You know, I could do without the arrogance."

"I'm not here to please—"

A twig snapped in the distance.

I shot up from my sprawl into a crouch. Aven tensed at my side. It could be nothing.

My ears strained as the forest went still but no further sound followed.

My shoulders relaxed, and I released the breath I'd held.

A rustle of leaves broke the silence, sounding much closer than the first disturbance. It was followed by a flap of cloth, then a quiet murmur. Another crack in the bracken, and the hair of my arms rose on end.

I exchanged a quick look with Aven, who gave a nod. I went for my sword. They went for their bow and slid an arrow from the nearby quiver.

Whatever was out there was approaching our camp and had either given up on the pretense of being quiet or was awful at sneaking around the woods in the dark.

"We should check it out," Aven whispered at the same time I said, "We need to leave."

Aven's mouth flattened. "Leave?"

Wait, oh no. That was obviously not what Ellinore the Brave would do. She would totally check out the strange noises in the dark and brave the creepy forest. Yes. That's right, she would suck it up and face whatever was out there with her sword and her sense of righteousness. Or whatever.

"I mean," I said with a shrug, "I should check it out." I jerked my head to the side. "I'll go this way, and you stay here." If I was going to don the Ellinore the Brave mantle, I couldn't let Aven join me. They would inevitably see the truth, and then they'd leave and report back to the king. There would be dungeons involved. I couldn't let that happen.

Aven frowned. "Stay here? No. I'm coming with you."

"Look," I said quietly, "as we established before this jamboree, I'm the leader. I go. You stay. End of conversation."

"That's ridiculous. I can help you. You know I can."

"You know all those ballads are about Ellinore the Brave, not Ellinore and her band of merry cohorts. I work alone."

They blinked. "Are you serious?"

I didn't have time to argue. "Do what you want, then. I'm going this way."

"Fine. I'll go that way."

"Fine."

Aven gave a sharp, aggravated nod, then they crept to the right. I went to the left, sword drawn. Aven melted into the shadows of the trees, arrow nocked, and I did my best to step softly as I moved away from the fire. I paused after ducking behind a tree, allowing my eyes to adjust to the darkened forest barely lit by the moons above, then slowly inched toward the sounds. My hands were tight around the hilt of my sword, palms sweaty. Treading lightly, I went deeper, until my own fire was a flicker of orange between the trees behind me.

The farther I went, the more the forest quieted. Not even my own steps or my harsh breaths reached my ears. The area was blanketed in a cloud of silence, almost as if it was magic.

I immediately tensed. Crap. It *was* magic. It had to be.

I straightened from my hunch and looked for Aven, hoping to spy them through the trunks of the trees and the drape of vines, but they weren't there. I dropped the tip of my sword, knowing that hostility was no way to approach a magical being, if that was what I was dealing with, but I kept a tight grip on the hilt just in case.

I drew on my years of questing and the authority I usually faked when in such situations, and cleared my throat. "I know you're out there," I called, though the dampening magic made it sound like a whisper.

A flicker of twilight-blue light appeared to my left, emerging from a hole in a tree, and flew toward me. A forest faery. I should've known.

"Hello," she said, voice high and tinny. While not an ancient like Dave, and certainly not a primordial like the Elder Beast, a faery still possessed potent magic for a folklore.

She bobbed at eye level while glowing a dizzying mix of purples and blues. She was about the size of my arm from elbow to fingertips, but she was powerful, especially here in her grove. Her long hair covered most of her tiny body, save for her wings, face, and feet. A feral, terrifying thing.

"Hello," I greeted. "I apologize for trespassing."

She flew to my other side while giggling. An arm no bigger than a twig appeared from her hair, and she held her hand to her mouth as she laughed. "So funny," she said softly. "There's no need to apologize."

I squinted at her. "Still, I shouldn't have disturbed you. I'll go back to my fire now."

"You can't," she said with another giggle, this time more mocking than humorous. My stomach knotted. "Not until I tell you a secret."

My fingers strained around the hilt of my sword. "No, thank you. I don't want to know. I'd like to just leave."

Her expression dropped into a pout. "Please? I have something to say to you, Ellinore the Brave."

I froze. My throat went tight with fear. Oh, that wasn't good. That wasn't good at all.

She laughed again, more sinister than airy. "Oh yes," she said with a twirl, her hair fanning out around her as if she were a dandelion puff in the wind. "I know your name. I heard them talking about you. It's not every day that the greatest quester the kingdom has ever known graces your grove with her presence."

"My reputation precedes me."

I slid my foot backward along the ground, trying to test how far the boundary of her influence extended behind me. But she noticed. Her pout became a pronounced frown, then her eyes narrowed. She flew over my shoulder and grabbed my ponytail in her small hand and tugged.

I bit down on a yelp and resisted smacking her away with the back of my hand.

She huffed in displeasure when I didn't react, and flew around to face me again, her hand still tangled in the strands of my hair. "Don't you want to know what I know?"

I did, but I wasn't about to say so or ask. That way lay tricks and trials. "No."

"You're no fun, Ellinore." She released me and crossed her arms over her torso, her long hair tangling around her ankles as she hovered. "I only wanted to play a game and have a little fun. It's so rare that I get to have fun with humans nowadays. Not since the road became less traveled."

I took another step backward. Something snapped beneath my heel, loud enough to break through her silence. I chanced a glance down to find the bleached bones of a human hand gleaming in the moonlight, the finger bone cracked cleanly beneath my boot. No doubt the rest of the skeleton loitered beneath the flora of the forest floor. I swallowed. "What about them?" I croaked, jerking my chin in the hand's direction.

"Oh," she said, covering her mouth again and letting out another giggle. "Oops. Well, that human wasn't as fun. He tried to use his sword instead of his brain. Like most of the human rabble that tromp through my grove carrying weapons. Always attacking before engaging in conversation." She clucked her tongue and shook her head. "He was too easy, honestly. At least you're giving me a challenge."

I swallowed, suddenly certain there was more than one skeleton on the forest floor. A drop of sweat ran down from my temple, and I wiped it away with my fingers.

She strangely stilled and her large eyes widened, glossy and silver beneath the moons. She flew closer, hovering near my wrist.

"Now, where did you get that?" she asked, voice soft with awe.

I looked down, and the slim silver of Dave's bracelet glinted in the light emanating from her. "From a good friend."

"Oh," she said. "Well, that changes things."

None of the other minor magical creatures had seemed phased by the presence of the bracelet before. Or if they had been, they didn't mention it.

"It does?"

"Yes," she said sadly. "I can't play with you and risk the ire of a dragon. A dragon is an ancient, and far more powerful than a second being like myself. They breathe fire, you know." She cupped her hand around her mouth. "That's dangerous to forest faeries."

Relief washed over me. "I understand. I'm leaving now." I turned, intent on running as fast as I could. I didn't know if she would allow me to go that easily, but it was worth a try.

"Wait!" She flew in front of me. "I still want to tell you a secret, Ellinore. I'll make it a gift, since you didn't try to trick me or capture me or threaten me with your friend's power." She zipped to a branch and sat down, crossing her legs and wiggling her dainty toes. "You're being followed."

"What?"

She smiled, wide and eerie, her teeth sharp, little glistening points. "Something is pursuing you. It's on the other side of the forest right now, and it is speaking your name. It wants something from you."

"It wants something?"

"Yes," she said, wings fluttering. "It's not friendly and it's not far."

This was a trick. It had to be. She was attempting to frighten me, to get me to make a foolish move so she could trap me, as she had the person before. I mean, I hoped she was. Otherwise, I was in more danger than I assumed. "How do I know you're telling the truth?"

"Why would I lie?" she asked with a melodic hum. At my raised eyebrow, she added, "I wouldn't lie to a friend of a dragon. I know better."

I gulped. Okay. That was terrifying information all the way around. "What is it, then? What's following me?"

She plunked her chin on her fist, elbow propped on her knee, and tsked. "I already gave you a gift. Any further information would constitute a game." She pointed to the skeletal arm on the forest floor. "Those are the rules. Dragon or no."

I took the hint. Okay. No more questions.

"Thank you."

She perked up, her expression easing into one more friendly. "You're welcome, Ellinore the Brave." She cocked her head to the side, as if listening to a sound I couldn't perceive; then her smile sharpened again into something threatening and wild. "Though I should warn you, if one of your companions crosses over the boundary of my grove as you did, I can't promise their safety."

Zig! Aven!

She waved her tiny hands. "You should go."

I didn't need any more prompting. I ran, uncaring that I crashed through the underbrush, snapping twigs and generally making too much noise. The fire still burned in the distance, much lower than when I'd left it, but a guiding light all the same. As I approached it, the sound of the forest came roaring back in—the hoots of an owl, the scurrying of animals underfoot, and the sound of Aven calling my name. Oh, thank the ancients. I quickly glanced over my shoulder, the flickering blue of the faery disappearing between the trees, but I didn't slow my pace. I had to keep Aven and Zig out of the forest. Not only was that feral faery terrifying, but she knew of my friendship with Dave. She could reveal my secret to Aven or Zig. And that would be worse than trapping them in her grove.

Whipping my head around, I let out a strangled yell as I smacked right into Aven's chest.

We tumbled to the dirt. I had the awareness to drop my sword, lest I skewer them as we slammed to the forest floor. Their back slapped against the ground, and they let out an "oof" as I fell square on top of them, my chin bouncing against their collarbone.

They groaned. "Ellinore?" they rasped.

I scrambled off them, fully aware of how I'd landed on them with my full weight and how we'd pressed together in interesting ways, and fully embarrassed about it. However, I'd have time to freak out later. Right then, knowing Aven was relatively safe, I had to get to Zig.

I grabbed their hand and tugged them upright.

"Ellinore?" they asked again.

"Yes. It's me. Let's go."

"Where have you been? I've been calling your name. I never found the source of the noise and—"

"Doesn't matter." I picked up their bow and shoved it into their hand, then yanked my sword from a pile of leaves. "Don't go farther into the forest. Come with me!"

Aven huffed. "I know you're the leader but—"

"It's not safe, Aven! We have to leave! Now!"

I didn't have time for them to second-guess, and Zig—oh my ancients, Zig!—was all by himself. What if he woke up and wandered away, looking for us? What if something else stumbled upon him? I linked my fingers with Aven's and took off, pulling them along behind me.

"What's gotten into you?" they asked, panting. "Did something happen?"

"I met a wild forest faery," I said. "She tried to trick me, but when I didn't succumb to her game, she told me that there was something in the woods following us and it's hostile."

"What's following us? Did she tell you?" Aven asked, stumbling after me.

"No clue."

"And you trust her?"

"I don't want to take the risk of not believing her." I couldn't very well explain to Aven that the faery wouldn't lie to someone under the protection of a dragon. That would just ruin everything.

"But—"

I whirled on them, finger pointed at their chest. "'Ellinore the Brave' does not mean 'Ellinore the Foolish.'"

Their expression morphed into one of confusion. "I never said it did."

Right. They hadn't. Well, fine. "Good. Let's go."

We lurched into the makeshift campsite, and my knees went weak to find Zig right where we'd left him—asleep in his bedroll. But my relief was short lived at the sight of our bags tossed about. Someone or something had been here and had clearly disturbed the soil, though there were no discernible footprints.

"Did you do this?" I whispered to Aven.

They shook their head. "No. I've been searching for you." They picked up their open saddlebag. "Our bags have been rifled through."

"Please tell me they were looking for gold."

Aven held up a purse that clinked when they jostled it. "Not quite."

Shit. That could mean several things—that whatever had done this wasn't something swayed by gold. Maybe another faery or a curious sprite had stumbled into our camp. Or, if a human, they were looking for something else other than coin.

"The scroll you found . . ."

"At the castle. I didn't bring it with me."

"Good," I said, picking up my saddlebag. I shoved my hand inside to find my own bag of gold hadn't been taken. Thankfully, I'd kept the countdown scroll in the small bag attached to my sword belt. "Believe me now?"

"I always believed you," Aven said without hesitation.

The unwavering truth in that statement made me pause. I'd expected a snarky comeback, not blind acceptance.

Aven continued, despite my internal confusion. "But yes, we should go." They cleared their throat. "The king would not want our quest to be hindered."

Oh, right. The king. I'd almost forgotten that the only reason Aven was even with us was to report back to the Crown. Well, at least they'd hear about an exciting encounter with a faery. I'm certain the bards could spin it into something long and fanciful and utterly untrue.

We quickly packed our things. I woke Zig with several hard shakes. Luckily, because of the travel, he had slept like the dead; otherwise, whatever had done this might not have wanted to leave a witness behind.

"What's happening?" Zig slurred.

"We're leaving."

"What? Why?"

"A faery tried to kill me," I said simply.

Zig's eyes shot open. He rushed out of his bedroll. "Are you serious?"

"Deadly. Come on. We have to move. It's not safe for us out here."

We woke our mounts, quickly saddled them, and tied our bags. I bent my head to Zig as Aven led their stallion out of the trees. "Do you still have it?" I whispered.

Zig's eyebrows drew together. He slipped his hand under the collar of his tunic, where he kept a bag tied close to his chest, and took out the cloth. I wilted in relief.

"Good. Keep it hidden."

He nodded. "Yeah, okay. Did a faery seriously try to . . ." He made a slashing motion with his fingers over his throat.

"Yes. I stepped on the bony hand of her previous victim. It wasn't great."

His wide eyes reflected the moons. "Wow. Okay. Glad I was asleep."

"Yeah. Me too."

Bluebell and Carrot plodded slowly to the road to join Aven and their steed. We mounted and rode toward Ashin by the light of the moons and stars. I kept my sword within easy reach, and I noticed that Aven had slung their quiver across their back instead of tying it to their horse.

I hoped that whatever had gone through our bags was merely a curious creature and not whatever malicious entity the faery had warned me about. It had not been motivated by gold, but it had been searching for *something*. At least it hadn't found the scrap of magic cloth.

But that didn't do much to allay my worries. The faery had heard my name spoken in the forest, which meant that whatever was tracking me had to know what I was after. Which made this whole journey even more dangerous than I'd initially feared.

10

AVEN, ZIG, AND I CAMPED IN A SMALL CLEARING A STONE'S THROW AWAY
from the boiling river that we would need to cross to enter the town of Ashin. I
set a watch rotation with Aven, taking the first shift. I knew I wouldn't be able
to sleep anyway, not with the words of the faery ringing in my head.

I brushed my fingers over the slim silver bracelet I used to summon Dave.
Yet again, he'd come to my rescue, even if he wasn't aware of it this time. And
yet again, it only served to highlight the fact that I could never have become
Ellinore the Brave without his help. It stung to think about—that even on a
quest to save my brother, I had to rely on someone else to step in, and the inabil-
ity to live up to my own hype swirled in the pit of my stomach.

The sun barely skimmed over the horizon, painting the sky with pinks and
purples, the rays beginning to break through the low-lying fog of the mountains
in the near distance. I took the countdown scroll from my pack and grimaced.
Another mark had disappeared, more wax dripping down the taper.

"You didn't wake me," Aven said, sitting up from their bedroll and rubbing
their eyes.

I shoved the parchment into my bag, then rested my chin on my hand as
nonchalantly as I could.

Aven pinned me with a questioning stare.

"I couldn't sleep," I said.

"Unsettled by the faery?"

"No," I immediately shot back, then sighed. "Maybe."

Aven's blue eyes softened into something akin to understanding, and I looked away, unable to take their concern this early in the morning.

"Hey," they said, voice low, "exhausting yourself won't help Zig. It won't make us go quicker or find the witness faster. In fact, it will hinder us."

I closed my eyes and breathed, somehow more rattled by Aven's empathy than anything the faery had done. "Thanks for your advice. But I'm good."

Standing quickly from where I'd been propped against a tree, I bit back a groan as my joints protested from being in the same position too long. I twisted, my spine cracking loudly enough for Aven to frown.

They ran a hand through their hair, the black strands a little less glossy than normal but still relatively flawless. I winced at the tangles at the ends of my own hair and quickly pulled it into a ponytail.

"I'll wake Zig," I said, flinching as I caught a snarl with my fingers. "Then we'll get going."

I crossed the meadow to where Zig had rolled into his blanket, using his saddlebag as a pillow. I prodded him with my toe. He didn't stir.

"Zig," I called. I applied more force to my nudge.

The lump groaned. "What?"

"Time to get up, Brother."

"It's scarcely dawn, Sister."

"Don't blame me. You wanted an adventure. As adventurers, we get up in the morning."

Zig yanked the blanket from over his head and glared at me. His hair stood on end like a rooster comb.

"Good morning. You look like a disgruntled chicken," I said, stifling a giggle.

His glare intensified. "Not my fault you made us relocate in the middle of the night."

I could have bitten back that it wasn't my fault we were on this quest to begin with, but I wasn't cruel, at least, before dawn. "Just get up."

Zig grumbled but managed to pull himself from his bedroll. In a few minutes the three of us were ready. Aven changed their tunic to another non-descript black one, but with a much longer hem, which fell to their knees. They belted it at their waist, then tied their leather guard over their forearm with practiced ease.

With no sign of whatever was following us, and no faeries in sight, we saddled our mounts and started the day's journey.

The river was only a short walk away. The bubbling water rushed over a combination of obsidian and sedimentary rocks. It was beautiful, if you liked frothing water that could boil the flesh right off a living creature. The heat was almost unbearable the closer we approached, the air shimmering with it, creating mirages in the morning sun. Steam rose in soft clouds, misting the bank and the ground around it, so that no grass or trees could thrive and offer shade along the river's edge. The muddy ground was slick and dangerous. One wrong step and we'd become boiled meat.

"Are you serious that this is the best way into this town?" Zig asked, still half asleep, his hair a brown, fluffy mess that was quickly becoming damp with humidity and sweat.

"It's the quickest," I said. "We didn't have time to travel a less treacherous way."

"Well, I won't have to worry about dying by the hands of magic," he replied, wiping his brow. "I'll just die here."

I shot him a glare. Aven snorted a laugh.

"There's bridges," I said. "Somewhere in the steam. They're not widely traveled."

Zig tapped his chin. "I wonder why? Maybe it's the death water."

Aven scanned the bank. "There," they said, pointing. "See the trail? That must be one."

"Good eye," I said, impressed.

"I use a range weapon," they responded with a smirk, tugging on the strap that held their quiver to their horse. "It's kind of my thing."

"Whatever. Let's make crossing bridges your thing. Okay?" Zig said, brushing past us, leading Carrot.

I hurried to catch up.

The bridge was made of wood that had been warped by the heat. It arched over the water, high enough that the Simmer wouldn't melt the soles off our boots, but not high enough to escape the burning mist, which was so thick that the far end of the bridge was obscured. The bowed planks were wide enough for a carriage to pass, but one of the side railings was missing, which meant we'd have to go single file for safety.

"How was this even built here?" Zig said, and gestured wearily.

"The bridge was built before the event that created the Simmer," Aven replied, tilting their head and scanning the crossing. "There were several that dotted the length of the river, but this may be the only one left. It might be dangerous, but your sister is correct that it is the quickest way into the town."

Treacherous as the way might be, we couldn't dally on the bank.

"Okay, let's get going." I tugged on Bluebell's reins, but she dug her hooves into the soft ground and pulled backward, uneasy and afraid. I rubbed her nose to calm her, but I knew that would do little. "We should get our horses over first, before they become more skittish," I said, eyeing the bridge. "They will follow each other. And then we'll go."

"One of us should go first to receive them," Aven said. Their own stallion was huffing from his nose, ears pinned down and eyes wide. "Or we might lose them."

"I'll go," Zig said before I could volunteer.

"No, Zig, I'll go. We don't know what's at the end of this thing."

"Nope," he answered, rolling his shoulders. "I got this. I'm inherently lucky, remember?"

"This whole quest is to save *you*. It's too dangerous for you to—"

"Look, if I die, then you can retire to the coast like you want. If I don't, we continue and you get more time with Princet Heart Eyes. It's a win-win for you."

I glared, but I didn't want to argue and delay our crossing further, so I stepped aside and gave Zig a grand bow. "Fine. Go ahead."

"With pleasure."

He gingerly stepped onto the first plank, and surprisingly the bridge didn't sway under his weight. Zig released a nervous laugh and stepped again. Then again. He grabbed the remaining railing when one of the boards creaked, but otherwise, he disappeared in the steam without incident.

"Ha!" I could barely discern him on the other bank in the thick, rolling haze, but his triumphant yell told me all I needed to know. Inherently lucky indeed.

"We're sending the mounts!" Aven shouted.

"Okay! I've got them!"

"Bluebell will go first," I said, grasping her reins tightly in my hand. "Then Carrot and lastly your stallion."

"Mouse," Aven mumbled. The stallion's ears perked up.

"His name is Mouse?" I snickered. "This magnificent creature fit for royalty is named Mouse?"

"I was four. I liked this fairy tale about a mouse and—can we talk about this later?"

"Oh definitely, because I'm not going to let that go."

"Fine!"

Bluebell was a good horse. She'd been with me for a long time, and she liked Zig well enough because he snuck her treats. So she'd go to him, and Carrot, as a pack mule, would surely follow. It was Mouse I was most worried about.

I led Bluebell to the first plank, tied her reins to the pommel so she wouldn't trip, and smacked her rump. "Go ahead, girl."

"Come on, Bluebell!" Zig yelled from the other side. "I have treats!"

Bluebell's ears pricked forward, and she stepped onto the bridge. After the first few tentative steps, she boldly walked across. Carrot followed easily. Once the mule was over in Zig's hands, we readied Mouse.

Aven rubbed Mouse's nose and whispered in his ear, trying to calm him, but it didn't help. Mouse still danced nervously, picking up his hooves and stomping, neighing in distress.

"You'll have to lead him," I said, after Mouse gave no indication that he was going to go quietly.

"Yeah, I know." Aven grasped the lead, their fingers twitching, their expression pinched. "Come along, Mouse. We can do this."

Aven guided Mouse to the first step of the bridge. Mouse neighed and huffed, blowing from his nostrils, but after a few gentle words and pets from Aven, they began their crossing. They made it over half the bridge, to the high arc, without incident, but then the bridge creaked.

Mouse reared with a high-pitched whinny, knocking Aven into the railing, then took off, hooves thudding hard against the planks.

Aven righted themself while on the bridge, hands gripping the cracked wood, chest heaving, but otherwise okay. They gave me a wave and a weak smile, but then the ground shook and the bridge buckled.

11

ɘ৵

"Aven!" I yelled from the shore.

The ground lurched sickeningly beneath me, and I stumbled, falling flat on my stomach right on the edge of the bank.

The bridge pitched like a boat in a storm. There was a loud crack, followed by a splash and a hiss, indicating the other end had dislodged from the shore and crumbled into the river.

Aven held on to the railing with determination, but the wood began to splinter, a deep crack running across the bottom at a dangerously fast speed.

Gritting my teeth to keep them from clacking, I pushed to my hands and knees as the world around me quaked, the tremors shaking up my palms into my arms and taut shoulders, rattling into my core. Standing meant risking falling into the Simmer, which sloshed along the shoreline, waves splattering up the bank, but I had to get to Aven.

I lunged forward and crawled along the boards. My fingers burned, and the wet heat scalded the fabric of my trousers at the knees. Once near the peak of the arch, I flattened my body across the planks of the bridge, hooking my leg around one of the remaining pylons to stabilize my swaying body as best I could. I reached out my hand to Aven.

"Come on!" I yelled, fingers outstretched.

Aven pushed off from the railing just as it partially fractured and fell into the river, popping and crackling before the wood was swept downstream. They sprang toward me and grabbed my forearm with a death grip, and then they dropped from sight as the surface gave way. I yelped in surprise as the bridge split in the middle and toppled.

Aven fell with a shout, my shoulder jerking over the edge with their weight, my body sliding with them until my knee caught and the jagged edge of the bridge bit into my chest. But I held on. *They* held on. And now Aven, a royal of the kingdom, dangled several feet above the Simmer and certain death, and I had no leverage to pull them back up.

Okay, new rule of questing: When crossing a bridge, cross it quickly.

My shoulder burned. Broken wood dug into the flesh of my bicep, and my fingers tingled with pins and needles, threatening my already-tenuous grip.

"Ellinore!" Zig's voice thankfully came from the other side of the river.

"Zig!" I yelled. "I need . . ." Help. I needed help. Aven's boots were surely melting, and my skin was slick with sweat and mist, and I knew both of us were going to die right then, because I wasn't going to let go. I couldn't let go. But as suddenly as it had all begun—the quaking ceased.

I gasped, releasing the scream I'd held behind my teeth in a loud, ragged breath, before sucking in air. I choked on the hot mist, sputtering, as I looked over the edge of the remaining wood. Aven peered up at me, blue eyes wide.

The boards beneath me groaned and cracked.

"Let go," they breathed. "Don't die with me."

"Are you kidding?" I said, strained. "I'm Ellinore the Brave. Sometimes I'm even Ellinore the Strong. I'm never letting go."

"Save Zig. Not me."

"Shut up! I'll figure something out."

I didn't know what. My bracelet to call Dave had slid down my wrist and was trapped between our forearms. He wouldn't arrive in time anyway, and I knew the potion he'd given me couldn't heal boiling to death. I had no purchase or grip to pull Aven up. Best-case scenario would be for me to stand slowly, but strong as I was, I didn't think I could lift Aven's weight in that way without my entire shoulder giving out. Maybe if I swung them—

"Let me help."

I startled at the light, calm voice coming from behind and almost dropped Aven right then. Whoever it was crouched next to me and reached down to grab Aven's other arm. I caught the barest glimpse of golden-brown skin before her sleeve fell to her wrist, but I couldn't risk looking at her and taking my eyes off Aven for a second.

Aven looked up at her with a questioning furrow in their brow.

"Why don't we discuss once you're out of harm's way, Princet Aven," she said. "Lift on three?" she asked me.

The boards beneath my body squeaked with her extra weight.

"How about lift on now?" I reached with my other arm, grasping Aven at the elbow.

"Okay. Now!"

She rose from her squat, taking the lion's share of Aven's weight, while I scrambled to my knees, then stood quickly to balance us out. It wasn't pretty—I ended up grasping the back of Aven's tunic to haul them over the brink—but we succeeded in not dying.

Once Aven was back on their feet, I grabbed their hand with my sweaty one and yanked them off the rickety remnants of the bridge and didn't let go until we were on solid ground. The mystery girl followed and stood with us on the muddy bank. Only the first few steps of the bridge remained intact; the rest had been swept downstream or dangled off in splintered pieces. I shuddered at how close we'd come to an agonizing death. But we'd made it. We'd made it.

I bent over, my hands on my knees, huffing and puffing from the exertion. Aven stood next to me, their body pressed into mine as they trembled. I wanted to ask them if they were okay, if they were hurt, if they needed a hug, but I didn't. I couldn't. That was not the relationship we had. And I wasn't going to break protocol with the mystery girl there. I settled for taking their hand in mine and giving it a quick squeeze. Aven met my gaze and mouthed, *Thank you.*

"Ellinore!" Zig's voice floated over the chasm. "Are you okay?"

I sucked in a breath, straightening, and yelled back. "We're fine! How about you?"

"Same! Thank the ancients you're alive. I thought I would have to finish the quest by myself."

I chuckled and shook my head. The loose hairs from my ponytail clung to the back of my neck and my temples and the side of my face, wet with sweat and condensation.

"Do you have Mouse?" Aven called, voice pitched high with adrenaline.

"Mouse?" Zig asked. "Who's Mouse?"

"Aven's horse!"

Zig's raucous laughter was probably the sweetest sound I could've heard at that moment. "Your horse is named Mouse? Seriously? That's hilarious."

"Zig!" Aven's tone cut through his levity like a knife.

"Yes," Zig said with a chuckle, undeterred. I imagined him wiping tears of laugher out of his eyes. "I have all three of our mounts."

"Great!" I called, elbowing Aven lightly in the arm. They pouted, then glanced at the girl and schooled their expression. Huh. Interesting.

"What are we going to do now?" Zig asked. "I'm on one side and you're on the other, and that is not going to work for me for very long."

That was a good question.

The girl gently cleared her throat. "I know another way. It will take a few hours, but you'll be in Ashin before nightfall."

I whipped around to face her, my hand drifting to where the hilt of my sword should rest, and grasped air. Oh no! My sword . . . was on the other side of the river. Okay. Must recalibrate.

"Who are you, anyway?" I asked, doing my best to figure out where my hands should rest. Hips? No. Crossed? That felt confrontational toward someone who had just helped me rescue my . . . competitor? Frenemy? Rival-slash-situationship? Whatever. I went with the always-awkward one-hand-on-hip move.

"Yeah, who is that?" Zig asked. "That doesn't sound like Aven."

Aven sighed and pinched the bridge of their nose. I just knew they were wondering what had possessed them to sign on to this traveling circus. Well, their fault for inserting themself into the situation in the first place.

The girl merely smiled. She was about our age. She was dressed in clothes that looked like she thought they might do well for traveling but actually made her stand out—a stylishly embroidered deep-green cloak that highlighted her bronzed skin and her brown eyes, and a flowy light-blue blouse that wouldn't survive an encounter with a gnome much less any creature with claws. Her shirt was tucked into a pair of trousers with elegant stitching at the hems, and her soft leather boots had never seen a speck of mud in all their existence. Each detail marked her as a noble, as did the lift of her chin and the jeweled pins that kept her styled dark-brown hair in place. She clutched a quarterstaff in one hand and had a travel bag looped across her shoulder. She looked like she'd stepped out of the pages of a fairy tale.

"Do I know you?" I asked, squinting at her. "You look familiar."

"We've met," she said quickly. She smiled, obviously pleased, her cheeks dimpling. "Only once, but I've followed all your adventures."

Oh. Oh no. A *fan*.

Aven stood by my side and crossed their arms. "Ellinore," they said flatly, "meet Farrah. A lady of the court. The queen's sister's daughter."

Oh no times ten. I swallowed around a tight throat. "You're royalty?"

"No," Aven said.

Farrah giggled and pressed her fingers to the base of her throat, her nails manicured, though one was broken, and her fingers sported calluses. Interesting. "Not a royal. My mother is noble, but the line of succession comes from the king's family. You could say that Aven and I are cousins by marriage."

"Or you could not say that. What are you doing here?" Aven asked, without any of the courtly manners they used when in the castle.

I glanced at them. Though their tone displayed annoyance, their expression was back to that neutral one they always used at court. Except when bickering with me, of course.

"Saving you, apparently." She batted her eyelashes. "The polite thing would be to thank me."

Aven's jaw ticked. "We're not at court, so I don't have to be polite. So again, *why* are you here?"

"I think the better question is why are you here, Princet Aven?"

Aven stiffened. Their glare hardened. "I'm here on order of the Crown." They bit out every word with tense diction, making it sound almost like a threat.

"Really?" Farrah asked in an exaggerated drawl. "I don't remember hearing anything official . . ."

"It was a closed-door meeting. Family only."

"Uh-huh. Is that a fact?"

"Yes. And you'd do well to remember that even though you are the queen's family, I'm the royalty here."

Oh. And that *was* a threat. What was going on there? Other than Aven tapping into something surprisingly attractive. If I weren't already parched from the steam, my throat might have gone dry. Wait, ew. I could admit that Aven was objectively pretty . . . They had always stood out in the sea of people at court . . . But attractive? To me? That was . . . definitely not needed.

"I'll keep that in mind," Farrah said, clearly unbothered. "But now that you mention it, I have a vague memory of a royal order. That's not where I found out about Ellinore's quest. Gossip moves fast, you know."

Aven's face turned red—either from frustration or the heat of the boiling water. I couldn't tell. "I'm only going to ask one more time. What are you doing here?"

Frustration it was!

Farrah's sly smile bloomed into something genuine and maybe even a little bit adoring. "I'm here for Ellinore."

"Me?" I squeaked.

"I followed Aven from the castle, and I've trailed you for the past few days, and—"

"You've been following us? *You're* who the faery was talking about?" I blurted in disbelief. "The hostile entity?"

She frowned. "I'm not hostile." She glared at Aven. "Though I don't know about Princet Aven."

"Just Aven. Like I said, we're not at court. No titles here." Somehow their defensive posture tightened, and I worried their spine might snap. "So you went through our bags to see if—"

"What?" She crossed her arms as well, the staff placed in the crook of her elbow. "What are you talking about?"

"Oh, don't play coy. You went through our bags, looking for clues to figure out where we were going. And where is your horse?" Aven said, looking past her shoulder. "How did you catch up to us so fast?"

"I *had* a horse, but it was stolen last night! Or it wandered off, or whatever, I don't know. Anyway, I did *not* go through your things."

"Hey!" Zig called. "What's going on? What am I supposed to do now?"

I broke away from their argument and walked close to the bank. "Go to Ashin," I called. "Lead the horses and Carrot. And we'll meet you there when we can."

"What should I do when I get there?"

"Wait for us."

"But—"

"Do *not* do anything that I wouldn't do! Understand?"

There was a pause. "But what if—"

"No!"

"Fine," Zig said, resigned. "I'll be at whatever tavern or inn I find first. I hope to be handsomely compensated for being entrusted with the care of . . . *Mouse*."

"Just be careful, Zig," I said. "And no magic mirrors!"

"That was one time, and I was six!"

I sighed heavily and headed up the bank. Aven and Farrah were engaged in a staring contest that I did not want to deal with.

"You know another way?" I asked.

Farrah nodded. "Yes! I've studied *all* the maps! I know all the kingdom shortcuts." Oh, not only was she a fan, but she was absolutely *too* bubbly. "There is an outcropping a few miles north that I know we can traverse."

"We could always backtrack and take the other fork south," Aven said, ducking their head close to mine, their earrings glinting gold in the rising sun.

"We might even find a closer bridge. We can ditch Farrah there and send her home."

"Might," I replied. "Look, my sword is on Bluebell. Your bow and quiver are on Mouse. If she isn't the person the faery warned us about, that means someone or something else is still out there. She at least has a way to defend herself . . . and us."

"I'm good with it too!" she chirped while twirling the staff. "I learned from a knight."

Aven shifted uncomfortably, apparently feeling as naked without their weapon as I did. "You barely tolerated me, a verifiably good quester, and now you're okay with her? A noble that you don't even know?"

"I'd like to remind you that you basically threatened your way into this quest. Your presence wasn't exactly my choice."

They blinked. "Okay, but that's different because—"

I cut them off. "For the record, and you can report this back to the king, I didn't want *any* of you to join, because as I said before, I work alone. But she's what we have. And we're wasting time. There's no telling what kind of trouble Zig can find unsupervised in a new town."

"Fine," they said. "But I'm warning you, she can be a little much to take."

"I grew up with Zig. I think I'll be fine."

12

"So like I said, my favorite is 'The Ballad of Ellinore and the Golden Dragon,' but my second favorite is the one of your very first adventure with the Ursa. Or wait, no, I forgot about the one where you dive down and trick the Lady in the Sea for her pearl. Or wait, I think it's the one where you defeat a griffin. Or is it the manticore? Oh, no! It's where you retrieve the jewel from the cliffside for the queen! Or is it? I don't remember. But anyway . . ."

I didn't think I'd be so vividly reminded about why I preferred to travel by myself. But here I was. I rubbed my temples as we hiked, a headache born of equal parts exhaustion and Farrah's chattiness throbbing behind my eyes. My legs burned from exertion as the path grew steeper and rockier. And there was a nice long scratch down my entire shin where my trousers had ripped from scurrying across the bridge on my hands and knees.

There wasn't really a path, as the grass had begun to overgrow the area with the rains and sun of spring, patches poking up between rocks, playing peekaboo. Birds chirped overhead, perching on the few scraggly branches of the smattering of trees. Bees buzzed, frogs croaked, rodents scurried. It was a nice spring day save for the constant noise of Farrah's babble.

Aven strolled smugly beside me, a grin on their face that told me they knew exactly what I was thinking and an *I told you so* was forthcoming as soon as Farrah took a breath.

She finally did.

"We could've gone south," Aven said with a gleefulness that was frankly unbecoming of someone so pretty.

"I will stab you when I have my sword back," I replied through clenched teeth.

Aven laughed heartily.

The Simmer gurgled off to the right of us as we climbed, cutting a path through the rocks, and somewhere to the left a mountain goat bleated a greeting. I had an inkling that I had been here once before. The whole area appeared vaguely familiar to me somehow, but it was the base of a mountainous path. They probably all looked the same anyway.

As Farrah prattled happily, I nudged Aven with my elbow.

"What's your beef with Farrah?" I whispered.

Aven frowned. "I don't have a beef."

"You looked like you wanted to rip her head off after we pulled you up and were out of harm's way. What's that about?"

"Nothing."

"You can tell me. Do you . . . like her or something?"

Aven mimed vomiting. "Absolutely not!"

I was a little surprised and concerned at the relief that statement brought me.

"What was that?" Farrah said, spinning around on her heel. Her dark-brown hair in its twisted noble style didn't move an inch. It was quite impressive, compared with my ponytail, which sagged in the damp heat.

"Nothing." I smiled sweetly. "Farrah, do you happen to remember all the words to that one about . . . the sea pearl?"

"Yes. Of course!" She began walking again, singing as she did so. At least she had a nice voice.

I allowed a few minutes of the song before poking Aven again. "Now talk."

"What? No."

"I'm literally listening to a song about myself. I hate songs about myself. So either you tell me what's going on or . . ."

"She's from the castle," they said, then sighed. "When I'm out adventuring, I don't have to . . . be the pinnacle of who my family expects me to be. I can just . . . be. I'm not a *princet*." Their expression pinched at the term. "I'm just Aven."

Oh. That sounded so . . . relatable. I knew how that felt. I could be myself only around Dave. Around everyone else I was the girl from the ballads.

I swallowed thickly. "I'm sorry. I should've thought of that before—"

"No!" They waved their hands and shook their head, their black bangs sweeping across their forehead. "No, it's fine. You didn't know."

"Well, now that I do, I feel awful about it."

"It's okay." They grinned, though it looked like a grimace. "You were right. She's the best way to get to Ashin. And she is armed." They looked like it truly pained them to admit it.

I bit my bottom lip, then took a breath. Aven had offered me empathy that morning; I could extend it back to them.

"You . . . don't have to be anyone but Aven around me—Aven the quester, my fiercest rival, the second-best competitor in the kingdom!"

The smile that tugged at the edge of their lips was genuine. "Thank you."

I might not be the best socially, but I recognized the weight of Aven's gratitude and refrained from offering a flippant remark in return. "You're welcome."

"Just don't believe anything she says about me!" they blurted.

I raised an eyebrow and clamped down on a laugh. "Well, now I'm intrigued. Maybe I should ask her about—"

"No! I will stab you with your own sword if you dare," they said, echoing my earlier words.

I smiled. "Okay. Noted."

"Also, even though I now have to endure Farrah's singing of bard ballads, thanks for not letting go." They gulped. "On the bridge."

My heart somehow fluttered and ached at the same time. "You're welcome." I nudged them hard in the ribs. "Besides, you have the information about the eyewitness. I couldn't very well let you die."

Aven frowned deeply, as if I'd personally insulted them. Which I had.

"What are you two gabbing about back there?" Farrah asked, spinning around on her heel in an elegant move.

I grasped on to the interruption. "Just wondering what you were doing following us," I answered quickly. "You never really said."

"I told you," she answered, twirling her staff while she walked backward. "I'm here for you, Ellinore."

I opened my mouth, then shut it, exchanging a confused glance with Aven.

"I know I'm not doing it correctly," she continued, facing forward but dropping back to walk beside me. "I mean, you're the best adventurer in the kingdom. I'm certain you receive requests like this all the time."

Aven stiffened beside me.

But I had no clue what Farrah was referring to. "I'm sorry, I still don't—"

"Oh! Look! This will help." Farrah ran off to a patch of vibrant wildflowers that swayed in the light breeze. She plucked several and rushed back to where Aven and I had paused in bewilderment.

She stood in front of me. Clutched in her hand was a scraggly bouquet, clumps of dirt and roots still hanging from some of the flower stalks. Her brown eyes crinkled when she smiled, and her cheeks bunched, and still somehow her hair remained perfect.

And for some inexplicable reason, she thrust out her arm, fingers clenched tightly around the stems of the flowers. "These are for you."

I took them, bemused. "Thanks?"

"You're welcome!" She wiped the dirt from the flowers on her trouser leg, wincing when it left a smear, then clasped her hands together in front of her, tucking her staff in the crook of her elbow. "So," she said with a bounce on her toes, "like I said, I know you receive a ton of propositions like this. But I was wondering if you would want to maybe—"

Oh. Oh no. Oh nooo. "No!" I shouted, cutting her off. The flower stems bit into my hand. Were there thorns on these?

She blinked. "No?" She said it with a duck of her head, shy and coy. "You didn't even let me finish."

I swallowed, my palms suddenly sweaty. "I'm not accepting suitors! At this time! Not right now. Not that I wouldn't . . . I mean, you're beautiful. But I'm moving! Trying to move. Away. To the coast. After all this is settled. This is my last quest ever. So . . . it wouldn't work out."

"Oh," she said, her fingers fluttering to her mouth. "Oh."

"Sorry?" I offered.

"No. It's okay." She shook her head, her face flushed. "It's fine. But"—she bit her lip, gaze casting toward Aven, who was as still and silent as a stone—"if we could just talk, I think I could make a case for—"

"I don't think that's a great idea," I blurted. I'd not really had to deal with love interests before, other than a few heirs of the older lieges asking me to dance at feasts. Honestly, the only person who really talked to me at the castle was Aven, and it was all pointed barbs and sarcastic remarks, things I knew how to deal with. I didn't know what to do with . . . this.

I looked to them for help, but that blank mask was back in place, maybe even a little colder and harder than before.

"I just want to learn from you!" Farrah shouted.

"Wait, what?" Aven asked, voice far too loud for how close we all stood next to one another. They rolled their shoulders, composing themself. "I mean, what?" they said, somewhat calmer.

"Learn from me?" I asked. "This wasn't about . . . love?" As soon as I said it, my cheeks burned with a blush.

Farrah laughed. And okay, that hurt a little bit. But she giggled, hiding her mouth behind her hand as if that would somehow keep me from hearing her. "Why would you think"—she snorted as she continued chuckling—"this was about me courting you?"

"Flowers," I said weakly. "Following us. You cornered me at the castle that one time."

"I gave you flowers because you always receive flowers from the court when you accomplish a great deed. I thought it was a thing to give flowers."

"I mean, I guess. I'm not really a flower type of person." Speaking of, I lowered my arm so the bouquet dangled somewhere near my hip, instead of out in front of me like some wilting manifestation of this misunderstanding.

"Anyway," Aven soldiered on, "you want to learn from Ellinore? Why? You've never shown any interest in questing. You barely attend the feasts."

"I don't have to explain myself to you. But if you must know, I . . . want to learn. I want to have adventures. I want to experience new things." She turned her face to the sun and blinked dreamily. "Just not in a romantic way!" she hastened to add after her pause. "Sorry. No offense."

"Oh, solid offense taken," I said, though I grinned to try to offset the sting. "So you somehow heard about this last quest, shadowed Aven when they left the castle, and then followed us all the way here?"

Farrah slowly tilted her head the side, gaze flickering toward Aven. "Yes. I heard about the quest from court gossip . . . and maybe the gossip originated with the king and queen, who tasked Aven to—"

"Supervise and record," Aven said quickly, cutting Farrah off.

"Sure. Anyway, I tried to talk to you, Ellinore, at the last feast, but you ran out of there like your hair was on fire."

Oh. Right. I'd forgotten. "I was a mess," I said, patting down the flyaways escaping my ponytail, because I was still a mess, figuratively and literally. "And I wanted to get home. That was all."

"You announced your retirement. And I saw my last chance to talk to you slipping away. So I took my shot. But you blew me off."

I grimaced. "Sorry. Again."

"Does your mom know where you are?" Aven asked. Their expression had softened slightly, but their tone was clipped and strained.

Farrah rubbed the toe of her expensive boot into the dirt, small bits of gravel popping underneath the leather. She pouted, twisting her staff in her hands. "No?"

"No?" Aven threw up their hands. "Great. Once your parents realize you're gone, they'll come looking."

"I left a note," she said. "That said I was with you and Ellinore."

Aven face-palmed. "I can't believe you would be so irresponsible to—"

"Follow a famous quester on a dangerous mission that may result in injury or death?" She batted her thick eyelashes.

"I was ordered by the Crown!"

"Uh-huh."

Okay. There was something weird brewing between these cousins by marriage, but I was not interested in family drama other than my own. And speaking of, Zig was traveling on his own. And the countdown parchment at my hip was no doubt burning steadily, taking another mark off the timeline. We needed to continue on our way.

"Well," I said as diplomatically as possible, "if the king and queen think it's okay for Aven to come gallivanting along with me without a bodyguard, maybe they'll deem it okay for their niece to come along too."

Farrah's face brightened. "Does that mean you'll let me join? You'll teach me?"

Great. Another one.

"This isn't fun and games, Farrah. This is life or death. I need you to understand that."

She nodded quickly. "I do. I heard that you're looking for the Elder Beast. I don't know what that is, but I'm certain we will find it together."

"Fine, but only if Aven agrees," I said.

Aven jolted. "Really?"

I handed them the bouquet as a gesture of passing off the responsibility. They eyed it as if it were poisonous.

"Yes. Look, it's a big responsibility keeping someone safe. And it would be on both of us, just like Zig."

"If she really does know all the maps, she could be useful," Aven muttered. They puffed up their cheeks and blew out a breath. Farrah shifted on her feet, her lower lip sucked between her teeth, her hands clamped around her staff. Her big brown eyes wide and pleading. "Are you really good with that thing?" Aven asked, nodding toward the quarterstaff.

Farrah perked up. "Yes. I told you I practiced with a knight."

"Which one?"

"Sir Pellam."

"He's not a bad fighter." Aven narrowed their eyes, crossed their arms, and tapped their chin in thought. "Okay. Fine. I agree."

Farrah pumped her fist and let out a whoop. "Best quest ever! You won't regret it, I promise!"

Oh, I already regretted it, because it was difficult enough to keep two people in the dark about my so-called amazing questing record, and now it was three. But I could do it. I could. I just had to keep in mind what Ellinore the Brave would do.

No big deal.

I'd be fine.

Maybe.

We walked for hours.

As we ascended, the sound of the Simmer grew distant, now rushing somewhere below us. The space we needed to cross was no longer a surging, boiling river, but a deep canyon that dropped . . . intimidatingly far.

The sun had reached its zenith about an hour ago, and a gentle breeze blew from the mountains, ruffling and drying my sweat-damp hair. Despite the whole bridge incident and the constant concern about Zig being alone in a new town, it was a nice day. The sky was bright blue, and even though we'd risen in elevation as we walked, we were still in the foothills below the mountains that towered above the landscape. The path was lined with a smattering of vibrant green grass and small flowers blooming in purples, yellows, and pinks. The scene was almost idyllic, and if things had been different, it would've been a perfect place to have a romantic picnic.

Or a nap. Normally, I wasn't one to complain, but having spent the whole night awake, I was exhausted. And I hurt all over from the events of the bridge. I was ready to collapse in a bed by the time Farrah pointed to the outcropping ahead of us.

I was so ridiculously tired that I must have hallucinated that this all looked absurdly familiar.

"Is this the source of the Simmer?" Aven asked, peering down into the canyon, where the river bubbled.

Wait. I rubbed my eyes and looked at a rock formation in the distance that sported the distinct shape of a cow.

"Yes," Farrah said, clapping her hands. She pointed to a trickling waterfall in the distance. "The water coming over the falls is quite cold because it's snow fed, and then it hits a hot spring down there"—she pointed to a pool below us—"and it boils."

Oh no. Oh nooo.

I quickly glanced around, my mind whirling. The cow rock pinged a memory of a joke Dave had made about wanting to eat it but how it would cause indigestion. I shook my head, pushing my palm against my forehead to quell my burgeoning headache.

"I've never been up here," Aven mused as we approached the outcropping.

The path ahead of us was a slab of blackened rock that at one point may have been a natural bridge, carved by the stream over the years. But the ground had since shifted, and the end of our route was several feet above the other side. We'd have to jump. If we made it that far. I peered tentatively over the edge, looking for a glimpse of red or a slither of a tail, but luckily saw only the rush of water.

"Have you, Ellinore?"

I jumped. "Have I what?" Aven had joined me by the beginning of the bridge, while Farrah had wandered off to a plateau a few feet ahead.

Aven raised an eyebrow. "Been up here before."

"Oh, I don't believe so. I think. I'm not sure. Maybe." That sounded convincing. I smiled as winningly as possible. It didn't work.

"Not sure, maybe?" Aven asked.

"Uh-huh."

"Are you okay? Do you need to rest?"

"No!" I cleared my throat. "I mean no. We should keep moving."

"Ellinore," Aven said, expression too sincere, too caring, too honest for me to handle. They gently touched my shoulder. "We can rest if you need to. It's not a crime to be human. I promise."

No, it wasn't a crime to be human. But as Aven had jokingly told me in the past, it was a crime to lie to royalty.

"I'm fine. I'm good. I swear."

"Oh my," Farrah gasped. "What are you? You're so adorable."

I froze. When I returned to my blank parchment on my table at my house to write my memoir, I would make it abundantly clear that I was not responsible for the creation of the Simmer, and that it was the result of an earthquake that had split the ground beneath the river and created a geothermal spring because there was liquid earth not far from the surface. There was a whole underground river of the stuff, and it followed the same path as the stream, heating up the water for miles. I would, however, take the blame for the reason that Farrah's "you're so adorable" struck fear in my heart. Because *this* was the location where Dave and I had herded the troublemaking fire salamanders years ago. This was their territory, and we had unknowingly encroached on it. Maybe if I weren't sleep deprived, I would have realized sooner, but it was too late now.

I ran to the flat area where Farrah stood in a bed of tall grasses and wildflowers, an ecosystem rife with bugs and small animals, perfect food for fire salamanders.

When I crested the incline, it was worse than I'd thought.

There wasn't just *one* baby fire salamander staring at her with its big, filmy eyes, but *two* baby fire salamanders.

And where there were babies . . .

"Farrah," I said calmly, staring at the two youngsters, who blinked adorably at her. They were bright red, about the size of small dogs, but much more dangerous. "Please back away."

"But they're so cute!"

They *were* cute—in this form. They were less cute when they grew to their adult size, which was frighteningly large, and, oh yeah, developed the ability to *spit fire.*

Fire salamanders were distant cousins of dragons, according to Dave—not ancients like him, but second beings, folklores. They grew to about ten feet in length, including their tail, and were more vibrant in color—usually red with yellow or black markings. They mostly inhabited places near still or slow-moving water and were drawn to warm locales, which was why they preferred the hot spring's basin. The Simmer itself couldn't support life other than the fire salamanders, so they had to venture out to find sustenance. They couldn't fly like dragons, but they were amazing at climbing with their long, knobby toes.

Oh, and they flicked their elongated tongues to capture their prey, then rent its flesh with their sharp teeth, and did I mention that the mucus on their skin was toxic? It was their natural defense from predators, though they wouldn't find many now that most varieties of folklores had dwindled to a handful.

Aven jogged up and stopped at my shoulder. "Are those—"

"Yes," I said, cutting them off. "Farrah, come on. We need to get across the rock before their mother appears." I shoved Aven behind me and pointed toward the outcropping. "Go."

"Oh, do you think I could pet them? Really quick?" Farrah clucked her tongue before I could answer. "It's okay, little ones. Don't be scared."

What did I do to deserve this punishment?

"Don't touch them!" I snapped.

"Farrah! Get away from them!" Aven yelled, also *not* running across the rock like I had ordered them to, in the direction of *away*. Had Aven already forgotten that they had had one brush with death today? Did they feel like having another?

Crap. Crap. Crap. Crap. What would Ellinore the Brave do?

Before I could figure that out, one of the little salamanders flicked out its tongue. Thankfully Farrah hadn't touched its head and was able to bat the tongue away with the end of her staff. The baby cried out, whimpering and skittering slightly back.

A growling hiss from over the hill in front of us answered any questions I had about where the parent was.

No time to question now. I grabbed Farrah's upper arm, tugging her harshly behind me before either of the babies could strike again. She stumbled, loosening her grip on her staff, which I gratefully plucked from the curl of her fingers, then swiped in front of me, just in time to deflect another curious tongue lick from the little bugger.

The mother salamander made another terrifying noise, calling out to her misbehaving children.

The second baby salamander whipped around toward the noise of its parent, effectively smacking its tail into my leg. Its slimy, mucus-covered skin slithered across the rip in my trousers, right into the open cut I had there.

The burn of the toxin tingled into the wound and slowly seeped into my leg, but the pain was dull enough to ignore for now.

Which was good because the mother salamander appeared from between two large boulders, stalking toward us on her short, thick legs, her tail dragging behind her. She was large even for an adult, and she spotted us immediately. Her tongue flicked out, small cinders falling into the grass in bursts of light and sizzles. The little ones ran back toward her and hid under her belly while emitting small cries, as if we had caused them great bodily harm, the little whiners. But at least their antics took her attention off us.

"Back away slowly," I said, holding the staff in both hands, knowing it would do little against an enraged momma salamander. But the illusion of safety was at least comforting.

The trio of us shuffled in the grass toward the outcropping, Farrah and Aven practically plastered against my back. The mother salamander inspected her offspring, seemingly having forgotten about us, thank goodness, because my leg stung, and I didn't know how long I had left before the toxin took actual hold. My foot was already half asleep.

"How close are we?" I whispered, not daring to take my eyes off the salamander family.

"Almost there," Aven replied, voice pitched low.

"Good." I licked my dry lips. "Once we get to the rock, run and jump. Salamanders are fast and great climbers, but they can't jump to save their lives."

"How do you know that?" Farrah asked.

Experience. "I just do."

"Don't question," Aven snapped. "Listen to Ellinore."

"If I don't ask questions, how am I supposed to learn?" Farrah shot back.

"Well, maybe you should've listened *the first time* and not tried to make a baby fire salamander your pet!"

"Oh, get off your high horse. You're just annoyed that you have to share Ellinore's attention with me."

"Will you two quit it!"

And that did it. The mother salamander whipped her head around and stared at us with her black, round eyes. She opened her mouth, showing off her rows of razor-sharp teeth, and hissed a threat. Okay. That was fine. She wasn't moving toward us, and even if she ran, we'd be able to get across and jump . . . probably. And it would take her time to follow—she'd have to crawl all the way down, then back up the other side. We'd be fine. Totally. I had this.

An answering growl rumbled to my left.

I whirled in the direction from whence we'd walked. Oh, there was the mate. Much bigger and much, much closer. I had no idea where he had emerged from; maybe he had climbed up the wall of the canyon or hidden behind some of the larger rocks. No matter, he was there, and he was poised to attack. He didn't perceive us as threats to his children like the mother did. He perceived us as meals.

Bursts of flame shot from his nostrils. Oh yes. We were snacks. A tasty treat for his family.

He charged, his short legs a blur of motion.

"Run!" I said, shoving Farrah with my free hand.

I swiped the end of the staff in the nick of time, striking the salamander's nose hard enough to knock him off track. He paused, stunned, which gave me enough time to glance over my shoulder. Farrah had taken my instruction and was poised to jump off the end of the outcropping to the other side.

Aven had not, and hovered.

"Go!"

"But—"

The salamander attacked again, catching the end of the staff in his teeth, the sharp points carving furrows into the wood. I played a fierce game of tug-of-war, trying to dislodge the weapon as flames licked up the shaft. The last thing I needed was for Farrah's staff to catch like kindling. Then I'd really be in trouble.

"Go, Aven! You're unarmed and in the way!"

Aven took a hesitant step toward the edge.

"I'll follow as soon as I can create some distance!" I couldn't take my eyes off the salamander, but I waited anxiously for any sound that suggested they were listening to me.

Their footsteps quickened, their heels thumping against the rock, and then silence as they jumped. An "oof" followed, which told me they had landed safely on the other side with Farrah. I breathed a sigh of relief.

I switched my focus from holding the salamander off to escaping. I wrenched the staff from the salamander's jaws of death and fire. He changed tactics as well and whipped his tail at my knees. I jumped out of the way, my leg threatening to crumble beneath me as the toxin worked its way through my veins. I brought the staff down again toward the salamander's head. At the last second he retreated, and the staff struck the stone.

"Ow!" I yelled as the force reverberated into my hands and elbows.

It *hurt*, but the loud crack was enough to frighten the creature into scrambling a few feet away.

Before it could mount another attack, I turned and took off running. My wound throbbed. My head hurt. My vision swam. I didn't even know if I was going to make it across without injuring myself further, or falling to my boiling death, but it was a risk I was willing to take to avoid being killed and then eaten, or worse, eaten and then killed.

With a last burst of adrenaline, I pushed off and jumped. I flew through the air and miraculously landed on the other side. Somehow I kept my footing with the help of the staff, stumbling only a few steps.

Whew. I'd survived. And so had my companions. Mission accomplished. Yay.

"Wow," Farrah mouthed. "That was just like in the stories."

Aven crossed their arms. "You almost got us killed," they muttered. "What in the ancients were you thinking?"

"That the baby lizard things were cute. That's what I was thinking. I'd never seen anything like them before. How was I supposed to know that their parents were fire-breathing, hissing, large lizard things?"

I tuned them out as they argued. My chest heaved. My knee throbbed. My head pounded. My wound *burned*. Oh, yeah, *there* was the toxin. Felt great.

I dropped the staff and hunched over.

"Can you two pause arguing for one second?" I asked, catching my breath, hands on my knees. "We may be out of immediate danger, but that doesn't mean we should stop here."

"Ellinore?" Aven asked, tentatively patting my shoulder. "Are you okay? You're flushed."

I straightened and placed my hands on my hips. Wow. The whole world wavered. I swallowed, then coughed. "I'm fine," I croaked. "Absolutely perfect."

Judging by Aven's narrowed eyes, they didn't believe me.

"Third rule of questing, Farrah," I said, still panting. "Don't touch things. Especially if they're cute."

"Okay. What are the first two rules?"

I waved away the question. "I'll tell you later. Let's get going."

I took a step.

Then my leg gave out.

13

ℰℛ

"You should have said something," Aven said for the thousandth time as we hobbled toward Ashin.

And for the thousandth time I considered ditching both them and Farrah and limping into Ashin on my own. Because *yes*, I should have told them that I'd been exposed to the toxin. I had been *hoping* to use the little vial that hung around my neck when they weren't looking. But the two of them hovered like mother hens, and I did not want to explain how I was in possession of a magic potion, when I so obviously despised mages and couldn't share that I was friends with an ancient magical creature without blowing my cover, since I'd supposedly offed him years ago. It was all too sticky, and I was too tired to come up with some feasible untruth. Also, the thought of racking up another lie was uncomfortable, especially with Aven so close.

Farrah scoffed delicately.

"What?" Aven asked, voice gruff and right next to my ear. One of the many disadvantages of hanging between the two of them as they supported me on our walk, other than not being able to take the potion, was that I was literally stuck in the middle of their bickering.

Farrah shot a look at them over my head. "Oh . . . nothing." She smiled in a way that looked as if she was trying for sweet, but the smugness was too strong to camouflage.

"It doesn't sound like nothing," they countered.

She feigned innocence. "I was merely agreeing with you. We shouldn't keep secrets from one another."

Ha! If she only knew.

Aven's shoulders stiffened under my arm. They glared at her, their blue eyes gleaming dagger sharp, but said nothing.

Okay. Well. I guess we were completing the remainder of this journey in awkward silence. Which, honestly, was better than the arguing.

"By the way," Farrah continued, and I bit back a groan. So much for silence. "Who knew Ellinore the Brave could wield a staff as well as a sword?"

"Well, you pick up skills as you go," I said. Which was true. Like knowing when to bargain and when to *run away*.

"It's unfortunate you didn't have your sword. I really could've witnessed Ellinore the Brave in action! Those salamanders wouldn't have known what hit them." She raised her arm, miming a sword. "With a whack and a swoosh and a stab and a—"

I stopped abruptly, jolting Aven to a halt as well, my heels sliding in the grass. My stomach plummeting at her insinuation that I would hurt or kill the fire salamanders for the crime of protecting their children and their own territory. I opened my mouth, then closed it, unsure of what to say.

"Do you need a rest?" Aven asked.

I nodded quickly, and they guided me to a large, flat rock and helped lower me to sit. I stretched out my injured leg and winced. The fancy hem of Farrah's cloak had been ripped off and was now tied tightly above my knee to keep the toxin from traveling any farther upward. A bandage, also made from Farrah's cloak, covered the wound, though it didn't do much. From the tourniquet down, my leg tingled unpleasantly, like a thousand little pins and needles poked into my skin. It wasn't enjoyable by any means, but I'd experienced worse.

Aven sat on the ground next to me as I rested, while Farrah pretended her staff was a sword and made clanging and whooshing noises as she danced around.

"We could still leave her in Ashin," Aven muttered.

But that was not what was on my mind by any means. "I wouldn't have killed the fire salamanders," I blurted.

Farrah suddenly stopped, the remainder of her cloak swishing around her. Her full eyebrows pulled together in confusion. "What do you mean?"

I glanced to Aven, who appeared just as intrigued.

I licked my dry lips. "We encroached on them. What happened was our fault. That doesn't warrant a whack and a stab and a whatever."

"But you've killed beings before. The Ursa. The manticore. *The Golden Dragon.*"

Ack. Right. The toxin must have gone to my head for me to forget that Farrah had been singing the ballads the whole way and that Aven was reporting back to their uncle, who could easily throw me in a dungeon.

"That was for quests!" I said quickly. "That's different."

Farrah appeared even more bewildered. "But—"

"If you hadn't tried to *pet* one of them," Aven broke in, "Ellinore wouldn't have needed to use her sword or your staff in the first place. So maybe pay attention to what Ellinore the Brave says."

I couldn't look at Aven. I couldn't let them see the surprise painted on my face, or the heat in my cheeks, so I ducked my head.

Farrah huffed. "Fine."

"It doesn't matter what I would've done with my sword anyway," I said, awkwardly pushing the conversation in another direction. "You wield a staff, which is very different."

"I do . . . ," she said, drawing out the vowel.

"And did Sir Pellam teach you anything other than how to whack and bludgeon?"

Once again Farrah appeared confused. "What else would he teach me?"

Aven sighed dramatically. I ignored them.

"If you come across a human wearing armor, or a creature with natural armor like a griffin, a staff isn't going to land a significant enough blow to neutralize them, no matter how much force you put behind it."

Farrah stared at the staff in her hands. "So what would I do?"

"Hope one of your travel companions uses a bow and arrow," Aven quipped.

I knocked my good foot into their leg, then continued. "You'll have a longer reach, so it will be easy enough to deflect their attack, disarm them if you can, and if you are alone, without a quest companion with a bow or a sword . . . flee."

She blinked. "That doesn't seem very . . . brave."

Great. "Well, if the choices are to be brave and dead or smart and alive, I'm going to choose the latter." I heaved myself to my feet, annoyed and done with the interaction.

I took a step and immediately stumbled, my leg achingly weak, but Aven jumped up and caught me before I hit the ground. They slung my arm over their shoulders and gripped my waist. "I've got you," they said, voice low.

Swallowing my overwhelming embarrassment and the sudden lump in my throat, I choked out a subdued "Thank you." Then I added, "Please do not put this in your account to the king. I have a reputation to uphold."

Aven chuckled. "No promises."

"Fine. But come on," I said, hobbling forward. "We're wasting time."

Farrah joined on my other side, her face flushed and her countenance somber. As we started back on our path, Aven didn't say a word, as if reminding them of our quest had sapped the humor out of the situation. Neither spoke or argued; they merely supported me as we continued on our path.

Huh. Maybe we would complete the rest of the route in awkward silence.

With one arm slung over Aven's shoulders and the other over Farrah's, I hobbled along until we staggered into the town as dusk was falling.

Ashin was about the size of Traveler's Rest, maybe slightly smaller. Which was good, because we found Main Street and a number of taverns within minutes.

With a grunt, I slid my arm from Farrah's shoulders and hopped over toward the rowdiest tavern, pulling Aven along with me until I settled against the wall of the building. I used Farrah's staff to steady me, then I gestured to the door.

"Zig is in there."

"How do you—" Farrah asked, eyebrows pinched together.

"I just know. Okay? Trust me. It sounds exactly like his kind of place." I yawned, covering my mouth with my grubby fingers. "Please find him so I can sleep."

"Will you be okay out here by yourself?" Aven asked.

I gave them my best withering glare. It must have worked, because they shrugged and went inside. Farrah followed, slipping through the crack of the door with her hands up as if she was afraid to touch anything. Huh. No fear when she wanted to pet a creature that could kill us, but touching a doorknob was too much. I wondered if she'd never been in a tavern before. She was noble, after all. Well, it was a day of new experiences for everyone.

Hopefully, the two of them would be occupied for a few minutes, so I could fix myself. I pulled the vial from beneath my shirt and eyed the magic liquid in the light of the streetlamps that had already been lit for the evening. Despite the ornateness of the vial, the stopper was a plain cork. I swished the potion to ensure it was adequately mixed (because who knew how long it had been in Dave's secret stash), pulled the top off with a pop, and touched the dripping cork to my tongue.

The relief was instantaneous.

The tingles immediately ceased, and the respite from pain was so quick, I went light-headed. Feeling returned to my foot, and for the first time in hours, I could feel my toes when I wiggled them. I untied the strip of Farrah's cloak from around my leg, which helped to release the rush of blood and potion throughout my body, and I sagged heavily against the post. My shoulder ceased hurting from the strain of saving Aven, and my headache immediately eased.

"He's not here. The barmaid said he'd left. I don't know why you insisted on continuing to look."

"Didn't you literally tell me to not question Ellinore? She said he'd be in here, and I wanted to be thorough . . ."

Their arguing drifted from the door, and I hastily plugged the vial and slipped it back under my tunic, right as they walked out.

"Are you okay?" Aven asked immediately, seeing me slumped against the post and admittedly a little loopy from both the potion and the pain relief.

"I'm amazing." Ha. Perhaps a lot loopy.

Aven looked me up and down, noticing that the fabric was now in my hand instead of tied above my knee. "What's going on?"

"Nothing."

"Ellinore," they said, hands on their hips, their tone dripping with disapproval, "didn't we just have a long discussion about telling us things that are important?"

"I am!" I bent my knee and wiggled my toes, and it took me too long to realize that they couldn't *see* me wiggling my toes. "Oh. I'm fine. All healed."

"You're fine?"

"Yes."

"How is that possible? You could barely walk when we went inside."

"Uh . . . it was a baby salamander. Not as venomous as an adult." I waved my hand lazily. "The toxin must have worn off."

"In the five minutes we were gone?"

"Yep." I laughed nervously. "It's a miracle. Yay!"

"Zig is not in there," Farrah blurted, cutting off whatever questioning by Aven was to follow. "He was there. But he left. He asked about an inn, though, and they directed him to one down the street."

Aven slung my arm over their shoulders and pulled me from the wall. "Not just any inn, but the most expensive one in town."

"Sounds just like Zig," I said, holding on way too tightly to Aven's shoulders. Even after two near misses with death, Aven's hair was somehow still glossy, and they smelled great, and they hadn't even lost an earring in all of it. Also, the longer tunic over the tighter trousers was such a good look on them. Like a whole other vibe than what they showed at the castle. They were unfairly *pretty* even after an altercation with fire salamanders and lugging my dead weight for several hours.

Okay. I didn't know if it was the pain relief or the effects of whatever was in that elixir, or maybe it was the unrelenting exhaustion, but I was a little out of it. Waxing poetic about Aven was one thing, but losing time was another.

Because one minute we were in front of the tavern, and the next we were in the lobby of the inn.

"Sister!" Zig yelled, tossing himself at me, almost taking both of us to the ground. Aven managed to catch us before we fell. "I thought the worst had happened and I would die of a broken heart before I actually died of a removed heart," he said, ever dramatic.

"Brother," I said evenly, though by the way Zig's eyebrows twitched, I think I may have slurred it. "Glad to see you're okay as well."

He regarded me, his hand on his chin, then reached out and poked me in the cheek. "What happened to you?"

"Salamander toxin." Aven tugged me upright as I wavered.

"Is he . . . ," Farrah started as she pointed at Zig, "always like this?"

"Yes. Humor is my coping mechanism," Zig said with a grin. "Otherwise, I may have to actually face my mortality. And anyway, who are you?"

"This is Farrah," Aven replied. They hauled me closer to their side again. "She helped us cross the river."

"Oh!" Zig said. "The disembodied voice. Great. Okay. So I got us the most expensive room they had."

"Let me guess. You used the money you just acquired in the tavern," I said.

Zig scoffed. "No. I would never." He jerked his thumb at Aven. "I used theirs. Consider it my fee for guiding Mouse here. And yes, all of our stuff is already safely stowed, and our three mounts are living it up in the stable. So let's go."

We followed Zig upstairs. He unlocked the door with a key and opened it with a flourish.

The inn's most expensive room wasn't much bigger than a regular room at an inn. Except it had two beds instead of one, and two nightstands, and Zig had already lit a smattering of candles around. He had even taken the liberty of rolling out my bedroll on the floor, the presumptuous jerk. Okay. He was correct in that I would have offered to take the floor—Aven's gold had paid for the room, so they deserved a bed, and Farrah had probably never slept on the floor in her whole life. It only made sense. At least he'd given me one of the bed's pillows; it was quite luxurious to have four feather pillows in one room. Maybe that was what made it expensive.

I unhooked myself from Aven and stumbled toward my bedroll, but Aven caught me by the elbow and guided me to the mattress. They gently pushed me, and my legs folded like cheap furniture beneath a giant.

"This is yours," I said as soon as I plopped onto the sheets.

"You need it more."

"I'm not taking your bed. You paid for the room."

Aven pinched the bridge of their nose. "Ellinore, please don't be stubborn. Just take it for the night. You can argue with me later."

"Fine. I will take you up on both offers." I flopped theatrically back onto the pillows, blinked at the ceiling, and then was out.

I woke up in the morning to the sun piercing through the window right into my face. Despite that, I was the most comfortable I'd been in forever. The mattress and the feather pillows felt like I was sleeping on a cloud. I didn't want to wake up, but if the sun was already that bright, I'd slept too long. I squeezed my eyes shut, groaned, and rolled over, knocking right into a body.

I froze. Peeling one eye open, I let out a relieved breath to find Zig next to me, just as asleep as I'd been, face smushed into his pillow. Oh, thank the ancients it was him. And not . . .

I rolled again and peered toward the other bed. Farrah was spread over the whole mattress, one foot hanging off, her dark-brown hair all over the place. Which meant . . . I inched toward the edge and looked down. Aven slept on the floor, curled into a ball on their side, blanket tucked up to their chin.

Sitting up gingerly, I noticed my leg propped up on a pillow, my boots off, and the makeshift bandage that had been placed on my wound was missing. I knew for certain I hadn't removed my boots before falling asleep, and I surely didn't take off the bandage, either. I reached down and touched the place just below my knee that had torn open on the bridge, to find it completely healed.

"The wound is gone," Aven said, scaring the daylights out of me.

I clapped a hand over my mouth to keep from screaming and waking the others. "Why did you do that?" I whispered back.

"Do what?" Their voice was raspy from sleep, and my gut lurched, which was not an entirely unpleasant feeling.

"Surprise me like that?" I cleared my throat. "I mean, come up behind a fierce fighter like me. If I had my sword, I could have skewered you."

Aven shrugged. "I can think of worse ways to go."

"What?"

"Nothing. I hope you're feeling better."

"I am."

"Good."

I waited for them to elaborate further, or question me about the disappearing wound, but they did neither. They merely went about gathering their things and getting ready for the day.

Zig snorted in his sleep, then rolled over to the other side, pulling all the sheets with him.

"I'm sorry if he kept you up," I said to Aven.

"He didn't. He actually didn't come into the room until the small hours of the morning."

"Yeah. He usually stays up most of the night. Then drags himself back in the morning to sleep for a few hours until he's up and out again."

"I can't imagine," Aven said, rubbing a hand down their face. "I dropped off right after you."

My cheeks heated. "Well, it's been a trying few days."

"You might want to wake these two," Aven said, pausing at the door. "We need to find the witness today, and I don't know how long that will take."

"Yeah. I will."

The door opened and closed softly. I swung my legs over the side and stopped short when I realized that Aven had slept without a pillow.

14

ZIG RUBBED HIS HANDS TOGETHER AS WE STOOD OUTSIDE THE INN. "SO what's the plan?"

He was unusually chipper for someone who might die if we didn't find a random person in a random town—his smile wide, his countenance glowing despite the light shadows beneath his eyes. I didn't know how or why Zig was so happy. Even his slouch looked more put together than my whole person, his hair artfully tousled. It had to be a combination of coffee and the sugar from the pastries he'd shoveled down earlier for our breakfast. He plowed through any and all awkwardness or friction that existed between the group in his usual Zig way, with a skip in his step and a snide comment on the tip of his tongue.

I, on the other hand, was annoyed that I couldn't rid myself of the grimy feeling that came with travel, though I'd washed up, changed my clothes, brushed my hair, and eaten breakfast. It didn't help that smoke from the mountains, which spat small bursts of flame in the distance, was swirling through the air. As I stood in the shimmering heat, despite the fact that it was barely morning, sweat beaded at my neckline even with my hair pulled into a ponytail, and particles of ash and pollen gathered on my tunic and trousers.

"The last person who saw the Elder Beast lived in this town," Aven said, adjusting the quiver on their back. They had their bow slung across their body and their armguard strapped in place.

"And?" I prompted. I'd left my armor with Bluebell the night before and had not retrieved it. I didn't want to be too intimidating to the witness, and I didn't want to draw attention. At least this way, I had a bit of anonymity if we needed it. Although I felt pretty inadequate standing next to Aven in my plain tunic and trousers. Despite Aven's more subdued clothes, they still looked every inch a royal, with each lock of black hair in place and not a smudge of dirt on their boots. Luckily, Aven wasn't exactly the most well known of the royals, being the cousin of the heir and last in line. They and Farrah just looked like nobles playing at peasants.

Aven scratched the back of their neck. "They were a smith."

"And?" I asked again. "Do they have a name?"

Aven tugged at their collar. Were they nervous? "William."

"William Smith?" I asked, deadpan. *Don't get frustrated. Don't get frustrated.* "That's the information you have. A teenager named William Smith." Okay. Frustrated. "Our only hope of finding the location of an *invisible* realm rests on a person with the most common name and the most common occupation in this not-so-small town."

Farrah snickered, her perfectly styled curls bobbing gently. She'd somehow managed to do her hair, apply her makeup, and drink her coffee at the same time. A skill that I could never hope to master.

"Well, it's better than any information you had, Ellinore," Aven said, defensive.

"Aven," I shot back, "we can't spend days asking around for the correct William Smith!"

Zig rubbed his temple. "I swear this unresolved sexual tension is going to kill me. Literally." He clapped his hands before I could even deny having any amount of tension with Aven at all. "Fine. You two bicker while Farrah and I start asking around. Come on, Farrah."

She gleefully brushed past me and skipped to Zig's side.

With all the confidence of someone who had neither an ounce of self-consciousness nor self-preservation skills, Zig sauntered up to the first person he encountered on the street and flashed a winning smile. "Hi," he said, hands clasped behind his back. "We're looking for a William Smith. Do you happen to know someone by that name?"

The man, who was stooped with age, stroked his grizzled beard. "Oh, for sure," he said in a crackly voice. "I know a William Smith."

Zig looked over his shoulder at me with a smug expression in a true *I told you so* manner.

"I also know a Bill Smith, a Billie Smith, a Will Smith, and a Liam Smith."

Zig blinked several times in succession but managed to keep his smile plastered on, though it went a bit stiff. "Oh."

"That's a lot of Smiths," Farrah said quietly.

"There is also William Smith Jr. and his son, who is the Third, and a cousin who is also a William Smith Jr."

Zig's frozen grin slowly thawed and fell into a grimace. "Oh."

Farrah rubbed his shoulder in sympathy.

"And there is a Guy Smith whose given name is William."

Aven stepped in before the gentleman could continue. "Could you tell us where we can find . . . one of them?"

"Depends on which one you want. Unless you want to know where all of them are."

This was going nowhere. Time to intervene like Ellinore the Brave would. "Is there one that might be an adventurer or a scholar? Maybe a bard?"

He cocked his head to the side in thought. "Oh, you want *William* Smith."

I bit my tongue to keep from screaming and merely nodded.

"Well, he's dead. He died fifty years ago at the old age of sixty-five."

Zig's shoulders drooped.

A hundred years ago. If our witness was fifteen when he saw the Elder Beast, that meant the account was a hundred years old. I shot Aven the most lethal look I could muster. They shifted nervously, tugged at their collar again, and ran a hand through their hair, mussing up the style.

"How old was that scroll?" I whispered fiercely.

"It wasn't *ancient*?"

"That's specific," I shot back.

"You know, for someone who had no plan before I showed up, you're being awfully picky."

Ugh. They were right. I had no other option, save for the cloth that would take three days off the quest, if we could even figure out how to activate it. We were back to square one.

"Thank you for your time," Farrah said sweetly.

"Yeah. Thanks," Zig echoed, clapping the old man on the arm, a cloud of dust puffing up as he did.

We turned away, each of us quiet. I had no idea what to do next. What could I do? We'd ridden all the way to Ashin and—

"He has a grandson."

I perked up from my disheartened slump and spun around. "He has a grandson?" I asked. "Where would we find him?"

"He's an odd one, just like his granddad," the man continued as if he hadn't heard me. "Always fiddling around with magic. And talking about heroes and writing songs with his lute."

Okay. The grandson was both a mage and a bard. The two worst occupations ever. But no one was perfect. And I could look beyond that if he knew the location of the Elder Beast.

"What's his name?" Zig butted in.

Please not another William. Please not another William. Please not another William.

"Rylan."

"Oh, thank the ancients," Aven muttered.

I shoved my elbow into their side. "Where can we find Rylan?"

The older man squinted up at the sun. "Oh, he's a late riser, so I've heard. About this time of day he'd be at home, I think. It's just on the outskirts of town, on the far side, past the old quake gauge. The one with the statue, not the one on the other side of town. That's the new quake gauge. Once you pass the statue, go down the path and it'll be the first farm on the right."

"Thank you," Zig said, grabbing the man's hand and pumping it up and down vigorously. "Here is a gold coin for your time."

The man immediately stuck it in his mouth and bit down. "Oh, it's real," he said as we took off briskly down the street.

"That's the wrong way! The old gauge is south."

The four of us skidded to a stop, then sheepishly turned as a group and went back the other way.

"Well, well, well," Zig said as we stood in front of the old quake gauge. "It's so nice to see the positive outcomes of my famous sister so wonderfully and hilariously documented by this town."

I stared in horrified awe at the shoulder-high statue and plaque placed next to the broken quake gauge. The statue was an . . . interpretive piece, to put it nicely. It was supposed to be me, per the small sign at its base, but . . . it looked more like an indistinguishable lump of volcanic glass that had been fashioned and shaped into some kind of cylinder. The slate next to it had the story of the broken gauge, and my bit part in it, engraved on the surface.

Farrah tilted her head to the side. "Well, it's . . . something. I mean, it's nice they wanted to commemorate your achievement."

Aven was looking everywhere but at the statue.

I wanted to *die*.

The quake gauge itself was a pendulum, a heavy ball on the end of a stiff rope that hung over a pit of sand. When the earth shook, as we had already experienced and which happened in and around Ashin often, the pendulum would swing, and the residents would measure the force of the earthquake by the length of the etches made in the sand. However, this one was broken, forever immortalizing the day Ashin felt the worst quake in its existence.

Not to mention the creation of the Simmer. But that was something I'd keep to myself.

"It says here," Farrah said, finger trailing over the lines on the plaque, a smile twitching at the edge of her mouth, "that a few years ago Ashin had experienced increasingly violent earthquakes, resulting in the breaking of this implement. Which indicated a potential eruption of the nearby peak. Until

Ellinore intervened, wrestled the fire elemental of the mountain, and stopped the eruption from happening."

I covered my face with my hands in abject embarrassment.

"My sister is so reserved and humble when it comes to her accomplishments," Zig said, poking me in the side. "Wouldn't you say, Aven?"

"No!" I dropped my hands. "Do not answer that! We're leaving!"

"But is it true?" Farrah asked, blinking her big brown eyes. "Did you wrestle a mountain spirit?"

I froze. That was the first time anyone had ever asked if something was true. I wanted to applaud Farrah for her critical thinking skills, but I also wanted to sink into the ground.

"Of course it is," Aven said.

I startled. Oh. They believed in me. They had faith in me that I didn't deserve. They unknowingly saved me by intervening in what could've turned into a tense and revealing conversation. And suddenly I could forgive them for their shoddy information about a witness that almost didn't pan out. And for some weird reason, my face heated with a blush, and my stomach lurched with a feeling that made me want to vomit.

I pointed my finger at them. "Do not put this in your report to the king!"

They slowly smirked. "But he would want to know about this historically important event that occurred in his kingdom."

Zig cackled. My face was on fire. "Aven, I will—"

"Stab me with your sword. Yeah. I know." Their eyes sparkled with mirth. And oh, I couldn't decide if I did or did not enjoy being on the other side of our teasing relationship.

"Shut up," I mumbled.

"Oh!" Farrah said, straightening from where she'd been poking at the lump of metal with my name on it. She twisted her fingers, her staff in the crook of her elbow. "This reminds me. I thought about it last night, Ellinore, and I do want to learn a disarming move."

"Oh," I said, grateful for anything to take the attention off that awful statue. "Okay. That's great."

"Good! When will you teach me?"

"Um . . . not right now? We're kind of in the middle of something . . ."

"Oh! Right." She nodded in understanding.

"Anyway, we're wasting valuable time," I said with a tight grin. "Let's go."

Zig didn't move. "Already? But I want to bask in your glory! After all, this statue is a stunning reflection of—"

I pushed Zig forcefully away, shoving him toward the path at the edge of the town that led to the farms, as he laughed wildly.

"First farm on the right, jerk. Keep walking."

15

To call the first farm on the right a "farm" was maybe a little too generous. It was probably a farm in a past life. The spring season was far enough underway that crops should have been sprouting. What we found was an unplowed and seedless field covered in grass, and a smattering of roaming farm animals.

A nearby sheep bleated, and Aven surreptitiously took a step closer to my side.

A small broken fence lined the path that had brought us there. A hinged gate swung open easily, though with a squeak that made me wince. A long lane lined with wildflowers led to a quaint clapboard house. It was much nicer than the house Zig and I had grown up in, with a painted covered porch and a roof that appeared to be well maintained.

"Shall we?" I asked, pushing through the gate and walking briskly down the lane. A donkey ambled close but took one look at us, a clump of grass in its mouth, and left, unimpressed.

Farrah giggled.

We climbed the small set of stairs and gathered on the porch. A two-seater swing hung on one side, lazily moving in the breeze. A woven mat was at our feet, and a horseshoe was nailed above the heavy, rounded door. Huh. The inhabitant was superstitious.

Aven stood at my back, Farrah and Zig to my left, leaving me in front to knock.

I took a breath. I had no idea what to expect. How old would the grandson of a sixty-five-year-old man who'd died fifty years ago be? At least middle-aged. Right? What the ancients were we doing? This was a wild goose chase. I should've taken Dave up on his offer. Screw my reputation. Zig was going to die because I'd trusted the wrong person and—

Aven reached around my body and knocked.

I glanced at them.

They shrugged. "You hesitated."

Shuffling came from the other side, then a thump, followed by a muttered curse. The door swung open.

"Yes?"

It was a teenager. A teenager who had obviously just awoken, with a blanket draped over his boxy shoulders, a line from a pillow across one cheek. His messy brown hair fell into his eyes, and he ran his hand through it, pushing it back to squint at us.

"Hi," I said, smiling in the most open and friendly manner I had.

"Oh shit," he said, voice low and gravelly. Then slammed the door in our faces.

I blinked. Okay, so of all the things I had expected, that was not one of them.

"I don't know about you guys, but I think I'm in love." Zig clasped his hands over his heart and mock-swooned. "He's *hot*."

Farrah elbowed him on my behalf.

Aven frowned. They reached around me and banged on the door.

It creaked slightly open, and the kid gazed out from a sliver.

"Hi," I said again.

He squeaked.

Okay. I didn't know what was going on with this guy, but we needed answers. I shoved my foot between the edge of the door and the jamb so that the teen couldn't close it again.

"We're looking for Rylan Smith," I said. "Know him?"

"I can't believe this is happening," he said.

Farrah twisted, looking around. "What's happening?"

"Princet Aven and Ellinore the Brave are in Ashin, and they are on my porch. It's a dream come true. I can't believe I manifested this with my vision board."

"Oh no," I muttered.

The door opened wider. "Sorry," he said, shrugging off the blanket and throwing it behind him. He wore a pair of tattered trousers and a long sleeping shirt, which he hastily tucked in. He ran his hands through his hair several times and cleared his throat, before puffing his chest out and dropping his voice. "To what do I owe the pleasure?"

Zig snorted. Farrah cackled.

I was one hundred percent certain that Aven and I shared similar sentiments, in that we hoped this was not Rylan Smith.

"Uh . . . ," I said, eloquent as ever. "Does that mean *you're* Rylan Smith?"

"Oh!" The teen took a step back, opened the door wide, then bowed at the waist, gesturing for us to enter. "Yes. I am Rylan! At your service. Please enter my grandfather's humble abode."

Aven bent their head toward me. "What *is* happening?"

I shook my head. I had no clue.

I stepped inside and immediately sneezed. The sickly sweet smell of degrading parchment pervaded everything, and it was mixed with the musty scent of dust and aged leather. Farrah raised her sleeve to her nose. Zig's eyes watered.

Aven rolled their shoulders. "Smells just like the castle archives," they said, voice low and awed as they stepped into the house.

The house itself was . . . interesting. One window was made of artful stained glass, and the other of bottles glued together. Both cast sparkles of light across Rylan's brown skin as he gestured to us to follow farther inside. Every flat surface was covered with . . . trinkets? Maps? Spoils from adventures? Was that a stuffed sprite cadaver? Dragon bones? Dave would not be happy about that. And not only was there clutter all around us, but all manner of things hung from the ceiling—more horseshoes, for one, as well as strings of vibrantly painted rocks, wheatgrass woven into certain shapes, coins with holes bored in the middle, and the spine of some kind of creature. Stacks of parchment with writing or sketches of various things wobbled with our footsteps. Rows of salt and ash lined the windowsills, and the shutters were hammered into place with iron nails.

"Oh, my Lady in the Sea," Farrah whispered. "We are going to die in here."

My sentiments exactly.

Rylan led us through the house—past a sitting room with a grand fireplace, a cushioned settee, and a rocking chair. All of which were covered in items and a thin layer of dust. He guided us through a kitchen area, with a table and chairs and a hearth. Again, all messy. And through a door to a back porch, then outside.

"Um . . ." Zig said. "We're outdoors again." He jerked his thumb back at the house as we followed Rylan down a stone path. "Should we be in there?"

Rylan hummed. "Do you want to be in there?"

"Not particularly."

"Fair. This way."

We followed a stone pathway through a barrier of trees that then opened up into a meadow. In front of us sat a second cottage, more picturesque than the first.

"This is my home."

Rylan pushed open the door with his shoulder, and I let out a relieved sigh when we found the interior neat as a pin. He brushed off imaginary lint from a cushioned couch in front of a fireplace and guided Aven and me to sit, leaving Zig and Farrah to their own devices. In the corner, propped on a stand, holding a place of honor among all the belongings, was a lute made with lacquered wood and decorated with a beautiful design of small birds flying around the edges. Several parchments with writing and musical notes were tacked to the wood of the walls. A lone cushioned chair sat in the far corner, with a pair of knitting needles and a basket of yarn by the side.

"Drinks?" Rylan called from a kitchen area, hands fluttering around a cabinet next to a small, round table. "Water? Tea? Wine? I have some mead, if you're interested."

Zig raised his hand, and I smacked it down.

"No, thanks. We . . . uh . . . just wanted to talk."

Rylan bobbed his head. He pulled over the chair from the corner and sat across from Aven and me.

"It's about the letters, isn't it?"

Aven raised an eyebrow. "The letters," they said evenly.

Rylan winced. "I'm sorry." He rubbed his brow, then stood and started pacing the small space. "I just think if the tales are going to be held as the accounts of authentic historical record, they should at least be accurate."

Okay. What really was happening? Who was this kid?

"I'm sorry?" I asked.

"No, I'm sorry." He dropped to his knees in front of me, as if imploring my forgiveness. "I just find it hard to believe that you defeated the Golden Dragon at thirteen when knights three times your age and skill level had been trying to kill it for a century. And all of a sudden you show up with a fast horse and a shoddy sword and take down a fully grown ancient?"

My mouth fell open. My heart thudded hard. *Excuse me?*

"And the fire deity of the mountain. Are you telling me I'm supposed to believe that you"—he gestured to me—"a teenage girl, were able to wrestle a fire spirit into submission? And that statue and plaque in town? Absurd."

I mean, I agreed with that. But he didn't have to *say* it. Great. Just great. Rylan was calling me out. In front of Aven, no less. With Zig standing right there. I chuckled nervously, not believing that the bard-mage kid had a desire for truthfulness in his folktales. This was not what I had on my list for today.

"Don't even get me started about diving down to the depths and fighting off a shark to confront the Lady in the Sea and trick her into giving you her pearl." Rylan chuckled, shaking his head. "It's preposterous."

This little shit. It was one thing to question the validity of the details, but of the whole event? He was not wrong, but still. I was Ellinore the Brave, Strong, Wise, and sometimes the Easily Annoyed. On rare occasions I was Ellinore the

Beautiful. To be fair, that last one was more in my own head. But anyway, the nerves of steel this kid had.

"Your objections to my feats seem to rely on sexist and ageist stereotypes that went out of fashion generations ago except in small-minded provincial individuals."

Rylan blanched, his amber eyes growing wide and horrified. "No! That wasn't what I meant."

"It sure sounds like what you meant."

"No! I was merely pointing out that since the dragon was only your second quest and you were barely trained, it was a skill issue."

"A skill issue?" My voice cracked with indignation. He was correct in a way, but insulting me? *To my face?* It was one thing when Aven did it teasingly, but entirely another when some guy I barely knew had the audacity. I put my hand on the hilt of my sword. "I'll show you a skill issue, you little—"

"Are you calling the bards liars?" Aven interrupted, placing a calming hand on my arm before I could stand. Rylan blinked, appearing slightly relieved that Aven had intervened. That is, until Aven continued. "The bards employed by the monarchs of this kingdom?" The way they said it, accusatory and harsh, made it sound like they were flat-out asking if Rylan thought *I* was a liar.

"Yes!"

I flinched but played it off by swatting at my ponytail. "Sorry," I said after a moment. "There was a bug in my hair."

"I think," Aven said, sitting on the edge of their seat, "that you need to be careful who you say such things to, including present company."

Rylan suddenly realized he'd said that to a royal and threw out his hands, palms up. He jumped to his feet. "No! I mean, no! I mean . . . um . . . maybe?"

"Anyway, I'm uncertain that anyone should be relying on the songs of bards for factual information," Aven said diplomatically. "We don't really have standards for accuracy and uniformity when it comes to their lyrics. Different bards interpret stories differently, but the source material is the same."

"But we *should* have standards! For two reasons. One—it's the main avenue for common folk to receive news. And two—the tales are considered to be the main purveyor of history." A beat of stunned silence followed, and Rylan shrunk into himself. "Look, I wrote the letters merely asking for the chance to interview you about your adventures so that there is a factual accounting of what really happened in a few of your quests."

"How many is a few?" I asked, voice a croak.

"All of them."

I made an affronted noise.

"Just to clear up minor details! Or the major ones. That's all! I meant no disrespect. I didn't really expect you two to travel all the way here. I mean, I hoped."

"Your vision board?" I offered.

"Yes." Rylan snapped his fingers. He patted the parchment tacked up on the wall behind the lute, apparently his vision board. "I hoped you would, but I never in a thousand years thought . . ."

His gaze flickered between me and Aven on the couch. Then he seemed to take in Zig and Farrah as well. Zig had found a spot of wall to sag against, and Farrah stood behind me, hands on her quarterstaff like she was ready to whack heads if she needed.

Rylan sighed. "You're not here about the letters."

Aven clasped their hands. "No. We're not here about the letters."

"Oh."

"We're here about your grandfather."

"Ah," he said, nodding, sinking back into his chair. "I should've known. That was his house we walked through."

I swallowed down my irritation and focused on the task at hand, which was finding any information about our current quest. "He had quite the collection."

"He was well traveled. He encountered a lot of things and knew even more."

"That's what we're hoping," I said. "Did he ever mention the Elder Beast?"

Rylan's demeanor shifted suddenly from welcoming to wary.

"Why do you ask?"

I leaned forward in my seat, gripping my knees, and poured every ounce of sincerity into my words. "It's important. We *need* to find the invisible realm." I hoped I'd imbued my sentence with the appropriate amount of pleading.

Rylan narrowed his eyes. "Find it for what?" He stood again and wrung his hands. "Is this an adventure for the king and queen? You've defeated quite a few of the remaining ancients and folklores. Is this a step up? Is this for some *sport*, so you can say you've defeated a primordial being?"

"A what?" Zig asked.

"Yeah, a what?" Farrah echoed.

Rylan pointed at them but stared at Aven and me, his eyes as hard as stone. "They don't know?"

"It's not for a quest. It's not for the royals." I gently placed my hand on Aven's forearm, then dug in my nails because I didn't need them to chime in at that moment. "It's for my brother, Zig. The one standing back there who looks exactly like me but not. He made a mistake and a council of mages—"

"Duo," Aven corrected under their breath.

I stabbed my nails in harder.

"Mages are going to take his heart unless I—"

Farrah cleared her throat.

"*We,*" I amended. "Unless we bring them the horn of the Elder Beast."

Rylan's eyes widened. "The horn? You're going to try for the horn? That's . . . Not only is that the most irresponsible thing I've ever heard, handing over a piece of a primordial being to a council of mages—"

"Duo," Zig said weakly.

"Fine," Rylan continued. "A duo of mages, not knowing what they intend to do with it. But do you think that the group of you have *any* chance of not only finding but overpowering a being that is older than time?"

"Older than time? What does that mean?" Zig asked. He pushed away from the wall. The chipper Zig from that morning had all but disappeared and been replaced by one with a wan expression and a faded smile. "What's a primordial?"

"Um . . . okay," Rylan said, hands on his hips. "So you know the beings we call ancients, right? Dragons and Harpies and griffins, et cetera. We call them ancients because they were the first beings that populated our world. Some even view them as gods or deities because they are so powerful, like how the Lady in the Sea is worshipped or how villagers used to leave offerings for the Golden

Dragon." Rylan gave me a knowing smile. "Their numbers dwindling over time has only added to their mystique."

Farrah tilted forward, pushing her body over the back of the couch so her face was right between mine and Aven's. "What about fire salamanders?"

"Good question. Those are second beings, like the faeries and sprites and gnomes—magical but with diminished capabilities. We call them folklores. They're not as powerful as the ancients."

Ha! Tell that to the murderous faery in the forest and the fire salamanders that wanted us as meals.

"Then there are the third beings. The ordinaries. That's us. And common animals like horses, fish, lizards, bugs, sheep."

Aven snorted at the mention of sheep. "I still think that thing was magic," they muttered.

Zig drifted close to Rylan, expression pinched. "That doesn't answer my question about what a primordial is."

"Doesn't it? Who do you think created the ancients? The faeries? Us?"

"The Elder Beast?" Zig whispered, tone tinged with awe.

"Yes. Primordials are creators. The Elder Beast is maker of all the creatures in our world."

"You used the plural. Like there is more than one," Farrah said, still leaned over the back of the couch.

Rylan grinned. "Well, there is more than one, of course. The other primordials were responsible for the wide seas and the high mountains and the heavens above us."

Zig whirled on me. "You knew?"

I stood, releasing my hold on Aven that I had embarrassingly never let go of. I grabbed Zig's upper arm to steady him as his willowy form swayed in the face of all the overwhelming information.

"Sit," I said, pulling him to the couch.

He sank into the cushion.

I swallowed. "Yes, I knew. I knew before I agreed to the quest. But it's *fine*, Zig. We can do this. I *will* do this."

Zig placed his trembling hand over his heart. "Why didn't you tell me?"

"It wouldn't have helped for you to know."

"It's an *impossible* task."

"Maybe," Aven interjected before I could attempt to reassure Zig. "But your sister has accomplished many impossible tasks before, so there's no reason she can't do this as well."

For the second time that day, my stomach twisted for some inexplicable reason and my face heated with a flush. Once again Aven *believed* in me. A pleasant shiver ran down my spine at the thought. But I didn't deserve Aven's utter faith or the concern that furrowed their brow or the fatigue that had set in the line of their mouth. I didn't deserve the sincerity of their words. And that's why they couldn't know the real me, find out about anything I'd done before, because I didn't think I could handle them thinking *less* of me.

I pushed those feelings aside. They didn't belong here.

I crouched down to meet my brother's brown eyes, a mirror of my own. "I took on this quest knowing the risks," I said. "I will see it through. You're my brother. I'm not giving up until the flame burns all the way down on the last day. Okay?"

Standing, I spun to face Rylan. We were the same height, though his body was broader. But he couldn't intimidate me. I might not have done everything the bards had concocted in their stories, but I *did* face down a dragon at thirteen.

"As you can see," I said, hand on the hilt of my sword, a growl in my throat, "this is no ordinary quest. If you have any information, now is the time to tell us."

Rylan swallowed, then squared his shoulders and lifted his chin, as if facing down a manticore. "You'll take me with you on the quest," he stated. "And you'll tell me all the details of your adventures and allow me to write an exclusive tale about this one."

I tipped my head back and groaned. Not another one. But if this was what I had to do … "The information better be good. If so, then yes. I agree to your terms."

He nodded, coming to his decision.

"There is a map."

16

"HE WAS MY GREAT-GRANDFATHER, ACTUALLY," RYLAN SAID AS WE RODE to a secondary location. "He kept his most prized possessions away from the house because he was worried about being robbed. Especially once he realized what he had found."

"And what was it that he found?" I asked, riding Bluebell. We had gone back to town to gather our mounts and belongings from the inn. I chose to don my armor once I knew we'd be traveling a few hours to retrieve the map. Who knew what we'd encounter along the way? We weren't really doing great in the avoiding-magical-creatures department.

Anyway, the whole process of packing up, Farrah buying a new horse, and Rylan ensuring he had everything he needed had taken too long for my liking, but Rylan assured us there was a safe place to camp for the night.

"He found the Elder Beast," he said bluntly. "And the location of a few of the others."

I sat up straighter in my saddle. "The others, too?"

Rylan nodded. "Yes."

He rode behind Zig on Carrot, not having a mount of his own. He had tied a pack behind the cantle, adding even more weight to the already-burdened mule. His lute was currently strapped to his back. I'd done my best to hide my grimace when he brought it along, though unsuccessfully if Aven's snort was any indication. But a deal was a deal.

"How far is this other place?" Farrah called from her newly purchased black mare named Starlight.

"It shouldn't be long now," Rylan said.

We'd already ridden out of Ashin altogether, the air clearer the farther we moved away from the mountains. We thudded over the wide southern bridge, much sturdier than the one we'd found across the Simmer, and I understood why it was the preferred path to travel into the town. Maybe I should've gone with my gut and approached Ashin by the south, instead of worrying about what the façade of Ellinore the Brave would supposedly do. But . . . we all had survived. I counted it as a win.

The roar of the Eastern Sea drifted louder as we traveled; in some locations I could even spy the rolling waters and whitecaps. I couldn't help thinking about my parents. I hoped they were living a quiet, peaceful life. I couldn't wait for this nightmare to be over so I could join them.

As we traveled, Farrah maneuvered her horse beside mine. "So," she said, trying for nonchalant but failing, "about this disarming move. Can you show me?"

"Now?" I gestured to my literally being on horseback.

Farrah smiled. "No time like the present."

"Fine," I said with a sigh. "Basically, you want to break your opponent's grip on their weapon."

"I know! That's the definition of disarming!"

"Right. So you target their wrist, and you want to make them bend it in a way that weakens their hold and, well, hurts."

"That's it?" Farrah asked.

"What do you mean, 'that's it'?"

She shrugged. "I thought there would be more to it. I mean, it's pretty obvious."

I sputtered. "That's only the general idea! Putting it into practice is more difficult, and making it fluid takes repetition and—"

"We're here!" Rylan yelled, cutting me off. We crested a small hill, and he suddenly signaled for us to halt, dismounting Carrot with a bounce in his step. His brown hair fluttered in the breeze coming off the water, and I shivered at the cool air, so different from the atmosphere in Ashin.

"We're where exactly?" Aven asked, dismounting and holding Mouse's reins. "This is a pile of rocks."

"Rocks" wasn't quite the correct term. The hill was composed of large gray-blue boulders that had smoothed from time and weather, stacked higher than most buildings I'd seen. I couldn't decide if it was a natural structure—a mountain worn down over time—or one that had been made by men or creatures. It could have been either, but it was indeed impressive.

Rylan huffed. "It's bigger on the inside. I promise."

From this vantage point the "pile of rocks" appeared to be solid, with no obvious way to enter. Ancients, I hoped this journey hadn't been in vain.

I hopped off Bluebell and grabbed my tattered cloak from my saddlebag.

Rylan led Carrot to a tree and tied him off on a low branch, before helping Zig down. Zig blushed, or maybe it was merely a flush from the chilly wind. I wouldn't pretend to know. But I passed off my cloak to Zig and wrapped it around him.

"The armor keeps me warm," I said when Zig lifted an eyebrow.

He didn't argue, clutching the cloak close around him. "Thanks. I'm a little chilled."

Farrah brushed past me and tied off Starlight, the hood of her own cape over her head to ward off the wet wind.

Once everyone had secured their mounts, I decided not to lash Bluebell, giving her leave to wander. She was used to roaming free and wouldn't go far, especially as there was plenty of long grass in the area for her to enjoy.

Rylan led us around the back of the rock pile. Aven stood close by my side, Zig and Farrah behind me. We walked to a well-hidden spot, and Rylan addressed me.

"We made a deal," he said, twisting his fingers nervously. "You'll keep it, won't you?"

"I gave my word. You give us the map, and you can follow us on the rest of the quest. And I'll help you with the details of the other stories."

At the time I agreed, I'd have done anything to procure this map for Zig. Now I wished I'd bargained a little harder. The truths and untruths had accumulated over the years, and detangling them with a bard was practically my own special hell. But seeing Zig's slender frame hunched over, his shoulders sticking out as sharp points even in my heavy cloak, hardened my resolve.

"This map better be the best map ever," I said.

Rylan gulped. "Yeah. It will be. And we'll go on the best quest ever."

Debatable, but whatever. "Fine. Lead on."

Aven suddenly stilled beside me. An icy gust ruffled their perfect hair as they peered around us. "Did you hear that?" they asked, gripping their bow.

I hadn't.

"Hear what?" I whispered.

Their sharp blue eyes scanned the landscape. "I thought I heard hooves. Maybe voices?"

"Well, I've let Bluebell roam, so it could be her."

"The breeze through the tunnels in the rocks can sometimes sound like murmurs," Rylan offered.

"And the sea is loud," Farrah said, spinning her staff in her hands.

Aven's brow furrowed. "Maybe." They ducked their head toward me. "Don't forget what the faery said."

"I haven't," I answered. How could I? "But we'll deal with it *after* we retrieve this map." I patted Aven's shoulder, and their muscles relaxed under my palm. They nodded in agreement, but their expression remained pinched.

Rylan beckoned us closer. "This way."

The stone face of the hill wasn't as impenetrable as it appeared. As we neared, I realized it was a mirage. It was two walls offset to create an entrance, which Rylan easily ducked through.

Aven raised both eyebrows. "Okay. Maybe not just a pile of rocks," they said when Rylan disappeared.

I nudged them with my elbow, and we followed. Zig and Farrah stayed close behind.

We entered a tunnel where my head brushed the stone ceiling above us, and Zig and Aven had to scrunch to walk through. My shoulders brushed the sides in places, and anxiety wedged in my throat as we squeezed farther into the cave. At least with Dave's place, I knew my dragon friend was on the other side and would help me if needed. Here, I didn't know what to expect. In fact, this was a bad idea. The whole group should not have come in here. Farrah and Zig, and even Aven, shouldn't have been subjected to this claustrophobic adventure.

There was a jangle of keys and the creak of hinges as a door opened in front of us. But I couldn't see it in the gloom. Thankfully, in just a few more steps, the area widened into a cavern. Where Dave's was beautiful and warm, this place was damp and dark. Here, the walls wept cold water, and with no sunlight to permeate the area, it was freezing.

"Rylan?" I called, unable to make out his figure in the dark.

A small flame bobbed in front of us, disembodied in the black, like the will-o'-the-wisps that led travelers astray. A torch flared to life, revealing Rylan with fire dancing along his fingertips.

"What? How?" Farrah asked as the flames flickered along Rylan's hand.

"I can do a little bit of magic." He wiggled his fingers after lighting the second torch. "Surprise!"

I sighed. Leave it to a mage to partake in frivolous pageantry. It was so wrong for one person to be two of the worst things ever at once.

"Great, can you light a fire? Because I'm turning into a block of ice," Zig said, pushing past me to join Rylan on the far side of the room.

"Sure. Just let me finish lighting the torches."

As each torch was ignited, more of the space was revealed.

A thick wooden frame buttressed the corners and reinforced the ceiling, and shelves were built into every single spot that could hold them. It settled my unease slightly, knowing there was more to the area than just a rock formation. In fact, there was a fireplace as well, with an oddly shaped chimney. Rylan pulled kindling and wood from a small stack next to the fireplace and piled it in the grate, then lit a fire with some flint. Zig settled close to it, sitting cross-legged on the floor.

"It's almost like a gnome dwelling," Aven said from their place beside me. "Much bigger and built from rock instead of a dirt mound, but close enough."

"And you've seen the inside of a gnome home?"

"Yes," Aven said. "Haven't you?" They grinned as they walked away to inspect a shelf.

I pointed to the ceiling above us. "Is that going to hold if there's an earthquake?"

Rylan smiled so brightly, it rivaled the lit torches. "Yes. It's bolstered with magic."

I raised an eyebrow.

"Not mine!" Rylan quickly clarified. "Great-Grandfather knew some mages. They did it. So yeah, if the beams give out, then we'll be protected by their magic. Great-Grandfather always had a fail-safe, or so I was told."

"Those mages didn't happen to wear awful hats, did they?"

Rylan shrugged. "I don't know. I wasn't born yet. All this has been passed through my family for generations. I'm the current caretaker."

"What about your parents?" I asked as I took in the objects on the shelves. Glass bottles filled with colorful liquids sat, carefully labeled with yellowing parchment, and scrolls were stacked in pyramids. A gnome's hat perched on a small hat stand. A faery's wing was encased in a cube of glass. A griffin feather floated in place on one of the higher shelves, suspended by its own magic. A small collection of gold emanated dragon magic, the caress of it a warm tingle against my wrist where my bracelet was clasped.

"Gone," Rylan replied.

"Huh?" I asked, snapping out of my own awe at the collection. "Oh. Right. I'm so sorry."

"No!" He ran a hand through his hair. "Not like that. They moved away. Got sick of the earthquakes."

"Ah, makes sense."

Farrah wandered the room wide-eyed and open-mouthed, taking in all the oddities and knowledge that this one room held. She paused at a low table near the center of the room and sat on the lone chair, then reached out to touch a bronzed goblet.

"Farrah!" Aven barked.

She startled.

"What have we learned about touching things?" I asked, walking closer, the steps of my boots softened by a large area rug decorating the floor.

She pouted. "I thought that was only creatures."

"Not only creatures. Apply it to everything."

She nodded quickly.

"So," I said, peering closely at a stack of parchments, the top one bearing a drawing of a creature I'd never seen before, "where is this map?"

"In here." Rylan gestured toward one of the mountains of scrolls. "Somewhere."

It's never easy. Why would it be easy? "Okay, new rule. You may touch parchments and scrolls, but that's it."

Farrah eagerly rubbed her hands together, darted from the chair, and touched every scroll in reach.

"Bring all the scrolls and parchments to the middle," Aven said, gathering a pile in their arms. "We'll go through them together."

We assembled in a half circle on the plush carpet. The first scroll was a recipe for a soup that could cure all ills. The second was a map focused on the migration of common geese versus the migration of Harpies. The third was a treatise on the worship of the Lady in the Sea by the people on the southern coast. The fourth was an itemized shipping receipt from a town that no longer existed.

And that's how we spent the next several hours. My knees started to ache, and my eyes began to blur in the low light of the flickering torches. According to Rylan, the torches would not burn out, since they were lit with magic, but the fire in the hearth had dwindled enough that the coldness of the cave seeped back into my bones.

Wrapped in my cloak, Zig huddled next to the dying fire. Farrah yawned. And Rylan hadn't blinked in at least fifteen minutes.

It had to be early evening by now. If we didn't find the map soon enough, we'd have to camp and try again in the morning.

I moved another scroll to the no pile and unrolled the next one. Immediately it had my attention. The map was yellowed with age, and at a quick glance I caught the position of a Harpy's nest at the top of a mountain and the accurate depiction of the location of the manticore. Both were ancients. Other locations were marked with single-colored dots and no descriptions, but there was a faded key at the bottom.

"This is it!" Rylan said, yanking it from my hand. "Each dot represents a different primordial. The key is a bit faded, but I'm certain in the sunlight we'll be able to discern the colors."

My heart soared. This was what we were looking for! This was what made the faery, the Simmer, and the fire salamanders all worth it. I could save Zig!

Giddy with the discovery, I looked up and met Aven's gaze, my cheeks hurting from how wide my smile stretched. Aven grinned in return, their expression softer than I expected, not near as excited as I'd thought they'd be.

"Okay," I said, brushing the dust from my hands. "Let's get out of here. It's cold and dark. We'll make camp nearby, and in the morning we'll study the map in the daylight."

Rylan quickly rolled the map back into a scroll. He tucked it into the travel bag at his hip. I pulled Zig to standing, slightly worried at how sluggish he'd become as the day had progressed. Was it the toll of the traveling? Or was the magic of the bargain affecting him? Whichever it was, the quest wouldn't take much longer. This misery was almost over. And I didn't even need to use that stupid scrap of cloth the mages had tried to trick me into taking. Suckers.

"Rylan," I said, slapping his shoulder. "Lead the way."

Rylan nodded vigorously. He stepped toward the edge of the room, near the way we'd entered, Farrah on his heels, Zig trailing behind.

As soon as Rylan's boots passed the threshold of the open door, the floor suddenly jolted beneath our feet. A deep rumble echoed around the space, and the shaking of the ground quickly grew into great lurching heaves.

"I thought you said this was earthquake-proof!" Aven yelled at Rylan as they tripped their way toward our escape.

"It's the magic!" he shouted back. "I don't think I'm supposed to remove the map from here. It must be a fail-safe!"

Objects fell from the shelves. Glass bulbs and vials burst into small shards as soon as they hit the stone. The scrolls in our no pile rolled about the room as the floor pitched. Dust rained down on us from the beams above, and they gave an ominous groan in response to another forceful tilt of the ground. When I glanced upward, a sheen of purple cracked down the middle, larger fractures spiderwebbing out from the center. Magic. The magic had broken.

Oh no. No. No. No. A few small rocks fell in front of the door. My heart pounded and I ran to Rylan, pushing him forward, because that map was leaving, magic or no.

"Go! Go!" I yelled.

Farrah stumbled to her knees. I grabbed her hand and yanked her upward. Rylan reached out for her and entwined their fingers, pulling her toward the passageway. Okay. Rylan and Farrah and—

A larger rock fell, and I dove out of the way to avoid being crushed into fleshy goo. I landed awkwardly on my shoulder, a loud crack echoing in my ear, but I didn't have time to evaluate injuries. Using my hands for balance, I scrambled to my feet. We had to get out of here. I could worry about snapped things later.

"Come on!" Rylan yelled.

Another epic quake shook the cave. Aven tripped on the carpet, slamming into a shelf. I slipped on liquid pouring from a broken vase and fell flat, knocking the breath out of my lungs. More rocks tumbled and slid down the sides of the room. The table fell completely over. A beam snapped in half overhead, raining splinters on us.

Rylan and Farrah shouted for us from their position on the other side of the threshold, their hands outstretched.

But I couldn't find my balance.

"Run!" I yelled at Zig.

He ran for the exit, jumping over a fallen beam, heading for Rylan and Farrah. But he stopped, hesitated, and looked back at me. A large stone overhead broke loose, and I watched in abject horror as it started to fall. I couldn't make it there in time. My heart pounded in my ears as my boots slipped on the slick floor, and I fell again.

Out of nowhere Aven lunged and pushed Zig hard in the back. Zig stumbled through the door and into the arms of Farrah and Rylan just as the stone struck the ground, sealing off our only exit.

The trio yelled in shock. But they were safe. I knew they were safe.

Then the rest of the wall came tumbling down.

17

WHEN THE DUST HAD SETTLED, THERE WAS A HUGE PILE OF ROCKS standing in between me and the map—and the rest of our group.

"Zig!" I yelled, climbing the pile, the stones rolling beneath my feet. I could feel my palms abrading as I clutched for purchase, and I was going to break an ankle if I tried to ascend this ridiculously large *pile of rocks*! "Zig! Can you hear me? Are you okay?"

Silence.

I rested my forehead on the cave-in. It was cold against my skin. A stark difference from the tears gathering and burning behind my eyes. Zig was safe. He had to be safe. I saw him make it through the door and into the passageway.

"Zig!" I yelled again, my throat clogged with regret and sobs and dust.

"Ellinore!"

I snapped my head up. The voice was faint, but I could hear him.

"Zig! Are you okay?"

"We're fine. The three of us are fine."

The knot in my stomach unraveled. Oh, I was going to throw up. Tears of relief slipped down my cheeks. Thank the ancients.

"Are you and Aven okay?"

Aven. I whipped around and found them sitting on the carpet, breathing heavily, with their elbows propped on their knees. They were covered in dust, but aside from a cut on the back of their hand, they seemed otherwise unharmed.

"You good?" I asked.

They waved.

"We're fine!" I yelled back. "Just trapped! Is there another way out of here?"

"Don't worry," Zig hollered. "Rylan is going to get you out. With magic!"

My eyes widened. "Can Rylan *do* that with magic?"

"Yes! I mean, maybe." That was Rylan's voice. "It might take me a little while because it's *a lot* of rock. And my magic and I tire easily." That must be why Rylan used the flint to start the fire in the hearth. He'd exhausted his magic lighting the room. This did not bode well for us. "I'll try a little tonight, but I think I'll do best in the morning."

"Oh my ancients," I whispered. I took a deep breath, rested my head on the stone again, and closed my eyes. Okay. I could hear them. There had to be a way for air to get in here as well. Or if not, there were only two of us. Suffocating shouldn't be a problem. I could weather this. And if I couldn't, I'd call for Dave. No big deal to summon the Golden Dragon, which Rylan correctly didn't think I had killed. But if that was what it came to, at least I had a plan.

I pushed away from the wall and opened my eyes.

Aven stood, wobbled, but then righted themself. They joined me by the rockslide.

"Set up camp," they yelled. "Sleep in shifts and keep a watch. Make sure you each get some sleep. Farrah, you're in charge."

Twin shouts of indignation followed, and then a small but clear "Yay."

"Why Farrah?" I asked.

Aven shrugged. "She has a weapon."

"True. But we've not seen her use it. Effectively."

"Point. But it's either her, your waning brother, or the mage who needs to focus on getting us out of here."

So Aven had noticed Zig's decline too. I hadn't imagined it.

I cleared my throat. "Fair enough."

Okay. While they were setting up a camp, it was time to investigate. That loud snap I'd heard when I fell was my pauldron finally giving way. I sighed. I'd known it was coming, but why did it have to happen in front of Aven? I unclipped the other straps, and the pauldron fell to the ground with a slap that echoed in the small space.

Aven raised an eyebrow. For the second time on the quest, they could've said *I told you so*, but they didn't. That was odd. Oh well. I divested myself of the rest of my armor. I didn't need it on right then, not while I was trying to figure a way out of our magic stone tomb. There had to be *something* in this museum of oddities that could help us.

Thankfully, one of the torches remained lit, offering some meager light. But what it didn't offer was *heat*. Without my cloak and armor, it was achingly cold.

"What are you doing?" Aven asked.

"Looking for something to help."

Aven sighed. "Don't you think you should let our companions work on getting us out?"

I scoffed. "I would if I wanted to die in here. But that's not my plan."

"Ellinore," Aven said softly. "It's late. They need to rest. *We* need to rest. And in the morning we'll give them a chance. They can do it."

I paused in my perusal of the glass bottles that hadn't broken. Maybe Aven was right. Again, if worse came to worst, I could always summon Dave. That would open a whole other can of worms, but maybe it would be worth it. I didn't want to waste the time it would take for Rylan to fish us out, but also we had a map now. Unless the entrance to the Elder Beast's realm was in one of the kingdoms across the seas, we'd make it in time.

"Trust them, Ellinore. It'll be okay."

"Fine," I said, crossing my arms to hide my shivering. "They can have at it for a few hours in the morning."

"How gracious you are," Aven said playfully.

They crossed the room, then tossed more wood on the fire and coaxed it back to life. The reds and oranges from the flames danced across their fair skin, glinted against the gold earrings lining the gentle curve of their ear, and created a shimmer on the lush pout of their mouth. My breath caught. It was as if one of the paintings in the castle had come to life or the lavish words of a poem had woven together and coalesced, turning a lovely phrase into a corporeal form.

I'd seen Aven limned in firelight before, noting how pretty they were, but for some reason this time was . . . *different*. Maybe because they had been willing to die in the Simmer if it prevented both of us from falling. Maybe because they'd pushed Zig out of the way from being crushed. Maybe because they had shown in just a few days that they weren't the pouting royal rival they pretended to be at court—they were far wittier, kinder, more willing to listen, and generally just . . . a good person.

It was no secret they were strikingly beautiful and wholly unobtainable due to their royal status and my ever-growing pile of lies. My heart twinged with an unfamiliar ache at the thought that they would never truly know me.

"This should warm the room a bit," they said, standing and brushing off their hands. "Hopefully, the flue hasn't fallen in, or the cave will fill with smoke, but we should know that shortly."

I didn't respond, tongue-tied by the slowly developing, horrible realization that I *liked* them. Not as a rival. Not as a friend. But in an *I want to kiss them* way. But I also wanted to hold their hand and listen to them talk about their day and know their favorite flavor of tea. Did Aven even like tea?

I shouldn't be thinking about this. I was on a quest to save my brother! I didn't need feelings!

"Ellinore?" Aven prompted.

"What?" I yelled. "Yes. I'm here. Um . . . what?"

They frowned. "I said, come on, let's get comfortable."

My stomach did that weird flipping thing again and my heart joined it. I had already suffered a cave-in and a near-death experience for both me and my brother; I didn't need an aneurysm from close proximity to Aven. If this quest didn't kill me from rockslides and fire salamanders, then I'd surely die from crush-related heart palpitations.

"Okay." I sounded choked.

We settled against the wall near the cave-in so we could still hear the others if they called for us. We had removed the remnants of the splintered table and a few other objects to free the carpet and pulled it close for us to sit on. We found a ship's sail rolled up in a corner and spread it behind us. Then we propped our backs against it, a barrier between us and the damp stone. I set my sword within arm's reach, and Aven did the same with their bow and quiver. I drew my knees to my chest, while Aven spread out their cloak and ensured it covered both of us as much as possible.

"Are we really going to wait right here and let a mage teen we hardly know figure out how to get us out?" I asked, because I had to get my mind off this abhorrent crush.

Aven sighed. "Yep."

I shifted, pushing my shoulder against theirs to leach body heat. I shivered.

"Are you really that cold?" they asked.

"Yes. Otherwise, I would not be cuddling with you." *Good one, Ellinore.*

Aven hummed. They took my hands and hissed. "Your hands are freezing," they said, rubbing them between their own. Their hands were warm and soft even with the calluses on the tips of their fingers and . . . I should not be dwelling on their gentle touch.

Deflect, Ellinore. Use snark. "Did you miss the part where I said I'm cold?"

"Oh, ancients, come here." Aven put their arm around my shoulders, pulling me closer. Then they grabbed the edge of the cloak with their fingers and tucked it around my body as best they could.

My cheeks heated with a burning blush that I hoped Aven would take for embarrassment. But honestly, if I absolutely had to be tucked next to Aven in order to not die in a cold cave, I was going all in. I relaxed against them, laying my head on their collarbone. I kept my hands tucked in close to my chest. It wasn't that comfortable, but I wasn't about to fling my arm across their torso, even though I had a fleeting thought that it might be nice.

"Thank you," I whispered. "You saved Zig."

"I knew that's what you would want."

Ancients, how were they so perfect? And how did they know me so well? Okay, they didn't really. Kind of. Ugh, I hated this feeling, the lies piling up into a barrier between me and them.

"You can report your thrilling heroics to the king," I said, mustering feigned magnanimity. "I don't mind."

Aven chuckled. "Thank you for the permission. I'll be sure to include them."

I huffed in amusement. We basked in the light from the fire and in our companionable silence.

"You know I hate this, right?" I did and didn't. I was curled in close to the person I admired, to the person I begrudgingly but desperately liked, to the person, if I knew they wouldn't report it back to the king, I might show the real me. Maybe. But I was stuck . . . waiting. Add to that all the lies, and I was a muddle of conflicting feelings.

Aven rested their chin on the top of my head. "I know."

A faint tumble of rocks sounded on the other side of the slide, followed by a muted cheer.

"That's a good sign," Aven said.

"Maybe." I squirmed to unbend my knees slightly and fit my body better against theirs. After a few adjustments I was completely cozy and, with Aven's body heat, quickly working my way toward warm. "Who knew Princet Aven was an incredible cuddler?"

"Just Aven," they replied.

Curious. "I've noticed that you correct everyone when you can. Why is that?"

"Titles aren't necessary on a quest," Aven responded almost rotely. It echoed what they'd told Farrah when she arrived at the Simmer. But I could tell it wasn't all there was.

"No, they're not."

They sighed deeply. "Also, sometimes folks get the title wrong, and it makes me uncomfortable."

"Oh. I didn't realize." I'd always known Aven as Princet Aven. Their cousin, the heir, was Princet Avia. Another one of their cousins was Princess Avriel, and there were a few other princes and princesses in there. I'd never questioned any of their titles, and it was a shock to hear that some did.

"It's fine," they said quickly. "You didn't know."

"But now I do."

They laughed. "Okay."

I shifted so I could stare at the underside of their jaw.

"I can feel you staring at me," they said, eyes fluttering shut. "When I was younger, much younger, I tried to fit into the frame of prince or princess. And neither . . . felt right. Luckily for me, Avia was years older and far bolder than I could ever be and adopted 'princet.' Which made it easier for me to do the same." They shifted. "I'm aware that some of the court refer to me as the Pointless Princet." I winced when they said the nickname, the disillusionment that surrounded it. "Once my cousins marry and potentially have children, there will come a time when I will be able to leave the castle and adventure or quest all the time and just be . . . me. But for now I am Princet Aven in court. And on quests I'm just Aven."

"Ah. Well, I like just Aven." I panicked when realized what I'd just said. "I mean the name. Aven. It suits you." Good save.

"Thanks."

We lapsed into silence. The flickering of the torch played along the walls, the dips and grooves of the rocks, the lines of the shelving, even across the parchments and scrolls that had fallen to the ground.

"Do you think one of those parchments has a way out?" I asked, jerking my chin to where some had fluttered to the carpet.

"You literally can't handle not having control of a situation, can you?"

I shrugged, the action causing Aven's tunic to bunch slightly. "It's a character flaw. I'm working on it."

Aven laughed. "Fine. To occupy your time, tell me the story about your first quest."

My whole body tensed. "Ha!" I said, far too loud for how close I was to them. "You know this story. You've heard it. Ancients, you were *there*."

"I was attending court and saw you brought in. I didn't witness what happened."

"Well, you heard Lord Ethan tell the story. That's what happened."

"Okay. But I want to hear it in your own words."

I froze. I thought back to the blank pages of my journal sitting on the table in my home. The unused inkwell. The desire to tell my own truth, to *know* my own self. And Aven . . . it sounded as if they wanted to know too.

I licked my lips. "My own words, huh?"

Aven nudged me. "Yes. It'll be a good bedtime story."

I laughed. But I relaxed further into them. And I told them.

"Zig and I were playing on our favorite hill outside of our village . . ."

I told Aven the whole story, every detail, because that day would forever be seared into my memory. I told them of how twelve-year-old Zig and I had ventured out to our favorite little hill on a sunny day. We rolled ourselves down the gentle incline, inhaling the sweet perfume of the flowers we crushed along the way.

We chased butterflies, and it didn't take long for me to scrape my knees and get my dress dirty. I was stung by a bee and cried a little over it, and Zig ran over to see if I was okay. He removed the stinger and kissed my finger. We were almost ready to head home for lunch when we heard a yell. And a roar so loud, the earth shook with it. A bear crashed through the tree line nearby, felling thick pines and oaks like they were twigs. It was the largest bear I'd ever seen.

"It was an Ursa," Aven murmured.

"I know that now. I didn't know it then."

The bear's brown-and-black fur was matted with blood, its claws as sharp as knives, and its curved yellow teeth were dripping with frothed saliva as it roared again. It was the most terrifying moment of my life.

The bear had been angered by the knights chasing it, and it raced toward us. Zig ran one way, and I ran the other, and the bear ran after Zig. When I realized, I turned around to find Zig had tripped. So I picked up the first rock I could find and threw it as hard as I could, and it hit the bear on the side of the head. Then it turned to me, roared so loud that the very air quaked, and charged.

Before it could attack me, Lord Ethan, on his white steed, burst from the forest with his sword drawn and stormed between me and the bear. But he galloped too close. And with one swipe of its mighty paw, the bear unhorsed Lord Ethan and gravely injured his mount. I ran over to the knight, thinking he'd protect me, and dropped to his side. But he was injured and had lost his sword. So I crawled on my hands and knees and found where his broadsword had fallen in the grass. The bear charged at us, and without thinking, I grabbed the hilt and, still crouched on the ground, swung the blade around right as the bear attacked.

By a stroke of luck, the sword pierced through the bear's heart as it fell on us to maul us. It collapsed on top of me, covering me completely.

Other knights arrived soon after to find Lord Ethan on the ground, his horse dead, and the Ursa unmoving. And when the five knights had managed to hoist the bear off Lord Ethan's legs, they found me underneath, still clutching the sword in both my hands.

"You were covered in blood," Aven said into my hair.

"I was. It was gross. My dress was ruined. I didn't care, but my mother was livid."

Aven chuckled.

"The group of knights who were in pursuit of the bear witnessed that I was under the Ursa, holding Lord Ethan's sword. I learned that it had been terrorizing some farmers' pigs and cows, eating them and leaving the carcasses, so the knights had been sent to kill it."

"But you did instead."

"I did instead. They plucked me from the ground, put me in front of one of the knights on a horse, and took off for the castle. Zig thought I had been kidnapped and ran home to tell our parents."

"Poor Zig."

"Poor me! I was terrified. I had to stand in front of the king and queen! And the knights told them of my supposed great deed, because I'd saved Lord Ethan from the Ursa!" I waved my hands for emphasis. "They dubbed me Ellinore the Brave and then brought out a bouquet of flowers and this sack of gold. It was the most wealth I'd seen in my *life*."

"It was your reward."

"It was the best thing to ever happen to my family. So I decided right then that I would go back and take on another quest. And I've been doing it ever since."

"And Lord Ethan has harbored resentment toward you ever since as well."

"That noticeable, huh?"

"I notice everything about . . . the quests." They coughed.

"Right. I forgot that you know it all."

"Not everything," they said. "At twelve, you'd never held a sword, and merely a year later you defeated the Golden Dragon."

My whole body went taut. "You sound as skeptical of my skills as Rylan!"

Aven laughed. "No, I don't."

"You do!" I accused. "You absolutely do." I pointed at my own chest. "I trained! With knights!" That was partially true. The squires at the nearby keep had taught me a few basic lessons and had always been up for a sparring session, especially when they knew they'd win. "And I studied with . . . masters." If being attentive during the jousting and sword matches at the castle counted, then that was also true. "There was an entire year between those two events, you know."

"Okay! I wasn't disparaging you."

"Yeah, sure," I grumbled, crossing my arms beneath the drape of Aven's cloak. I don't know why it upset me. I knew I was not nearly good enough with a sword to defeat a dragon, but I could hold my own if absolutely necessary and all avenues of negotiation and/or fleeing had been exhausted.

Aven chuckled. "And now you've retired at the ripe old age of seventeen."

I knocked my elbow into Aven's ribs. "I know you don't understand, but I finally finished what I had set out to do, which was give my parents a good life. And now I'm tired. Of it all."

"I'm tired too," Aven replied. "In a different way."

I sighed. "Then we should rest."

"We should."

I know we both meant it metaphorically, but I was exhausted right then as well. And with Aven's tacit permission, I snuggled closer.

18

I WOKE UP TO THE SOUND OF ROCKS SHIFTING.

Somehow I was sprawled on the carpet with Aven's cloak and the sail covering me from chin to toes. I blinked sleepily, and the blurry room came into focus. Aven sat next to the hearth, a small, cheery fire burning beside them.

"What time is it?" I asked, my voice a morning croak.

Aven shrugged. "I don't know. But Rylan has been working on moving the stones for a few hours now."

Yawning, I stretched while still on the floor, pushing my hands above my head and pointing my toes.

Aven looked away, the fire heating their cheeks to a rosy red.

"Have you talked to the kids?"

Aven huffed a laugh. "They are literally our age. Zig is your twin."

"Yeah, but they act like children."

"And we don't?" Aven asked, raising their eyebrow.

"Point taken." I pushed myself from the comfort of the makeshift bed and shivered when I stepped into the cool air. Leaning against the cave-in, I yelled to the other side, "You okay over there?"

"We're great!" Zig answered, and my anxiety eased at the sound of his clear, strong voice. It came from far closer than the night before. "How about you two?"

I checked with Aven, who gave me a lazy thumbs-up. "We're fine!" My stomach growled as soon as I said it. Okay. That was a problem. "Is there anything edible in here?" I called to Rylan. I received a laugh in return. Great.

I wandered away and plopped down on the carpet. Maybe I could mend the strap on my pauldron while we waited. I hated not being able to do anything to fix the situation. I held on to the fact that at least we had a map. A real map to the invisible realm. And sitting idle was a small price to pay for that.

Time passed slowly, punctuated only by the occasional rumble of rocks knocking about and the grumble in my stomach.

"Um . . . Ellinore? Aven?" Farrah called some interminable time later.

"Yes?" I answered from my bored sprawl on the makeshift bed.

"Hypothetical question. What should we do if someone approaches us?"

Alarm bells rang in my head. I jumped to my feet. Aven joined me by the wall, their shoulder brushing mine. "What do you mean?" they asked.

"Like if a group of people are riding in our general vicinity? And they're, like, pointed toward our camp?"

That didn't sound hypothetical. "Um . . . are you sure this situation *is* hypothetical?" I asked, digging my fingers into the dirt and gravel of the rockslide.

"I didn't want to worry you, but no."

Aven and I exchanged a nervous glance. "How many?" Aven called. "And what do they look like?"

"Six or so on horses. And they have swords and bows. Their faces are covered."

The faery's words rang in my head.

"Run!" I yelled. I clawed at the rocks, hoping to magically bring them all tumbling down. "Run! Do you hear me, Farrah?"

"But what if I try my new disarming move? I've been practicing with Zig."

"No! Are you kidding me? Run!"

I pressed as close as I could, straining to hear. Farrah barked orders to Zig and Rylan. The scuffling noises of breaking down camp followed.

"Don't worry about the camp!" I yelled. "Get on horses! Take the map!"

But it was too late. The thunder of hooves echoed on the rocks, too many to be just our mounts. A gruff voice that I couldn't make out. A scream that was maybe Farrah. More voices, more shouts, more chaos.

"Catch him! Disarm her!" There was the unmistakable metal scrape of a sword being drawn from a scabbard. The commotion of horses whinnying in agitation, and people shouting, and voices overlapping one another.

And then a loud shout breaking through it all, followed by an ominous silence.

"Zig!" I yelled. "Farrah! Rylan!"

A throaty laugh was my only response. The horses departed, the sound of their hooves decreasing as they rode away.

"Zig?" I called, closing my eyes. "Zig?"

Aven hadn't said a word. They rested their hand on my back, their gentle touch a sharp contrast to the jagged fear coursing through me.

I wrenched away from them and paced the length of the room.

"You said to trust them!" I pointed my finger in the general direction of Aven, not wanting to meet their eyes, the anger within me welling quick and hot and ready to burst at the nearest target. "And now! Now they're gone! And the map is gone!"

"We don't know that."

I whirled on them. My hair fell into my face in wild tangles. My tunic was bunched oddly from how I'd fallen asleep, and my breath was horrible. I had broken armor and was trapped in a paranoid man's absurd hidey-hole full of magical snares. My brother was gone. Our means of escape was gone. The one clue we had to the invisible realm of the Elder Beast was *gone*.

How could they be so calm?

"We do know that! Did you not hear? Those weren't helpful people. They were thieves or bandits or someone with ill intent who has been tracking us since day one! They knew we were here!"

Aven sat down at the hearth, expression placid. Like it didn't affect them at all. In fact, it was almost like we were in court and that flat, royal personality they used around everyone else had taken hold. "If they've been trailing us that long, then they have to be other questers who heard your outburst at the inn with the mages."

I crossed my arms. My hands were freezing. "What?"

"Think about it. I heard the rumor within hours all the way at the castle. They could've heard it too and are also looking to cash in on the Elder Beast's whereabouts."

I didn't like how they'd worded that, but it was no secret that all my quests before this one, barring the very first, had been about winning gold. I breathed out and started pacing in a circle. "That's a large jump in logic. *If* it's other questers, why wait until now?"

"Remember when someone rifled through our bags? They didn't take the gold because they didn't need it. They were looking for a clue and didn't find one, which means they knew we didn't have one either. Until today."

That was sound logic. "Okay. So they've been following us for a while."

"They scouted us yesterday," Aven said. "I heard them but didn't see them. And they obviously knew we were here to retrieve something for the quest. Something that would help us. And when you and I weren't present, they took their chance."

"I never should have trusted Rylan to get us out. I shouldn't have *waited* on a rescue. I never should've listened . . ." But the damage was done.

Aven's face flushed. "You mean you shouldn't have listened to *me*."

The statement had bite to it, more animosity than I'd ever heard from Aven, even when we were playing at rivals. And that blank mask slipped into anger.

"I didn't say that!" I shot back, shame curling in my gut.

"But you meant it! You didn't trust me to stand watch. You didn't trust me enough to tell me you'd been poisoned by the fire salamander. You didn't even trust my advice about having your pauldron fixed." They threw up their hands in a gesture of complete frustration. "When are you going to realize that I'm only trying to help you?"

"Trying to help me by reporting back to the king?"

They flinched hard, face paling. "That doesn't negate the fact that I'm on your side and want to see you succeed! If only you'd listen sometimes!"

"Hey, this is not *my* fault. I didn't want you or the others tagging along while I figured this all out to save my brother. I have historically worked alone, you know." Not completely alone. But not with humans. Not with anyone who would judge me.

"It's not weakness to rely on others, to take advice, to *trust* people." Aven sighed wearily. Their shoulders slumped. "You're not alone now, Ellinore."

"I know! And look where it has led me! Led us!" I rubbed my brow, a headache brewing in my temples. "Whoever was out there now has a map to not only the Elder Beast but all the primordials." And if Dave had lectured me merely about the horn of the Elder Beast, imagine what he would think about pieces of all the other creators of our world. I would have to call him, and face the consequences with Aven and the monarchs and whatever dungeon I ended up in later. My hand drifted down to my wrist, fingertips brushing the bracelet.

"If only the fail-safe spell had actually worked," Aven said wryly. "The map would be trapped in here with us."

I stopped my pacing on a coin, pulling my fingers away from the bracelet. "Say that again."

"The fail-safe spell—"

I snapped my fingers. "That's it! The spell Rylan triggered was a fail-safe to keep the map hidden, presumably. He said his great-grandfather always had a fail-safe."

"And?"

"There is no way there is only one exit out of this place." I peered around the room with new eyes. "If I were an old adventurer with prized possessions hidden in a cave, where would I conceal my other means of escape?"

The shelves had miraculously stayed upright, bolted to the stones. Several of the objects had fallen, but not the ones that possessed real value—like the griffin feather and the faery wing. But other than the shelves, the rolls of maps, and the table and rug, there was nothing that pointed to a way of escape. Maybe there was another optical illusion like outside.

I walked along the walls, running my hands over every inch, looking for a stone to press or a trick of the light that would lead to a hidden door. But every rock I touched only left scratches and grit on my fingers. Every corner I investigated turned up nothing. Minutes turned into an hour, the thieves fleeing farther and farther away, but I could not find another exit.

I slumped to the carpet, tugging the ends of my hair in frustration. Goose bumps bloomed on my skin, the sweat I'd built up cooling rapidly, and I shivered.

"Are you cold?" Aven asked once I'd stopped. "I can throw another log on the fire."

I paused. The fire had been burning on and off since we arrived in the cave the day before. But the air was clear; smoke hadn't built up in the room.

The flue.

"Put it out," I said, running over. Hope bubbled under my skin as we snuffed the fire with the sail we'd used in our bed last night. Even with the logs smoldering beneath it, I dropped to my knees and wiggled into the fireplace. The hood was plenty wide for two people to fit if they wanted, and it arched in such a way that I didn't even need to bend down far to squeeze in. I peered upward.

"Aha!" My voice echoed, bouncing off the stone.

A thick rope dangled from above, high enough to avoid the flames, but low enough for someone standing to reach it and climb out. The corridor was small, but we could both make it through. I could even see a flicker of daylight above.

"Can we get out?" Aven asked.

I ducked out of the chimney, soot-smeared and grinning. "I hope you can climb a rope."

Climbing out of a caved-in gallery of oddities through a chimney, carrying a sword and wearing armor (minus the broken pauldron, which I sadly left behind), while my crush was hanging on to the same rope inches below me, was not on my top-ten list of things to do on any given afternoon, but I did it.

Aven and I emerged from the chimney onto the top of the pile of rocks that Rylan had led us to in the first place. I basked in the warmth of the sun and breathed in the clean, salty breeze from the ocean. And then the anxiety of the situation crashed into me.

Farrah, Rylan, and Zig had been taken. Our mounts had been stolen.

But from this vantage point, I could make out the tracks the others had left behind, leading south, running parallel to the beach.

By Aven's logic, they were presumably other questers looking for the Elder Beast, but we didn't know for certain. All we did know was that they had our friends, they had the map, and we had no way to follow them except on foot.

Aven breathed heavily next to me, shoulders rising and falling. They sat on the rock peak, elbows on their bent knees, hands dangling. They winced as they rolled their shoulders.

"Never climbed a rope before?" I asked, stretching out my own arms to relieve the soreness and tension. Ugh. I smelled horrible, like sweat and charred wood.

"No," they said. "And it's not something I wish to repeat."

"Well, let's try not to get trapped in a cave again."

"Good plan." They heaved themself to their feet, dusting off their hands on their trousers. "So what do we do now?"

"We track them. They have more than an hour's head start and we're on foot, so that's not great, and—"

Aven grabbed my arm. "Look!" they said, pointing into the distance. "Is that your horse?"

I squinted in the direction they pointed, then gasped. I recognized that brown blob walking at a tree line. That *was* my horse! "I didn't tether Bluebell," I said, dizzy with relief. "She must have roamed far enough away that the thieves didn't see her."

"Well then, what are we waiting for?"

19

THE SKY WAS DARKENING BY THE TIME WE'D FETCHED BLUEBELL, EATEN
the provisions I had in my saddlebag, drunk my canteen nearly dry, and, after
a small argument about wasting time, washed up in a nearby stream. In hindsight, it wasn't time wasted, as we were pressed very close to each other riding
double, and now I smelled of soap instead of dank cave.

"They're still heading straight south. Following the coast," Aven said,
leaning toward the ground from their position behind me in the saddle. Any
other time I would not have been able to focus beyond the feeling of Aven's
hands around my waist, but my brother was in trouble, as were our two other
companions, and that put a damper on any sense of romance or attraction I
harbored. "They haven't changed direction."

"There's a port town at the mouth of the next river," I said, absolutely not
thinking about Aven's body behind me, "but I doubt they would want to be
seen. Especially with three unwilling members of their group." What else could
be in that direction? A hideout? A lair? Had they had time to read the map?

"They'll have to camp at some point. Maybe soon."

"That will give us time to catch up."

"Ellinore . . ." Aven sighed. "We need to rest as well to keep our strength.
And we don't want to lose their trail in the dark."

They were right. "A while longer. We spent all day in a cave. We're fairly rested."

"Fine."

So we rode. I urged Bluebell faster than was probably wise. But when the stars emerged as pinpricks in the night sky, I reluctantly agreed to stop.

We set up camp under the next tree we found a few steps off the path. I tied Bluebell off, leaving her to snack on the grass around the base of a spreading oak. Even in the night the leaves were vibrant green, a sign of the coming summer. Luckily, the trunk had a spot between two roots that created a natural cradle large enough to fit us both. Aven and I tucked in side by side, shoulders pressed together, weapons within reach. No blanket, as the night was much warmer than the cave.

I tipped my head onto Aven's shoulder and fell asleep to the sound of the breeze rustling the leaves overhead.

I woke earlier than Aven the next morning. It was barely dawn, just the faintest tendrils of light starting to break over the horizon. But as I blinked awake, shaking off the blanket of sleep, I caught sight of smoke curling against the backdrop of a dahlia-colored sky.

I sat up instantly.

A fire!

That had to be the thieves' camp.

I shot to my feet, waking Aven with my movement.

"What's happening?"

"Smoke," I said as the only explanation. I untied Bluebell's reins from the tree and grabbed my sword.

Aven ran a hand down their face, still half asleep, and used the trunk to leverage themself to standing. They rubbed their eyes and yawned. "Smoke?"

"Yes! Smoke. Remember? Thieves? Our friends? The map?"

That broke through Aven's drowsiness immediately. "Smoke!" They grabbed their bow and quiver.

I swung up into Bluebell's saddle and reached down for Aven. They climbed up behind me, and we took off. Every possible scenario ran through my brain. Had the questers had time to read the map? Had they released our friends, but we hadn't seen them? Worse—had they killed them? This whole quest was to keep Zig safe, but what if I had failed at the hands of some thieving adventurers?

I didn't even want to consider it. And I didn't have time to because I pushed Bluebell hard, her hooves kicking up dirt and grass as we covered the distance to the smoke in record time.

The trail of gray was originating from a thick copse of trees that created a barrier between the shore of the Eastern Sea and the main road, then jutted inland. It was composed of spindly pines that managed to thrive in the sandy soil, dense enough to hide a band of thieves. The sea at high tide had encroached far enough inland that the sound of the waves slapping against the pebbled sand covered the noise of our approach. Fortuitous for us. Bad planning by the people who had taken our friends and our map.

Aven patted my leg, and I slowed, not wanting to risk riding too close. We broke off toward the end of the woods nearest the rolling waves. It would take us farther from the smoke, but we'd be able to approach from the ocean side, which they would not expect. Skirting the long way around the trees would be our best shot, though it was going to take precious time. With the rapidly rising sun, we knew we didn't have long until the bandits readied for departure.

We left Bluebell by a grassy dune and crept toward their encampment. The layer of pine needles over soft sand muffled our footsteps, and the clustered trees provided cover as we approached. Stealth was important, but so was speed, and I didn't want to lose what might be our only chance. Moving quickly, we made it to a patch of tall spring-green grass on the outskirts of the woods and hid among the stalks. Crawling on our bellies, Aven and I approached the outer edge of the camp. I peered through the trees, and my heart leaped when I spied Zig, Rylan, and Farrah tied to a tall stump, ropes crossing their chests, pinning them. They were off on their own, away from the small clearing of the main campsite, where the firepit was spitting as one of the thieves stoked the flames.

Aven poked my shoulder and jerked their chin toward the inland border of the woods.

Our mounts.

"We need a plan," Aven said, right into my ear, voice pitched low.

I nodded. We had to hurry. The rest of the camp was waking up, and our window of opportunity was closing.

"I counted fifteen bedrolls," Aven said, which was impressive, as they were scattered among the roots of the trees. I had no idea how the poor saps who had camped there last night had even found enough ground to stretch out. "And two are awake. That means seventeen."

Pretty and smart. Be still my beating heart.

Okay, being aware of my crush made it way more difficult to focus. How inconvenient.

"Ellinore?" Aven whispered, knocking their shoulder into mine.

A plan. Right.

"We'll make for the port village once we have the map and our friends. I have a feeling the bandits won't want to follow us there."

"I agree," Aven said, propped on their elbows. "But how do we actually accomplish that?"

My first thought was to pull the thieves away from their camp somehow— maybe frighten them with a fake monster? Or what if I lured them away? That would allow the others to get free and give Aven plenty of time to look for the map. That was the smartest course of action, but . . . was that what Ellinore the Brave would do?

Well, no. Based on the tales, she would confront all the combatants and vanquish them with her sword while one hand was tied behind her back. But that wouldn't work.

Yet a more-realistic variation might.

"I'll distract the bad guys. You get the map."

"What about the others?"

I huffed quietly. "Are you kidding me? There's not a knot or lock invented that can hold Zig. He's just been waiting for us. He only needs a signal."

Aven patted around on the ground and pulled a smooth ocean shell from the tangle of grass, about the size and weight of a skipping stone. With a grin, they hopped up on their knees and threw it as hard as they could, before dropping back down onto their stomach. The shell sailed through the air and smacked the tree bark right next to Zig's ear.

Good shot. How attractive. Yay for us.

Zig startled awake, wide eyed, and immediately spotted the shell where it had landed next to him. He wiggled, peering around the area, looking for us. I cast a quick glance to the camp; the two thieves who had roused were now moving about, but they weren't paying attention to anything beyond eating breakfast.

I raised my hand above the grass and pointed toward the mounts, hoping my meaning was clear.

Zig's smile was a sight to behold.

Okay. This was going to work. The trio of captives would free our mounts. Aven would grab the map and the saddlebags. And I would be the distraction.

This would work. I could do this. *We* could do this.

A third member of the camp roused, throwing back the cover of his bedroll. I tensed. We were running out of time. The thief stood, yawned, and stretched his hands above his head, his back to us. His clothes were . . . much finer than what a bandit would wear, on par with Aven's and Farrah's attire. He sat on a fallen log and rummaged through what I recognized as Aven's pack, his long blond hair falling into his face. He removed a strip of salted meat and chewed loudly, then reached in again.

Aven stiffened beside me as the man pulled out a leather-bound journal and flipped through the pages. They frowned, fingers tightening on their bow.

Huh. I wondered what was in that journal. Furthermore, I wondered why the thief was interested in reading it and—

The man lifted his head, shook his hair from his face.

I sucked in a harsh breath.

Son of a *bitch*.

I'd recognize that ostentatious mustache anywhere.

Aven was right. These weren't common thieves. They were questers. *Noble* questers.

I should have known. The poor choice of campsite was a dead giveaway, as that fool was terrible at adventuring. And he had *our* map. Oh. I was beyond mad now. Righteously so. Anger boiled right beneath my breastbone, burned in my core like dragon fire. My hand twitched on the hilt of my sword. Because not only had this pompous jerk risked my brother's life and taken our hard-won map, but this was a direct challenge to me. To Ellinore the Brave.

It took every ounce of self-control to hold on to my composure lest I stab that man. Maybe I *would* fight them all with my sword.

It was time for my dramatic entrance.

And it was going to be a *magnificent* one.

"Map. Friends. Flee," I whispered.

Aven nodded sharply, jaw clenched.

I rolled away from them, putting space between us so the questing group wouldn't clock them right away. And then I ran in a crouch, darting from tree to tree, until I was just a few feet from their campsite.

Okay. Here went nothing.

I unsheathed my sword, the blade gleaming in the morning light.

And I stepped out from behind twin pines into the campsite.

"Lord Ethan," I called. "What a coincidence!"

20

THE FACT THAT LORD ETHAN—THE MOST AWFUL QUESTER OF THEM ALL, the man who had brought back the corpse of a bat during the spider challenge—had somehow orchestrated the kidnapping of my brother and friends and had stolen the map to the Elder Beast was something I couldn't stomach.

I was going to kill him. Or at least punch him in the chin.

At my appearance, he dropped the pilfered journal in the dirt, his face paling upon meeting my furious gaze. Standing, he clasped his hands behind his back and strode forward until we were only a few feet from each other in the small clearing. His white surcoat swished around his legs as he walked, his puffed-out chest displaying his coat of arms, which included a winged horse—a symbol of fame. He wished. I held him at sword point, my arm as steady and solid as a rock.

"Ellinore," he said evenly. "I thought you were trapped in a cave."

"Oh, I was." I smiled, cheerful and wide. "But I escaped. Because I'm Ellinore the Brave."

He huffed a courtly laugh, the same one he used when the king made a bad joke. He peered over my shoulder. "Where's Princet Aven?"

"Left them behind." I shrugged. "They slowed me down."

His mouth dropped open in surprise. Good. Let him be caught back on his heels. It gave me control of the situation.

"Anyway," I said, flipping the tip of my sword toward his neck. "You've been following us for quite some time. You searched through our bags in the woods on the first night."

He sniffed. "I would not deign to rifle through your belongings. I sent guards to do that."

"Any particular reason?"

"I knew Princet Aven had information I didn't."

"Ah. Well, since you didn't find what you were looking for, you've now kidnapped my brother and stolen my map. And I'm going to skewer you and your band of charlatans with my sword for daring to do so."

Ethan coughed into his fist. He wiped his hand on a kerchief he pulled from the interior of his tunic, instead of on his trousers like an ordinary person. He was nobility through and through. The other two of the band who were awake (squires, it looked like) stood on either side of Ethan with their own weapons drawn and aimed at me—a sword and a pike. Yikes about the pike. I wasn't a fan. But at least I had their focus.

"That's not very honorable of you." He sighed and shook his head. "But I should've expected that from a *peasant*."

I scoffed. "Is that an insult? Because you'll have to do better. That's so old news, friend. No one at court cares. They only care that I *win*. And I have been winning since I killed that Ursa with *your* dropped sword when I was *twelve*. I mean . . . ," I continued, glancing over his shoulder. Zig, Farrah, and Rylan were free from their binds and slowly creeping toward the saddlebags. And Aven was . . . retrieving the journal? They were prioritizing recovering their account for the king over finding the map? "I have *you* to thank for even sparking my interest in questing. So thank you. So much."

Aven shoved the journal down their tunic. Rylan threw two saddlebags over his broad shoulders. Farrah retrieved her quarterstaff, and Zig had his hands on at least three canteens. Okay. Great. But where was the map?

Lord Ethan chuckled demurely. "Funny you should mention the Ursa. Five years ago you stole prestige and acclaim from me. And now I plan to steal them back."

I narrowed my eyes. "I was a child who got lucky with a sword. There was no intent to steal anything. It was merely good fortune we weren't both mauled to death."

"And since then? You've won almost every competition in the last several years. You stole the right to rescue Princess Avriel from me. You accumulate wealth far beyond your station. You win favor from the king and queen, receiving gifts like that sword you're wielding. The Pointless Princet even likes you, despite the fact that you are so uncouth as to defeat them in their birthday competition."

Oh, and there was one of those consequences for my actions that I had been warned about. Zig was right. I had made a faux pas with that one. But whatever, I had to keep Lord Ethan and the two squires focused on me.

"At least I'm not so uncouth as to refer to a royal by that awful nickname," I spat.

Lord Ethan smiled, realizing he'd struck a nerve.

Damn him. I plowed past the minor slip. "And Aven knows I'm sorry about their birthday."

Aven snapped their head up from where they searched through Lord Ethan's bedroll. They flashed a quick acknowledging smile before returning to picking through the campsite for the map. "I made a mistake," I continued. "I'm big enough to admit it."

"Well, then maybe you'll be big enough to admit that I have the upper hand. I have a map to the beast you're so desperately attempting to find. The Elder Beast, correct?"

I didn't move a muscle, because he already knew. I wasn't going to play his game.

"Excellent," he said, taking my silence as an affirmation. "That is wonderful to know, because I'm going to find it first. I will kill it, sell off its parts to the highest bidders, and watch as the mages harvest your brother's heart. And then I'll locate the other primordials and kill them all as well and do the same." He smiled. "I think the king and queen would love to display the horn of the Elder Beast. It would look amazing next to the pelt of the Ursa in the great hall."

"You are making a grave mistake, Lord Ethan."

Lord Ethan smiled. "No. I think you'll find that *you* have made the mistake."

That was ominous. A chill swept down my spine. I cleared my throat, grabbed the hilt of my sword with my other hand as well, and readied myself. "Look, *sir*, I only want my brother, my friends, and the map. Hand them over and I will walk away without shoving this through your neck."

"No." He cleared his throat. "Guards!"

Ah. There was my mistake. The lumpy bedrolls we had assumed were Ethan's sleeping entourage were actually . . . empty. All the previous inhabitants had risen before dawn and had been lying in wait, hidden in the shadows cast by the pines. I was surrounded. *We* were surrounded. And oh, there were more of them than we'd thought. Crap.

The squire to my right lunged, and I easily knocked the point of his pike away with the flat of my blade. I crowded in against him, the end of the pike useless in such close quarters. I swung my blade and sliced through the wooden handle like it was paper. I quickly spun and dodged the other's clumsy attack, then tripped her as she passed, her sword ending up wedged in between the twin pines.

There was a cry of "They've escaped!" obviously referring to the troublesome trio.

Lord Ethan stomped his foot. "Then capture them again!"

Before the guards had even moved, Farrah jumped into the fray with her staff, smashing heads and stomachs with surprising grace and speed. Zig slashed out with his knife as he danced away from the guards. Rylan pushed out with his palms, and a rush of wind swept over the campsite, kicking up sand and dirt and toppling two of the smaller trees, temporarily trapping several of Ethan's guards.

What the ancients were they doing? They were supposed to be running away! Yet when Farrah smashed her staff into someone's face, giving them a bloody nose, and Zig used trickery to steal a short sword from the hands of a guard, I couldn't help but feel grateful they were with me.

But Aven? Where was Aven? Where had they gone?

I blocked another sword thrust, then another, making my way close to

Lord Ethan as he fled toward the middle of the camp, picking up his own sword and brandishing it as I approached.

The whiz of an arrow flew by my ear, followed by a clang of metal on metal. A grunt sounded behind me, and I whirled to find a squire I'd not noticed with their sword on the ground and an arrow sticking out of the tree behind them. I kicked them in the stomach, then kneed them in the cheek. They fell like a sack of grain.

I blocked another weak strike from a guard who'd freed himself from the magically felled trees, and . . . the guards weren't really fighting us. I glanced around as they attacked but didn't finish their strikes, pulled back when Farrah made a mistake or failed at her new disarming move, or when Zig tripped over a branch, or when Rylan's magic was weak at best. They were *corralling* us, forcing us toward the middle of the camp. Despite my friends' best efforts, they'd been backed up close to the center of the encampment, unable to flee to the mounts. And because of my pursuit of Lord Ethan, I too was surrounded by trees and weapons.

"Ellinore," Lord Ethan sang.

I turned to face him. "What is this? What are you doing?"

"Enjoying my victory."

He pulled a parchment from the inside of his tunic and flapped it in front of my face. My breath caught when I saw the flash of the drawing of the world and the colored dots that marked the locations of the primordials.

The map!

"So this is all to gloat? Great. Fine. You won. Hand over the map."

He tsked. "Have a little imagination, Ellinore. My plan isn't just to gloat. My plan is to capture you, tie you up, and throw you in the ocean. Maybe the Lady in the Sea will rescue you. Who knows? But for certain you'll be out of my way."

"You are sorely mistaken," I said through gritted teeth, "if you think I won't stick the pointy end of this weapon right into your ribs and watch you bleed out."

"That doesn't sound honorable at all."

"Just trying to fit in with the crowd."

"Well then. So should I." He jerked his chin to another guard. They walked over, holding a lit torch, which he accepted. He pinched the map at the edge, allowing it to unroll fully, the longest point dangling only a few inches from the ground. He waved the flames closer to its surface. Smoke caressed the face of the map, curling around the frayed edges. One ember, one errant flame, one spark, and the entire parchment would light.

Fear seized my limbs. My heart pounded harder than it had during the brief fight. I trembled as sweat rolled down my spine, gathered in the hollow of my knees. That was the only clue we had to the Elder Beast. The only way to save Zig. The one tangible item that could help my brother.

Lord Ethan then nodded to someone behind me, but I didn't dare look away.

There was a scuffle, followed by a yell from Farrah and an indignant "Hey!" from Zig.

"Let me go!" Rylan yelled, his boots scuffing in the sandy soil, grunting as he fought.

A tall, beefy guard dragged Rylan in front of me, right next to Lord Ethan's side, a knife blade pressed against his neck.

"You light that," I said, voice thick, gaze locked on the map and the flicker of the flames, "you kill my brother."

"Oh no! Well, that would be an unfortunate side effect."

My pulse raced, and it felt like my heart had migrated to my mouth. "Listen to me. Defeating a primordial is nearly impossible. They are more powerful than the ancients. They exist outside of time. They are *gods*."

Lord Ethan smiled, oily and insincere. I was going to pummel him as soon as I had a chance. *Come on, Aven. Where are you?* An arrow would not go amiss at this point.

"I'll give you a choice, Ellinore the Brave." That name had never sounded so ugly. "You can choose to save your friends, and I'll allow them to go on their merry way back to their homes. Or you save yourself, and yourself *only*, and the map."

"That's not a choice. Either way my brother dies."

"Well, you can't win all the time, Ellinore."

"Neither, then. Fight me." I flexed my fingers around the hilt of my sword. "A fair fight. If I win, we go free and get the map. If you win, you keep the map and we'll back off."

He laughed. "What do you take me for? I'm not a gullible creature. And I've grown weary of your attempts to stall." He cleared his throat. "The mage," he said, gesturing to Rylan. The guard holding him pushed the edge of the knife against the thin skin of Rylan's throat, blood welling along the blade. "Or the map."

Ethan wiggled the parchment in a sinister tease.

"You wouldn't," I breathed. "Then you wouldn't know the locations either."

Ethan chuckled. "So you think."

I froze. I didn't know what to do. I'd tried my way—to talk and bargain— but Lord Ethan hadn't budged. If I were the Ellinore the Brave of the stories, I'd choose the mage. Right? But that would doom Zig, and I couldn't . . . I couldn't do that. I was Ellinore the sister first. The twin. And I had promised Zig I would release him from the mages' wager. I'd promised him I would do everything to save him.

"Come on," Lord Ethan said, waving the map closer to the torch with an airy laugh. "Make a choice, Ellinore. Or lose both."

I licked my lips. "The m—"

An arrow sank deep into the forearm of the guard holding Rylan. She yelped, dropping the knife and clutching at the wound. Rylan rammed his head backward, colliding with her nose, and blood spurted from her nostrils. He ran. She shouted and stumbled, careening right into Lord Ethan. Another arrow burrowed into the handle of the torch, knocking it from the surprised noble's grip.

Chaos erupted as more arrows flew. Shouts rang out. Guards dived to the ground to avoid being hit.

An arrow buzzed right in front of Lord Ethan's face. He staggered, tripped on a fallen log, and fell on his backside next to the campfire.

He dropped the map . . . directly into the flames.

21

FLAMES LICKED AT THE PARCHMENT, BLACKENING THE SURFACE AND curling the edges as it burned.

I lunged and grabbed the remnants. Falling on my knees, I cried out as I frantically smacked handfuls of soil to smother the fire, words and routes rapidly disappearing as embers ate their way across the kingdom, across the world, across any hope I had of rescuing Zig. The whisper of the destruction and the crackling of ruined paper filled my ears, drowning out the chaos around me.

Hot air and smoke blew into my face. My vision blurred with tears as the map fragmented between my dirt-smudged fingertips, the smaller pieces turning to cinders and ash as the breeze picked up and carried them away.

"No!"

My voice cracked in desperation and pain. All that remained were burned tatters. The map was unsalvageable, unreadable, unusable, *gone*.

"Ellinore," someone said behind me, grabbing the edge of my leather cuirass and tugging. "We have to go!"

"No!" I cried, clawing at the dirt, gathering the remaining slivers of parchment.

The person yanked me away with force, hauling me upward. "We have to leave! Or we have no chance."

I wrenched away from them and picked up my sword from where I'd dropped it on the ground, the leather-wrapped hilt digging into the burns on my hands. Through the smear of my tears I spied Lord Ethan running. I released a guttural noise of fury and surged forward.

"Ellinore!" the person yelled, holding on, their boots scuffing through the dirt as they restrained me. "Ellinore! Zig needs you!"

That broke through my haze of wrath, and I shook my head, taking in my surroundings. The forest was on fire, the fallen torch having lit everything around it. The flames spread quickly through the pine needles, the fire licking up the trunks of the trees, the very ground molten. The guards ran in circles like startled chickens, gathering what they could before the flames consumed it all.

I blinked, tears running down my hot cheeks, as Aven released my armor and grabbed my wrist instead, dragging me behind them. They had picked up a short sword at some point, but they didn't need it. Everyone was running from the flames.

We emerged from the burning trees, choking on smoke, to find the other three already mounted and ready. Aven jumped up onto Mouse and hauled me up to join them. They took my sword from my limp grip, and I settled behind them, curling my burned hands toward my body.

I hid my face between Aven's shoulder blades as they shouted at the others and we tore away from the devastation. I cast one last glance at the burning pines, gray smoke billowing in large columns upward, and noted the irony that it was smoke that had drawn us there and smoke that marked our departure.

Aven found Bluebell where we'd left her and grabbed her bridle. They turned in the saddle, their face covered in ash, their expression drawn in concern, and offered me the leather reins and the chance to dismount. My mind was blank. I couldn't process what had happened, much less ride. I shook my head, then tucked myself against Aven's back.

If Aven was surprised, they didn't show it. They lashed Bluebell to Mouse, and we rode toward the port town.

I was grateful; I didn't want to leave the comfort of pressing my cheek to their shoulder. Closing my eyes, allowing the tears to stream in angry rivulets, I buried my sobs in the fabric of their tunic.

22

_~~_

I DON'T REMEMBER MUCH OF THE NEXT SEVERAL HOURS. IT WAS AS IF
THE anguish of losing the map had swallowed me whole. I heard the goings-on
around me—how we traveled slowly to ensure the mounts hadn't been injured,
the fact that Lord Ethan had stolen nearly all our gold, how Zig took what was
left to the tavern to see if he could multiply it, and how Rylan and Farrah went
to procure us any kind of cheap food.

That left Aven and me in the only room we could currently afford at
an inn.

I sat heavily on the bed, my hands on my knees, palms facing up, as Aven
knelt in front of me and stared down at them in horror.

"Ellinore," Aven whispered.

"It's okay," I said, my voice clogged from sorrow and disuse.

They studied my face. "No, it's not. This is ... bad. I'm not sure what to do,"
they said, hovering, their brow furrowed.

My hands were burned and blistered from the bends of my wrists to the
tips of my fingers, the shiny, swollen skin an angry red. They _hurt_ like nothing
had ever hurt me before. And that included a few of the closer calls I'd had.

"I think I may have some bandages in my saddlebag, but it's still on Mouse
and—"

"I lost," I whispered. Tears burned behind my eyes, blurring my view of the small room with two beds and barely any floor between them. The sea crashed against the shore somewhere outside the tiny window. The late afternoon sky darkened, sliding toward early evening. Sounds of footsteps echoed up and down the stairs, and laughter wafted up from the dining room below. The air tasted of salt and smelled of fish and mead mixed in a noxious odor at which I'd normally wrinkle my nose. My mouth was parched, my tongue sticking to the roof. My entire body *ached*, and all I could think of was how the map had disintegrated in my hands. How I'd watched Zig's only chance burn to ash and waft away on the breeze.

Aven stilled, waiting patiently for me to continue.

I opened my mouth. Closed it. Opened it again, and a breathy voice followed. "I lost," I said again. "To *Lord Ethan*."

Aven snorted a laugh, though it wasn't funny.

I shook my head. It had been a long time since Ellinore the Brave had suffered a loss. Years even. But Ellinore the Brave, the one in the songs, didn't exist. Just Ellinore the Fraud. Ellinore the asshole who beat a royal at their birthday celebration in a game, not understanding the social faux pas of doing so. Ellinore the absent sister and daughter who had spent her teenage years winning gold and acclaim but at the cost of her relationship with her family, with her brother.

"I lost," I said again. "I'm lost."

Aven rested their hand on my knee, a gentle, reassuring touch. "All of us escaped unharmed except for you. We retrieved our mounts, if not all our things. It wasn't a total loss."

Tears stained my cheeks when I finally met their worried gaze. "I don't know what to do. I don't know how to move forward from here."

They offered a smile, small and genuine and sad but still somehow tinged with promise. "We'll figure it out. The group of us. I know you didn't want all of us following you, but give us a chance and I think we might work well as a group." Their warm fingers dimpled my skin when they gave my leg a comforting squeeze. "You might not have seen it in all the fighting, but Farrah can wield that quarterstaff even if she can't pull off a disarm. And Zig is so smart. You're right, no knot or lock can hold him. Rylan just needs some practice and a little confidence, and his magic will be as fine a range weapon as my bow."

"I'm sorry I defeated you on your birthday. I wasn't lying about that."

Aven paused. Their blue eyes caught the candlelight like jewels in the queen's crown but were adorned with dark circles beneath. Their forehead creased, and their shoulders drooped as if they were so, so tired.

"It's okay," they said. "I would've been suspicious if I'd won. I wouldn't have liked it if you'd lost on purpose."

"Still," I said. "I should've sat out. Or something. The point is, I'm sorry."

Aven sighed. "Apology accepted." They took a breath and looked down at my hands, gently cradling them in their own. "We need to do something about these."

I wanted to tell them that they didn't need to worry. That I had a potion from a dragon's hoard beneath my tunic that would heal the burns in a moment. I wanted to tell them *everything* in my own words, like they had wanted with the story about the Ursa. But even though the truth sat heavy on my tongue, I *couldn't*. I couldn't tell them. Not until Zig was safe.

I'd just lost the map. I couldn't suffer losing Aven as well. That might break me.

Their thumbs gently caressed my wrists. "Ellinore?" they prompted.

"Um . . . I—"

The door swung open and Farrah, queen of lifesaving interruptions, stuck her head inside. Somehow, after everything, her hair remained perfectly styled and her makeup was flawless. I was so envious. Her eyebrows shot up at Aven holding my hands, but Aven didn't move.

"Don't you knock?" they muttered.

Farrah grinned but abstained from responding with a biting comment. "Zig made some winnings, and we have food downstairs when you're ready."

"Thank you," I said.

Farrah's gaze flicked between me and Aven, her eyes narrowing. "Aven," she said sweetly, "there are bandages and I think a potion for pain downstairs. Why don't you come and get them for Ellinore?"

Aven frowned. "Can you bring them to me?"

"No. I have been tasked with taking care of our mounts. Mouse, Starlight, and Carrot need extra love. They were kidnapped too and have been through a traumatic experience."

Aven looked as if they were about to argue, but I jumped in first.

"It's okay. I'll be fine by myself for a few minutes."

They tilted their head and assessed me. "Are you certain?"

I drew myself up from my slouch and cleared my throat, trying my best to project an image of someone who hadn't just had a breakdown. "Yes. I'll be okay."

Aven grumbled but stood and followed Farrah.

I listened for their steps to descend the stairs, and once I was certain Aven wasn't returning imminently, I pulled the vial from beneath my tunic. The liquid swirled a cooling blue, and I'd never been so grateful for magic in my entire life. My hands and fingers were swollen, so removing the stopper was almost a lesson in futility, but I finally uncorked it and was able to shake a few drops onto my tongue.

As with the salamander venom, the relief was almost instantaneous, and I sagged on the bed, exhausted but healed. My head spun, and I contemplated lying back on the mattress and giving in to the fatigue.

But I wasn't finished with what I needed to do.

The tiny room came equipped with a pitcher and a shallow porcelain bowl. The water was cold, but it worked well enough to rinse the ash from my face and body. And a linen pillowcase ripped into ribbons made adequate bandages to hide my now-healed hands. I tied them off with my teeth just as I heard Aven's and Farrah's voices coming up the stairs.

"You should tell her," Farrah said.

Aven's response was short and clipped. "No."

I perked up. Tell me what?

"Aven, you need to tell her before this whole quest goes much further. Or gets more dangerous."

Aven laughed at that, bitter and sharp, footsteps pausing outside the door. "*More* dangerous? That's impossible, Farrah."

"Ugh. You're being so *you*."

"I'm not taking attention away from the purpose of the quest, which is to save her brother. Anything beyond that just makes things complicated."

Farrah groaned. "Excuses, excuses. You can't keep the secret much longer. She's going to figure it out. And then she'll be pissed you lied."

I flinched. Aven had lied? Farrah had hinted before about secrets, but I hadn't given it much thought, chalking it up to her relentless teasing of Aven. But this sounded like Aven was keeping something from me. Something that would *hurt*.

There was a world-weary sigh. "It doesn't matter. This is her last quest."

"That makes it matter more, you royal fool!"

The door swung open before I could move from the center of the room, where I was obviously listening. Aven stopped in the doorway, mouth falling open. We stared at each other, the atmosphere tense.

"You're back," I said, voice a croak. I blamed the smoke from the forest fire and not the fact that this was the most awkward interaction that had ever happened in all of time. I held up my bandaged hands. "I took care of them. On my own."

Aven blinked. "Oh."

I swallowed. "Yeah." Should I address the chimera in the room, or should I let it go?

Aven opened their mouth, then shut it. They scratched the back of their neck and hummed. They glanced at Farrah, who nodded encouragingly. "So, Ellinore—"

"No!" I said quickly. "No. I don't want to know."

Aven's brow furrowed. "You don't?"

"No. You keep your secret. And you let me keep mine."

"Oh."

"Deal?"

"Yeah."

"Great. Let's not bring it up again." Okay. I couldn't take much more of Aven's hurt bewilderment. I was already fatigued from my absolute emotional collapse. I could not handle anything else. Especially if it would heap more unhappiness and stress upon me. "Uh . . . let's go have dinner," I said, brushing past them quickly.

I descended the stairs into the inn's dining area to find Zig and Rylan around a table with chairs left open for the rest of us. They chatted, their voices low, while they shoveled stew into their mouths, dipping warm bread into their bowls as well to sop up the gravy. The scrape of my chair along the rough-hewn wooden floor alerted them to my presence.

Zig startled, then jumped to his feet.

"Sister," he said, rounding the table.

"Brother."

He collided into me with a breath-stealing hug. I couldn't tell who clung harder. I fisted my hands in the back of his tunic and buried my face in his shoulder. He squeezed so tightly, my ribs creaked. We embraced for a centuries-long minute, before pulling away.

"I'm glad to see that you're aware again," he said. "I would've hugged you earlier, but I didn't know if you'd remember it."

"Thank you. I'm better now," I said, though Zig could tell I was lying.

Zig's regular pale complexion had dimmed to a waxy gray. His lips were almost blue, and his eyes, deep brown like my own, had become cloudy. His usual enthusiasm for life had leached out of him. Whatever magic bound him to the mages' bargain was draining him as each day passed, and I couldn't do anything about it, not anymore.

My stomach twisted in a knot as we both sat down at the round table, the stew no longer as tempting as it had been before.

Rylan also appeared a little worse for wear, as if the travel and the fighting had sapped all excitement out of him. His hands shook as he took a drink, and he frowned down at his stew, lost in thought. Farrah joined us, uncharacter-istically somber, from either the events of the day or the conversation from upstairs, I wasn't sure. I didn't look at Aven when they sat at the table, unsure of what I'd find.

Instead I took a hearty slurp of the stew, then a drink from the water cup in front of me.

"Um . . . Ellinore?" Rylan asked. "What do we do now?"

I dipped a piece of bread into the bowl, then shoved it in my mouth. I kept my head bowed, my hair hanging in my face.

"I don't know," I said, a confession.

"We should go back to the cave," Farrah said. "To find another map. Not everything was destroyed, right?"

Rylan sighed. "That map was exceedingly rare. The only way there would be a duplicate is if my great-grandfather made one. And we searched through all the scrolls already and only found the one."

"Did any of you hear Lord Ethan speak with his retinue?" Aven asked. "They obviously had a plan if they would allow the map to be destroyed."

"It was a mistake," I said, chewing around a tough bit of stew meat. "Lord Ethan made a mistake. He had no intention of seeing the map destroyed. It was just to . . . humiliate me . . . and taunt me into making a choice. He stumbled during the scuffle. He didn't mean to drop it into the fire."

"They did talk often about the southern part of the kingdom," Rylan said, trying to ease the despair. "They mentioned a river and possibly a waterfall. I'm certain I saw a dot in that area of the map."

"His fief is to the north, on the edge of the Dark Wood. There would be no reason for him to travel south." Aven rubbed their brow. "Unless he was questing."

"I had a chance to look over the map too, though I couldn't quite figure out the key." Farrah tapped her spoon on the edge of her bowl. "If we head that way, though, I do know a good route. Like I told you, I know all the shortcuts this kingdom has."

"I know what we should do," Zig said.

I snapped my head up to find Zig shoving his hand into the folds of his tunic and removing the scrap of cloth.

"No," I said. "No, Zig."

He ignored me and slapped it in the middle of the table. The scrap was still blank, save for the coffee blob. No lettering or information had magically appeared since Zig stole it from the mages. It held nothing, other than a way to lose three days of Zig's life, if we even found a way to activate it.

"No. Not an option."

Aven's eyebrows pinched together. "What is it?"

"A clue," Zig said, sitting back in his seat. "The mages I made the bet with offered it to us at the start of the quest. But Ellinore refused to take it."

"How'd you get it, then?" Farrah asked.

"Oh, you sweet, naive child."

"I'm only a year younger than you."

"Well, how do you think I got it? Ellinore refused it. So I stole it, right from underneath their noses."

Farrah's eyebrows shot up. "Really? You stole from mages?"

"Though I don't condone stealing mostly," I said into my stew, "it was a pretty good move."

"Thank you, dear Sister."

"Why wouldn't you take it?" Aven asked.

"Because if we find a way to activate it, then it will take three days off the timeline of the quest." I gulped a swig of water. "Three days off Zig's remaining time."

"Oh," Aven breathed.

Farrah poked it with a long fingernail. "It doesn't say anything. How is it a clue?"

"It has to be soaked in magic first," Zig said.

"Saturated," I corrected. "Saturated with power."

Zig shrugged, excruciatingly nonchalant for someone discussing taking three days off having their heart. "Okay. Whatever that means." He tapped Rylan on the shoulder. "I was hoping you could figure it out?"

"Me?"

"Yeah. You know a little bit of magic, right?"

"Yeah, but," Rylan started, gaze darting nervously around the table, "I'm not really a mage. I'm just a bard. I don't have that kind of power."

"But you said you've studied it. You had access to a house full of magical crap. You could totally figure this out."

Rylan licked his lips. "Maybe? I guess I could try."

"Then it's settled." Zig smiled, though it wasn't as bright as usual. "Rylan will work on saturating the clue with power or magic or whatever it needs."

"And?" I prodded. "What if he can't figure it out? What if time runs out while we sit around and do nothing?" Aven wrapped their fingers around my hand, and I realized that I was holding my spoon in a clenched fist so tight that I had cracked the wooden handle. I relaxed, then pulled my hand away. "My first mistake was allowing all our eggs to be in one basket," I said, voice low. "I'm not doing that again. We're following Lord Ethan."

"What?" Aven clenched their fists. "Even if he did have access to the map, he's the worst quester ever, Ellinore. I think together we could come up with a better course of action than following him. Maybe Farrah is correct, and we should go back to the cave, or maybe we travel to the castle and look through the archives or—"

"No." I loudly cut them off. "Lord Ethan didn't mean to drop the map into the fire, but he did say he knew where the Elder Beast was when he was goading me. You said yourself he has no reason to travel south unless he is on a quest. Rylan heard him talk about a river and a waterfall. He'll lead us to the invisible realm, and we'll step in and cut him off. Then we'll find the Elder Beast first."

Aven frowned. "But—"

I hit my fist on the table. "But what? We all agreed I was the leader of this group! You're here by order of the king," I said, biting the words out at Aven. "And you"—I whirled on Farrah—"wanted an adventure." I pointed at Rylan. "You wanted to witness a quest so you could write a song. None of you are here to save Zig. Only I am. And this is the best way to do it."

The silence after my outburst was deafening. I pushed away from the table and stood, not meeting any of their eyes.

"I need some air."

I left the inn and walked down the wooden boardwalk of the port town all the way to a dock that jutted out into the glittering sea. The sister moons cast ripples of light along the rolling water. Fishing equipment littered the dock, the smell of dead sea life overpowering the clean, salty air.

At the end I sat down, dangled my feet high over the water, and took a deep breath. The one thing I had always prided myself on was my composure, my ability to allow things to bounce off, like the snide comments at the court or the jibes sometimes in the bards' songs. I never allowed anyone to see that their opinions got to me. Even with Aven, I kept them at a distance. We competed. We bickered. We leaned on each other in a cave. But Aven didn't know the real Ellinore. And I apparently didn't know the real Aven.

I ran my fingers through my hair, my bandages catching on the snarls. What was I going to do? What was the best course of action? I had so little time. Maybe I should break down and summon Dave. He'd said he didn't know where to look, but maybe he could help in another way.

I fiddled with the thin bracelet on my wrist. If I called Dave, Aven would know everything I'd done was a lie. Could they live with that? Could I?

"Wow, you must really be in your head if you didn't hear me stomping down the dock."

I sighed as Zig settled next to me. He put his arm around my shoulders and pulled me close like he used to do when we were young.

"I'm sorry," he said, resting his cheek on my hair.

I scrunched my nose in confusion. "You're sorry?"

"Yeah. I dragged you into something you didn't even want to do. I made a stupid bet with mages because I was reckless and gold-hungry and, well, a tiny bit jealous of your acclaim and adventures. I kind of wanted to be part of your"—he made a vague hand gesture—"quests and friends, I guess."

"Not all fun, is it?"

Zig huffed. "Not really."

"I would have never wished any of this on you." I turned in his embrace and wrapped my arms around his body. I hid my face in his chest as tears gathered in the corners of my eyes, and squeezed as hard as I could. "I don't want you to die."

Zig shrugged. "I don't want to die either. But I won't blame you if that happens, Ellinore. You're doing everything you can to save me." Guilt settled in my stomach like a stone. "And I appreciate it so much. But you don't have to shoulder everything alone. I promise the others are here to help."

"I can't risk it. I don't want to lose you."

"You have me right now. And I'll be here until the last flicker of that candle. How many marks are left, by the way?"

I reached into the bag at my belt and pulled out the parchment. I unrolled it, and we both stared at the candle. In the dark it emitted a soft glow. We counted the marks that remained.

I gulped. "According to this, when the sun rises tomorrow—nine."

"Oh. Well. That's not so bad." He shrugged as I put the parchment away. "Do you think Rylan will date me for the last nine days of my life?"

I punched Zig in the ribs. "Don't distract him while he's trying to activate the scrap of clues."

"Good call. I'll date him after he cracks the code. If, you know, I'm around."

"Please don't joke like that."

"Like what?" He rubbed his fist on the top of my head, knotting my hair. "About how much I'm going to haunt you as a ghost? You'll never be rid of me. Even if you move into the castle with Aven and become noble by marriage, I'm going to haunt those halls and bemoan the fact that I never lived in a palace with tapestries."

I disentangled from him. I wiped the tears from my cheeks, rolling my eyes at the implication that Aven would even want to date me, much less marry. "You're insufferable."

"You're my twin. So if I'm insufferable, so are you."

"That's not how that works."

He laughed, but it came out as more of a wheeze. "Hey, listen," he said, tugging on my hair, "you're kind of in the doghouse with everyone else, so you'll totally be sleeping on the floor tonight."

Ah, well, that made sense. "Okay. I won't argue."

He grinned. "And don't worry, okay? If you say we need to follow that stupid lord-of-winged-horses guy, then that's what we'll do. We trust you. *I* trust you. You're Ellinore the Brave."

My heart dropped. Oh. I tucked the bracelet under my long sleeve. Zig wanted Ellinore the Brave, so I would be Ellinore the Brave. For him. She'd accomplished amazing things before. She could do this, too. Maybe.

23

I spent a rough night on the floor of the room. Everyone was tucked in and asleep when I finally entered, and I merely took off my boots and armor and crawled into my bedroll, with no pillow in sight.

The next morning I waited until everyone else had left before rising. I pulled off the bandages from the night before, the skin of my hands healed and new. Then I washed and dressed and met them down at the inn's dining area.

"Hey," I said, sliding into a chair.

Aven, Zig, and Rylan looked up from their bowls.

"Just wanted to say I'm sorry for yelling. And I didn't mean what I said. It was cruel. So yeah."

"It's fine," Rylan said, accepting my words eagerly. "We understand that you're stressed."

"Thanks."

Zig pushed a bowl toward me, flashing a soft grin.

Aven gave me a cold shoulder, which I returned only because I was petty.

And Farrah . . . Wait. Where was Farrah?

"Has anyone seen Farrah?" I asked, shoveling what counted as breakfast, a bowl of some kind of ground corn, into my mouth.

"She left the room early this morning," Zig said, nibbling a piece of bread.

"She asked for some gold, so I gave her a few pieces." He shrugged. "She might be getting supplies."

"We need supplies," Aven grumbled.

"So does Lord Ethan." I took another bite. The stuff kind of grew on me as I continued to eat. "A lot of his things burned in the fire. He'll have headed for the nearest town to regroup."

Rylan squinted. "Which is here. Right?"

"No," Aven said, rubbing a hand over their face. They looked tired. "He headed inland."

Farrah burst into the inn, her long hair disheveled for once. Her smile was as bright as the morning sun, her brown skin glowing with excitement and purpose.

"Here!" She slapped a parchment down on the table, the tips of her fingers stained with ink. It was a map.

"What is this?" I asked, sliding my bowl out of the way.

"It's a map!"

"We can see that," Aven said wryly.

"A map of the kingdom. I found it in one of the shops. And I added all the shortcuts I know." She beamed.

Rylan leaned over the table, his chest on the surface, his face right against the parchment. "Here is that river in the south that Lord Ethan talked about. I remember one of the"—he dropped his voice—"primordial dots being near there." He pushed the tip of his finger and made an indent with his nail. "Right there," he whispered.

"With Rylan's memory of the other map, and my knowledge of the kingdom, we don't even need to follow Lord Ethan. We can find our own way to the southern river and find the waterfall ourselves!"

Aven pulled the map closer to them and peered at the routes with their brow furrowed. "The towns and roads around the castle appear correct, which means this is an accurate rendering of the kingdom," they mused. "I think this could really help."

Zig raised an eyebrow. "So in theory we could even beat Lord Ethan there and find the invisible realm before him?"

"Yes!" Farrah bounced on her toes.

"What do you think, Ellinore?" Aven asked.

What *did* I think? I wasn't sure. My judgment was *off*. I'd done what I thought Ellinore the Brave would do at the campsite, and I'd lost the map. I'd almost lost my friends and myself in a *fire*.

Lord Ethan may have been the worst quester ever, but he was better than me right now. He'd had the map for a whole day and had an entire retinue of squires and guards who could assist him with deciphering it. He held all the cards, and I had a group that included the second-best quester in the land, my gregarious brother, a noble girl who had barely ever left the castle, and a mage with weak magic and a penchant for writing songs.

"I think," I said slowly, "that we only have nine days remaining and we're right back where we started. Our best chance is following Lord Ethan. It's still the safest course of action. Just for a day or so, to ensure he *is* heading in that direction. What if we went south and he suddenly took a turn north?"

Farrah's face fell. Rylan shrunk back in his seat. Zig cocked his head to the side, eyeing me with a frown. Aven pushed their bowl away and stood.

"I'll ready the mounts and make sure we have enough supplies."

"Wait! Aven!" I stood and reached to grab their arm, to stop them from leaving. I didn't want them to be angry with me. But at Aven's fierce expression, I stopped mid-motion, my fingers outstretched, almost brushing the fabric of their tunic.

Aven glanced down at my healed hand. And I could see their thoughts in the clench of their jaw. Our deal from the night before.

My stomach knotted. But Aven said nothing.

"I'll go with," Zig said, jumping up, breaking the tension.

They walked out.

That left me alone with Farrah and Rylan. I sat down and gulped water from my cup and wiped the dribbles from my mouth with my sleeve. Farrah and Rylan were gracious enough not to ask what that was all about. So I carried on. "I really appreciate your initiative with finding the map, Farrah. And I know you both mean well. It's just . . . he's my brother."

Rylan nodded in understanding.

Farrah sighed. "We get it."

"Look," I said. "I know what I said last night was borderline mean, but you two have to realize, questing isn't always fun. It's not like in the tales."

Rylan perked up at that, eyes wide, and oh, I was going to regret that later.

"And it's not always adventure-type things either, like battling salamanders or surviving a cave-in. Sometimes it's boring. And more often than not, it's gross. And sometimes it's making the hard and unpopular decisions." I grimaced. "Whatever romantic notion you have, temper it, then add, like, ten times more sweat and bucketloads of mysterious goo."

Rylan nodded like his head was on a string. Farrah raised her chin.

"I know from the songs it sounds like you can hack your way through the world with a sword and that's the best and only way to do things. That's what guys like Lord Ethan think. It's what they do." I took a breath. "But it doesn't have to be like that. It *shouldn't* be like that."

Farrah frowned. "Like the fire salamanders. You only used enough force to defend us, and then we ran."

"Yes. Exactly."

"But the bards' tales," Rylan said, brow furrowed.

I rubbed my forehead with my fingers, a headache burgeoning behind my eyes. "You weren't wrong in believing that not all the facts are completely accurate."

He snapped his fingers. "I knew it! You promised to—"

"Yes. I did, and I'll keep my word." I grimaced again. "Maybe not in front of Aven. If we can avoid it."

Farrah's eyebrows shot up, and her smile pulled into a teasing grin. "Oh. Something *did* happen in the cave."

I straightened from my slump. "What do you mean by that? Did Aven say something?"

Farrah merely smiled brightly.

"Thank you for explaining everything, Ellinore." She rolled the map up, then tucked it into the bag at her side. "I'm going to get ready."

Rylan stood. "Yeah, me too."

"Wait . . . what?"

Farrah laughed. Rylan squeezed my shoulder in a friendly gesture as he passed.

And then I was alone. I closed my eyes and thought of the child who had accidentally defeated an ancient, and wished she'd never taken up that sword at all. But then she'd . . . *I'd* be dead, so that wouldn't be great either.

A faint strum of strings broke the silence of the inn. "And now it's time to listen to the story of the mighty Ellinore at the start of her glory."

"Oh my ancients, no." I abandoned the remainder of my breakfast and left.

We rode out shortly thereafter. Zig and Aven had replenished the supplies we needed for travel, so our saddlebags were fairly bursting. I led our group, the others dropping back to ride behind. Rylan still rode with Zig, his lute strapped to his back. Farrah rode next to Aven, which was an odd pairing, as they continued to snipe at each other over trivial things.

I'd been frozen out. My outburst the night before had done its damage. As did my decision to continue trailing after Lord Ethan's retinue. It . . . surprisingly hurt. But no matter. This gave me what I'd wanted in the beginning—quiet so that I could think about our next steps and ultimately complete the quest.

We stopped in the next town to confirm Lord Ethan had been there. It was easy. We merely asked if a man with a winged horse on his chest had strutted around like a peacock, flashing a sigil of nobility and demanding things, which he had, and then we found his trail.

We continued on, heading inland, crossing over a slow river late in the afternoon. The grassy plains of the flatland stretched out before us much like an ocean. Long stems swayed in the breeze, brushing against our legs. The land hummed with the sound of insects and the whistle of the breeze through the long stalks. The fragrance of wildflowers wafted from patches of blooming bright blue, deep purple, and a blushing pink. The birds chirped and squawked as we passed, some following to see if we'd throw food, others flitting from small clusters of saplings, mostly short serviceberry trees and the occasional fruit tree.

Lord Ethan's group was much larger than our own, and their trail cut a swath through the empty land. They moved slower due to needing more supplies and pack animals than we did. We'd catch up with them within a few hours if we kept at our pace. Not that I wanted to catch up. I wanted to stay half a step behind. I didn't want them to know we were following. Lord Ethan thought I was defeated. I didn't want to disavow him of that notion.

Aven moved beside me and shielded their eyes from the bright sun. "Do you see that?"

"Oh, you're talking to me now?"

They frowned. "I've been talking to you."

"Not since last night."

"Well, maybe there is a reason for that."

"Oh? Really? Are you suddenly allergic to apologies?"

Aven sniffed. "Only insincere ones."

I pulled my horse to a stop. "What? Insincere? What are you even talking about?"

Mouse paused next to me, bringing Aven and me eye to eye. "The fact that you lied."

I froze. Uh-oh. Which lie were they referring to? Because there were many of varying degrees of severity. "I have no idea what you mean."

"Uh . . . Ellinore? Aven?" Rylan asked, voice soft.

"No idea what I'm referencing, huh?"

"Yeah, no idea."

"Of course."

"Now, what does *that* mean?"

Zig cleared his throat. "Hey, Ellinore?"

"Never mind. It must not be important enough for you to remember."

I threw up my hands. "Aven, I don't know what part of my apology was insincere, but I apologize for that, too."

"Oh, nice. Insincerity on top of insincerity."

"Can you just speak plainly?"

"Guys!" Farrah yelled.

"What?" Aven and I yelled back in unison.

She pointed at the sky. "What's that?"

I snapped my head around. A large, dark cloud undulated in waves several lengths in front of us. I squinted and leaned forward in my saddle. Upon closer inspection it appeared to be a flock of birds, flying on an updraft, then diving back down, moving in agitated unison. But they were small for most local fowl, about the size of insects, and the sound of their wings buzzed over the landscape. My eyes tracked to where they hovered above a large grove of flowering bushes and plants, the bright crimson of buds stark in the distance and . . . oh no.

"Are they . . . coming toward us?" Zig asked.

"Turn your mounts," I yelled. "Follow me."

I made certain that Farrah and Zig had heard me before I took off, knowing Aven would be right next to me, but it was too late. We'd galloped only a length before the cloud descended upon us, and we were enveloped in a swarm of pixies.

They were tiny creatures, about the size of butterflies, and they usually weren't aggressive unless disturbed.

The mass swooped down, the number so dense, they blocked out the sun. Hundreds of them zipped like hummingbirds over us and around us, bumping into one another as they crowded the sky and the ground. Their little blue and purple bodies smacked into our mounts and our saddlebags, moving so quickly, they were streaks of indigo and silver.

Our horses whinnied and huffed, stomping in circles, rearing and shaking their heads. I yanked Bluebell to a halt so she wouldn't bump into any of the others as the mounts panicked in the chaos. The low visibility made it difficult to discern the surrounding area, increasing the likelihood of a misstep. The hum of the pixies' wings filled the air with white noise, vibrating in our eardrums, disorienting as it drowned out all other sounds.

The pixies crawled over everything—my brother, my friends, our mounts, the ground. Farrah yelped as they pulled her hair, plucking out the ornate pins, burrowing into the thick strands. They ripped the feathers from Aven's arrows, tugged on their golden earrings, climbed into their quiver and under the hem of their tunic. They strummed Rylan's lute, ducking into the sound hole, wooden thumps emanating from inside. They pulled cards from Zig's sleeves, pushing their way up his arms, deeper into the fabric.

They hovered over me, but even the most curious only came within a few inches before darting away to join the others.

"Get off me!" Farrah shrieked, her voice cutting through the interminable buzz. She batted them with her staff, knocking a few away, but as soon as she did, others took their place. "Ow! One bit me!"

"If we're aggressive toward them, they'll be aggressive in return!" I yelled.

"More aggressive than they're already acting?" Aven shot back.

Mouse reared, and Aven held on by the skin of their teeth, the pixies agitating Mouse's mane and tail. Aven covered their head with their arms, trying to prevent even more from crawling into their hair and tunic.

"What do we do?" Zig asked, swatting at them, knocking several away. "If we can't fight them—ow, ancients, their teeth are sharp!—are we supposed to let them crawl all over us?"

"I'm thinking!"

Rylan pulled off his lute and shook it, several pixies falling out, hitting the strings with their wings, causing discordant sounds amid all the humming. Then he started taking swings with the instrument to keep them away, with little result, only succeeding in almost braining Zig several times.

"Rylan! You almost hit me!"

"Ow! Ow! Ow!" Farrah shrieked.

Aven tugged on Mouse's reins. "Can we outrun them?"

We could if we were careful. But there had to be a reason why they were swarming like this. Pixies were normally docile creatures that minded their own business, tending flowers and fostering growth of bushes and trees. They even cared for animals—small rodents, birds, insects, and lizards.

"We don't need to fight or run. They're agitated," I shouted.

"Really?" Zig asked. "I hadn't noticed."

"But they're not usually dangerous."

Starlight bumped into Carrot, and the mule kicked back with both legs, grazing Starlight's side. Farrah yelped and gripped the pommel to stay saddled.

"Is this one of those not-hacking-our-way-through situations?" she asked.

"Yes! Exactly! Lord Ethan's trail cuts through that grove," I said, swiping my hand out to point toward the flowering bushes cresting the small hill a few minutes' gallop away. "Which means his entourage probably disturbed their nest."

"Is that why they're trying to burrow into my hair?" Farrah asked. She screeched suddenly and grabbed one from the collar of her blouse.

"We need to find the queen and put her back in their hive, and the rest will follow."

Aven maneuvered closer to my side, clinging to their horse's neck, wincing when a pixie yanked on their shining hoops. "How will we even do that?"

"Rylan," I shouted, "play a tune. Any tune."

He didn't answer but swung his lute around and started strumming a ballad I recognized. Thankfully, he didn't sing. But the music did what I thought it might. It cut through the noise, and the swarm calmed, the frenzy gradually slowing into a sway. The pixies didn't disperse, but they gave us a little distance and were no longer bumping into everyone and everything.

"Farrah."

She pulled another pixie from her hair. "Yes?"

"See those pink bushes? Ride over and look for a hole in the ground or a burrow in a tree. Somewhere that might be their original home."

"Oh. Okay. Got it." She knocked her heels against Starlight's sides and galloped off, a small portion of the swarm breaking off to follow her.

"Aven, you're used to finding small targets," I said, gesturing toward the pixie cloud. "Find the queen. She'll be wearing a crown."

"How do you even know about pixies? We never had a pixie quest!"

"Just do it! We can argue later!"

Aven sighed in disbelief, but they straightened to their full height in their saddle and shielded their eyes as they searched the pacified swarm. It took several minutes of peering into the group until they spotted her.

"Ha! I found her. There!"

I followed their line of sight. And there was the queen, flying in a daze. Her figure was slightly larger than the other pixies, her hair a stunning silver, her skin a deep purple. Her golden crown twinkled in the light. But one of her legs dangled at an awkward angle.

"Worst quester ever," I muttered. Lord Ethan should have known not to lead his group through what was obviously a pixie grove. He had hurt their queen, which had led to the whole frenetic horde. If we had been any other travelers, the pixies might have been hurt worse, or might even have hurt others.

"Zig. You have the quickest hands. Can you catch her?"

He rifled in his saddlebag and yanked out a tunic. He tied off the sleeves, fashioning it into a crude sack with a wide mouth. He slipped off the back of Carrot and positioned himself in the middle of the circling mass.

"Rylan," he whispered, gaze locked on the queen, "stop playing."

As soon as the last note faded, the vibrating energy of the swarm increased again, the buzz rising to a deafening level. The pixies swirled once more, diving toward us and the ground. The queen, though hovering in the middle of it all, bobbed downward in the chaos, close enough for Zig to catch her. It took Zig three tries, especially since pixies tried to climb up his sleeves again, but he captured her, as well as a few others, in the makeshift bag.

"I got her!"

"Hand her here," I said. He carefully offered me the bag with the queen, and I spurred Bluebell toward the grove.

The entire swarm followed, but once again they didn't dare fly too close to me, deterred by the magic of an ancient that radiated from the bracelet around my wrist.

Farrah stood in the grove, waving her hands above her head. "It's here! I found it here!"

As I'd thought, the pixies' hive was partially underground. The hooves of the horses and mules had collapsed the soil, forcing the pixies to fly out or be crushed. I jumped down from Bluebell, not wanting to add to the mess.

Farrah pointed toward the base of a small tree. "There," she said. "I think one of the entrances is in that hollow."

"Be careful, she's hurt," I said, holding the queen in my hand after extracting her from the tunic, the other trapped pixies flying off. She seemed to know she was safe, her purple body stretched the length of my fingers, her short wings fluttering, but not in an attempt to fly away.

Farrah's eyes widened in awe. "She's beautiful."

"She is," I agreed.

The scent of crushed flowers and disturbed earth was overwhelming as I knelt by the tree.

We placed her inside the hollow, and as soon as we did, some of the pixies burrowed into the soil, creating new tunnels and pathways to rebuild their underground kingdom. The others hovered around my shoulders and above my head, waiting.

"Go ahead and join the others," I said to Farrah. "I'm going to stay with her for a minute. Just to make sure she's okay."

Farrah led Starlight away, and once she was out of earshot, I pulled out the chain around my neck and shook the vial of healing potion. The queen would need little, so I offered the end of the wet cork to her.

"Here. This will help. It's from a dragon."

She propped herself on her elbows and took a sip from a drop pooling on the edge. Instantly, a small flash of magic burst from her body, and her broken leg straightened and healed.

"I'm sorry," I said. "For my fellow humans. They should've known better than to cut through your grove."

She flew up from the hollow, floating in front of my face. She darted close, kissed my cheek with a tinny giggle, then hovered in front of me. This close, I could see her tiny smile. Then she flew away, the remainder of the swarm following her into the tree.

24

"HOW DID YOU KNOW WHAT TO DO?" FARRAH ASKED AS WE SETTLED down in our camp for the night. A small campfire was already burning, and we'd had dinner from our rations and water from our canteens a few minutes prior. "That the pixies had been disturbed and that we just needed to help them?"

I laid out my bedroll and stretched along the thin material, sword within reach. I had already tried to spy Lord Ethan's fire in the growing dark, hoping to glimpse it in the middle of the flatland, but I hadn't. The event with the pixies had delayed us, so he was farther ahead than I wanted, but we'd catch up the next day, and we'd only need to stay on his tail for a while longer.

"A mixture of experience and fairy tales," I said. Which really meant a lot of listening to Dave talk about the old days, when magical ancients and folklores roamed the land and humans were few. "A little studying."

"You lied, though," Farrah said, tapping her chin.

Ugh. "Uh, what now?" I couldn't hide my exasperation. Being accused of lying when I was actually being truthful about some things (while still lying about others) was growing tedious.

"There was no mysterious goo," she said with a mischievous grin.

I blinked, then smiled. "Next time."

"I'll take first watch," she said, standing from her own bedroll near the fire, quarterstaff in her hand. "Someone told me that adventuring isn't only about the fun things. Sometimes it's about the boring stuff, so I'm first."

"I'll go second," Rylan volunteered before I could say anything.

Aven brushed past me to sit against a tree near the fire. "Third."

Huh. Okay. I guessed that meant I didn't need to stand a watch that night. That was . . . kind of nice.

I flopped onto my bed, tucking my arm behind my head, and relaxed.

Rylan had his lute across his lap, strumming the strings, and I didn't have the heart to tell him to stop.

"We worked well together today," he said, plucking out a melody. "It was neat how Ellinore told us what to do."

Zig leaned on Rylan's shoulder, stars in his eyes. "We *did* work well, didn't we?"

I wanted to puke. My brother was besotted.

"You hear all the stories about how Ellinore the Brave vanquished this or beat that or shoved her sword through another thing. It was nice to help instead." Rylan shook his lute, something dinging around on the inside. "I think one of those pixies left something in here."

I laughed quietly. But Rylan was right. I hadn't thought about what Ellinore the Brave would do at all during that encounter. I'd acted on instinct, on what I knew. I hadn't second-guessed myself or tried to be who I thought Aven wanted me to be or what the bards had portrayed me as. It had all come naturally, and it had worked out in the end. The pixies were safe. No one in our party was hurt, other than a few superficial bites and scratches. And we had emerged victorious.

For the first time in days I felt . . . hopeful. Like maybe we had a chance. That we could still save Zig.

I stretched my arms over my head and caught Aven observing me.

"Are you finally going to tell me what I did wrong that you're so mad at me about?" I asked.

Aven frowned. "You lied."

Ah, there went that good feeling. "So you've said. But I still don't understand."

Their shoulders rose and fell with a sigh as they watched the flames of our campfire. "When you apologized, you said you didn't mean the things you yelled at us about our motives for why we were on the quest. But you *meant* them. And you weren't wrong."

I gulped. "I wasn't?"

"No. Farrah wanted an adventure, and Rylan wanted to write a song. You shouldn't apologize for pointing that out."

They conveniently left out their own motive of reporting to the king, and while I wanted to know why, I bit my tongue. They were finally talking to me without venom behind their words, and I'd rather have that at the moment than an answer.

"Oh."

"You *should* apologize for shouting and for not realizing that those weren't our *only* motives. But I wouldn't want you to say sorry for calling us out and doing your best to protect your brother. I . . . don't want . . . You shouldn't diminish yourself for anyone else. Especially not me."

"Oh," I said, softer.

"And I think I can safely say that we all want to help however we can. That we want to save Zig, too."

Why did they have to be so *perfect*? I'd always been physically attracted to Aven, and I liked that they bickered with me, but why did they also have a good heart? Why couldn't they be . . . heinous? Or a selfish noble like the ones I'd encountered in the castle? Or vaguely callous like the king and queen? It would help save my own heart from stuttering all the time.

"And that's why you wouldn't speak to me for half a day? For my own good?"

Aven shrugged. "I also don't like liars."

And my heart stopped spluttering. It stopped altogether as fear and guilt gripped it. I cleared my throat. "Any particular reason?" *Hypocrite,* I wanted to tack onto the end, but again I restrained myself. Because, of the two of us, I was the bigger liar. I was certain of that. And if the secret they had would jeopardize Zig, then I didn't want to know.

They threw a twig into the fire. "Because I encounter them often in court. Even as the Pointless Princet"—I cringed when they spoke that awful moniker—"I still must be wary of people who want to be close to me. Just in case."

"Ah. I understand."

They propped their chin on the heel of their hand. "I don't mean you. I . . . haven't ever thought that about you."

No. Too earnest. Too intimate. Deflect. Deflect. "Good to know. And I'm glad that you've come around and want to save my brother and not just observe and learn from the greatness that is Ellinore the Brave."

Aven scoffed playfully. "And that's my cue to work on my arrows. Those pixies pulled off their fletching." They stood and walked away.

"And speaking of work," Rylan said, setting his lute aside. "I should study the scrap of cloth."

Zig woke from the half doze he'd been in on Rylan's shoulder. "Oh yeah." He removed it from his inner pocket and handed it over. Rylan inspected it with a furrowed brow and pinched mouth, then set it on the ground. He waved his hand over it, and that was when I decided not to watch.

If Rylan figured it out, that meant the candle would drop three marks.

We still had *days* of our journey remaining, even if I wasn't certain of how many exactly.

We were running out of time.

25

ை

"ELLINORE! ELLINORE!"

I jolted awake, instantly reaching for my sword. "What's happening?" I said, slurring. I sat up and shook my head, shaking off the clinging vestiges of sleep and dreams. "What's wrong?"

Farrah dropped next to my bed, giddy with excitement, her whole body vibrating.

"I have a plan!" She unrolled the map, setting stones at the edges that she had pulled from the pocket of her trousers to hold it in place. Then she paused, bottom lip sucked between her teeth.

Oh, she was waiting for permission. "I'm listening."

"Okay!" she shouted, then winced. "Sorry. I'm just excited."

"I can tell."

"So, Rylan, Zig, and I went over what we heard from Lord Ethan while we were prisoners in his camp. And all three of us remember the same things—a southern river and a waterfall. Before Lord Ethan stole the map from us, I did have a chance to look over it in the light of day. The key and the colored dots were faded, but there definitely was a dot in that direction."

She dug her broken nail into the map on a spot at the southwesternmost point of the kingdom, where a thin river flowed from a cluster of mountain peaks down to the sea.

"This is where we need to go," she reiterated. "This is where we are, approximately." She tapped a point a few inches outside the port town we'd left the day prior.

"Okay. And?"

"The most direct route from one point to the other is right through this forest." On the map were small symbols for trees that resembled triangles on sticks. The words *The Climbing Wood* were written in delicate cursive. "But Lord Ethan has a large retinue, and they won't be able to traverse it."

"They'll have to go around," I muttered, trailing my finger around the wood. To the south was a town and then a wide river; to the north was more forest. "But we could go through."

"And if we did, we would then cross this river at the narrowest spot"— she pointed to a skinny blue line directly on the other side of the wood—"while the winged-horse lord would have to cross at the widest. Our route would be the most direct path."

My heart lodged in my throat. "We'd beat them." To the waterfall. To the invisible realm. To the Elder Beast. I swallowed. "We could do it."

Farrah nodded. "I know a way."

I closed my eyes. I had only glimpsed the map, and I didn't remember much. But if Farrah was correct, then it would save us time, time that was ticking down. But I'd have to trust her expertise. I'd have to trust what Rylan and Zig supposedly heard and that it was correct. I'd have to trust that she knew the way. I'd already established that my judgment during this quest was off, skewed in some way. Thinking and planning like Ellinore the Brave wasn't working. Maybe I should lean on the judgment of others?

"You knew about the outcropping over the Simmer."

"I did."

I opened my eyes. "Are you certain?"

"I am."

"Will you bet my brother's life on it?"

Farrah glanced over her shoulder to where Zig and Rylan were readying Carrot. She nodded sharply. "I will."

"Okay," I said, voice a whisper. "Okay."

Farrah beamed. She rolled the map tightly. "I promise you won't regret this." Then she scurried off to tell the others.

Once everyone was busy, I reached into my bag and pulled out the magic countdown. The candle flickered, drips of wax running down the sides, pooling on the two-dimensional table where it sat. It had burned another mark away.

"Are you ready, Ellinore?" Aven asked.

I shoved the candle into my bag. "Almost."

Aven raised an eyebrow and crossed their arms over their chest. They were wearing the long tunic today, the hem falling past their knees, with splits up the middle and back to allow for riding. It was black with red stitching, the colors of the kingdom's banners. They had black trousers on beneath, and their shiny boots. "Are we really trying to beat Lord Ethan?"

My mouth went dry, so I nodded, not trusting I wouldn't squeak.

"Good. I think it's a smart plan."

"You do?"

"Yeah. It's good to see you . . . having faith in someone." The edges of Aven's lips twitched into a smile. "Also, I never liked Lord Ethan much. Pompous jerk. I want to defeat him almost as much as you do."

"Is that any way for a royal to speak about their vassal? Tsk, tsk."

Aven's smile broke free. And how I'd missed it the past few days. "I won't tell if you won't."

"Cross my heart, hope to . . ." I trailed off. "Hope to make it through the forest and to the Elder Beast."

"Nice save."

I laughed. "Thanks. Are you ready?"

Aven took a drink from their canteen. "Yeah. Let's go piss off a lord."

26

WE REACHED THE FOREST BY MIDDAY.

If I had known that the Climbing Wood on the map was referencing what I knew as the *Haunted* Forest, I might not have agreed to this course of action. "Might" was doing a lot of heavy lifting. I would have said no. Absolutely, unequivocally no. Because according to legends, this wasn't an ordinary forest.

The trees loomed in front of us. Their trunks were thick, larger than the girth of my horse, and they butted against one another closely enough that they left little room for passage. Their leaves created a canopy so thick, the ground was in constant shade, almost comparable to the Dark Wood. But while the Dark Wood housed a small number of man-eating spiders, this forest was said to house things much more sinister.

I had explored most of the continent, but I had never walked beyond the barrier of this wood. I had avoided it at all costs. Even Dave didn't dare to fly over it, instead choosing the longer way around. Because it was haunted or cursed or plagued or blighted or whatever word the locals used. There was something *wrong* with it, and not in an it's-just-misunderstood way. Ominous eeriness seeped from the edges, literally, as a rolling fog crept along the ground at the periphery.

Aven paused beside me, reining Mouse next to Bluebell. "Oh," they said. "I didn't realize—"

"Me either."

They gulped. "Are we going in? Or should we go south to the village?"

"What?" I asked, my voice as shaky as theirs had been. "Are you scared of ghost stories?"

"No. I'm scared of ghosts. Actual ghosts. You know what lurks in there, right?"

"What *does* lurk in there?" Zig called. He hunched over the neck of Carrot, patting the mule absently.

"Things," I said. "It's not called the Haunted Forest for nothing."

Rylan looked suddenly as if he might faint. "This is the Haunted Forest?" he said, pointing a trembling finger. "I thought it was the Climbing Wood."

Farrah had the map out across the pommel of her saddle. "It's the Climbing Wood on the map. That's strange."

"The Climbing Wood may be its official name, but that is certainly not what the locals call it," Aven said.

"Climbing Wood, Haunted Forest. It doesn't matter," I said, waving my hands. This was no time to question. I had to trust my gut . . . well, Farrah's gut. And I, ancients help me, trusted Farrah. "We're going in as soon as Farrah finds the path. If she can't locate it in a reasonable amount of time, we'll head south and hope to—"

"There it is!"

Ack.

Farrah triumphantly rolled the map and slid it into her saddlebag. She hummed. "I wonder why we didn't see it when we first approached? Maybe the branches hid it."

"Or," Aven said, whispering into my ear, "it opened for us and is coaxing us inside to kill us and eat our corpses as they sink into the ground."

Goose bumps popped up along my arms. "What is with you?" I asked. "Are you really afraid? Of a forest?"

Aven lifted their chin. "I'm allowed to be afraid. I am a bit . . . scared of ghosts. Happy?"

"Not really, since I'm counting on you to remain calm while we are in there!"

"What? Does Ellinore the Brave not have fears?"

"I do. And it's watching my brother die." I slid off my saddle and gathered Bluebell's reins in my hand.

The path was narrow, the mouth of it the widest section before it disappeared into the darkness of the trees. We would have to lead our mounts single file. Aven paled as they dismounted from Mouse, almost as if they were about to faint, and they stood beside me, peering into the crushing gloom. I moved closer and nudged them with my shoulder.

"Hey," I said, voice low, my head tipped toward theirs. "If you really don't want to go in here, I can order you to ride south and look for Lord Ethan and his entourage at the town. The others don't have to know."

They took a deep breath. "No. I'm okay. Really."

"Aven, I don't want to force you to do something that you don't want to do."

"It's okay. No time like the present to face your ultimate childhood fear that is deeply rooted in your subconscious."

Oh ancients.

"Okay." I squeezed Aven's hand. They squeezed back. "Rylan?" I called.

He dismounted from Carrot. "Yes?"

"We need torches. Magical torches."

"Oh. Okay. Yes. I can do that."

"Great." I clapped my hands. "We're going in. Aven and I will lead. And you three will follow. Stay right behind Bluebell."

We hitched Bluebell to Mouse, and Carrot to Starlight. The trio would lead Starlight, which meant Zig would be in the middle, the most protected.

I held the magical torch above my head, peering into the gloom as we stood on the edge of the path. Aven tangled one hand in Mouse's reins and held their bow in the other, quiver on their back. Though I don't know what they thought an arrow would do to a ghost.

"Ready?" I asked with a trembling grin.

"If I die," they said, glaring at me, "I'm going to be very upset."

I patted their shoulder. "You'll be fine. I'll be right with you."

They heaved a sigh. "Fine. Let's go."

Entering the forest was an experience that I did not want to repeat. Ever. Again.

Aven walked through the barrier first, into the rolling mist, and disappeared in the dark, as if the shadows swallowed them up.

I took a breath, centered myself, gripped my sword with one hand and my torch with the other.

I stepped through.

The forest engulfed me. On the other side my torch flickered, the light of the magic flames barely penetrating the dimness.

From what I could see of the narrow path, it wound thinly through the trees. I hoped our horses would be able to traverse it.

"Ellinore?" Farrah called, her voice muted in the thick atmosphere and the weight of the shadows.

"We're up here."

"We're right behind you!"

I twisted to peer behind Bluebell, where their two torches bobbed. "Let's go," I said with a nod to Aven, who looked like they were going to be sick.

The pace of our procession was agonizingly slow. The path was treacherous, full of gnarled roots, snaking vines, and scratching branches. The more we walked, the more I learned to keep my gaze locked on the path in front of me, for every time I glanced at either side of us, I saw a terrifying shape in the darkness, or a bobbing ball of green light, or movement within the shadows.

The forest knew we were here, and it tracked our progress.

Time warped. It felt like we'd been trekking for hours, while also seeming like we hadn't moved at all. The plods of the horses' hooves were deadened thumps. The grunts and curses of the others faded to whispers when they reached me, though I was only a step ahead. The very air was oppressive, pressing down on my knotted shoulders.

I glanced back, trying to see if I could view our entrance for any kind of reference point, but all that was there was the stretching dark, the trail we'd walked gone, overgrown and taken back by the forest. Vines appeared as if they slithered along the ground. A large blur streaked across the path, silent as the grave, despite running over bracken.

My throat tightened with fear. I strangled my sword in my grip, the leather creaking under my fingers.

"Ellinore," Aven's voice sounded, as if on a breeze.

"Yeah?"

"Are you . . . seeing things?"

"Yes."

Aven's breath left in a whoosh. "Good. I mean . . . I'm glad I'm not the only one."

"Yeah. Hooray! I'm a partner in your misery." Even treading through a creepy forest, I couldn't help but poke at Aven. Teasing was my love language.

"That's not what I meant!"

"Sounds like what you meant."

They huffed in annoyance. "Even in a haunted wood, surrounded by ghosts, you can't help yourself, can you?"

"No."

Aven groaned. "I don't even know why I li—"

A growl sounded in front of us, low and menacing.

We stopped in our tracks and our teasing. Aven immediately nocked an arrow. I held my sword at the ready and lifted the torch, revealing a massive black dog. Its shoulders were easily the height of my own, and its fur was made of wisps of curling shadow. Its glowing red eyes glared at us as it released a warning growl, unveiling rows of yellowed, razored fangs.

The hair on my arms stood on end as I readied myself, gulping down my terror, adjusting the grip on my sword. Aven trembled beside me.

The beast stepped forward.

It left no paw print or tracks even with its substantial size.

"Hey! Why did we stop?" Zig yelled from behind us.

"Aven needed to retie their boot strings," I called back.

"Well, hurry up! I thought I heard a growl or something."

He wasn't wrong.

I shuffled closer to Aven, not daring to take my eyes from the dog but unsure of what to do. Ellinore the Brave would attack, would not wait for the beast to make the first move, would give it no chance. But Ellinore the Brave's decisions had really sucked the past few days. The real Ellinore knew that sometimes pixies only needed help and that dragons didn't want to die over bad jokes and dead sheep.

I didn't move. The ghost dog growled again, the sound of it so low, it vibrated through the ground, into the soles of my boots, and up into my body, rattling the trees as well as my bones. But the dog didn't advance. If it had wanted, it could've torn through us and the horses by now. But it hadn't. Instead it waited.

"I don't think it's going to hurt us," I whispered. "I've read before about forest guardians, and I think it may be one."

Aven didn't respond. Their body was drawn tight, muscles locked, their bowstring taut. I could only glimpse their profile, but they seemed . . . scared.

"Aven," I said softly. I gently rested my hand on their shoulder, which was a giant mistake.

They startled and released the arrow. It flew from their bow with a twang, and if the dog had been corporeal, Aven would have shot it right between the eyes. As it was, the arrow passed through it and embedded in a tree deeper in the forest.

The dog growled, louder this time, and hunched down, coiled as if ready to attack. Trees of the forest shook around us, bending toward us, the spindly branches reaching out as if to pull us off the path. Vines crawled along the ground, closer to Aven's legs. Howling erupted in the distance. The beat of leathery wings filtered down from above. The rolling mist gathered, muted my already-dim torchlight, and hid the path in front of us until only the barghest was visible.

"What's happening?" Zig shrieked in the distance.

"Ellinore!" Farrah yelled.

I craned my neck, and the two torches were barely as bright as glow bugs. "Stay together! It's okay!"

The forest was alive . . . literally. And Aven had been correct—we were going to be sucked into the earth, and our corpses would be eaten by trees or bats or whatever else called the woods home. Unless I did something.

Aven staggered back as roots pulled from the earth and lurched toward them.

I jumped in front of Aven, my arms outstretched, the tip of my sword pointed toward the ground. The roots recoiled but remained ready to attack.

"They didn't mean to do it," I said to the ghost dog. "It was a mistake. We're very sorry. We ask for your forgiveness."

The dog didn't rise from its attack crouch, but it didn't jump and rend our flesh, either. My heart thumped hard in my ears, but I had an idea. If I was wrong, it would end in my very messy death, but that might happen anyway.

I took a breath and I bowed. I'd done weirder things in my life. But if the dog was the ghostly guardian of the forest, that meant it garnered respect. It was only manners.

I kicked Aven in the shin, and they hastily followed. "I'm sorry," they murmured. "I meant no harm. Honestly."

After a year-long minute, the dog barked.

I straightened, and though the ghost dog was still as terrifying as before, it wagged its tail. The mist receded. The trees swayed back to their original positions. The echo of bat wings faded as they flew away.

"We would like to pass through your forest," I said as politely as possible. "We want nothing from you or your friends. Only safe passage to the other side."

The dog tilted its head, red eyes assessing us. It yipped in what I could only conclude was agreement.

It stepped from the path, and the forest reshaped around its paws. Trees bent and twisted, bracken parted and cleared, vines slipped away. It peered with glowing eyes over its shoulder, and the ghost dog yipped again.

"You want me to follow you?"

It moved forward, the woods parting, the route opening and widening substantially, allowing the others to join us at the front and the mounts to traverse the wood comfortably. Well, that seemed to be a good sign.

"We're moving," I called to the group behind us.

They maneuvered themselves and the mounts so they could walk with us. Zig was at my side instantly. "Are we following a ghost dog out of here?" he asked.

"Yes."

"Oh, thank the ancients. I think I speak for all of us when I say I would like to be out of the creepy forest now."

The dog walked on, the forest bending to its will with every step it took. In what felt like no time at all, I spied the light of day peeking beyond the perimeter of the wood, though I imagined that had more to do with how time warped in the haunted wood, rather than how far we were from the edge.

But before we reached the exit, the dog stopped at the bottom of a tall flowering tree. It tilted its head and looked up toward the branches and whined. I stepped closer and peered upward, and spotted a large leather ball.

"You want us to get down your ball?" I asked.

The ghost dog wagged its tail.

"Why can't you just get the tree to shake it out?"

At my question, the tree wiggled, but the ball was firmly stuck between the trunk and two thick branches.

"Okay. I guess I can—"

The dog butted its head against my leg, which nearly knocked me over, and barked. It grabbed the edge of my trousers with its teeth and pulled me away from the tree trunk.

Then it barked at Aven.

Ah. This was Aven's penance for shooting the arrow.

"Oh," they said. "I don't know if I can climb a tree."

The tree offered a low branch and Aven sighed. "I can't believe I'm doing this," they grumbled as they hopped on the branch and grabbed another for support as the tree assisted them with climbing.

"Are we really watching your rival-slash-situationship climb a tree and retrieve a leather ball for a ghost dog in a haunted forest?" Zig asked. He rubbed his eyes. "Or am I dreaming?"

"No," I said with a laugh. "This is happening."

"This has been so fun," Farrah said, clapping her hands. "In hindsight. While I was living it, it was too scary. But now? It's great!"

Rylan scratched the back of his neck. "I wouldn't say 'fun,'" he said. "But it will be amazing for the song."

Within a few minutes, Aven was able to wiggle the ball loose and toss it down, much to the dog's delight. It wagged its tail and hopped after the ball, like a puppy at play. The tree assisted Aven with their descent, and once their feet hit the forest floor, they cleared their throat.

"Let's just get out of here," they said, tone low, sounding defeated.

It was almost sunset when the edge of the forest came into view and we could see the sky beyond the shadows. The forest guardian paused a few feet from the demarcation, and I stood next to it as Aven and the others crossed the barrier into the light. Farrah curtsied in her wide trousers as she passed. Zig gave me an incredulous look, his hand tangled in Carrot's reins. Rylan smiled widely and waved.

"Thank you again," I said to our new friend. "I appreciate your help."

The dog whined and leaned into my side, its head knocking against my shoulder. I laughed and scratched behind its ear, its fur surprisingly soft for a ghost. It licked my hand, then picked up its ball and bounded into the trees. Huh. Well. We'd survived the Haunted Forest.

Good job, us.

27

ONCE WE STEPPED OUTSIDE THE TREE LINE, I TOOK A HUGE, RELIEVED BREATH.

Farrah danced over to me, staff in her hand. "Hold still," she said, reaching up and tugging on my hair. "Here," she said, holding out a small pink flower. "A souvenir from our harrowing experience."

I laughed. And immediately handed it to Aven. "For you," I said, offering the flower with a flourish. "For bravery in the face of a ghost."

Aven took the flower with a thin press of their lips.

"Come on," they said, clearing their throat. "I want to cross the river before we camp, so we don't have as far to travel tomorrow."

Sometimes I didn't know when to stop teasing. "Admit you just want to be as far as you can from the Haunted Forest before you sleep tonight."

Rylan raised his hand. "I admit it."

Zig shook his head. "I mean, we did almost get eaten at one point. I don't think Aven has a monopoly on wanting to be as far away from it as possible."

Aven gave a half-hearted smirk, but I could see there was no humor in it. "See? Everyone agrees. For once."

"I don't," Farrah said, raising her hand. "I don't think it's haunted. I think it's misunderstood."

I bit down on a laugh.

Shaking my head, I brushed past the group. "Anyway. Let's cross the river."

Compared with previous experiences of crossing rivers, this time was surprisingly easy. We found a spot to camp on the other side, in a meadow at the base of a small hill. Aven volunteered for the first watch and disappeared shortly after in the dark.

The three others were busy recounting their harrowing journey in the forest for Rylan's song. So I ducked away to find Aven, wanting to apologize for my teasing and make sure they were okay.

I found them leaning by a spindly tree, near where we'd tied the mounts, the leather journal in their hand. They carefully opened the pages and slipped something inside, though I couldn't make out what because of the turn of their body. But the leather cover matched the one they'd saved from Lord Ethan's camp.

"Hey," I called softly.

Aven startled, their shoulders jumping. They snapped the journal shut and tucked it away. "Oh, hey."

I joined them at the apex of the hill, where we could look out at the area surrounding us. We'd been traveling across flat plains as we moved inland, away from the coast, but once we'd left the forest, the land had become hilly as we approached where the map showed a potential waterfall. If everything went according to plan, we'd find the Elder Beast sometime tomorrow and the quest would be done. With little time to spare, as the marks would tick down to seven remaining.

"Writing down our latest adventure for the king?" I asked. "And how the forest wanted to, and I quote, 'kill us and eat our corpses as they sink into the ground'?"

"No."

Aven took a breath and squeezed their eyes shut, as if preparing to face down a knight in a joust instead of talking to me.

"I have to tell you something," they said, clenching the journal in their hands. "But first, I want to apologize for today. I shot that arrow and almost killed us all."

My heart skipped a beat. Were they going to tell me *the* secret? I swallowed down the tightness in my throat. If it was going to change my perception of them, then I didn't want to know.

"Well," I said, pulling at a loose thread on the hem of my tunic, "it was your turn. I think the last almost-life-ending mistake was when I started a whole forest fire trying to retrieve a map."

Aven opened their eyes and stared at me. "What?"

"Before that, we almost all fell into a boiling river. And before that, we almost got killed by a feral faery." I shrugged. "But who's keeping track?"

Aven's brow furrowed. "I almost pulled you into the river. I was the one who told you to wait for Rylan to fix the cave-in with magic, which led to the kidnapping. I shot the arrow that made Lord Ethan stumble and drop the torch, and I almost just got us killed now because I was frightened of a ghost dog."

"Look, neither of us can be blamed for that cave-in fiasco. That is solely on Rylan's great-grandfather. And the fire salamanders was—"

"Farrah," we said in unison.

"The rest was all circumstance."

They shook their head, strands of their black hair hanging in their face. "Don't make excuses for me, Ellinore."

"I'm not! Seriously. I never would have made it this far without you." I threw up my hands helplessly. "Everything *I've* accomplished on this trip has been due to luck and timing."

They rubbed their forehead. "That's somehow even worse."

"Oh, come on. You saved Zig in the cave-in. You kept your head when we lost the map and pulled me back from the brink. I would've died in that fire. Ancients, I would've died at least three times during that fight alone."

"It's not good enough." They crossed their arms over their chest. "I've worked so hard to overcome the Pointless Princet mantle. To prove myself, and I just . . . It's never enough."

My heart hurt to hear it. Because I knew the truth about my success, the deception of it all. They didn't, so they were holding themself against a false metric. The truth tasted awful as it sat on my tongue, and I wanted to spit it out, to tell them. But I couldn't risk it. Not when we were so close to the end. But maybe . . . when we were done, and I was retired again. And I had a place to flee afterward.

So I settled for a different truth. "You're the best person I know."

"That's not—"

"It is. It is true."

"You must not know many people."

"Truthfully, I don't." They huffed in weary amusement. "But I do know that for all the people in that castle, you're the kindest, most gracious, nicest even when you don't have to be. When you probably shouldn't be. I . . . admire that about you." I shuffled awkwardly, looking around the landscape so as not to meet their eyes. "So there."

"Thanks," they said quietly.

"You're welcome." The silence stretched, an uneasy tension building between us, as Aven shifted, their eyes darting between the dark landscape and my boots. The strain was unbearable, but I . . . I didn't want to leave. I wanted to bask in Aven's presence for a while longer, no matter how uncomfortable it became, because the next day it could all change.

I scuffed the heel of my boot in the grass. "Now that's out of the way, are you going to show me what you've written about me in that journal?"

Aven paled in the low, flickering light. "The journal?"

"Yeah. I assume it's the notes you're going to tell the king."

Aven's fingers flexed around the leather cover. They licked their lips. "I . . . the king . . ."

"What?"

"The king didn't really send me. There's no royal order."

I stilled. "What?"

Aven winced. "I heard about the quest. And I came of my own volition. I made up the story about the king because I couldn't tell you the real reason I wanted to join."

"Ah. So that's the secret Farrah has been teasing you about."

They nodded. "She knew I lied. As you said, the king and queen are ruling an entire kingdom; a random quest isn't high on their list of concerns, even if it involves Ellinore the Brave."

Aven's reveal was a little underwhelming. I mean, I was hiding a whole dragon. What's a little white lie to join someone on a quest? Except, well, having Aven along did influence my decision-making—thinking about their perception of me the whole time, trying to live up to the stories in real time. But I wasn't wrong earlier; Aven had saved me several times. And without them, there was no telling what would've happened with Lord Ethan or if I would ever have found Rylan or the map.

"So . . . what's the real reason you came? To prove yourself?"

Aven released a breathy laugh. They ran their hand through their hair, then tugged on one of their earrings. "I came because I had to see you again."

Oh. That was . . . not what I was expecting. "What?" I asked weakly.

"Are you upset?" they asked, far too timid for themself.

"Upset? No. I'm confused."

They made a high, indignant noise before flipping through the journal, landing on a page, and thrusting it at me.

"Here."

The leather cover was worn, smooth as if it was frequently handled, the pages made of stiffer parchment than a scroll. I stared down at the paper in bewilderment.

"It's a flower." A single yellow flower, perfectly pressed and preserved.

"Yes."

"Okay?"

Aven fidgeted. "Flip the page."

I did as I was told, the thick edges of the leaf digging into my fingertips. It was two flowers this time—blue and white.

Still confused, I went to the next. The flower from the tree in the Haunted Forest was pressed between the pages, still fresh, the crush of the petals fragrant.

"What?"

"You've handed me a lot of bouquets over the years."

I snapped my head up.

They shrugged nonchalantly, but it didn't quite cover up their nervousness. "I know you meant it as a joke most of the time. All of the time. But you gave them to me, so they're special."

What?

"You accused me of only coming on this quest because of the king, which wasn't true," they hastily added. "But . . . ," they continued in a voice so quiet, I barely heard it over the hoots of the owls and the chirp of frogs, "but I just . . . when you retired, I realized I might not see you again. And I had to see you again, Ellinore. Even if it was one last time. Even if I couldn't convince you to return for the summer tournaments."

"You . . . you kept the flowers?"

Aven frowned in exasperation. "That was several sentences ago, Ellinore. Please keep up while I'm trying to tell you about how much I like you."

"I literally said you were the best person I knew, like, ten minutes ago, Aven."

"So?"

"So if that was not the biggest signal in the world to kiss me, then I don't know what would be!"

Without hesitation, they swooped in, pressing their lips to mine, their fingertips nervous and trembling as they slid along my jaw. My heart pounded. My mind went utterly blank. Aven kissed me! I was kissing Aven! Our mouths were touching in a romantic way!

Before my brain could even process, Aven pulled away.

The journal slipped from my hands, and I gripped the front of Aven's tunic and brought them close. They leaned in, and we kissed again.

I wasn't very experienced with kissing, but I could say that our second kiss was better than our first. And our third kiss was probably the best kiss in the history of kissing. Until our fourth, when Aven dropped their hands to my waist, and then again until our sixth, when I looped my arms around their shoulders and sank my fingers into their hair.

After our ninth or tenth, honestly, I began to lose count, because once we started neither of us made a move to stop. But at some point Aven gathered enough sense of responsibility and paused our kissing.

"I dropped the journal," I whispered.

"I'm supposed to be standing watch."

I blinked. Watch. Oh! Questing! The quest thing. Yes. That.

"Right."

They smirked. "You forgot, didn't you?"

"Shut up. No, I didn't."

"Admit it. The world disappeared while we kissed."

"And you call me arrogant."

"It's not arrogance when it's true."

"Yes, it is, and for the record—"

They kissed me again.

And yeah, they were not wrong. The world indeed ceased to exist beyond us, beyond where their lips touched mine, and all my worries about the quest, about my lies, about my life beyond the moment, faded away.

28

TODAY WAS THE DAY.

According to the map, we were almost to the reaches of the Southern Mountains and the waterfall that marked the entrance of the invisible realm of the Elder Beast. That should have been the only thing on my mind as I saddled Bluebell and readied our group to finish the quest.

It wasn't.

Aven's kisses were a solid second occupier of my thoughts. But we had agreed that whatever was to happen between us needed to wait until *after* I had the Elder Beast's horn in my hands and had freed Zig from the mages. Then we could talk.

It was nice to live in this pretend bubble, imagining a future with Aven. A future that would never really happen. Because when we eventually talked, I would have to tell the truth about . . . everything. But that was for future Ellinore to figure out. Present Ellinore had to focus on navigating the tricky terrain of the foothills.

"If we find the next river," Farrah said, trailing her finger over the map, "and follow it toward its source, we should find the waterfall."

I agreed. "That sounds like a good plan."

Farrah's eyes twinkled with pride as she grinned. "Yeah, it is."

I clapped my hands to get the group's attention. "Okay. Listen up, friends.

If the map is correct, we're finding that waterfall in a few hours. And as much as I hate to admit this, there is no way I'm going to defeat a primordial alone. So be ready when we get there. We'll need all capable hands."

Farrah gave me a determined nod, her fingers clutching her quarterstaff. Zig didn't look well, but he had the pilfered short sword strapped to his waist, and I knew he had at least one knife hidden up his sleeves. Rylan grasped Zig's shoulder; his other hand was tucked in his pocket, his expression serious. It was no secret that I hadn't wanted any of them to follow me on this quest, but I was glad they were with me now as we headed into the veritable realm of the beast.

"We're with you," Aven said softly. They hooked their pinky finger with mine in a quick, reassuring gesture.

"I know. Let's go."

We found the river easily enough, a winding shimmer of clear snowmelt that weaved through the hills, swiftly following the path of least resistance toward the Southern Sea. We rode upstream along the bank for several hours, and just as I began to question our plan, a roar in the distance chased away my doubts, and soon I spotted the rising mist of crashing water.

The waterfall.

Bluebell must have felt my excitement that we were so close to our goal, so close to finding the prize and ending the journey, because she danced beneath me, galvanized by my own energy. I clicked my heels and took off at a gallop, outpacing the others, even Mouse.

My pulse thumped in my temples as I leaned over Bluebell's neck, her mane whipping in the wind. I'd forgotten how much I enjoyed this part of questing, the thrill of approaching the finish, the knowledge that there was only one more piece of the puzzle to find and there would be a win at the end—be it a purse of gold, a bouquet of flowers, or in this case, the ability to save my brother's life.

I was almost there. So close. Just around the next bend and—

The river spilled over the craggy top of a plateau in ribbons of whitewater, splashing into a large, clear pool below, before rapidly continuing downstream in the carved bed. Tears welled in my eyes in utter relief.

The waterfall was the tallest I'd ever seen. Thousands of gallons of water poured over the falls daily, traveling down from the mountains to feed the farmland and the towns all the way to the coast.

"We made it," I breathed.

Aven pulled up beside me. "So did someone else," they said.

I whipped my head around and my heart sank. Lord Ethan's retinue was on the other side of the river.

"They beat us. How did they arrive before us?" I can't accurately describe the combination of despair and loathing I felt at losing to him a second time. But whatever that emotion was called, it left a bitter taste in my mouth.

"It doesn't matter," Aven said, clambering down from Mouse, whose sides were still heaving from the climb. They looped their quiver around their body and grabbed their bow. "We didn't come this far to be defeated by a haughty lord."

I jumped from Bluebell and clipped my sword belt around my hips. "Just so you know, that was unfairly attractive of you just now."

Aven shook their head. "Flirt later. Now it's time to win."

"If we win, there will be much more than flirting later."

Aven's face turned beet red. "Ellinore."

"What? Just speaking facts. That said, let's go."

Like the previous time I faced Lord Ethan, this called for a direct confrontation.

Glancing at his camp, I saw only a few of the organizational members milling about—cooks, scholars, even a bard—but there was no sight of Lord Ethan himself or his squires and guards, which meant that his team was already behind the falls. A slippery ledge jutted from the face of the rock cliff above his camp, providing a route to whatever lay behind the wall of water. I only hoped that Lord Ethan had not found the entrance to the invisible realm yet and that we could somehow get to it first. Or if we'd truly lost, then I would fight Lord Ethan and take the horn by any means necessary.

Unfortunately, there was no outcropping or path to the backside of the waterfall on our bank of the river. But no matter, there was another way in.

"Can you swim?" I asked Aven, knee-deep in the water already.

"Passably," they said, splashing as they entered the pool. "I'll keep up."

The stream was freezing as it lapped at my waist. Goose bumps covered my arms, and I had to fight every instinct I had that wanted me to curl into a ball and try to get warm. I shivered as I half walked, half swam until the water came up to my shoulders. The clear water was deceptively deep, and once I was up to my neck, the bottom dropped away, and my toes lost touch with the smooth rock floor. It was terrifying. The things I did for my brother.

Speaking of, both Aven and I were treading water before the rest of our group arrived. They hurriedly dismounted behind us and ran to the bank.

"What do you want us to do?" Rylan called.

"Feel free to join anytime," I said, teeth chattering. Ancients, this was frigid. Colder than the cave. "We'll have to swim under the falls, so meet us on the other side! But be careful!"

I turned my attention to the churning froth of the falling water. Aven joined me, their shoulder touching mine, the ends of their hair wet and clinging to their pale skin.

"Ready?" they asked.

"Let's go."

I took a huge breath, preparing to dive beneath the surface, but a sudden wave slapped me in the face and pushed me away from my destination. A wave that shouldn't have been in the pool at all. A wave that had emanated from behind the falls.

I inhaled water in a surprised gulp. I coughed, choking and freezing. Another swell followed, then another, as if something large had dropped in and the ripples were spreading out, pushing Aven and me toward the current of the river.

Crap. Crap. Crap.

We couldn't get sucked in and swept downstream. We'd certainly lose to Lord Ethan then and potentially drown in the process. I reached for Aven's hand and grasped their frigid fingers, both of us struggling for the shore.

Screams and shouts erupted from the bank, though I couldn't see why with the water smacking me in the face every few moments. Using all the strength I had, I yanked Aven close to me in the water, my biceps straining, and looped my arm around their waist. I hauled us to where we could find our feet, and then we stumbled for the shore, slipping on rocks. I banged my knee and cut my hand as I scrambled out of the freezing pool.

Farrah offered the end of her staff, and I took it gratefully, using it for balance. Rylan and Zig had Aven, pulling them out as well.

Before I could even ask, Zig answered my question.

"Um . . . a few people just ran downstream screaming," he said.

As I watched the chaos on the other side of the river, dread settled in my stomach. The squires and guards who'd made it out of the pool were on the bank with their weapons drawn, others were in the river, struggling to reach the shore, while the rest had been swept downriver. What was going on?

My armor was waterlogged, my hair was plastered to my neck, and everything was unpleasant and heavy and so cold that I could barely breathe. But it was all the least of my worries.

A roar split the air, so piercing, it almost burst my eardrums. I flinched as another followed, clapping my hands over my ears as stabbing pain infiltrated my senses.

The ground trembled, throwing us all off balance. I fell to my knees, the others staggering around me.

Then the waterfall parted, like curtains peeling away, to reveal an utter nightmare.

Even with the height of the falls, the monster needed to duck its head to emerge from its lair. Aven grasped my arm as the first head was followed by another. And another. I felt Aven's grip tighten as I lost track of how many heads there were, all of which sat atop long necks that merged into one snakelike torso, which slithered out from behind the falls.

"That's not the Elder Beast," Rylan whispered.

Stone-cold fear lodged in my middle. It certainly was not.

This wasn't the correct primordial, the one we were meant to find. It was literal death, the stuff of bad dreams and fairy tales that warned of dangers in the water.

Which meant we had failed. I'd failed. In the most crucial moment of this quest, when I'd decided just to be Ellinore for once, to trust my gut, to follow my good quest instincts, I'd made the most egregious error of all. A mistake that may have condemned my brother to death.

One of the heads roared again.

It hurt. Like being stabbed in the temple. Well, at least Zig wouldn't die alone, because that thing would easily destroy us all.

The many heads bobbed and surveyed the area, whipping around and snapping at the frightened horses of Lord Ethan's retinue. They reminded me of dragons' heads, with the same type of snout and nostrils, filmy eyes, and rounded ears, but they sat atop long, serpentine necks. The scales were a deep blue at the top and transitioned into black as the necks merged at the torso and continued to the snakelike tail. I'd never seen something so large, so literally monstrous, in all my quests, in all the parchments I'd read. It was truly a creature from before the concept of time.

"What is it?" Farrah asked, voice shaking.

"It doesn't matter," I said. "It's not what we're looking for, so let's get out of here before it notices us."

"Agreed," Aven whispered.

We had unconsciously moved backward as a group as we watched it in awe, but now we really needed to retreat strategically. As in, run.

"That foolish asshole," Aven spat.

I dragged my gaze from the monster to the shoreline. Lord Ethan stood there, his squires and guards at his back, brandishing their weapons at something they could never hope to vanquish. His archers had arrows nocked and ready. A few squires wielded long pikes, but nothing that would pierce the scaled armor of the monster.

Aven shook their head. "He's going to get them all killed."

The primordial glided out farther, the movements of its snake tail pushing another wave of water downstream. It lowered one of its many heads and released a soul-shaking roar at the other shore.

"Ellinore," Zig said, tapping my shoulder, "there's a town downriver. If that thing has been awakened, what's to keep it from traveling and destroying anything in its path?"

Fuck. It was a primordial being, which meant it had shaped our world. It had probably created the river, or hell, the entire coastline, maybe even the width and breadth of the seas. It could easily level anything in its path and reform our world anew.

"We wouldn't have to kill it," Rylan added. "Only drive it back to its lair."

Aven sighed heavily. "And maybe keep the king's vassal from meeting his unnecessary demise."

"If there aren't people trying to kill it, it might even just go back to sleep or whatever it has been doing for the last several centuries," Farrah said, ever the optimist.

One of the monster's heads swiveled in our direction, while another's teeth clacked, and another huffed water from its nostrils. I shivered with cold and with fear. "I don't know," I said. Every instinct screamed at me to run, to take my friends and ensure their safety, and damn whoever might be in the monster's path, as long as my brother and Aven and Rylan and Farrah were protected. Ellinore the person wanted to *run*.

"Ellinore, I don't want people to die because of me," Zig said quietly.

Damn. I had really come to hate Ellinore the Brave. "Fine. Keep away from its teeth. Rylan and Aven, distract it. Zig and Farrah, let's go save folks."

29

FARRAH, ZIG, AND I RAN DOWNSTREAM, AWAY FROM THE POOL, AND found a line of stepping stones that weren't completely submerged, to cross to the other bank. Once on the other side, we whistled to Aven and Rylan and began our approach.

"You two get the support staff out of here, then start with the back row of squires and guards. I'll take care of Lord Ethan."

"Okay. Good plan," Zig said, hands on his knees. "Just try not to get killed."

"You too," I said. "And try not to steal anything."

"No promises." Zig's usual smile didn't reach his eyes. "Seriously, be careful. That thing is . . . monstrous."

"I'll be fine. You two go before this gets worse. And, Zig, no magic rings."

His smile turned genuine. "That was one time, and I was eight." He turned to Farrah. "Ready, partner?"

She pursed her lips. "Yes. Let's go."

They shook hands, and then they crept to the camp, ushering the noncombatant members of the retinue onto horses and sending them to safety.

I rolled my shoulders, unsheathed my sword, and headed into the fray. Aven shot arrows from the other side of the river, focusing on bouncing them off the heads that were trained on Lord Ethan's group. Rylan stood in the water, gathering waves with his magic and pushing them at the snake body in an attempt to nudge it back under the waterfall.

Okay. The heads were directed elsewhere—time to hero.

"It's distracted!" Lord Ethan yelled over the chaos. "Charge it!"

Oh ancients, no!

I ran forward, darting between the lines of squires and guards, knocking aside their swords and pikes, until I could reach Lord Ethan at the front.

"No!" I yelled. "Don't do that! Run!"

"Don't listen to her! She just wants to steal our victory!"

"I don't want you all to die!"

Lord Ethan swung his sword, and I brought mine up barely in time for the blades to clang against each other.

"What are you doing? I'm trying to save you!"

"You're trying to interfere!"

One of the heads swerved toward us and opened its mouth. I expected another roar, but instead I was met with a focused jet of water. I ducked and rolled out of the way just in time, the intense stream slamming into trees, splintering them to pieces. Shards of the trunks and branches flew in all directions.

Okay. No. Because what? I didn't know it could do that! I'd thought we were only dealing with many heads, and teeth, and the possibility of a lethal tail. I didn't know this was basically a water dragon.

Obviously, neither did Lord Ethan's followers, because they all turned tail and ran. Yay. Great. One mission accomplished.

I gained my feet on shaky legs and staggered back to a stunned Lord Ethan. I grabbed his arm. His mustache was wet and uncurling, his blond hair plastered to his head and neck. His eyes were glassy.

"What is that thing?" I yelled.

"I thought this was the Elder Beast's realm," he replied, dazed. "But we must have read the key wrong."

"No shit!"

"I think it's the Hydra."

"I don't care!" I shook him and he flailed, as lax as a rag doll. "Where is the Elder Beast on the map? Can you show me?"

The Hydra roared again. Aven continued firing arrows, but they bounced harmlessly off its scaled armor and only seemed to annoy it. Rylan did his best to manipulate the water, but it had little effect. He switched to balls of fire, but they only aggravated the Hydra more. We needed to get out of there. We needed to run.

But my quest wasn't over.

"Where is the Elder Beast?" I yelled again.

One of the heads bent low and snapped at Aven. They barely managed to dive out of the way. Another shot a glob of snot out of its nostril toward Rylan, and the blob landed at his feet, splattering all over him. The head pointed in our direction opened its maw, and another rapid froth of water shot out. I tackled Lord Ethan, flattening him to the ground.

I shook him again, my hands gripping his surcoat, because we were losing. We would lose again. Against this thing.

"Tell me!" I demanded.

Lord Ethan's eyes snapped open, and he sat up, grasping my arm, his fingers digging into my flesh, almost as hard as I held him. I yanked him to standing, and he wavered on his feet. "Don't wake them up, Ellinore."

"Just tell me where the Elder Beast is!"

Lord Ethan squeezed his eyes shut.

I caught movement in the corner of my eye and managed to shove Lord Ethan away as another current of water erupted from the mouth of one of the heads, shooting between us. The stream was too quick, and the outer edge of the spray clipped my side, knocking me backward like a puppet with no strings.

I struck the ground harder than I ever had in my life, the air whooshing out of my lungs. My head connected solidly with the dirt, and the world went dark.

30

I BLINKED AWAKE TO A BRILLIANT GOLDEN SKY, THE SHIMMER OF THE
iridescent color reminiscent of the glint of coins or how firelight cast a soft glow
along the gilded curves of Aven's earrings. It was like a painting, completely
and utterly beautiful, moving in a sinuous, calming undulation. I'd never seen
a sky so stunning. I was in awe as I peered upward, my body resting on the wet
ground.

Wait. Skies didn't move like that.

I blinked again, the wash of color coming into focus as interlocking scales,
almost like dragon scales.

Huh.

Wait.

Dragon scales.

Dave!

I was *under* Dave's belly!

Turning my head, I saw my arm lying awkwardly next to me, the bracelet
broken, the links snapped into pieces, now scattered across several leaves of
grass. Oh. I'd called him. It might have been an accident, but I chose to celebrate
the small wins at this point. Go me.

Okay. I needed to get my bearings.

Moving *hurt*. Not just my head, but my legs, my arms, my back, *everything*.

Bones were definitely broken in places. My armor was beyond repair, the leather blasted apart by the power of the Hydra's stream. I hoped I'd managed to push Lord Ethan far enough away. Though no one could accuse me of not trying to save that winged-horse jerk.

As I took stock of my surroundings, things didn't seem good. Not the loud roars, nor the occasional burst of heat near my feet, which meant Dave was breathing fire at someone or something. He was fighting. The Hydra? Lord Ethan? Aven?

Only one way to find out. Bracing myself, I rolled from beneath Dave and, with great difficulty, made it to my hands and knees. I shrugged off the remnants of my armor, my tunic fortunately intact. Luckily, my sword hadn't flown far, and I grabbed it, using the blade to help leverage myself to my feet.

Dave's wings were fully spread. He looked even more menacing than when I first met him, when I was sent to kill him all those years ago. He was indeed breathing flames at the Hydra, driving it beneath the falls. And . . . what were those black clouds flying around several of the heads? Were those pixies?

The Hydra had backed mostly behind the waterfall, the few heads that dared to poke out from the whitewater curtain surrounded by pixie swarms. I didn't want to startle Dave, but I also wanted him to know that I was awake. I pressed my hand on a scale under his spread wing, knowing he'd be able to feel it there.

He didn't look at me, but he took off into the sky, using the wind from the flapping of his magnificent wings to drive the Hydra back farther.

Okay. That nightmare appeared to be under control.

Where were the—

"Ellinore!" Zig ran toward me and caught me in a bone-jarring hug that made me bite down on a cry of pain. "Oh my ancients, are you okay?"

"No," I said through gritted teeth. "Please let go."

Zig immediately released me, but his hands hovered over my shoulders. He was pale and soaked to the bone, and I couldn't tell if those were tears on his lashes or droplets from the Hydra fight. I chose to assume the latter despite his reddened cheeks, because I didn't know if I could handle Zig crying over me.

The others gathered a few steps behind. Aven and Rylan had their hands on a very disgruntled Lord Ethan. Rylan dripped Hydra snot—there was the mysterious goo Farrah had wanted so badly. Aven was drenched, their clothes sodden. For the first time on the quest, Farrah looked like she wanted to go home, wearily leaning on her quarterstaff.

"We thought you were dead," Zig continued. "And we couldn't get near you because this fool," he said, gesturing to Lord Ethan, "kept antagonizing the monster. But out of nowhere the Golden Dragon"—he swept his hand to where Dave and the pixies continued to corral the Hydra—"flew in and protected you."

I glanced at Aven. Their expression was that horrible blank mask they wore at court. My stomach swirled; vomit bubbled in my gullet. And it wasn't only from the head injury.

"I can explain," I said softly to Aven, to everyone.

Aven's jaw clenched.

A gust of hot wind blew over the group, knotting my damp hair even worse, and I didn't need to turn around to know that Dave had landed behind me, the heat from his breath and the thump of his legs and tail alerting me to his presence. As did the wide eyes, and the way the group skittered back. All except Zig.

"Is that the Golden Dragon?" Rylan breathed. "The one from the tale of Ellinore and the Golden Dragon?"

"His name is Dave," I said. "And yes."

"The Golden Dragon you supposedly killed," Aven bit out. "The one that you took a scale from and brought back to the castle."

I gulped. "Yes."

Lord Ethan burst into mocking laughter. He wrenched his arms away from Aven and Rylan, which didn't take much effort with how shocked they both were.

"You're a fraud," he said, stumbling and laughing like a fool.

I flinched.

He waved his arms. "Ellinore the Liar! Ellinore the Imposter!"

"Hey!" Zig shoved Lord Ethan hard in the chest. "Watch it, prick. She saved your life."

"And she's going to wish she hadn't when I tell the king and queen that Ellinore the Brave defrauded the Crown of gold. She seduced young Aven, the Pointless Princet, and even led the queen's niece astray on a dangerous quest when she didn't even have the credentials to protect either of them!"

Farrah protested with a "Hey!" at the same time I ground out "Do *not* call them that!" through clenched teeth.

"I joined of my own accord, thank you," Farrah said, lips pursed in anger.

Lord Ethan ignored her, laughing again, his features twisted into an ugly smile completely focused on me. "Or what? You'll skewer me with your sword? Do you even know how to use that?"

"Want to find out?"

"No, thank you. I'll take my chances at court, and after I tell everyone the real story of Ellinore, maybe Princet Aven will come visit you in the dungeon."

"I would think twice," Dave rumbled, causing them all to jump, his breath a warm gust, "about threatening a person who is friends with a dragon."

Lord Ethan's face drained of all color. "It speaks."

"Of course he does." I crossed my arms. "All the ancients and folklores speak if you listen."

Aven's gaze cut like a knife. "You speak to ancients and folklores often, then?"

I gulped. "Aven, please. If you just allow me to explain."

"What's there to explain?" Lord Ethan continued. "How many other quests have you lied about?"

"The quest," Dave rumbled, "was to stop the Golden Dragon from eating the sheep and terrorizing the villagers. If you've noticed, after Ellinore and I became friends, the dragon disappeared, and the village's sheep prospered, and the humans were terrorized no more with harmless pranks."

"Semantics!" Lord Ethan yelled.

A buzzing sounded nearby, growing louder by the second, until a massive swarm of pixies hovered over us. They flew in a synchronous wave, like a flock of birds in flight, blocking out the sun. The pixie queen dropped in front of me; her crown sat atop her silver hair, and her purple body twirled like a dandelion on the wind.

"Thank you," I said with a nod. "We appreciate the assistance."

She fluttered close to my face and gently touched my cheek, her grin wide and happy. Then, as quick as a hummingbird, she darted away, taking her subjects with her.

"Friends of yours?" Lord Ethan taunted.

"As a matter of fact, yes. We helped them after you rode through their grove and destroyed half of their kingdom."

He huffed. He opened his mouth to speak, but Zig shoved him again.

"Okay. We've heard enough from you. Why don't you scurry along like the rat you are and try to explain to your followers how you read a map wrong and almost got all of them killed? And how they are only alive because of us and our magical friends." Zig went to push him once again, tripped on a broken branch, and stumbled into Lord Ethan.

"Get off of me, you peasant!" Lord Ethan howled.

"Sorry. Sorry. I'm just so clumsy." Zig staggered and grasped Rylan's arm to steady himself.

Lord Ethan tugged on his surcoat, lifted his chin, and turned on his heel, then stomped away.

"Wait!" I yelled. "Where is the Elder Beast? You have to know. You had the map!"

Lord Ethan paused. "The map burned," he called over his shoulder. "Thanks to you."

"But you *must* know," I cried out, hobbling after him. "You have to know!"

He scoffed. "Even if I did, which I don't, I wouldn't want to awaken any more of these *monsters*. Not for all the gold in the kingdom." He turned then and smiled, oily and smug. "I have stronger morals than *others* when it comes to monetary gain."

The dig would've stung two weeks ago, but now it only came across as petty.

"Oh, are you still talking?" Zig said, crossing his arms. "I thought I heard a donkey braying."

Lord Ethan glared, then walked off with a huff.

"Do you want me to crisp him?" Dave asked.

"No. It's okay." I patted Dave's nose. "Thanks for offering, though."

Farrah peered over Zig's shoulder. "What did you get?"

"You remembered!"

"Of course. First rule of preventing pickpockets: Never allow anyone to get too close."

Zig beamed. "You're a quick study." He tugged at his sleeves. "Let's see. Oh, a purse of gold. He's not going far without that. Um . . . this noble sigil thingy." Zig held up a thin circle of silver about as large as his palm that had a winged-horse cast on the surface. "Oh, an embroidered handkerchief. Fancy. A comb, probably for his mustache. A . . ."

Zig's voice faded away as Aven left the huddle, moving toward the river and the stepping stones. I followed, body aching, vision swimming, but I couldn't let them leave. Not without an explanation. I had to get them to understand.

"Aven, wait!"

They kept walking. They hopped the stepping stones to the other side, and despite being wobbly and unbalanced, I followed, slipping only once.

"Please, Aven. Let me explain."

Once on the other side, Aven strode quickly, looking around.

I couldn't keep up. My legs protested every step. My head pounded. Every breath was agony. "Aven!"

They whirled. "Fine. You have until I find Mouse. So explain."

"I wanted to tell you. For a long time."

"Tell me what? That the spider was already dead when you found it?"

My mouth dropped open. "How did you know?"

"I suspected, but . . . Ellinore the Brave wouldn't *lie*. She's the standard, the pinnacle, no way she'd be deceitful to the *monarchs of the continent*." They let out a breathless, bitter laugh. "Now, with the blinders off, it was obvious. But I stupidly trusted you. What did I know, anyway? I wasn't as good and knowl-edgeable as you. Maybe massive spiders decompose quicker than other dead things. Maybe a thirteen-year-old can slay a dragon all on her own."

My heart twisted. "Aven."

"What else have you been lying about, huh?" They pointed at Dave. "The

Golden Dragon is obviously alive. What about the pearl from the Lady in the Sea?"

"I found it on the eastern beach after a storm."

Aven blinked. "And the quill from the tail of the manticore?"

"Dave helped me solve a riddle, and I asked for a quill when we told the manticore the correct answer."

"The jewel for my aunt's crown?"

"Made a deal with a gnome."

"When you wrestled the gods?"

"It was the fire salamanders that were disturbing the volcano. Dave and I moved them. I wasn't even on a quest then. I was trying to have some downtime."

"A vacation in a place known for earthquakes and volcanoes?"

I shrugged. "Well, there was this cute girl I met on another quest who lived—"

"I don't want to hear it!" They shook their head. "Do I even want to know about the swamp sprites?"

"I did save Princess Avriel! That happened! I promise. I just ... did a few chores for them and fixed a mess the princess had made with her carriage. I didn't need to swing my sword around like Lord Ethan."

"So all of it? Every quest? Every great deed? They were all a lie?"

"Yes."

They clapped their hands. "Great explanation, Ellinore! Really informative. Don't worry, I won't tell my uncle. But I can't promise Lord Ethan won't." They threw up their hands. Their face scrunched; their ears turned red. "I can't believe I wanted to learn from you! I can't believe that all this time I held you up as the unrivaled peak of questing, and you were a fraud." They spun in a circle, still looking for Mouse. "Just *why?*"

"For my family. So my parents and Zig could have a better life."

"The fame and glory had nothing to do with it, I'm sure."

"It didn't! Ask anyone. I *hate* the songs. I *hate* the attention. But I endured them because that was what I had to do." I tugged on my hair, my fingers tangling in the damp strands. "After I killed the Ursa, which was all luck, I was in over my head. I didn't know how to fight with a sword other than what a few squires taught me. I barely knew how to ride a horse. So I had to find a better way to accomplish things. I didn't have to *kill* ancients or folklores. I didn't have to trick them or steal from them. I talked to them. Like the ghost dog and the pixies. I just . . . found a different approach to complete the tasks that were asked of me."

"So you could talk to them, but you couldn't talk to me?"

"Hey, you kept a secret too."

They blinked. "Don't even pretend they are the same order of magnitude."

I swallowed the lump in my throat, tears burning behind my eyes. My stomach cramped with grief. "I didn't lie about liking you."

Aven rolled their eyes. "Sure."

"I didn't! I think deep down I've liked you for years, but I was distracted by the quests. And I couldn't entertain any thoughts beyond winning until I had enough gold to—"

They snorted, cutting me off. "Priorities, right?" Their shoulders slumped, exhaustion weighing them down. I saw it in their eyes, in the clench of their teeth, their clasped fists. "Where in the ancients is that horse?"

They marched off again, and I followed, pursuing a flash of white through the trunks of a few trees. Mouse grazed on a patch of grass, currently unbothered by our argument, and by the events with the Hydra. Aven approached him, rifled through the saddlebag, then turned to face me. They thrust out their arm, the leather journal in their fingers.

"Here," they said, staring at the ground. "Have your ill-gotten bouquets back."

"No. Those are yours. I couldn't. Aven, you have to—"

"Take them." Their voice was soft but firm.

Tears spilled down my cheeks. The leather was cold and smooth in my palms as I held the journal. "I'm sorry."

"Well, so am I." Bowing their head, they wiped at their eyes.

We stood in awkward silence for a moment, until they cleared their throat. They shoved their foot in the stirrup and swung up onto Mouse's back.

If it was possible, my stomach sank even further. "Wait, you're leaving?" Fear, real fear—more than what the Hydra had elicited, more than the faery, more than the salamanders, more than the cave-in—real, unadulterated fear swirled in my gut, gripped my throat. "What about the quest? That was the wrong primordial. The map is gone. We have no leads. We have no idea where to look."

Aven closed their eyes and pinched the bridge of their nose. They appeared as defeated as I felt. "Well, now that you have your real quest companion here, I'm sure you'll figure it out. And you won't have to worry about hiding anymore."

"Aven . . . that's not . . . I need . . ."

"When this is over, don't come back to the castle. Stay retired." They didn't look at me when they said it; instead they tugged on Mouse's reins, gaze fixed on the ground, unable to look me in the face. "Good luck, Ellinore the Brave," they said softly, then clicked their heels against Mouse's sides and galloped off.

I collapsed to my knees. My entire body throbbed with pain, from my hair to my toes, but out of everything, my heart hurt the worst. Every beat was agony.

I buried my face in my hands and cried.

31

My sobs were so forceful, it was difficult to pull in air. I pressed my forehead to the dirt, wrapped my arms around my torso, and wept great, heaving, hiccuping cries into the grass.

I'd thought hitting the ground as hard as I did from the Hydra's waterspout was the most stunned and wounded I'd ever been.

I was wrong.

This moment was worse. So much worse.

Like a thousand arrows plunged into my heart.

I curled on the ground and pulled my knees into my chest, trying to protect myself from the hurt, but it had burrowed into me and left a hole so cavernous that I couldn't fathom its depth. I ached with sudden loneliness, with the loss of what might have been. I wished I didn't know what it was like to be kissed by Aven, to be held by them, to be *seen* despite the lies, because maybe it would make this parting less intense, less jarring, less anguished. And while the existence of whatever had burgeoned between us had given me warmth, the absence of it was as cold as a magical cavern or a river fed by snowmelt.

Everything had gone wrong. I had *nothing*. I would lose my brother. I'd lose my friends. I'd let *everyone* down. Ellinore the person couldn't save anyone, not even herself.

I stayed there, rolled into a ball of pain, gazing into the sky. I'd met a god earlier that day, a primordial being, older than time, one who had carved the rivers and filled the oceans; maybe there was one on high who would be willing to give me guidance, an answer, *anything*.

"There you are." Dave landed lightly near me, his large frame curling around where I sprawled, his body lowering to the ground. "The others were worried."

I didn't say anything, but I reveled in Dave's warmth. His belly scales glowed with fire and provided a comfort I'd missed. I closed my eyes and pressed my body close to him.

"Where's Aven?" he asked.

"They left," I replied. My voice was a hoarse scrape from crying. "They couldn't suffer another moment being in the company of a fraud."

Dave huffed. "Their loss."

I pushed myself to sitting with a groan and leaned on Dave's neck. I settled against his scales, tipped my head back, and sighed.

"Thank you for coming to save me," I said.

He nudged me carefully with the tip of his wing.

"You're injured. Take the potion."

I didn't argue, too drained physically and mentally to do so. I shook a few drops onto my tongue, then slumped against him in relief and exhaustion as my bones knitted back together and my bruises healed.

"Thank you. For saving us."

"Of course. I came as soon as I felt that you were in trouble, *real* trouble. I'd felt the few times you almost summoned me, but I held off."

"You could feel those?"

"Yes. But when the bracelet *broke* . . . I knew you were in danger. Being seen was the last thing on my mind. I focused only on getting to you."

I patted Dave's cheek. "Thank you. I would say that you shouldn't have, but there was no way we would have gotten out alive, much less been able to force the Hydra back to its lair, without you."

"You would have thought of something, I'm sure."

I shook my head. "No. Aven was right. I'm a fake. Ellinore the Brave doesn't exist in any incarnation."

"What do you mean?"

I swallowed another round of tears that threatened behind my eyes. "I tried. I tried so hard to be who Zig needed, who Aven wanted, the person the bards had written about, the one admired by others. But every time I tried to do what I thought Ellinore the Brave would do, it went wrong. Horribly wrong. But when I trusted my gut, that went wrong too." I tugged on a tangle of my hair. "And now neither Ellinore the person nor Ellinore the Brave will be able to save Zig. I truly am a fraud."

"I still don't understand. Explain it to me like I'm fifty."

"They all needed something from Ellinore the Brave. Aven wanted more time from her. Farrah wanted to learn from her. And Rylan wanted to record her stories. So I tried to become her. I couldn't very well show them the real way I'd done things."

"Why not?"

I lifted an eyebrow. "Are you being obtuse for a reason?"

"No. I sincerely want to know why."

"Because I'm *not* Ellinore the Brave!" I shouted, throwing up my hands.

Dave smiled, as large as a dragon could smile, revealing his rows of razor-sharp teeth. "Exactly."

"What?"

"You're not Ellinore the Brave. Why would you try to act like someone you are not? Why would you attempt to live up to an expectation of an archetype? Of someone who isn't real?"

"Um . . . because I was afraid of being found out and getting arrested—"

"It doesn't matter," Dave said, cutting me off. "What matters is what you do *now*."

"Okay. You say don't be Ellinore the Brave, but I also tried doing what *I* thought was correct. I followed my gut, and I *still lost*."

"You can't win all the time, Ellinore. That's not how life works." Dave knocked his wing into my leg, jostling me. "It's the law of averages. You've won all the other times doing things your way. There was bound to be a loss. It just happened at an inopportune time."

I snorted. "Yeah. Like, the worst time ever to fail miserably."

"The question is, what is your plan now?"

Tears welled in my eyes again. "I don't know," I murmured.

"Yes. You do."

Hypothetically I did. But I was scared. What if I tried and failed again? What if the others left me like Aven did? What if they got hurt? What if I lost Zig? I scrubbed my face with my palms and took a deep, centering breath. At the end of the day, the what-ifs didn't matter, because I *would* lose Zig if I didn't do something. Anything. My brother was worth any risk.

When I fought the salamanders, I didn't second-guess myself about trying to save Farrah and Aven. When I intervened with the pixies, I didn't think about Ellinore the Brave, only what needed to be done. Maybe it was time to stop doubting myself and my methods. It was time to stop trying to be the hero from the tales that I thought everyone wanted me to be.

It was time to be just Ellinore.

"I can't give up," I said to myself as much as Dave. "If I do, I lose my brother. But I'm not sure where to start, and we're running out of time." I bit my lower lip. "But maybe my friends have some ideas."

Dave hummed in agreement. "Maybe they do."

"Ellinore!" Farrah yelled, sprinting toward us through the meadow in a panic. "There's something wrong with Zig!"

32

"I'M FINE," ZIG SAID, WAVING THE CONCERN AWAY WHILE THE GROUP OF us gathered around the fire. I'd run all the way from my meadow of sorrow, across the stepping stones, and to the camp the others had made. My breath heaved. Dave landed and circled his body around us, and I couldn't deny the relief of his presence. "Don't worry about it. It was only a little discomfort. Nothing to bother Ellinore the Brave and the Golden Dragon with, honestly," he said with a weak chuckle.

He wasn't fine. His skin was sallow, his brow furrowed with pain. He pressed his mouth into a firm line. And though he tried to hide it by scrunching his body and pulling his knees close, I could see how he clutched his chest, his fingers curving over where his heart lay beating beneath.

"What happened?" I said, lowering myself to a log across from him, the flames of the campfire dancing between us.

Rylan rubbed Zig's shoulders to try to comfort him, Zig's tunic bunching beneath Rylan's large palms. "I don't know," Rylan said. "I'd gone to wash off the monster snot, and I heard Zig yell out. I ran back and found him on the ground, writhing."

"I wasn't writhing," Zig said, shrugging off Rylan's touch. "Don't exaggerate. I was merely rolling in the dirt."

Rylan frowned. "You were writhing."

"Yeah? What do you know of writhing?"

"More than you think."

Zig's eyebrows shot up. "Really. Because I was under the impression that—"

"Don't finish that sentence!" I said, interrupting. "Just . . . tell me what it feels like. And don't lie!"

"Ironic coming from you, dear Sister. Don't you think?"

"Zig!"

He rolled his eyes. "Fine. I was stoking the fire, and suddenly it felt like my heart was ripped from my chest." He waved his fingers, the edge of a playing card poking from his sleeve. "No big deal."

"No big deal?" Farrah asked from where she stood near Dave's tail. "Seriously?"

"Yeah. No big deal! I'm not dead, obviously. It was probably a glitch in the magic."

I froze.

The sounds of the trio chatting faded out while my thoughts whirled. Glitch in the magic. Why would the . . .

"Rylan?" I asked slowly. "What did you say you were doing when it happened?"

"Washing off dried Hydra snot. It was surprisingly difficult to scrub off. I had to immerse myself completely in the water, and even then it was hard to remove. It had soaked into my clothes." He frowned. "I think they're a lost cause."

I dived for my saddlebag, which was in a pile near where the others had tied the horses. I wrenched open the flap and yanked out the parchment. I unrolled it and my stomach sank.

Three marks were gone.

When the sun rose, I'd have three days left.

"Ellinore?" Dave asked. "I can hear your pulse racing."

I stood and brought the countdown parchment over to the others. I held it out, showing them the drawing of the candle that had burned down.

"Rylan, where is the magical scrap?"

"I keep it right here," he said, sliding his hand into his tunic. "In a pouch so I don't lose it."

He took it out and opened it. His eyes widened. Farrah gasped as she peered over his shoulder.

"What is it?" Zig asked.

Rylan held the worn cloth out for us to see. It was sodden, flopping over Rylan's hand. Golden cursive writing glittered on both sides.

"Saturated in power," I said, giddy with excitement. "The primordials are inherently powerful and magical. So when you were doused with Hydra snot, and it soaked into your clothes, it saturated the scrap and activated the clue!"

Rylan's eyes widened. "Oh. Well. I'm glad I kept it close."

"Me too." Okay, maybe bards weren't so bad after all. Still couldn't forgive the mage part, though.

Zig rubbed his palm over his chest. "So that's why my heart feels like it's going to fall out of my body? Because the magic took the three days?"

"Does it still hurt?" I asked, dropping to my knees beside him. The clues could wait a moment. My brother came first. He'd always come first. That had been one of my mistakes on this adventure, worrying more about his and Aven's perception of me than the stakes of the actual quest. I'd lost sight of what really mattered. Which was Zig.

"A little. Not as bad as when it happened."

"Zig."

"Fine! It hurts, okay? I could vomit I hurt so much."

I removed the potion vial from beneath my tunic and handed it to him, wrapping his fingers around the glass and silver.

"What's this?"

"A healing potion." I nodded toward Dave. "From Dave's hoard. I've been using it for injuries. But I want you to take it. Use it as you need to."

"It won't save you," Dave rumbled, making Zig and the others startle. "Not from the magic of the mages' bargain. But it will ease the pain until your sister can solve the riddle of the Elder Beast's location."

Zig took a sip and sighed, slumping down so his shoulders were propped on the log, and his eyes fluttered shut. "Good potion."

I took the vial from his limp hand, plugged the end, then tossed the chain around his neck.

"What do we do now?" Farrah asked. She studied the words on the cloth. "These phrases don't make any sense to me. Like 'through the eye of a needle.' Does it mean a sewing needle?"

I stood and gently took the magical piece of cloth from her, then settled down next to Dave so he could peer at the writing as well.

"'Begin at the Edge of the World.'" I lifted my head. "Does that mean anything to anyone?"

Rylan shook his head. Zig was practically asleep, eyes closed, features relaxed. Farrah ran toward me and spread out her map on the ground. We looked through all the names but found nothing that even came close.

She hummed. "It must be like the Climbing Wood and the Haunted Forest. Remember when Aven said that locals will refer to places differently? Maybe that's what's happening here."

I ignored the pang of guilt when she spoke Aven's name. "Yes. I remember. But that doesn't help us. We don't have time to run around every town in the kingdom and ask them if the Edge of the World is a colloquial term for anything nearby."

"Hey," Zig asked, awake but sprawled bonelessly, his head on Rylan's thigh, "where is Aven, by the way?"

I avoided his inquiring gaze. "They left. They must have gone back to the castle. I don't know."

Farrah took my hand. "Aven is stubborn. And surprisingly impulsive sometimes. Like leaving the castle to join you on a quest and making up a silly lie about the king ordering them to do so instead of just telling you that they missed you and wanted to see you again."

"Well, I don't blame them for leaving." I ran a hand through my hair. "I did lie. About a lot of things." I gestured to Dave. "The Golden Dragon, for one."

Farrah wrinkled her nose. "Yes. Well. None of us are perfect."

"And it does prove my hypothesis that the bard tales are exaggerated if not outright false," Rylan said with a shrug.

"You don't care that I lied? That I knowingly took gold from the kingdom under false pretenses?"

Farrah laughed. "If the gold didn't go to you, it would've gone to Lord Ethan." She said his name with a sneer. "Besides, I've witnessed how you handle situations, and I think your way of doing things is admirable. Like you said, we don't need to hack our way through the world."

"Rylan?" I prompted.

He smiled. "I'm just happy my theory was validated."

"But the gold?"

Farrah laughed again. "The king and queen don't use the kingdom's gold on their silly bets. That comes from their own personal wealth."

"What's the difference?" I asked.

Farrah gently patted my arm. "Oh, you sweet peasant."

Okay. I didn't know if I liked *that*, but at least my friends didn't seem to mind that I had lied my way to fortune and fame. But it didn't go unnoticed that Zig had remained quiet.

"Zig?" I asked softly, afraid of his response.

"I'm still processing. Ask me again later."

"Fair," I said. "At least you're willing to think it through. Aven just . . . left."

Farrah scooted closer to my side, as if sensing my melancholy, and looped her arm through mine. "They'll come around."

I didn't want to tell her how wrong she was, so I deflected. "So the Edge of the World. It might not be a location. Maybe the Edge of the World is a book or a song? Rylan?" I asked, my voice taking on a desperate edge.

He shook his head. "I'm sorry, Ellinore."

"Let's get some rest," Farrah said. "It's late, and I know I'm exhausted. We can revisit in the morning." She stood, brushed off her trousers, then rubbed the toe of her boot in the dirt. "Do we need a watch or will the dragon . . . ?"

"His name is Dave. And ask him."

Farrah cleared her throat. "Dave? Will you keep the first watch?"

Dave chuckled. "There is no need for a watch. No one will approach while I'm here. But if there is trouble, I'll wake everyone."

"Oh," Farrah said with a timid grin. "That sounds great. Thank you."

"You're welcome."

"I'm Farrah, by the way. That's Rylan, and that's Zig."

Dave laughed again. "I'm pleased to meet you all. I've heard a lot about you—Zig in particular."

"Ignore it all. My sister is a liar, if you haven't heard," Zig said from his bedroll, which Rylan had laid out for him.

A lump lodged in my throat.

Without saying good night, I curled up in my own blanket and fell asleep at Dave's side.

33

AN AGONIZED GROAN ROUSED ME.

I sat up, kicking off my covers, and crawled to where Zig writhed, hand over his heart, features twisted in pain.

The sun had yet to rise, though the sky lightened toward dawn. Farrah and Rylan were still asleep, Rylan snoring lightly. Dave lazily opened an eyelid and watched with a sharp green eye, though he didn't move.

I grabbed Zig's shoulder and shook.

"Hey!" I whispered.

He jolted awake, biting down on a cry, teeth sinking into his lower lip. I grabbed the potion, the chain having twisted from Zig's jerky movements, and slapped it into his palm. "Take some."

He nodded quickly, groaning as he pushed up onto his elbows. He uncorked the vial, then splashed a few drops on his tongue. Heaving a sigh of relief, all his tense muscles going lax, he flopped down.

"That bad?"

He nodded. "Yeah." He lifted his head and met my gaze. "I wish I'd known how much magic sucks before entering that bargain."

"I'm sorry."

"Not your fault that I made a foolish bet with a council of mages."

"Duo of mages."

"Right. Whatever."

I helped Zig ease back down to his bedroll, then bunched up my own blanket for a pillow, and he closed his eyes as he sank back toward sleep. I didn't want to leave him, so I sat next to him, intent on watching the sunrise. He grabbed my hand and squeezed.

"Are you mad?" I asked quietly.

Zig blinked his eyes open and peered at me with a squint, then shrugged. "About the lying? Meh. Not really. Maybe a little. But it's kind of awesome that you've been revealed to be a bigger swindler than I am."

"But—"

"You should really capitalize on your brand power now, before Lord Spoilsport gets the word out and those taverns stop knocking down your door for endorsements."

"I don't—"

"Also, you have a dragon for a best friend. I'm more upset that you didn't let me in on that."

"But, Zig—"

He cut me off with a wave of his hand. "Hey, take the grace of my forgiveness and run with it, Sister."

"Brother," I said, whining in return, "I want to make sure that we're good, that it's clear that it all was for the benefit of our family. It was never about glory or fame."

"Yeah." He stared at the coals of the fire. "I know."

"And I never would have thought you would make a bet based on all the lies."

"The bet was my own fault. I may have let the size of your reputation get to me a bit." Zig offered a grin, though it was pained. "But you have to admit, being on a quest was way more fun than staying at home and making stews of death."

"Hey, I tried, okay?"

"I know you did. But it's obvious you didn't belong in our small town. You belong out here, making friends with magical beings."

A tear slipped down my already-red cheeks. "I'm not sure about that. I had to quit because I was worried that the lies would all catch up to me, so I wanted to leave before they did."

"Makes sense. Though I doubt there weren't at least a few kernels of truth in those songs. The point is you belonged out here. Not in Traveler's Rest. Not baking."

"I never tried baking."

"Good. It would've been a waste of flour."

"You know, I'm trying to save you. I don't think you want to be insulting me."

He shrugged. "Whatever. Anyway, you were a hero. You *are* a hero. And you deserve to be out heroing and winning and collecting prizes, even if the reported versions of events are more flowery and gilded than the reality."

"That's a nice way to say 'defrauding the Crown.'"

"Whew, yeah. What *are* you going to do about Aven?" Zig propped up on his elbow. "Go after them? Declare your undying affection? Drag them to the house on the coast with our parents?"

"The answer would be none of those. Thanks."

"Shame. Especially after hearing about how they went out of their way to research the Elder Beast in the castle archives to give you a fighting chance, and made up a lie about the king ordering them to be there just to disguise their raging affection for you."

"Well, yeah, they're a . . ." Wait a minute. "What did you say?"

"That Aven did research as soon as they heard about the quest so they could come save the day for you. You know it was all for you, right? They didn't show up on our doorstep for me, though if they did, I wouldn't turn them down."

"Hey!" I said, shoving him lightly.

Zig plopped down in the bedroll and shoved me back with both hands. "What? It's the truth. But again, they're not interested in me. Their heart eyes are only for you."

I shook my head in denial, though my heartbeat quickened with the thought. "Whatever."

"Come on, I'm so right on this. They showed up with research in hand—well, not literally, they had one clue, but my point stands. No one else would do that."

I frowned. "Right . . . They did do that."

Zig cocked his head to the side, as much as he could while lying on a pillow. "Are you okay?"

"Yeah," I said with a nod. "Yeah. Of course. Better than you. No offense."

"Offense taken."

"You should rest. Save your strength. Drink the potion as you need."

Zig raised an eyebrow. "Why do I get the feeling that you're up to something?"

"Because you know me so well."

He hummed in acknowledgment. "Sister," he said, eyes drifting closed, "I know this was my first and probably last quest, but I must say, best quest ever."

"Last quest? Don't think you're wiggling out of this so easily. Now that I know you can cut it, you'll be the one heading out and competing against Aven in the summer tournaments."

"Nah. You've done all this for me—the least I can do is live at the coast with you. If you still want that."

I took Zig's hand. "No. If I don't belong in our town, you surely don't belong in a fishing village. I think you'd make an amazing adventurer."

He smiled lazily. "Sure. Zig the . . . Uninhibited."

I huffed in amusement. "Yeah. That will go over well." I tugged a blanket up to his chest. "Get some rest, Zig the Uninhibited."

Zig grumbled but squirmed around in his bedroll for a few minutes before quieting. I stayed next to him, holding his hand, until it went lax in my grip as he drifted off. I placed it gently on his chest, then stood.

I went to Dave and leaned on the warm scales near his neck. After taking the scroll from my bag, I unrolled it. The candle had burned down to a stub. Three marks remained. I had three days. I couldn't waste time.

"What is your plan?" he asked, voice low so as not to disturb the others.

I sighed deeply. "I need to talk to Aven." I scratched Dave's ear. "I have to ask you for a favor."

"I figured. What are you thinking?"

"I'm sending Zig home to Traveler's Rest with Rylan and Farrah."

"And what are we doing?"

My heart ached at the thought of what I needed to do. But it had to be done to have even a sliver of a chance of saving Zig. "We're finding Aven."

34

I WOKE FARRAH WITH A TAP TO HER SHOULDER.

"What's happening?" she yelled, shooting to a sitting position, hand on her quarterstaff, eyes closed.

Crouched next to her as I was, I had to flinch away or risk being head-butted. "It's just me, Farrah."

She peeled an eye open, then the other, and blinked rapidly.

"Ellinore?" She rubbed her forehead with her free hand. "Why are you waking me before dawn?"

"Because I'm giving you an important quest."

She tilted her head in confusion. "Aren't we already on one?"

"Yes and no." My throat went tight. I hated the thought of sending Zig home, the thought that it might be the last time I saw him, that I might fail and not make it back in time to stop the mages. But if there was any possibility at all of saving him, I was going to grab it. "I need you to take Zig to Traveler's Rest."

She shook off sleep, immediately becoming more alert. Her brown eyes snapped to mine, her mouth falling open. Even a tendril of her perfect dark-brown hair fell to frame her heart-shaped face. "What? Why? I thought—"

"I have three days to find the Elder Beast, take its horn, and bring it back to the mages. I can't be slowed down, so I'm going to travel with Dave. I need you to make sure Rylan and Zig are safe. Take all our mounts."

She yawned, then tucked the wayward strand back in place. "This is a lot to take in so early in the morning."

"Yeah, well, I trust you to take care of them and get them home with all your map knowledge."

Her eyes shone in the light of the rising dawn. "I can do it. But you take the map." She rummaged in her bag at the side of her bedroll. "You need it more than I do."

I took the offered scroll of parchment. "Thanks. You've been an amazing adventurer."

"You've been a great teacher. Don't pet creatures. There's always another way out. Listen to what nature tells us. Trust your gut and help when you can."

I blinked. "You learned all that from me?"

"Yes." Her smile blossomed into something sweet and genuine. "Don't tell Aven. But I learned from them, too. Don't hold yourself up to what you might know of someone else's achievements, because you don't know the whole story." She leaned closer to me. "They haven't learned that lesson themself yet, but hopefully they'll figure it out. Because—and again, do not tell them—they're pretty amazing too."

"They are," I choked out.

Farrah grabbed me into a hug and squeezed. "Don't worry. I'll take care of Zig. You can trust me."

I clasped her back. "I do. Please don't pet anything."

Her chuckle vibrated against me. "I won't," she said in a whisper. "Promise."

35

DESPITE OUR MANY ADVENTURES TOGETHER, I'D NEVER RIDDEN ON Dave's back before. Though he balked at a saddle, he at least acknowledged that having some kind of rope attached would be beneficial to keep me and my saddle-bags from falling off mid-flight. Using the straps from Bluebell's bridle, we fash-ioned a leather handle that wrapped around the bases of Dave's wings, where the bones emerged from his shoulders, then stretched across the middle, where I could sit astride his spine and hold on. It also allowed me to secure my belongings.

Once that was managed, we took off.

The sky lit up with pinks and yellows as dawn broke, the colors so beau-tiful from the back of a dragon, where the light reflected off Dave's scales in a vibrant shimmer. There were moments as we climbed to just below the clouds, my stomach swooping with the beat of Dave's wings, when I felt I could reach out and touch the sun as it broke over the horizon. But the joy was short-lived, as I craned my neck to watch the landscape roll by below us, my hands trem-bling with the sight.

"Hopefully, we'll catch Aven where they spent the night last night. Before they head out again." I had to yell or my words would be lost in the wind. I didn't realize how fast Dave could move in the air. I kept a grip on the leather strap with white knuckles, and the rough texture of Dave's scales snagged my trousers as I clenched my thighs tightly over his back.

"And you're fine with me being seen?" he asked, looking over his shoulder to where I perched.

We flew low to try to spot Mouse or Aven on the route back to the castle. There was no doubt Dave would be noticed, and there was no way the emergence of the Golden Dragon wouldn't cause a ruckus. But it had to be done. I had to find Aven.

"Yes. As long as you're okay with it."

"I am. It's been a while since I've had the opportunity to tell a few jokes to humans. Maybe play a few pranks."

"Well, try not to become a quest again. We don't need that hindrance."

He grumbled in acknowledgment and annoyance, a small wisp of smoke puffing from his nostrils.

I leaned over his neck, searching the countryside for any hint of Mouse's white hair or Aven's campsite. Fear settled like a stone in my gut the longer I rode and didn't spy any hint to Aven's whereabouts. Aven couldn't have traveled far, could they? It was almost evening when they'd left, and they would have needed to stop . . . unless they rode all night. Ugh.

"There's a town," Dave said, his tail swishing behind him. "Do you want me to fly over it?"

I took a breath. "Yes. Do it."

Dave dipped lower, and even with his legs tucked close to his body, the tips of his claws scraped the tops of the structures. A commotion followed, dozens of the townsfolk pouring out of the buildings behind us, all pointing at the sky.

We made a swoop down the main street, then turned around and did another pass. With one hand wrapped around the leather strap, I bent close to peer at the awed folks, hoping to spot the one person I needed. Who I missed even though it had been less than half a day.

We continued over the town, and at the end of the street was an inn with a stable right next door, and in front of that inn, with their arms crossed, and their expression incredulous as they stared at the sky, stood Aven.

I yanked on the leather, signaling Dave to stop.

He did, using his great wingspan to slow, then hover, stirring the dust of the street, until he landed lightly on the other side of the stable, right in a bed of flowers. How lucky.

I slid off, patted Dave on the side in thanks, stooped down for the quickest of moments, and then ran toward the inn before Aven could disappear.

Whispers of "Ellinore the Brave" and disbelief at the return of the Golden Dragon followed me, but I ignored them. I slid to a stop in front of Aven.

Dark circles adorned the skin beneath their eyes, and their normally polished boots were dusty. They looked more run down than they had during the entirety of the quest thus far.

A crowd gathered around us, and though I would rather not have this conversation with a dozen pairs of eyes staring at me and a dozen sets of ears listening, that wouldn't stop me.

"Aven," I breathed.

The crowd gasped, obviously not realizing until right then that royalty was in their midst.

"What are you doing?" they said, voice harsh and low, arms tightening around their body. "Everyone will see." Their brow furrowed. "You won't be able to deny . . . anything."

Even though they were angry with me, they were still looking out for me. But I didn't intend to lie any longer.

"I don't care. I need to talk to you."

"Well, I don't really want to talk to you, so . . ." They shrugged. "Maybe go?"

"I'm sorry," I blurted. "I'm sorry for everything, and I will spend my life apologizing if that's what you want me to do, just so you will talk to me again. But that's not why I'm here. Mostly."

Aven's eyebrows shot up. "Then why are you here?"

"I need your help."

They sighed, their frown deepening, which I didn't realize was possible. "I'm not in the mood to lend any more assistance, Ellinore the Brave."

Whispers surrounded us as Aven turned away. But I hadn't slept much, and my emotions were running wild, and I'd left my injured brother, and I could *not* let them leave. I reached out and grabbed their shoulder, spinning them back around, to the astonishment of the crowd.

"What are you doing?" they yelled, throwing out their arms. "Do you want to make things worse?"

"I'm not here as Ellinore the Brave!" I shouted. "I'm here as just Ellinore."

Aven's expression pinched.

"No titles," I continued. "No pretenses. No prize. No posturing." I fell to my knees and offered the scraggly bouquet of flowers I'd picked from Dave's landing site. A mixture of orange butterfly weed, bluebonnets, and one bright-pink rose. Clumps of dirt still clung to the roots, and the wild rose's thorns dug into my palm, but I held them out in my trembling grip and hoped. "I would rather not do this in front of a crowd, but since I don't have that option, here goes. I'm so sorry I lied to you. But you of all people know the pressure a reputation can put on a person. And I was so young when the Ursa happened, and it was overwhelming to have the power to change my family's life for the better. I never meant to hurt you. Aven, I adore you and I admire you and I still think you're the best person I've ever met. And I'm throwing myself on your mercy. If you can't forgive me, I'll find a way to understand. But right now, in this moment, I'm not here for me; I'm here for Zig. I need you."

Aven's cheeks blushed deeper than the pink petals of the rose. After a tense moment, when their eyes shone and their lips twitched as if they were suppressing a besotted smile, they rushed forward and grabbed my elbows, hauling me to my feet. "Ancients, Ellinore," they said, their voice low and fond, gripping my arms, "do you have no shame?"

"Absolutely none when it comes to you."

"This doesn't solve everything."

"I don't expect it to. I don't want it to. But I'm serious about it all." My voice shook and pitched high as I tried to hold back another round of tears. "Zig needs your help. I need your help."

They studied me, as if looking for any hint I might be insincere. Then their stare dropped to the flowers, and a timid grin curled the corners of their lips. "Okay. You have it."

The crowd clapped. I winced, having forgotten they were there. I wiped my hand over my cheeks, catching the stray tears that had fallen.

"Come on. We need to find a better place to talk." Aven took my hand and tugged me away from the crowd, toward the stables. Thankfully, no one followed us. Though there would be rumors about what we'd done in the darkened stables alone, that was the least of my worries right then.

The door creaked when Aven opened it. The heavy, cloying smell of hay and animal musk permeated the space, and I rubbed my nose to ward off a sneeze.

Aven guided me to Mouse's stall, and we stepped inside.

Aven cleared their throat. "I couldn't sleep last night," they said. "I debated with myself so many times to go back. I got to this town and decided I'd sleep on it. But I didn't sleep. At all."

And that explained the dark circles and rumpled clothing.

"I'm not one for public declarations," they said, running a hand through their hair, the tousled strands falling everywhere. "But I'm sorry. I shouldn't have left the way I did. I was so angry and confused, but that doesn't excuse that I abandoned the group, the quest, you. I apologize for that."

"You were planning to come back?"

They grimaced. "I don't know. I hadn't decided. And I'm still . . . I don't know how to trust you, Ellinore. I'm furious and . . . heartbroken. I needed time to process, and I still don't know what I'll do or say after the quest. But I also know I shouldn't blame you for my own insecurities. You may have been the standard I was measuring myself against, but you're not the one who made me feel pointless."

"You're not pointless! Don't call yourself that."

The corner of their mouth lifted into a smile. "I want to help. I will help."

My throat was clogged with tears. "Thank you." I dropped the flowers to the stall floor. "I wonder what the bard tales will say about that display? Ellinore the Fraud and her pathetic ploy to win back Aven the Scorned."

"Not the best title, but Rylan could make it work."

"Oh my ancients." I laughed in my hands, covering my face in embarrassment. "Well, I wouldn't put it past Rylan. He completed one impossible task, what's another?"

"What do you mean?"

"That's why I'm here. He activated the magical scrap of clues with Hydra snot."

Aven's mouth fell open. "Are you serious?"

I nodded. "Yes. It revealed a set of hints that I don't know how to decipher."

Aven's expression turned concerned. "You've lost three days."

My stomach clenched with the reminder. "Yes. I'm hoping you'll know what these phrases mean. You read the firsthand account; they might sound familiar."

I took the scrap from a pouch inside my tunic and handed it to them. The script glittered as they held it in a beam of light.

"'Begin at the Edge of the World,'" they read. "'Follow the gaze of the giant at sunset through the eye of a needle.'" They shook their head slowly. "I'm sorry, Ellinore. It doesn't ring any bells. I think it might be nonsense."

"Are you certain?"

They examined the words in the light, shaking their head as they did so, until they paused. A slight hitch in their breath and a scrunch of their brow alerted me that they'd thought of something.

"What?"

"I think . . . well . . . there was an old family castle called Brinkmount in the far northwest that sat at the base of the mountains that bordered the sea." They licked their lips in thought. "It was abandoned almost a hundred years ago."

"Why?"

"Because it was crumbling into the waves."

"Okay. What does that have to do with—"

"Before it did, all the contents of the library were saved and brought inland to the family castle. I found the account of Rylan's great-grandfather in the castle archive. It could be that the parchment originated from Brinkmount."

I crossed my arms. "I still don't understand."

"If my memory is correct—and I remind you that this all happened decades before even my uncle was born—that castle was sometimes called the Edge of the World."

36

⊷

AVEN YELPED INTO MY EAR AND CLUTCHED MY WAIST TIGHTER, squeezing the air from my lungs with a death grip. Their forehead pressed so hard between my shoulder blades, I was certain I'd have a bruise.

Dave flew us over the treetops but not much higher, knowing that both of us weren't used to actually flying like he was. But he moved quickly, understanding that we were in a time crunch—we needed to make it to the second clue before sunset, provided our hunch about the first clue was correct. His large golden wings flapped next to us, his scales almost blinding in the sunlight.

"I mean, the timeline makes sense," I yelled over the rush of the wind. "If William Smith was a teenager when he encountered the Elder Beast, then his account could have been dictated to a castle scribe and housed at the Edge of the World before the castle fell into the sea."

"But where did the scrap come from?" Aven's chin dug into my shoulder, their breath warm on the skin of my ear. It made goose bumps erupt down my arms.

"I have no idea. But he obviously knew mages, since he was able to set the magical traps in the cave. It could've been created by one of them with or without his permission. He wouldn't have needed it himself because he had the map."

"Unless it was another fail-safe."

"Huh. Good point."

Hours passed, the day pushing into the afternoon. Dave rose to avoid a tower of a lord's castle, and Aven squeaked, clutching me tighter. I chuckled, though my knuckles turned white from my own firm grip.

"That was the home of the lord of the northernmost fief," Aven said as the small castle disappeared behind us. "We should be at the Edge soon, based on Dave's speed." They'd removed their hands from my waist and now had their arms wrapped completely around my torso, the length of their body pressed against my back in a line of warmth.

"I can't believe I convinced you to ride a dragon."

"We didn't really have a choice," Aven answered. "There was no way we could follow the clues, find the Elder Beast, and make it back to your home in time riding on Mouse."

The truth of their statement stole my breath more than Aven's anxious clutch of my rib cage. This was it. If we were wrong, then the quest was truly over. Zig would die because of my lies, and I would . . . end up in a dungeon? Be on the run the rest of my life? Maybe I'd board a ship and sail off to one of the other continent kingdoms and try to make a fortune there. Well, that was future Ellinore's problem. Current Ellinore had to focus on saving her brother. And not on how comforting Aven's arms were clasped around her.

The farther north we traveled, the colder the wind blew. Massive white pillars of snowcapped mountains poked through wispy clouds in the far distance. And as the sun lowered in the sky and the dying rays cast an orange sheen on Dave's scales, the northwestern coast came into view.

I'd seen only the Eastern and Southern Seas—both of which rolled with gray waves against sandy, shell-strewn shores. The Northern Sea was wholly different. It gleamed a bright green, the tumult of the waves capping the water in white foam as they battered the rocky shoreline, splashing with force on the face of fallen mountains. Yet, in places, the water was transparent, allowing me to see straight down, where I spied the masts of ships and the shadowed shapes of creatures swimming in the murky depths.

Dave flew low, his tail dipping into the water every so often, sending up a frigid spray that made me hiss between my teeth. It was so mesmerizing watching the deep water pitch and roll beneath us, I almost missed that it was no longer the base of mountains it pounded against, but blocks of stone.

I perked up as I spotted towers and battlements sticking out from the heaving bright green, the last vestiges of a crumbling castle.

"It's almost completely submerged," Aven said in awe as Dave lightly landed on a wide path that connected the towers, water lapping at the edges of the crenellations.

"Who thought to build a castle here?" I asked, stretching my arms above my head, my joints creaking in protest from being in one position for too long. A red line from the leather of the strap crossed my palms, and my muscles ached from keeping myself seated on Dave's back.

"There once was a long spit of land that connected Avoury to the kingdom across the Northern Sea," Dave said. "It appeared only during low tide."

"Previous monarchs built castles at each corner of the continent either to foster trade with kingdoms and cities across the seas or as a defense against them," Aven said, peering over my shoulder toward the mountains in the distance. "This one just happened . . . to become unneeded once the spit was destroyed."

I removed the magical scraps from the pouch close to my chest. "As fascinating as the history of our kingdom is," I said to Dave and Aven, "do you see any giants?" I craned my neck and looked at the sun. It dipped perilously close to the horizon. "We don't have much time."

"Hold on." Dave pushed off from the castle, the battlement crumbling beneath the strength of his claws. We surged upward, Aven grabbing me again as we slid a few inches down the scales of Dave's spine.

We climbed higher and higher, touching the freezing clouds, until we were able to see the entire jagged coastline below us—the turbulent sea, the froth and foam, the castle keep beneath the waves, the surrounding abandoned town, the cliffs of the mountains that rose on the northernmost point of the coastline, peaks even higher than where we hovered. In the distance the submerged isthmus that had once connected our kingdom to another glittered like a golden road beneath the clear green.

"There!" Aven called, pointing so fiercely that they almost slid off Dave entirely. "To the north of the castle. Do you see it?"

Dave didn't answer, merely swooped down like an arrow, my stomach dropping with him as he glided along the shore, then turned inland to land on a grassy hill.

Aven gulped. "Please don't do that again," they said, complexion a vague green as they slid from Dave's back.

I followed and stood face-to-face with a giant monolith. It was a carved obelisk of shiny rock, with two smooth faces and two rough-hewn—a forgotten monument of some kind atop a lonely hill, surrounded by flat, barren land. Other than the mound, white-and-gray rock stretched as far as we could see in all directions—toward the beach and to the mountains.

"'Follow the gaze of the giant at sunset,'" I murmured. The deep pinks and oranges of sunset splashed across the sky. From where I stood at the base, the monument cast a long shadow that stretched across the rocky plain, disappearing between two mountains in the distance. "The shadow! Quick! Before the sun sets!"

Aven and I scrambled up onto Dave's back, and he took off, following the path, his wings beating quickly, eating up the miles, racing the sun as it sank. Wind whipped my hair, the cold of it stinging my skin, freezing the tears that leaked from the corners of my eyes. Beneath us the shadow faded slowly, merging into the gloom as the sun disappeared.

"Faster!" I yelled.

Smoke billowed from between Dave's teeth as he pushed himself, following the shadow until . . . it was gone.

He eased to a stop, landing gently at the foot of two mountains. I bent forward, my head on his back, my eyes closed. I couldn't look. What if the shadow didn't continue in a straight line? What if it bent in some way? What if we'd failed again?

"Ellinore!" Aven shook my shoulder. "Come on," they said as they dismounted. "Let's go!"

I tensed and slowly lifted my head.

We were surrounded by rock on three sides, with the monolith far behind us. The mountains towered above us, sheer surfaces that climbed higher than the clouds.

I jumped down from Dave's back, my bootheels clacking on the stone surface.

"No wonder this corner of the kingdom is uninhabitable," I murmured, hugging my arms to my body for warmth. "It's freezing, and nothing can grow in all this rock."

"Which makes it the perfect place for a primordial to hide."

"If it is indeed hiding," Dave said. "The Elder Beast may only be resting. After all, it created the ancients, the folklores, then the ordinaries. Maybe it has a fourth classification up its sleeve."

"I don't think the Elder Beast wears a tunic," I said.

Dave narrowed his eyes.

"Come on." I belted my sword around my waist. "Soon it will be too dark to see. And we have to find a needle in a . . . mountain range."

"I don't think it's going to be that difficult," Aven said from where they had wandered ahead.

"What?" I asked. An outcropping cut off my view of where they pointed, so I ran to them, my spirits lifting. I skidded to a stop next to them, grabbing their arm to steady myself, and gasped when I saw what they meant. "The eye of the needle," I breathed.

In front of us, wedged between two mountains, was a stone oval. It was tilted, so that the oval listed to one side, but there was no mistaking that it was our eye. The opening shimmered a slick silver, reflecting our images instead of the mountains beyond, and it was only big enough for a human to step through.

"The eye of the needle," Aven echoed, positively giddy. They bounced on their heels, their fingers gripping the crook of my elbow. "I can't believe we found the entrance to the invisible realm."

My breath caught and my throat went tight. "We're so close. We're going to retrieve the horn. We're going to save Zig."

"Ellinore," Dave said. "Do you have a plan for when you face the Elder Beast? Do you think a sword and an arrow will defeat a creature older than time itself? Did you not learn your lesson with the Hydra?"

I tore my gaze from the eye and faced Dave. "I did learn. I know what I need to do." I swallowed, then corrected myself, reaching out for Aven's hand. "What we need to do."

Dave nodded. "I can't help with this. I'll wait for you here."

I swallowed. "Okay. I understand."

Dave smiled, then pushed his snout into my torso. I lay across it and gave him a hug. "It's okay, Dave. I got this." I stood and gave him a reassuring smile. "After all, I'm Ellinore."

37

STEPPING THROUGH THE LIQUID SILVER WAS AN EXPERIENCE UNLIKE any other I'd ever had in all my years of questing. The magic poured over me like warm water, hovering over my skin but not quite touching, raising the fine hairs on my arms and the back of my neck.

One moment I was on the rugged, rocky ground, and the next I was in a ... meadow. But not like any meadow in our world. The grass was a soft blue and springy beneath my feet. The trees climbed dizzyingly high and had purple trunks and pink leaves and twisting violet vines. The sky was a bright green— like the Northern Sea I'd just flown over—and it rippled with frothy clouds. My eyes burned, as it was all almost too much to take in—the vibrancy of the colors, the flip of the sky and the ground, the warmth of the air, humid and damp, heavy in my lungs. Silver droplets of water slicked my skin, beading on my clothes, making them appear as if they'd been sequined.

Aven gasped as they stepped through the eye and joined me, their eyes wide, their grasp tight on my arm.

"What is this place?" they breathed, taking it all in.

"The invisible realm of the Elder Beast, I imagine." On the other side of the eye, I could see Dave waiting for us, though he was muted, like a painting where all the colors had washed out—or that could be the result of staring at the spectrum of color on this side of the needle.

They gulped. "Well then." They pulled an arrow from their quiver and nocked it on their bow. "We should be prepared."

I nodded and drew my sword, the weight of it comforting in my grasp, the leather-wrapped hilt plush against my palm.

Together we crept through the meadow, our footsteps flattening the blue grass. The air we breathed was sweet yet cloying, almost as pungent as the perfumes some of the lieges and courtiers wore in court. I wished for the canteen I'd left on the other side, and I didn't dare sip from the puddles of silver water we avoided.

We stepped around pink bushes with black buds, over sprawling white roots of trees, and past beds of green and deep-blue flowers. I wanted to pick one for Aven, but the petals were odd and waxy to the touch, and I didn't want to risk inciting the Elder Beast's ire before we'd even met it.

"We could get lost in here," Aven muttered as we came to a flowing river, the water tumbling over golden rocks. On the other side was another blindingly bright meadow.

We stopped at the bank. "Should we . . . call for the Elder Beast?" I asked. "Let it know that we're here?"

"You want to invite it to kill us quicker?" Aven asked, hands clenched around their bow.

"If William Smith lived to tell the tale, surely we'll be fine." I held on to that hope, because as Dave had said, there was no defeating a primordial in a battle.

"What's your plan, then? Care to let me in on it?"

"Well, remember how I confronted Lord Ethan . . . twice? That. That's my plan."

"Seriously? And what am I to do while you're distracting it?"

"Shoot it if you can, I guess. If things go wrong."

"Great. So I can die first."

"Love interests often do."

Aven stopped short. "Is that what you think I am? Because—"

A twig snapping near us silenced us both, and we tensed. I reflexively dropped into a battle stance, while Aven drew back their arrow. A rustle of bushes followed, and from between two purple-and-silver trees, the Elder Beast emerged, walking toward the river as if Aven and I didn't exist at all. Or, more likely, posed no threat.

It stood on slender legs akin to those of a bull. It had the face and torso of a brown spotted deer, and the wings of an eagle sprouted from its back. A black horse tail flicked behind it. But the most important detail was the bone-colored horn that sprouted from its forehead. It was long and sharp, gently curving upward.

The Elder Beast lowered its head and drank from the river, unbothered by our presence. Its magnificent, feathered wings flexed, then folded against its back, and its large hooves carved furrows in the dirt as it pawed the ground.

Aven and I stood frozen, unable to do anything other than watch as it drank.

It lifted its head and stared at me, and its eyes—dark, limitless pools—met mine.

"Ellinore the Brave," it said with a small bow of its head. "And Princet Aven of the kingdom of Avoury. It's an honor to make your acquaintance."

I dropped the tip of my sword, awkwardly standing from my crouch. "You know us?"

"Of course," it said, its voice high and soft. "I know all the heroes. Those who came before and those who have yet to come."

"Heroes?" Aven asked. They eased the tension on their bowstring. "But I'm not . . ." They motioned at me. "We're not . . ."

"Not yet," the Elder Beast said. "Someday."

Aven's mouth fell open. They dropped their arrow, blinked as if coming out of a daze, then scrambled after it. I'd have to tease them about it later. If there was a later.

"So," I said, "you know why we're here."

The beast made a noise like birdsong, as if in thought. "You're here for me." It nodded toward our weapons. "Those won't help you. I am immortal, like the Hydra you awakened."

I held up my free hand. "To clarify, that was not us."

It made another noise, this time like the bark of a fox, and I realized it was laughing. "Luckily for humanity, my fellow immortal returned to sleep until a time arrives when the world requires a new ocean."

My mouth went dry. "So the Hydra did shape the world?"

"Of course," the Elder Beast said, tilting its head to the side to regard me like one might regard a child. "All of the immortals had a hand in creating the world in which you live. Do you not know?"

Aven and I exchanged a glance. "No. Not really. A lot of that is . . . lost."

The Elder Beast blinked, its eyelashes long and curled, framing its large doe eyes. "A shame."

"Yes. But that's not why we're here." I had no idea if changing the subject was rude, but we had only two days left. And if sunsets worked here the same way they did outside, the sky's shift from a frothy turquoise to an eye-watering yellow indicated we might have even less.

"Please, tell me why you've disturbed my rest."

Oh. That wasn't quite hostile, but I did detect a little annoyance behind that statement.

"My brother made a bargain with a council of mages." Aven, thankfully, did not correct me. "He wagered that I could find the mythical, powerful, graceful, and beautiful"—no hurt in buttering it up a bit, though Aven's incredulously raised eyebrow might give me away—"Elder Beast and retrieve its horn. If I lose, he has to give the mages his heart."

The Elder Beast tilted its head at me once more.

"He'll die," I added. "My brother. He'll die if I don't bring back your horn."

It laughed again. "I will not willingly hand over my horn."

My whole body went cold. "But . . . my brother—"

"I'll make you a different sibling," it said, pawing at the ground. "Humans are easy to form."

I flinched. Aven stepped close to my side, seemingly as fearful as I was at how nonchalantly the Elder Beast had suggested swapping out one human for another. "No. No. I would like to keep the brother I have. He may be annoying, but I love him. We haven't been on the best of terms, but we've just started to rebuild our relationship."

The Elder Beast regarded me with a critical eye.

"Please," I said again. "I know it's a monumental ask, but is there any way you would . . . give me your horn?"

"No."

My heart sank. I tightened my grip on my sword. It would be a horrible idea to try to fight the beast, then take the horn, especially if the Elder Beast was half as powerful as the Hydra. But I wouldn't give up. We'd come so far already. The horn was within my grasp.

"I understand your attachment to your horn, but I am very much attached to my brother, my twin—"

"You humans. You take, and you kill, and then you celebrate it all. You have driven my other creations to the edges of the world. Among the ancients, only two dragons remain. A handful of Harpies. A single manticore. And I haven't felt or seen a griffin in years. And the others—the folklores—are just waiting to suffer the same fate. Why would I give you my horn when I am the only being who can right the balance that humans have threatened?"

Its eyes bored into me, and I had to look away. My face prickled with shame. And if Aven's hand squeeze was any indication, they were feeling ashamed too. I may not have joined the quests with the intent to harm ancients and folklores for sport, but I'd participated nonetheless (and won most every time, but that was the last thing the Elder Beast needed to know). Dave was living proof that I had done my best to protect them when I could. My head shot back up as an idea zinged through me. I found myself stepping forward, even as Aven tugged me backward.

"What if we struck a bargain?" I asked. The Elder Beast regarded me shrewdly. It jumped over the river, as easy as breathing, and landed on the bank next to us. Aven and I skittered back in unison. Aven's grip tightened on my wrist. I held my breath as the beast eyed us.

"What could you possibly offer me?" it said, and I could feel the warmth of its breath.

"Protection." When it snorted, I rushed to continue. "For the other creatures, I mean. Back in our world. I can work to keep them safe."

The Elder Beast tossed its head in irritation. "You two have killed your share. Why should I believe that you'd stay true to your word?"

I took a deep breath, swallowing down my fear. "I've never intended to hurt any creature. In fact, I've tried to find a way to protect them every chance I got. I restored the home of a grove of pixies. I transplanted a herd of fire salamanders for their own safety. And I rescued the Golden Dragon from being hunted by a pack of bloodthirsty questers. I can do this."

The Elder Beast stared at me for so long, I began to worry it was getting ready to pounce. But then it sat on its haunches and tilted its head. "That," it said, "is an interesting proposition."

I let out a shaky breath and pressed forward. "If you give me your horn, I promise to devote my life to this."

Aven's grip on my arm was crushing at this point. They stepped forward and interjected. "Before you decide, oh wondrous Elder Beast, may we have a moment to talk?"

The Elder Beast narrowed its eyes. "Certainly. But not for long."

"Thank you. This will take just a moment," Aven said, dragging me toward the way we'd come.

"What are you doing?" I whispered, though the Elder Beast could probably hear everything in this silent and frankly weird realm. "It was about to give me its horn. I was about to save Zig's life."

"In exchange for basically your own, Ellinore."

"I know!"

"You wanted to retire. Taking this bargain would be the extreme opposite of that. What happened to 'last quest ever'?"

I squirmed. "I could still have days off," I said weakly.

"Ellinore!"

"Fine! Yes, it would be the opposite. But come on! Zig said he wanted to join if he lived beyond tomorrow. And I'd . . . I'd have you. Right?"

Aven blinked. "Of course you'd have me," they said, sounding offended that I would question their participation.

"Well then, it wouldn't be so bad. No titles. No pretense. No competition.

It could even maybe become best-quest-ever good." I pushed Aven's shoulder. "I sucked at retirement anyway. You were right about that."

"Fine. How will everyone make money? There's no prize at the end here. If there is an end at all."

"The Crown has gold. *You* have gold."

They stared at me, eyebrows drawn together, mouth flat. "Let me get this straight. You want to spend the rest of your life protecting the ancients and the folklores of our world—which stretches beyond our kingdom's shores, by the way—and you expect me not only to join you but to fund it all?"

"Yes?"

"Okay. Just checking. Sounds great. I'm in."

They yanked me back to where the Elder Beast stood, not even giving me a moment to process what they'd said and what it all meant. But standing next to them, their hand in mine, our fingers interlaced, I couldn't help but beam.

"Does this mean we have an agreement?" the Elder Beast asked. "My horn for your devotion to protecting the ancients and folklores of your world?"

I swallowed down my apprehension and nodded. "Yes."

The Elder Beast shook its head, and its horn fell to the ground at my feet.

"Goodbye, Ellinore the Brave and Princet Aven of the kingdom of Avoury. I will see you again at some later time."

The Elder Beast pranced across the river, stretched its wings, then flew over the meadow and disappeared into the trees.

I dropped to my knees, the curved horn in front of me. It was as long as a deer antler, with velvet along the base, and ridges of growth that followed from the root to the tip.

"Here," Aven said, handing me a cloth.

I nodded, too overcome to speak, and wrapped the horn in the cloth, holding it reverently in both my hands.

"Ellinore," Aven said, hand on my shoulder, when I made no attempt to move. "We need to leave. There's no telling how much time has passed in our realm." They peered at the sky. "I can't even tell how much time has passed in here."

"Are we doing the right thing?"

"It's a little late to think about that now! We already pledged ourselves."

I shook my head, my hair falling in my face. "No. I mean"—I stood, my legs unsteady—"can I really hand this much power over to those jerks of mages? What if Dave and Rylan are right? What if it's irresponsible of me to do so? Now that I'm holding this horn, I can feel the raw magic in it. It scares me."

Aven regarded it, brow furrowed. "It might be irresponsible, but this quest was for Zig. Whatever comes from giving this to those mages, we'll handle it. You and me."

My eyes brimmed with tears. I clutched the horn to my chest. "When we get out of here, I'm going to kiss you on the mouth so hard."

They smirked. "We should go, then."

We followed the indents we'd left in the blue grass back to the eye. Dave awaited us on the other side—I could see him keeping watch through the shimmering silver.

I paused and handed Aven the horn. I reached into the slim pouch under my tunic and removed the scrap of cloth. I studied the glittering gold letters one last time, then dropped it.

Aven gave me a small smile.

Together we stepped through the eye.

On the other side, without preamble, I kissed Aven firmly on the mouth, just like I'd promised.

38

DAVE WAITED FOR US, HIS SCALES LETTING OFF AN ORANGE GLOW IN THE light from the setting sun.

"Do you have it?" he asked, after I detached myself from Aven.

I held the bundle out for him in both hands. "I can't quite believe it, but yes. We have the horn."

"Congratulations." His tone indicated he was less than enthused, his green eyes locked on the bundle in my hands.

My fingers clutched the cloth, the horn unbending beneath. "I know you're wary about what the mages have planned for this. But Aven and I will fix it. I promise. Whatever it is."

Dave acquiesced with a nod. "I know."

Aven hadn't moved from where I'd kissed them. They were staring confusedly into the distance. "How . . . how is the sun setting again?" They scratched along their jaw. "Did we . . . go back in time?"

Fire flickered out from between Dave's teeth as he released an annoyed sigh. "You've been gone a full day."

"What?" I asked, almost dropping the horn in surprise. I quickly pushed it into Aven's hands, then wrenched the parchment from my saddlebag. The candle had burned down to a puddle, the inked flame flickering, the wick almost completely gone. We had no time for moral dilemmas. I had to return to the Griff-Inn as soon as possible or all of this would have been for naught. "Can you fly us through the night?"

"I've been hunting only in the night for years. I think I can get us back to your village."

Aven frowned. They handed over the horn once I was securely on Dave's back, then climbed up behind me. Dave took off, flying low back the way we'd come—over the slabs of rock, the sunken castle, the rough, white-capped green of the Northern Sea, then inland across the rolling plains.

Aven's breath was hot against my neck as they held on. Their voice a whisper on the wind, so I almost didn't hear them when they said, "Take me to the castle."

"What?" I asked, twisting in my seat. "Why?"

"Because I need to go. I have something to do."

"But . . . the horn . . . the mages . . . *my brother*."

"I know. But it's important, Ellinore. I wouldn't leave if it wasn't." The moonlight lit their expression with a soft glow, and they smiled. "Trust me."

I did.

"Dave," I called, leaning over his neck. "We need to drop Aven off at the castle."

Aven kissed me after we had landed discreetly inside the castle walls on a patch of grass near the stable. They tugged me toward them with a hand on the back of my neck, making my toes curl in my boots and my mind go blank.

"I'll see you soon," they said, stumbling back as we finally parted.

"You better."

"I promise."

"Good. I don't know what's going to happen, but I do know I'd like to face the aftermath with you."

They smiled. "Same." They stumbled another step on the green grass of the lawn.

I clambered up onto Dave's back, one hand clenched on the leather strap, the other clinging to the horn.

"Goodbye, Ellinore the Brave," Aven called in the still night. "Have fun. Try not to die."

I laughed and shook my head at the echo of my own words from the day of my supposed retirement. "Just go. You're embarrassing me in front of Dave."

Aven waved and disappeared into the dark, footsteps fading as they crossed the courtyard into the keep.

Dawn broke just as we landed outside my childhood home.

Rainbow, Bleep, and Bloop were right where we'd left them in the paddock, joined by Bluebell, Starlight, and Carrot. They'd made it back!

The sheep bleated, and Dave's stomach rumbled, his tongue lolling out between his razored teeth.

"My brother would kill me," I said as Dave eyed them. I slid from his back, horn in my hand, saddlebag looped over my shoulder. I leaned against his side in my version of a hug. "Seriously. He loves those sheep. And we think that Rainbow might actually be a fauness."

Dave snorted, a curl of smoke rising from his nostril. "And I might kill your brother if I don't eat soon."

I paused. "Dave?"

"It's been too long. I must find food."

"Okay. Well. Let's get done with the mages, and then you can go hunt to your heart's content in the mountains. I promise. Just a few hours more."

"Ellinore," Dave said with a quiet rumble, "you don't need me. You can handle this."

"But . . . I don't have any way to call you if I need you."

He smiled. "Then don't need me."

"But—"

"You are Ellinore. That's all you need to be."

Flapping his wings, he took off. He lazily made a circle, the sun glinting off the gold of his scales in a dazzling sight. Then he flew toward his lair.

Leaving me alone outside with the sheep. I shook my head and pushed open the door to my home.

Rylan stirred a pot of something over the hearth that smelled amazing, while Farrah dusted the windowsill, humming a ballad I didn't recognize. As I entered, Rylan dropped his wooden spoon and Farrah squealed.

"Ellinore!" She tossed the rag and ran to me, barreling into me and enveloping me in a fierce embrace. "You made it! Do you have the horn?"

The relief at seeing them both alive and whole and *there* took me by utter surprise. "Yeah," I said, swallowing hard to keep the happy tears at bay. "I do."

Rylan's eyes widened. "You killed the Elder Beast?"

"Of course not. I made a deal with it. It's a long story, but the point is, I have the horn and we're going to save Zig. Speaking of, where is he?"

"Resting," Farrah said, fingers twisting in front of her. She pushed back a strand of dark hair. "We made it back late yesterday evening, even using Lord Ethan's gold to fund some bribes and flashing his sigil to get us privileges."

"And how is he . . . ?"

Rylan and Farrah exchanged a worried glance. "He finished off the dragon potion last night," Rylan said, brow furrowed.

"I'm fine." Zig drew out the vowel of the latter word. He stood propped against the doorway to the only other room, face drawn and pale, arms crossed to hide the tremble of his hands.

"Really? Then come over here and say hi."

Zig cocked his head to the side and squinted. "I'm comfortable where I am." He leaned most of his weight against his shoulder. "But did I hear correctly? You have it?"

"Yeah. I have it. I'm going to the Griff-Inn right now."

Rylan's mouth went flat, and he bit his lower lip. He turned away from me, his shoulders up to his ears. He flicked his wrist, and the spoon flew from where it had fallen on the hearth into his hand. Huh. That was a new trick.

"Rylan," I said. "I know you're worried about the fallout. But *we'll* handle it. You know, if you would want to keep questing with me. You and Farrah both."

He spun, mouth agape. Farrah blinked; then a beaming smile stretched across her face. She embodied the midday sun, her hands rising to her cheeks. "All of us?"

"Yeah. It seems like my retirement will be postponed for a while. And you will have to get permission from your family to be on the road."

She squealed again, jumping in place.

"And I have a specific job for you, Rylan, that I know would please the Elder Beast." His mouth fell even farther. I was scared a fly might buzz in. "I'll tell you more after this mage business is dealt with. But would you be interested?"

"Yes!" he yelled. Then he swallowed and composed himself. "I mean, yes. I would love to join."

I smiled. "Great. Well, I'm leaving now because our time is almost out."

"Oh!" Farrah gasped. "We have to ready the mounts!" She flung open the door and disappeared.

"That's assuming we're coming?" Rylan asked.

"I wouldn't mind the backup."

He grinned, then followed after her.

With those two out of the house, I approached my brother and engulfed him in a hug. He sagged into me, his forehead on my shoulder, his hands loosely clasped around me. Even though he was right there in my arms, he almost felt . . . insubstantial, like he could blow away on the wind. I held him tighter, needing the reassurance, needing him to stay corporeal.

"Where's Aven?" he asked into the fabric of my tunic.

"At the castle. We'll see them again soon."

"Good. So you've worked it all out with them?"

"Mostly."

Zig pulled away, his brown eyes dull but his lips ticked up at the corners. "You'll be a princess after all. You'll need an animal companion to complete the vibe. May I suggest Carrot?"

I laughed and pushed him gently. "Ew. I won't be a princess. Ever. Even if it were possible, I wouldn't entertain anything until after this is sorted. And I clear things up with the monarchs. And I take a short rest in or out of a dungeon. I'm tired from the stress."

Zig chuckled. "You and me both. I thought you pushed us hard. Farrah is a whole other level."

"Really?"

"Oh yes. Rylan and I were trying to come up with ways to get her to camp for the night, short of falling off our mounts."

"Oh, Zig."

He shrugged. "Do *you* have a plan for meeting with the mages? Last time didn't go so well for me . . . or you."

"I have an inkling of a plan," I said.

"Better than last time?"

"Marginally."

Zig snorted. "Great."

"Don't worry." I opened my arms and gestured to myself. "I'm Ellinore."

"Yes, you are. And you're my sister, so I feel obligated to tell you how bad you smell."

Mortified, I felt my face heat. I'd just spent several hours with Aven clinging to my back. "Really?"

"Oh yeah. Maybe wash up before you confront Forto and Quip," Zig said with a wan smile. "And comb your hair. You look like you've been flying on a dragon."

39

I ENTERED THE TWO-STORY CLAPBOARD BUILDING CALLED THE GRIFF-Inn through the open front door, flanked by Farrah and an unsteady Zig. A middle-aged woman stood behind a desk at the front, and a hooded bard sat in the corner strumming a lute, an unfamiliar melody filling the space.

And as before, the duo of mages sat at a table in the small dining area, drinking coffee and eating runny eggs, porridge, and burned toast.

"And then he cried, 'But where are my magic beans?'" Forto said, and laughed uproariously.

Quip followed suit, his ridiculous squashed hat falling onto his forehead, the feather wilting. Their twin staves of ash were propped in the corner, and I flicked my gaze to Zig, who gave me a short nod of acknowledgment in return.

They continued their conversation as we approached, steadfastly ignoring us, as they had the first time. I may have learned a thing or two on this quest, but old habits died hard.

I unsheathed my sword and smacked the blade on the table between them, the sharp edge slicing through a muffin. Quip flinched, but Forto merely turned his head toward me, his lips stretching thin over his toothy smile.

"Well, if it isn't Ellinore the Fraud," he said, steepling his fingers. "How pleasant to see you." He peered past my shoulder. "And your brother."

"Unfortunately, I can't say the same."

His eyes narrowed. "Because you failed?"

"No. Because I just don't like you."

He scoffed. "Your manners surely require refinement. Maybe the Pointless Princet can teach you when you're in the castle dungeon for your lies."

I did my best to school my expression, but I could feel heat rising in my cheeks.

He noticed, because of course he did. "Oh yes. News travels fast. Tell me, is the Golden Dragon still alive because of a moral compass you possess or because of lack of skill?"

I clenched my jaw and took a centering breath. "Do you want the horn or not?"

Quip perked up from his slump in his chair, robes swishing, boots thumping on the floor as he moved. "You have it?" He licked his lips. "You have the Elder Beast's horn?"

"I do."

"Let's see it, then," the other said lazily. "And remember, we'll be able to tell if it's a fake. Like you."

It took everything in me not to rise to his bait. "First, promise you'll release my brother."

"Of course. That was the bargain. Horn or heart."

"Say we made it in time."

Forto rolled his eyes. "You made it in time, Ellinore. If you truly have the horn."

"I don't trust you," I said, grip flexing on the hilt of my sword, my stomach in knots. "I don't want you to come up with some excuse to not release my brother."

"We are mages of our word. You've held up your end, and we'll hold up ours." He nodded toward Quip, who pulled a large purse of gold from his inner robe. He dropped it on the table, the clank of the pieces loud as the pouch struck the wood.

"Good." I nudged Farrah. She passed the wrapped bundle to me and took the hilt of my sword in exchange. I flipped off the top of the cloth and held the horn across my palms. "This is it."

The mages stood, chairs sliding back. "It really is it. It's the horn of the Elder Beast," Quip said with a tremble in his voice.

"It is."

Forto held out his hands and I passed it over. He inhaled sharply, fingers touching the velvet at the base and then the bone, running over the ridges. "The power is . . . incredible."

Next to my shoulder, Zig gasped. He staggered, falling forward onto the breakfast table. He rubbed his chest with his fist, coughing and wheezing, knocking over a chair in the process.

"I'm free," he said, voice a breathy shout. "It worked."

He flopped onto the table fully, then rolled onto his back, his hair falling into the plate of eggs, his wildly flailing limbs flinging cups and plates to the floor. One foot knocked over another chair. It was all wildly dramatic and exactly what I needed.

Forto clutched the horn, admiring it despite Zig's antics.

But Quip skittered away. "This is outrageous!" he cried, pushing from the table to prevent porridge from flinging on his robes.

The bard in the corner sang, "And now the mage is within reach."

Oh. Yes, he was. Farrah handed my sword back to me as I grabbed Quip by the front of his robes and slammed him against the wall of the inn. I held my sword edge to his throat.

"Now," I said, "consider this a robbery. Give me the horn."

Forto laughed. "You're not serious?"

"Oh, I'm serious. I'm very serious." Blood welled along the blade as I angled it for emphasis. "Now hand it over."

"Forto," Quip said, strained.

Forto's mustache twitched. He glanced at his staff propped in the corner.

"Oh, can't do the little disappearing magic trick without holding that, huh?" I said with a nod. "That sucks."

His face turned red. Quip made a choked noise.

The bard sang, "Ellinore the Brave has turned to a life of crime."

What the ancients?

"So she should *watch her back*."

What? Oh. I spun quickly, just in time to catch a chair that had been leveled at my head by one of the inn kids. He still gripped the legs, while I blocked the slats with my forearm.

"What are you doing?" I grunted.

"You . . . you said it was a robbery! I was trying to help."

Save me from do-gooding bystanders! I dropped my sword, the hilt clattering to the ground.

The whole inn paused, just for a moment, the space of a breath, then descended into utter chaos. With both hands, I was able to push the chair and the kid out of the way. The other bystanders scattered, yelling as they went, knowing better than to interrupt a fight.

But Quip was free and lunging for his own staff.

"Farrah! Zig!"

I dived across the table, grabbing Quip by the robes and dragging him down before he could reach it. He squeaked out a cry as both of us fell to the wooden floor in a heap.

"Get the horn!" I yelled as I rolled and scuffled.

Farrah twirled her quarterstaff, and with a flourish, she brought it down on Forto's wrist, breaking his grip on the horn. From the force of the blow, the horn went flying across the room.

"I did it!" she yelled. "I did the disarming move!" She jumped in place. "Ellinore, did you see? I did it!"

Forto took advantage of the lapse in Farrah's attention and grabbed his mage's staff from the corner. He aimed it at Farrah and sent a blast of power, which knocked her off her feet, right into another table, which collapsed into a pile of matchsticks.

The horn rolled across the floor. I lunged for it, but Quip grabbed my ankle and I face-planted, my nose slamming hard. I kicked backward, trying to dislodge Quip, while I stretched my arm for the horn. My fingertips grazed the bone.

"Ellinore wanted to save her brother."

I looked up to see Zig and Forto locked in a game of tug-of-war with his staff. The end was jammed into Zig's stomach, and having just witnessed Farrah flying across the room, I couldn't imagine what it would do at close range.

"Zig, let go!"

Forto pushed again, Zig stumbling as he released the staff. He fell into the bard, knocking into the lute with a thump.

With a mighty tug, Quip pulled me farther from the horn. I clawed at the floor, trying to move forward to no avail.

"Hey!" Zig yelled. "Let go of my sister!"

Quip screeched when Zig landed on him.

And suddenly I was free. I reached for the horn, and Forto stepped on my hand. He ground the heel of his boot on my knuckles, and I gasped in pain, unable to yank free.

"Well, well, well," he said. "This doesn't look like it's going to end well for you."

"Hey!" Farrah stood from the pile of rubble. She wiped the back of her hand across her mouth, blood smearing over her cheek and chin. She pointed her staff at him. "We're not done."

She charged, swinging her staff hard, and Forto stumbled backward as he raised his own, barely in time to block the blow.

As soon as he was off my hand, I scrambled to my feet and grabbed the horn. Then I tossed it to the bard, who hid it among his robes.

The bard strummed again. "And Ellinore and her band ran away!"

That was our cue. Zig bounced up from where he'd pinned Quip, and Farrah turned and ran away from Forto. Then the three of us sprinted out the front door.

The sounds of Forto's yells and Quip's footfalls were right behind us.

"Split," I gasped.

Zig ran off one way. I took another, and Farrah a third. They couldn't follow all three of us, but it didn't matter anyway. Because the Elder Beast's horn was securely folded into Rylan's cloak, and he very serenely stood from his chair in the corner and walked out the back door.

40

◦‿◦

I FOUND BLUEBELL WHERE I'D LEFT HER EARLIER ON THE OUTSKIRTS OF town. I swung up into her saddle and rode off to where I knew the Elder Beast's horn would be safely stored.

When I arrived, I was glad to see Starlight and Carrot already there. I dismounted, then squeezed my way through the cavern passage and into Dave's lair.

Farrah sat in my chair, wet cloth pressed to her mouth. Dave hunched over his small pile of gold.

"I told her I could wear a hat," he said to Farrah.

She took the cloth from her mouth. "You'd look dashing in a hat," she said, mildly slurring from the swelling in her jaw. "But I don't know how well it would do for a disguise."

Zig sat on my stack of blankets on the stone shelf where I often slept. He juggled two jewels and a golden goblet while Rylan looked on.

"I can't believe you stole the mages' jewels right from the ends of their staves," Rylan said, voice tinged with awe.

"Their fault for waving them all around. Honestly, they should have taken better care of their things."

Rylan laughed. "Sure. Their fault."

"Hey," Zig said, catching all three objects. "You can do something with these jewels, right? Maybe develop your magic further?"

Rylan's eyes widened. "Maybe."

I cleared my throat, announcing my presence.

Farrah shot up from the chair. "Ellinore!" she yelled, rushing over. She slapped a cold, wet cloth across my face. "For your nose!"

I winced, holding it with my fingertips. "Oh, thanks."

"Were you followed?" Rylan asked.

Zig stood and ran over to give me a hug. I hugged him back, squeezing until he wheezed.

"No," I said, releasing him. "I think we lost them. But if we didn't, they'd be foolish to follow us into a dragon's den."

"You'd think, but they didn't seem like the brightest mages in the council," Zig said with a wink.

"You're not wrong, but I think the Elder Beast's horn is safe here for the time being."

"Hopefully, they'll suffer consequences for their actions," Farrah said, sitting back in the chair.

"I doubt there will be any more than what was doled out by our hands." I rocked back on my heels. "Speaking of facing consequences for actions, are you all ready to come with me to face the music at the castle?"

"No, thank you, Ellinore," Farrah said politely. "I think I should stay here, guarding the horn."

"But . . . don't you need to go home at some point?"

"Oh yes," she said, leaning back in the chair. "And I'm going to be in so much trouble. So I'd rather wait a little longer before being grounded for my remaining existence."

Oh. Okay. "Zig?"

"Pass."

"Rylan?"

"Um . . . sorry. I don't think I'd be any help."

I deflated. "Thanks, guys."

"Hey," Zig said. "You made your bed. "

"I know." I kicked a loose rock.

Dave heaved himself to his feet. "I will go with you, seeing as I was your partner in crime."

"Thank you. You're a true friend." I said the last part loudly for emphasis.

The other three grumbled and waved me away. Ingrates.

"Come on, Dave. Let's go not get killed or thrown into a dungeon."

"Oh, I definitely won't," Dave said as he stretched like a cat. "I'll fly away before that happens."

There was no use hiding the famed Golden Dragon. Dave had been seen by dozens of people already, including Lord Ethan. I just hoped that Aven had found a way to spin Dave's continued existence in my favor.

We touched down in the courtyard and were greeted by screams from the castle staff. I slid from Dave's back and landed lightly on the stone as a retinue of guards encircled us with their swords and pikes at the ready. Not the most auspicious welcome.

But then Aven broke through the line and sauntered toward me, back to their impeccable self, hair styled and makeup on point. I wanted to run to them, kiss them, but I didn't think that was a good idea while surrounded by this many guards. So I stood in front of Dave, hands clasped behind my back, doing my best not to launch myself at them once they came near.

We were a stone's throw apart when their path was blocked by the head guard. He whispered to Aven, and then the both of them walked toward me. Aven was in the lead, with the head guard a step behind.

And, oh no. Was I going to be arrested? Surely, the king and queen would have me dragged in at least for questioning if not for a long vacation in the dungeon. Had Aven vouched for me? Would they sneak in and visit me in my cell?

The guard paused behind Aven. "So Princet Aven was telling the truth," he said with unrestrained awe. "Ellinore the Brave tamed the Golden Dragon."

I blinked. Annoyed smoke curled from Dave's nose.

"What?" *Wow. So articulate, Ellinore.*

"Yes," Aven said, moving to stand beside me. "She did. And the Golden

Dragon has been instrumental in assisting Ellinore on her adventures." Aven nudged their elbow into my arm.

"Yes!" I blurted. "That's true. He's become an amazing ally."

The guard shook his head, smiling to himself. "Wow. My daughter is a huge fan of yours. She won't believe that somehow you are even more amazing than the songs say."

My face burned with embarrassment, while Aven smiled with thinly concealed affection. "Right? I wouldn't have known either until I joined her on this quest. But yes, even more amazing than the bards tell."

Oh. I was going to make Aven pay for that. So much. Or maybe I'd just kiss them.

Aven cleared their throat. "The king and queen wish to speak to Ellinore. So we'll be on our way."

"Yes, Princet Aven."

Aven nudged me in my arm. "Tell Dave to fly off," they said in a murmur.

"What?"

"Do it."

"Golden Dragon," I said loudly, petting Dave's snout. "You may fly away for the time being."

Dave's eyes narrowed. But with a low rumble, he took off. Well, at least he was out of harm's way. Which was more than I could say for myself.

The guards oohed and aahed as Dave made a wide circle around the castle, then headed back toward his cave.

Aven guided me toward the throne room, our hands knocking together as we walked. I wondered if they wanted to lace our fingers as badly as I did. Once we were out of earshot of the guards, Aven stopped in the middle of a corridor.

They placed their hands on either side of my face. "What happened to your nose?"

"Face-plant."

They winced. "But everything else? Zig? The horn?"

"It all worked out."

They sighed, closing their eyes and bringing their forehead to rest against mine. "Thank the ancients. I haven't stopped worrying."

I grasped their wrist. "We handled it. While you were handling . . ."

They straightened. "Right. I did some preventative damage control after you dropped me off at the castle," they said. "Lord Ethan had yet to arrive, so I had the jump on whatever 'lies' he would tell. It seems traveling without his sigil and gold cache caused a few delays on his journey."

"Ancients bless Zig and his quick hands."

"Yes. He bought me some time to prime my aunt and uncle in your favor."

My heart fluttered. Aven had protected me once again. "Thank you. You didn't have to do that. I know you don't like liars."

They smiled softly. "Well, I like one. And I get why she did it. But I hope she doesn't feel like she ever has to again."

"I won't ever lie to you. I promise."

"I know." Their gaze locked with mine, and my cheeks heated even further. I must have looked like a strawberry at this point, but I didn't care. "But Lord Ethan made it back a few hours ago, and he has told anyone willing to listen about, well, everything. So be ready."

I nodded. I took a breath, raised my chin, and grasped the hilt of my sword. "How do I look?"

Their gaze was fond as they pushed back a strand of my hair. "Like Ellinore."

We continued on our way, and soon we were at the double doors that led to the throne room. The last time I was here, I had dragged in a dead giant spider. This time I was trying my best not to hold hands with my previous rival while facing down an angry lord and a king and queen who might throw me in a dungeon. I liked this time better.

We pushed open the doors to catch Lord Ethan in mid-rant.

"She's a charlatan. She's a liar. She's a fraud."

"And she's right here!" I said, striding down the carpet toward the thrones.

The king looked bored, rubbing his temple with two of his fingers. And the queen was annoyed, her lips pursed. I didn't know if this boded well for me at all.

"Your Majesties," I said with a bow. "Princet Aven said you wanted to speak to me."

"Lord Ethan," the queen started, "has been telling us quite a fantastic story about some kind of beast and a forest fire and a map that involved you somehow. I don't know, I've lost track." She took a sip from her goblet. "Dear Aven has already told us about the Golden Dragon and the misunderstanding that occurred."

The king perked up. "Yes. So remarkable you tamed the dragon. You should've told us that before. We could've had a dragon at our feasts. Can you imagine?"

I grinned with gritted teeth. Dave would hate attending a feast . . . or would he? "I'm sorry for the mix-up. I'll be more specific with details in the future."

The queen waved the remark away. "It was so long ago. Who cares now?"

Lord Ethan paled. I could tell he saw his chance to nail me to the wall slipping away. "Ask her about the other quests!"

"We shouldn't bother Ellinore with recounting those," Aven said smoothly. "We have bards for that."

"Oh, of course!" the queen said, delighted. She clapped her hands. "Call the bard. I'd love to hear the one about—"

"Wait!" Lord Ethan yelled. "That's not the point."

"Then get to the point, Lord Ethan," the king said. "We've been listening to you ramble for the better part of an hour."

"Did you tell her about kidnapping Farrah?" I asked, tone innocent.

Lord Ethan went translucent.

"Farrah?" the queen snapped. "My niece Farrah? What does she have to do with this?"

I might as well take the opportunity to help Farrah out. "She assisted us greatly on the quest to save my brother. She should be commended when she returns home. But during our journey Lord Ethan did indeed kidnap her."

The queen's expression turned murderous. "You kidnapped her, Lord Ethan?"

"Tell her how you threatened her and Princet Aven with throwing them into the ocean while bound."

"Is this true?" the king barked.

Lord Ethan raised his hands. "That is taken out of context."

"Then explain the context," the king said, voice low and dangerous.

"And if I do, are you going to listen? Or are you going to believe the lies of this peasant and the Pointless—" He cut himself off the moment he realized what he'd said.

But it was too late. The king turned purple with rage. "Choose your next words very carefully, Lord Ethan, or you might find yourself in a dungeon."

Ethan swallowed, his throat bobbing. "I apologize, Your Majesties."

"I believe it is time to see yourself out," the queen said. "And retire from questing. Return to your lands, Lord Ethan. And only come to the castle when called."

Lord Ethan scowled. He opened his mouth to respond.

"The next words you utter better be 'Yes, Your Majesty,'" the king said.

Lord Ethan squeaked. He bowed. "Yes, Your Majesty."

He cast one last murderous glance in my direction, then strode out.

"Good riddance," the king muttered. "Aven, was there anything else you needed to speak about?"

"No, Uncle. Thank you." Aven turned to leave, but I didn't go with them. Not yet.

I stood in front of the thrones. "Your Majesties, may I have a moment of your time?"

The queen smiled gently. "Why yes, Ellinore."

"Thank you. Over the last two weeks, I've traveled all over the kingdom. I've encountered a faery, fire salamanders, pixies, a ghost dog, and two primordial beasts. That's not even to mention the griffin feather or the gnome hat that I found in a cave." I paused, choosing my next words carefully. "I have enjoyed the quests you have devised over the years, and I've learned so much about our land and the creatures that inhabit it. But there are fewer and fewer of them. And I'm afraid that if the nature of the quests remains unchanged, then there will be fewer still."

The king raised an eyebrow. "Are you asking for us to cease the quests?"

"No. I just ask that they be geared more toward helping than hunting."

"Helping?" the queen asked. "I don't understand."

I took a breath. "Sometimes we just need to listen to solve a problem instead of hacking our way through the world."

The queen exchanged a confused glance with the king. "I'm sorry, Ellinore. I still don't—"

"Like the Golden Dragon!" Aven interrupted, coming to stand by my side. "Ellinore could have slain the dragon, but instead she helped him find an alternative food source to the village's sheep."

And another outlet for his horrible jokes, but the king and queen didn't need to know that.

"Ah," the king said with a nod. "I see."

"But what about the stories?" the queen asked, swirling the wine in her goblet. "The one about the Golden Dragon is my favorite."

"The current songs don't need to change," Aven said evenly.

"And I've made friends with a bard!" I blurted. "I'm helping him create new stories based on my previous quests. So you will still have new tales to look forward to."

"Oh," the queen said. "That sounds lovely."

The king hummed. "Now that the Golden Dragon is tamed"—Dave was going to kill Aven for that—"could you bring him to a feast?"

The queen perked up. "Oh! Could you arrange that, Ellinore?"

I glanced at Aven. "Uh . . . of course. As long as he feels safe."

"Which would mean vowing to change the quests," Aven added. "No more hunting of the ancients and folklores."

The queen leaned over to the king. "That would also mean no more spiders. The servants had a terrible time cleaning the stench out of the carpets."

The king nodded. "True. And we already have several grand souvenirs," he said, gesturing to the shelf behind him, where the spider's fangs now sat alongside Dave's scale and the pelt of the Ursa. He turned his attention back to Aven and me. "Fine. Consider it done."

"Then I think the Golden Dragon would love to attend a feast," I said, hoping Dave wouldn't mind. "As long as he has his own table and it takes place outside."

The king slapped the arm of his throne in excitement. "For the feast of the opening of the summer tournaments!"

"That would be perfect, dear," the queen said with a wide smile. "Ellinore, are you planning to return for the summer season?"

I winced. "Um . . . no."

The king frowned. "Even though we would change the nature of the quests?"

"I am exceedingly grateful that Your Majesties have considered all that Princet Aven and I had to say. And I'm very grateful for all the Crown has done for me and my family. But I've been given a new purpose . . . by a god."

The queen blinked in surprise. "A god?"

"Yes. A primordial being tasked me with taking care of its creations."

"Goodness! Well, we must respect the decision of a deity, mustn't we? Will the bard be accompanying you?"

"Yes. He will."

The queen smiled. "I look forward to the thrilling stories."

The king cleared his throat. "Well, Ellinore the Brave, I will miss your theatrics."

"Thank you, Your Majesties." I bowed. "And from now on, it's just Ellinore."

"Aven," the queen said with a smile. "Will you be joining her?"

I turned so quickly, the sheath of my sword banged against my leg.

"If I may?" they asked, hesitant.

"Of course," she said. "Just ensure you return for the holiday feasts so we can check in. But otherwise, go have fun."

Aven's grin matched my own. They grabbed my hand and laced our fingers together. And we strode, smiling, down the carpet.

"Not too much fun!" the king's voice echoed behind us.

Once outside in the courtyard, we stopped and took a breath. "I can't believe that went as well as it did," I said. "You must have really buttered them up before Lord Ethan arrived."

Aven blushed. "I may have told them that I loved you and that I was going to follow you whatever happened, even if that meant being thrown in the dungeon with you. And I hoped they wouldn't do that, because I'd rather love you out here," they said, gesturing to the wide world. "But I'd do what I had to."

"You said that?"

"Yes."

"That . . . that is good buttering," I said, my voice a breathy sigh. "Lord Ethan didn't have a chance."

Aven laughed. "So what now?" they asked, facing me and pulling me close. "We have a dragon, three friends, a horn, and a vow we gave a primordial being to protect the magical creatures of the world."

I frowned, my brow furrowing. "I think we have one more thing to do before we wrap up this quest."

"Can I kiss you first?"

"I'd be a little annoyed if you didn't."

"Good to know."

So they did, and I was far from annoyed.

41

"ARE YOU SURE YOU WANT TO DO THIS?" AVEN ASKED ME AS WE STOOD outside the silver eye that led to the invisible realm.

I took a breath. The Elder Beast's horn lay across my palms. "Yes. We can't allow this to fall into anyone else's possession."

"I agree, but we could protect it at the castle."

I rolled my eyes. "Until the descendants of one of your cousins uses it to usurp the throne. I've heard that ballad, Aven. Rylan's sung it for us."

"That's fictional." Aven crossed their arms. "They didn't use a horn, anyway. It was a different magical artifact."

"Come on, we agreed."

"If you two would like to hurry up," Dave grumbled, "I would like to find a mountain goat to snack on while you're in there. I'm hungry."

"Yes, Dave! We're going."

Aven and I had agreed that the Elder Beast's horn was too dangerous to exist in the outside world. Forto and Quip were still out there, and rumor was they were on the hunt for it. As well as a *real* council of mages who had heard about the debacle. We couldn't protect the horn and continue with our other quests.

It was determined that Aven, Dave, and I would be the ones to return the horn. That way, only the three of us would know where the invisible realm existed. And when we died, the secret would die with us.

We'd even burned the map Farrah had used to track our progress across the kingdom. It might not have had the Elder Beast's location noted, but it did mark where the Hydra lived. And we all knew it was best to leave that particular primordial alone.

Stepping through the shimmering eye was as weird as it had been the first time. The silver slid over me, and suddenly I once again stood on blue grass, this time beneath a light-purple sky.

"Huh," I said, bending down and retrieving the cloth with the clues. "It hasn't moved."

Aven popped through beside me. They shook their head, then ran their hands through their black hair. "Ancients, that's weird," they said, glaring at the eye.

"Okay. Where should we put it?" I asked, holding up the horn. "I don't want to leave it right next to the entrance, just in case."

Aven hummed. "Maybe we throw it in the river?"

"Perfect."

Amazingly, I remembered the way through the meadow, past the oddly colored bushes and trees, to the river. The world around us was silent, our footsteps the only sound. And there was no way the Elder Beast didn't know we were here.

Once we reached the river, I took a calming breath. Part of me couldn't believe that I had gone through so much trouble for this horn and that I was going to toss it into the river. Another part of me couldn't wait until it was gone.

Aven touched my fingers where they wrapped around the horn, my knuckles white. "It's okay," they said. "You're right. It's too powerful and too dangerous for our world. But the good news is, we can always retrieve it. If we have to. I hope we never have to, but you know what I mean."

I nodded. "I do." I swallowed, took one last glance at the ridges of bone, and tossed it in. It didn't even splash in this strange realm, merely sank to the bottom of the riverbed and blended in with the rocks. I tossed the cloth of clues as well, and it drifted downstream, out of sight.

"Okay. It's done." I tore my gaze away from it, only to find the Elder Beast staring at us from the other bank. I startled and grasped Aven's arm.

They inhaled a quick breath.

The Elder Beast didn't speak to us, merely eyed us, then turned and jumped away, hiding in between the trees.

"What do you think—"

"Nope," I said, cutting Aven off. "We are not pondering that interaction. We are leaving."

"Yeah. Okay."

We scampered out of there without looking back.

On the other side of the eye, the early afternoon had turned into the early hours of the morning. Dave slept soundly, a small fire flickering by him, providing warmth and light. The stars winked brightly, and the three sister moons all shone.

"Should we wake Dave?" Aven asked. "Farrah and Zig wanted to get an early start tomorrow. They want me to take them to the gnome village outside of the castle."

"Rylan wants me to help him with the song." I grimaced. "I'm bad at rhyming. I don't know why he keeps asking. He lived the quest. He knows what happened."

Aven chuckled. They grabbed their saddlebags and sat down by the fire, adding a log Dave had gathered for us. "Isn't that what you wanted, though? To tell your story in your own words?"

"Theoretically," I said, settling down beside them. "Writing is difficult, though."

Aven draped their arm over my shoulders. "And to think, that was supposed to be your last quest ever. But as Farrah would say, it turned into the best quest ever."

I laid my head on Aven's shoulder and snuggled close. "I don't know. Maybe our best quest ever is still before us."

"That's surprisingly profound."

I elbowed them in the ribs. "If we really think about it, all my previous quests were supposedly completed by Ellinore the Brave. That means the quest for the Elder Beast was my first quest ever as just Ellinore."

Aven smiled, their blue eyes shining in the firelight. "I like just Ellinore. She's pretty great."

"She is," I agreed.

And for the first time in a long time, I believed it.

ACKNOWLEDGMENTS

I'm incredibly happy and grateful to share *The Last Best Quest Ever* with readers, especially with anyone who has ever struggled with imposter syndrome. I wish I could offer some bit of salient advice that could ease self-doubt, but I think self-acceptance involves a journey, much like the one Ellinore takes throughout the novel.

Of course, Ellinore has a team that supports her. And I am lucky to have one as well.

I'd like to thank my agent, Eva Scalzo, who has been the champion of my work over the last several years.

Also, thank you to the team at McElderry Books. Kate Prosswimmer continues to draw the best story out of me even when I'm stubborn. Many thanks to Alex Kelleher, Thad Whittier, and Andrenae Jones. A million thank-you's to Sam Schechter for the beautiful cover art and to Rebecca Syracuse for the cover design.

Special thanks to my author friends DL Wainright and October Santerelli for being sounding boards and for offering encouragement and support during the creative process. Thank you to Jessica Parra, who has been such a delight to get to know and spend time with this past year. Thank you to CB Lee, who is an amazing author and friend.

Also, thank you to my internet family and pocket friends who have been there for me as I work through not only creative challenges but life ones as well.

My internet family always comes through, and I can't thank them enough for sticking with me this past decade. Special thanks to my "bestie" Amy Y and my BFF Kristinn.

I'd like to thank some wonderful independent bookstores who have been so great and helpful throughout my career, especially Malaprop's Bookstore in Asheville and Fable Hollow Bookshop in Knoxville.

Thank you to my family—Keith, Rob, and Chris.

Lastly, I'd like to thank everyone who either purchased this book or borrowed it from a library. Thank you for allowing me to entertain you for a few hours. I'm very appreciative of your time. I hope you enjoyed reading this story as much as I enjoyed writing it. Until next time, I hope you stay safe and happy.

Thank you,

—F.T.